FEAR.DEATH.BY.SWORD

To Jeanie,

Enjoy the book, and thanks for your support!

Cavanaugh James Welch

Copyright © 2018 by Cavanaugh J. Welch
All rights reserved. This book or any portion thereof may not be reproduced or used in any manner whatsoever without the express written permission of the publisher except for the use of brief quotations in a book review.

Printed in the United States of America

2nd Edition, 2018

ISBN: 9781976777196

This book is dedicated to my loving wife, Joy. Your unyielding will to persevere through life's problems while still exuding love for those around you has been my inspiration for this book. Without you, I would not be where I am today.

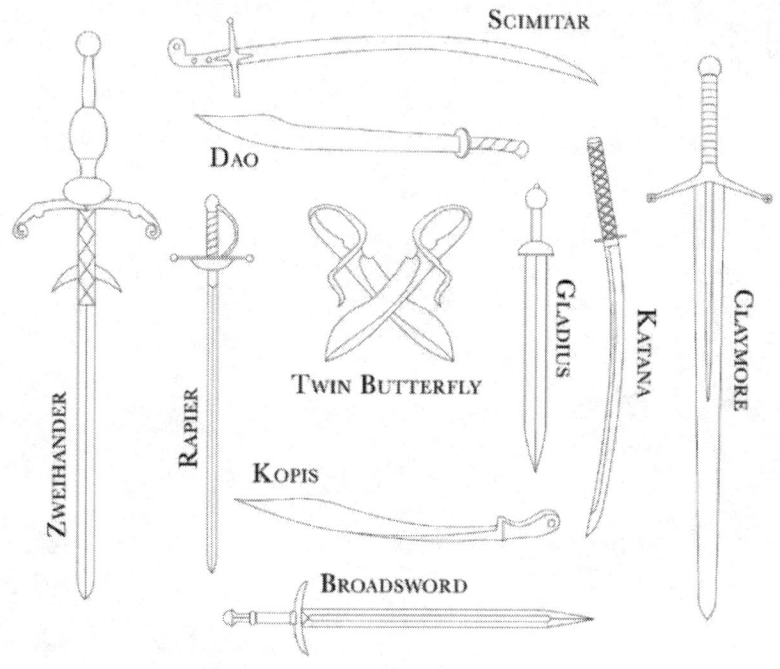

"When you pick a sword, it should feel like you're meeting an old friend for the first time"

-Neith

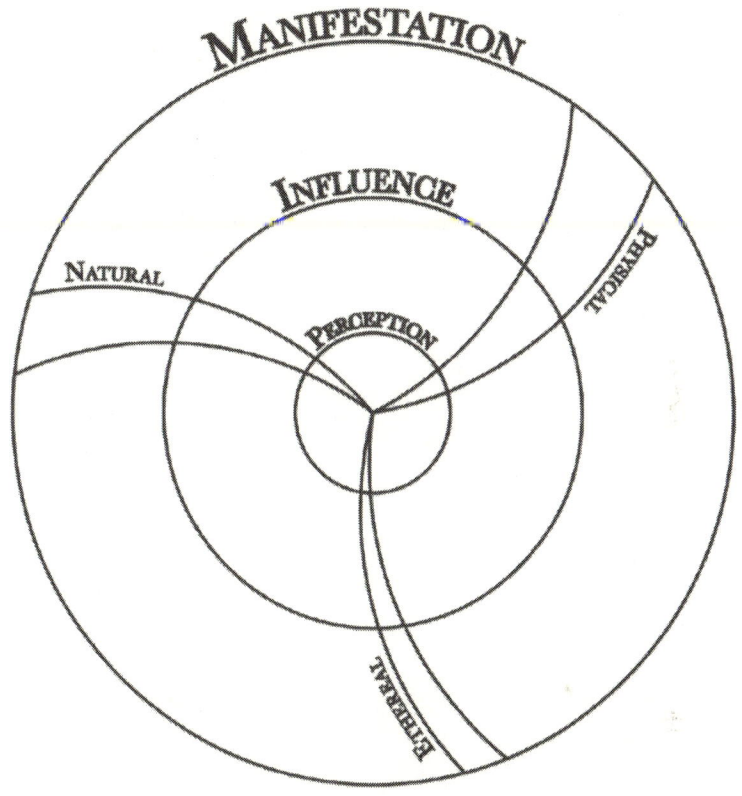

Three Tiers of the Soul Diagram

CHAPTER 1

As they walked solemnly, two by two, the iron black casket drifted between them, carried by six strangers. Anyone who had known the deceased didn't have the resolve to carry him to his final resting place. It would take hours before they all reached the burial plot. Every member of Fratello della Spada in the country came home to witness the funeral. A grand display like this was reserved only for those who died in combat, something that had not happened in a long time.

The cause of death was anything but natural. Two days ago they found Bulo's decapitated body propped up against a wall like a puppet with cut strings. His head was nowhere to be found, those that were closest to him had to identify the body. Despite the entire incident being caught on video, no one could see who killed him. The assassin's face was obscured the whole time, as if he knew where each camera was positioned. A murder within the walls of the Citadel was unprecedented. As one of the oldest buildings of Fratello della Spada it was true fortress, designed to protect against intruders and withstand sieges. Over the years many renovations were made, but it was never meant to withstand a threat from the inside. Few people knew the locations of the cameras in the Citadel. Even fewer had the skills to avoid them while murdering a man like Bulo. Still, no one was being ruled out. Everyone there was a suspect. Sadness and suspicion settled through the crowd like thick fog. They all knew that the killer was there with them, secretly gloating behind a guise of grief. That fact had everyone in attendance on edge.

"Neith, Bulo was one of your good friends, right?" Champ whispered as he walked beside Neith in the procession line.

"Yes" was all Neith could manage to say as memories of Bulo flashed through her mind. Champ wanted to ask how she was feeling after everything that had happened, but he already knew the answer and thought it best to leave her alone for now. She looked as if grief had taken hold of her soul. However, it wasn't grief that kept Neith from speaking, it was rage. The only thoughts that seemed to satisfy her were finding the bastard that killed Bulo, and what she planned on doing to him once she found him.

"Well, I'm here if you need anything." Champ said not expecting a reply.

The last funeral Champ could remember was at least five years ago, and the guy was in his nineties when he died. Everyone's mood was different now. It wasn't often one of them died so young. Anyone worth their salt that could call themselves a member of Fratello della Spada didn't die easily. It wasn't exactly an organization that welcomed people with open arms. Dedicated to preserving the art of the sword, masters of any style of swordsmanship were permitted to join, if they were good enough. They were all guided by the principle, 'Let every man choose his own fate'. All that mattered was preserving and passing on the knowledge so that it was not lost to history. Still, there were rules. Killing another member was strictly prohibited, especially within the walls of the Citadel. Whoever did this wanted to send a message to everyone. He wasn't playing by the rules, and no one was safe.

It had been thirty minutes since Champ last spoke to Neith. Everyone in the front of the line had taken their seats already. The back was still slowly filing in, but Champ felt now was as good a time as any to try and start a conversation again.

"Neith, I know how you must be feeling—"

"Just shut up." Neith said in a quiet yet serious tone. "Nothing you say can make this day any better, so you might as well save your breath."

Champ fumbled his words as tried to respond. He desperately wanted to say something that would comfort her, but as hard as he tried his mind was blank. She was right. Nothing he said would change anything. All that was left to do was watch as the iron black casket, Bulo's casket, was slowly lowered into the ground.

CHAPTER 2

"Nathaniel, did you forget the butter again!" screamed his mom.

"No mom, it's in the bag!" Nemo shouted back. Even though his real name was Nathaniel everyone but his parents called him Nemo. It was a nickname he picked up in first grade and it just kind of stuck with him.

Nemo's mom looked around some more before giving up.

"I don't see it. Why don't you come down here and look since you're so sure you didn't forget it"

"Ugh, ok coming" Nemo grunted, "I know I didn't forget the butter, she probably isn't looking in the right bag."

Nemo focused on the television, trying to catch the end of his show before he went downstairs. Rays of sunlight beaming through his window diverted his attention to the old birthday cards on the window seal. His fifteenth birthday was two weeks ago. He wanted to have a party, but all of his so called friends were 'too busy' or had 'other things to do'. When he really thought about it, there were only a few people he hung out with. None of them he could really call friends.

The glass from the window reflected his pale face and blue eyes through a mess of his light brown hair. Next to his birthday cards sat a medal, the only recognition he'd ever received in his life. It read 'Thank You Participant'. He got it just for showing up to his fifth grade class spelling bee. Sports didn't really interest him, and even though people thought he was smart in school his grades said otherwise.

"Nathaniel!" his mom shouted again.

Nemo rushed down the stairs in a hurry. The quicker he found the butter, the faster he could get back to watching his show.

"I know it's here." He thought to himself as he looked through each of the bags.

"I remember checking everything off the list mom gave me as the cashier scanned..." The sudden realization occurred to him that he left a bag.

"Mom I'm going back to store. I left the butter there." Nemo said as he rushed out the door.

"Ok! Be safe." she yelled, not expecting him to hear it before he left. She shook her head while she watched him run off. "I knew that boy would forget something, he always does."

The store wasn't far from Nemo's house. He could have walked, but he took his bike instead. It had been cloudy all day, and looked like it might rain soon. Nemo always looked forward to rainy days. Something about it always calmed him and helped him focus. It was as if the lack of people outside made the world quieter. As much as he would enjoy riding home in the rain, his mom would probably be upset if he came back home soaking wet. So he pedaled faster to hurry to the store.

Just as the grocery store was coming in sight, something else captured Nemo's attention. A woman, dressed in all black, was walking at a very fast pace on the other side of the street. She looked to be in her mid-twenties. Her bronze caramel skin glowed in the red and purple rays of sun that were slowly being overtaken by the dark clouds. A single long black braid of hair flowed down her back and swung side to side in the air as she walked. She had a deep scar above her left eye. Somehow that small imperfection only added to her beauty. As she came closer, Nemo noticed her black outfit was accented by gold jewelry unlike anything he'd ever seen before. He assumed she must be rich, or someone important, or both. The long stride of her legs made her look taller that she actually was. Knowing that, he was sure she would still tower over him. Just looking at her was intimidating. But it wasn't her looks that kept his attention. It was the expression on her face. A mixture of anger, sadness, and fear all showed in that woman's gaze. If he hadn't seen it himself, he wouldn't think it was possible to make a face that showed so many emotions at once.

Right as he was about to go back to thoughts of retrieving the butter for his mom, the woman looked at him. She didn't look at him as if she was casually glancing in his direction. She looked directly at him, almost as if she was looking through him. Nemo tried to focus on something else. He certainly didn't want to stare back at her. Before he could wrap his head around what would cause her to stare at him so intensely, she took off in a mad sprint. All the emotions on her face were replaced completely by fear. There was no doubt in Nemo's mind. This woman was running for her life.

The very first thought that popped into his head after seeing her take off was that he should just mind his business. That would satisfy all the mystery he needed for today, no need to worry about why a woman was running for her life.

Besides, if he followed her what was he going to do? What if she was in real danger, and what would he say if she wasn't and wondered why he was following her? He didn't have an answer to any of these questions. But the one thought that did stand out to him was, if he was ever running away like that he would want someone, anyone, to come to help. Against his better judgment, he turned his bike around and started to peddle after her.

CHAPTER 3

After the funeral, Neith went for a walk in order to calm herself. However, she was unable to do so while still thinking about everything that had happened over the past couple of days. Small drops of water were starting to fall from the clouds rolling in above. Rain was coming. The sound of her boots hitting the cracked concrete sidewalk with every step resounded in her ears. It was at that moment she heard something else, the sound of another person's footsteps. Someone was walking behind her. Neith considered herself an expert at tracking people without them noticing, so it was rare for someone to be able to sneak up on her. Judging by the sound of each step, she could tell that whoever was following her was still pretty far away. Most people would barely hear such a faint noise, but after years of practice Neith's senses were always on high alert.

She decided to walk a bit faster. If someone really was following her they would match her pace and give themselves away. Then, she could quickly hide and wait for the right time to ambush them. A brief wisp of hope crossed her mind that this person might actually know something about who killed Bulo. That simple thought reignited her burning rage that had just starting to cool. Neith walked even faster. Despite her anger, she was still keeping track of the footsteps behind her. They sped up to match her pace just as she expected. Everything was going according to plan until the faint sound of the footsteps disappeared. Neith kept walking, listening more intently than ever for the footsteps, but they were gone.

A thousand questions raced through her mind at once. Sounds didn't just disappear out of nowhere, especially when she was tracking them. Even when a person stopped walking it made a distinct sound, but the footsteps she heard just vanished without warning. Her thoughts quickly ran through every possibility she could think of, but they all came collapsing back together when a strong presence appeared across the street.

"There's no way that was there before" she thought. "I would have sensed it a mile away."

Someone was close, and they wanted her to know it. Whoever it was, something about their presence was suffocating. It made her hair stand on end, and her bones tremble. There was no time to question how it got there, or where it came from. She knew the one thing she needed to do,

RUN.

Immediately, Neith took off in a mad sprint going the opposite direction. At first, she was so focused on getting away from whoever was unleashing that murderous aura towards her that she didn't notice the boy on the bike, peddling his little lungs out trying to keep up. It was clear the aura wasn't coming from him, but that didn't explain why this kid was following her or what he planned on doing if he could catch her. She certainly hoped he didn't think he was coming to her rescue. It was people like him with the best intentions that made the worst decisions. The last thing she needed was some kid trying to play hero and getting in her way.

As she ran, the intense murderous aura followed. Neith's patience was wearing thin and she was already tired of running. Running was never her style, she preferred to stand her ground and look directly into the enemy's eyes. Thoughts of why she was even running faded to thoughts of Bulo's funeral and the image of his casket being lowered into the ground. The logic of survival was overtaken by her lust for revenge. Neith made up her mind that she would find out what was going on before she took another step, no matter who was in her way. Once she came to this resolution, she drew her sword.

A long single edged scimitar, engraved in Arabic symbols from the hilt to the base of the blade, appeared from the cloth covered scabbard that held it. The quickness of the draw was only matched by its silence. Time seemed to slow down as Neith once again went through the familiar ritual that was drawing her sword. She felt her grip tighten around the long leather wrapped hilt. It felt nearly weightless in her hand, the result of the countless times she had handled it. With her next step, she did an immediate 180 and bolted past the boy on the bike, searching for the source of the aura. Just as quickly as it appeared, it was gone. Like a faint smell in a breeze, there was no trace of it left. If she hadn't felt it so intensely before, she would have thought she imagined it. However, there was no imagining what she just experienced.

Neith was in a blazing rage by this point. She had been ready cut down whatever threat she was facing. Now there was nothing for her to direct her anger at. Someone was toying with her and she wanted to find out who. The only person left was the boy still following her. She didn't know if he was involved with everything that was happening, but at this point she wasn't taking any chances. She would have answers as to what was going on no matter what.

****

The next few seconds in Nemo's head all became a blur. One second he was riding his bike, chasing a woman he thought was in trouble. The next second, he felt himself being slammed against a wall and his feet dangling in the air. The woman's left hand held him by his neck against the wall. Her right hand held a long, curved sword close enough to him that the tip touched the center of his chest. Rain had started to fall, and anyone around was running for cover to keep dry. No one was around to see or hear them, leaving just them standing in the rain alone.

"Who are you, and why are you following me?" Neith asked.

"My... my... my name is Nathaniel but everyone calls me Nemo. You looked like you needed help, but I'm guessing now that you don't so if you put me down I'll leave." Nemo stuttered.

Neith paid no attention to his request. "What do you know about Bulo?"

"Who is that? I don't know anyone named Bu—" as soon as he started his last word Nemo could feel the sharp blade penetrate his shirt and press against his skin. The pressure behind it told him that she meant business. The calm intensity of her voice was only matched by the serious look in her eyes.

"I'm going to ask you one more time, what do you know about Bulo?" Neith said.

"I swear, I don't know anyone named Bulo!" Nemo screamed. "I have no idea who you're talking about." The last thing Nemo heard was "We'll see" before everything around him went black.

CHAPTER 4

Nemo woke up in a dark room with an awful pain in his neck. He was still trying to rationalize what had happened, but his first thought was about how upset his mom would be when she found out he wasn't coming back with the butter. He looked around and tried to identify where he was as the fog of unconsciousness faded from his head. After a few minutes, when his eyes adjusted to the darkness, he could see he was surrounded by four brick walls with only one window facing his direction. There didn't seem to be a door anywhere in the room, leaving him without a clue as to how he got inside.

The rusted metal chair Nemo sat in wobbled under him as he looked around. Down in front of him, he saw the sweat outline of his unconscious head on a matching metal table. On top of the table, sat a small speaker. If it weren't for the searing pain in his neck, Nemo was sure the uncomfortable chair would have irritated him by now. He tried scooting his chair back from the table, only to realize that he was chained in place. His legs and his chair were chained to the table, which was bolted to the floor, forcing him to stay seated in a very upright forward position.

As he was looking around, still taking in his surroundings, someone switch on a glaring light aimed directly at his face. The light was so intense that he could barely keep his eyes open, but through the slender gaps of his eyelids he thought he could see the silhouettes of people in the window.

A dull robotic voice came from the speaker on the table.

"What is your name?"

Nemo was still trying to find an angle where the light didn't completely blind him when the voice on the speaker repeated itself.

"What is your name?"

"My name is Nathaniel Lake but everyone calls me Nemo. Why am I here? I haven't done anything." said Nemo.

Instead of acknowledging his question, the voice from the speaker asked another one of its own.

"Where were you Tuesday between the hours of 6pm and 3am?"

"Why does it matter where I was, I haven't done anything!" Nemo shouted. "And why am I chained to this chair?"

"Just answer the question." said the voice from the speaker. "The quicker you answer our questions the quicker we can resolve all of this."

Nemo sighed and gave it some thought. "I was home the whole time. I get home from school around four, and I usually don't go anywhere else so I'm sure I was home the whole time."

The speaker went quiet for what seemed like hours, but it was actually only about twenty minutes. Finally, just as Nemo was thinking he wouldn't last another second sitting in this uncomfortable chair, the speaker came back on.

"Last question, what were you doing following Neith?"

Nemo's head popped up at the mention of the name. "Neith? Is that the name of the woman that brought me here?" he asked.

"Yes" replied the voice from the speaker.

"Well by the way she ran, it looked like she was in trouble. I didn't know if I could help, but I thought I'd at least follow her and see."

There was slight pause. Nemo heard men whispering in the background before the speaker shut off again. Just as he was dreading sitting there for another twenty minutes with the light shining in his eyes, the light shut off and he heard locks being opened. A section of the wall opened up like a door and four tall men walked in. The tallest of them needed to bend over to make it through the doorway. The other three were slightly shorter and could simply walk through. All of them wore black jackets. Black masks covered the top of their faces, leaving their mouths exposed. Their shirts and pants were different but they somehow managed to still look surprisingly uniform.

The tallest one stepped forward and spoke, "My name is A. These are my fellow interrogators B, C, and E."

Nemo could tell A, B, C, and E, were code names, but he wondered why they skipped over the letter D. Just as A was about to continue speaking, a huge dog ran in and jumped in the air. Its jaws dripped saliva on the table as they snapped closed right in front Nemo's face. If A hadn't grabbed it by the collar at the last second, Nemo wouldn't have much of a face left. The dog kept barking and aggressively snapping at Nemo until A gave the collar a tug and it finally sat down by its master's side. Earlier when the speaker was quiet, Nemo had thought to ask for a bathroom break. Suddenly he didn't have to go anymore.

"Whoops, sorry about that" said *A*. "This is *D*, the fifth member of the interrogation team. He gets a little jumpy around strangers."

"Nice dog" Nemo stuttered as he tried to stop his heart from beating so fast.

A continued, "I also would like to apologize for our interrogation procedures. We did a background check and verified your story, it seems you are innocent."

Nemo didn't know what crime they suspected him of, but innocent sounded good. "So, you're going to let me go?" He said with the hopes of getting out of his chains and finally being free from the uncomfortable chair.

"Unfortunately not" replied *A*

That was not the response Nemo expected to hear.

A gave Nemo a reassuring smile. "You see one of our members was murdered, and he was killed in this very building. Such a thing has never happened before, so we're being extra cautious until we find out who's responsible. Since you now know where this place is, I'm sorry but we have to kill you."

All the color drained from Nemo's face. He wanted to ask *A* to repeat what he said, but he already knew he had heard it clearly.

"But I was unconscious! I don't know where I am!" Nemo screamed with all the force his scared voice could muster.

"Doesn't matter" replied *A*

"You said yourself I was innocent!" Nemo shouted even louder this time.

"Doesn't matter" replied *A*

"Are you really going to kill an innocent person? What about the police? You'll go to jail for murder!" Nemo yelled as his last ditch effort to reason his way out of this situation.

A sighed, "Buried down here in these catacombs, no one will find you. No one will even look for you. The tunnels under the Citadel, the very building you're in, stretch on for miles. Other tunnels nearby stretch out even further underground". *A* looked down to see Nemo trembling in front of him. He put a reassuring hand on his shoulder.

"Look, it's not like I want to kill you. You just happen to be in the wrong place, at the wrong time, with the wrong people. It's an unfortunate task that none of us will enjoy, but must be done regardless."

Nemo couldn't believe what he was hearing. He had to escape, but with these chains still on he couldn't even escape out of his chair. He thought of anything and everything he could do to get himself out, but nothing was working. *B* stepped away from the other interrogators, who had been whispering among themselves, to speak to *A*.

"I have another idea. We can let him take the Trials."

"The Trials?" *A* responded as he looked in the air to ponder the idea. "Hmm, I guess that could work. Although I don't really like the idea. Usually candidates that aren't sponsored by a current member don't fare so well, but I'm always open to new ways of thinking. Let's put it to a vote, all those in favor of execution raise your hand."

Nemo breathe a slight sigh of relief as only *A* and *C* raised their hands.

"All those in favor of letting this young man take the Trials, raise your hand" the remaining interrogators, *B* and *E,* raised their hands.

A looked around at the hands in the air. "Hmm a tie, this is no good. Let me think about what to do"

Nemo didn't know what *A* might think of next. He was just happy that the dog didn't get to decide the tiebreaker.

"I know!" shouted *A*, "We'll let the person that brought him in vote to break the tie. Take him to Neith."

23

At the sound of *A*'s voice the other interrogators unlocked Nemo's chains and grabbed him from the chair. They dragged him up several flights of stairs and through a series of hallways until they arrived at a door. The door was cracked open, but *A* still knocked before entering. Nemo heard a soft, sweet voice say "Come in", before he was dragged into the room and thrown on the floor. A soft crimson rug in the middle of the room broke his fall. It was the first time he had a chance to rest in hours.

"Well are you just going to lie on my floor, or are you going to get up?"

The soft voice Nemo heard outside was now stern and commanding. In front of him, Neith was relaxing on a white chesterfield sofa, her braid undone and her shirt unbuttoned part of the way down. The seamless black boots he remembered were replaced by the copper hue of her feet dangling over the edge of the sofa. This was the first time Nemo had seen her up close and relaxed. It was the exact opposite of how dangerous he remembered her being. As Nemo raised himself to his knees on the rug, Neith sat up and stared at the interrogators walking in behind him.

"What are you idiots doing here and why did you bring that trash with you?"

A stepped forward unfazed by the insult, "We seem to be in a quandary over what to do with this boy. He is innocent and has nothing to do with the events that have occurred, but unfortunately we must kill him anyway. Two of my colleagues are of a different mindset and think we should allow him to participate in the Trials. We seem to be at a stalemate over which idea should prevail, so we came up here to seek your guidance on the matter."

"Idiots" Neith mumbled to herself. "Why are there four of you anyway, couldn't you all avoid this situation by having an odd number of interrogators?"

"There are five of us. *D* is an invaluable member of the team who assistance cannot be discounted." *A* said as he held *D* by his collar.

"That dog has more sense than all of you put together." Neith responded as she got up from the couch. "Fine, I guess I'll decide. So, the choices are between killing him and letting him take the Trials? What to do, what to do."

Nemo opened his eyes as wide as he could and looked up at her, trying to conjure up any shred of sympathy in her heart.

"Ah whatever, let him take the Trials."

Nemo almost jumped up and hugged her he was so happy. That feeling of hope was quickly shattered when Neith said, "He'll probably die anyway, but at least we won't have to kill him ourselves."

"Wait, what are these Trials?" Nemo asked. But as soon as Neith stopped speaking, he was dragged back out of the room by the interrogators. They carried him down the hall by both arms, while his feet dragged across the floor.

"I can walk on my own." said Nemo just as a long series of winding stairs came into view. This finally got *B* and *E* to put him down. While they were walking, Nemo figured he could use the time to ask some of the many questions he had.

"What are the Trials?"

A, walking in front, turned his head to respond. "The Trials are a series of tests for potential new members. They only happen once a year so you're pretty lucky to show up the day before they begin."

Nemo didn't feel very lucky at the moment, "Why did Neith say I'll probably die, are these tests dangerous?"

"The tests aren't designed to kill any applicants. However, accidents do happen. Most potential applicants train for years with a master before attempting the Trials, so your chance of accidental death may be a little higher than normal. Specifically, in your case since you weren't originally brought here for membership, but under suspicion of being an accomplice to a murder, know this. If you do not pass you will still be executed."

Nemo wanted to stress the fact that he was innocent and didn't know what in the world was going on, but he knew it would fall on deaf ears. Instead he decided to find out as much as he could about the Trials before they arrived to wherever the interrogators were taking him.

"How many people usually pass the Trials?"

"About twenty percent give or take, but if you happen to be part of that twenty percent you'll become a full member of Fratello della Spada with all the rights and benefits of any other member. Then you can leave this place at your leisure."

"Well isn't that just great. Can you at least tell me what these tests are?"

"No, I'm afraid not. I can tell you the three categories that the Trials focus on. Each Trial will test you either physically, mentally, or spiritually. You must be strong in all three to become a member of Fratello della Spada."

As they reached the end of the steps, they approached a large steel door. Nemo knew his time for questions was running out. "Is there anything else I need to know about the Trials?"

"No, everything I've told you is information all the other applicants know. It wouldn't be fair to have you starting at more of a disadvantage than you already are."

A unlocked the large bolt on the door and directed Nemo inside the room. "This is where you'll be staying tonight. Get some rest and someone will be here to wake you up for the Trials in the morning."

Nemo walked into the dark room. The door was quickly shut behind him. When he turned to ask how he was supposed to see, the interrogators had already left and headed back upstairs. He was alone in the dark, again. He slowly felt his way to the back of the room until he found something he didn't expect, a light switch. He quickly flipped it on to discover that what he thought to be an empty cell was actually a nicely furnished room. A bed with several layers of sheets was positioned in the middle of the room with small night stands on each side. Nemo thought maybe his pleas of innocence weren't for nothing after all. Still he didn't imagine he would get any sleep tonight with everything he had been through that day. He didn't even know what time it was, or what time someone would come to wake him up. Regardless he decided to climb into bed, fully expecting to be kept awake by thoughts of the Trials tomorrow. But as soon as he was snugly between the sheets, he fell fast asleep.

CHAPTER 5

The door swung open and hit the wall behind it with a loud bang.

"Wake up you lazy bum! Today's your big day" Neith yelled.

In a rush, Nemo woke up scared and confused. He halfway expected to wake up in his bed thinking about what a crazy dream he had. Unfortunately, it was not a dream. This day could be the last day of his life. Before he had a chance to fully awaken, Neith was already dragging him out of the bed.

"You should feel honored to be allowed to take the Trials, even if this is the last day of your life you should give it your all."

Nemo was pretty tired of hearing about his impending death. All he wanted to do was go home and continue living the boring life he was used to.

"How would you feel if you knew today was the day you might die, I doubt that you'd be so cheerful about it."

Neith looked at him with a confused look on her face.

"Every day is a day I might die, so why should I treat it any differently than the rest?"

Nemo wasn't sure she understood the point he was trying to make, but he didn't feel like bringing the topic back up.

Neith led him to the waiting area for applicants. There he was told to shower, given a change of clothes, and a token with his applicant number on it, number twenty. When he finished changing, he sat back down in the waiting area. It was torture thinking about the unknown obstacles that lie ahead. He thought just waiting there should be a trial in itself. Finally, after about an hour of waiting, someone he didn't recognize came up and spoke to him.

"Greetings applicant number twenty, my name is Rufus and I will be the moderator for this year's Tournament for Rating Initial Applicants Level of Skill or as you call it, the Trials. Now if you would please follow me to the first stage."

Nemo was led into a large round pit almost the length of a basketball court and nine feet deep. The walls of the pit were adorned by almost every type of sword imaginable, and they did not look to be decorative. Railing surrounded the top of the pit preventing anyone from accidentally falling in or purposefully climbing out. Screens hung overhead as if this were some type of sporting arena. It reminded Nemo of a modern version of the ancient coliseums he had read about. The other nineteen applicants were already there waiting. There were girls and boys of different races, all about the same age as him. All of them seemed to be much calmer than he was, although he probably was the only one that wasn't there willingly. At the top of the pit Nemo could see people standing around looking down at all the applicants. He also saw Neith and *A* looking directly at him. Nemo wanted to scream at them for putting him in this situation. He regretted trying to help Neith and thought to himself if he got out of this alive he might never help anyone again. As angry as he was, he realized thinking about the past would do him no good, he had to focus on what was in front of him if he wanted to stay alive.

The moderator approached the middle of pit and began to speak to the crowd above.

"Greetings all, and welcome to the annual Trials! This year we have one of the largest groups we've had in quite a while, an astounding twenty applicants! We will begin with the first stage, a one on one tournament. Defeat your opponent by surrender or rendering them unable to fight and you will advance to the next stage. The matches will be determined at random. A number representing each applicant has been placed in this hat next to me. I will draw two numbers at a time to determine who will fight whom. I will also serve as the referee for each fight. The only rule is that you must stay within the walls of the pit. There are no restrictions on fighting styles, weapons, or areas of the body you may attack. For our members watching above, betting will end after the first 30 seconds of the fight. The odds will be shown in real time on the screens overhead. Best of luck to you all!"

Hearing that the first round was a one on one tournament, Nemo looked around at his competition. He had never been in real fight before, and everyone there, even the girls, looked pretty intimidating.

"Why couldn't this have been a spelling bee?" Nemo whispered to himself. "At least I'd have a chance at winning that."

Again, he reminded himself that this was no time to worry about the problem, he needed to focus on a solution.

"I can probably pick up some useful moves while watching the other fights" He thought. "We're all about the same age so they can't be that much stronger than I am. As long as I don't go first I'll be ok."

Rufus the moderator pulled two numbers out of the hat beside him to announce the fighters for the first round. "Up first, applicant number eight and applicant number twenty!"

Nemo's mouth dropped open. He suddenly felt sick. Applicant number eight quickly moved to the center of the pit. Nemo, still trying to fight off the wave of nausea that just hit him, stared at his opponent enter the arena. She was a thin, young girl no older than sixteen. A cool wave of relief washed over him. His opponent might actually be someone weaker than him, but that didn't explain why she looked so confident. As Nemo walked toward the center of the pit, he heard the girl say, "Aww man why'd I get the weak one, I wanted show off my skills. This won't be any fun at all." Hearing that, Nemo's nausea immediately came rushing back. He wanted to turn around and run for the sidelines, but it was too late. As soon as both applicants were near the center of the pit, Rufus announced,

"Ready FIGHT!"

At the moderator's word, applicant number eight charged at Nemo. She was fast, much faster than he expected. Even though he could see her running at him, his legs refused to move. His arms felt like jello. Wobbling about as he tried to lift them in his futile effort to block what was coming. Number eight quickly transitioned the momentum from her run into a swift kick to Nemo's stomach, knocking him clear off his feet. For a few seconds, he lingered in the air confused about what just happened. He briefly thought it might have been easier to just be executed.

Nemo hit the ground hard, and rolled back into the wall of the pit. His head was spinning. Just opening his eyes made him dizzy, and the distinctive taste of blood filled his mouth. Number eight still stood in the spot where she had kicked him. It was clear she didn't expect him to get up. The crowd above erupted with noise as Rufus gave his commentary on the fight.

"Number eight starts off with a strong kick, sending number twenty flying back to the other side of the pit. Ladies and gentlemen take notice of the odds displayed on the screen above, they originally started as 2:1 but are now heavily favored in number eight's direction 15:1. Only ten more seconds of betting left so choose wisely!"

As Nemo struggled to gather his senses, the noise of the crowd finally registered in his ears. Quickly he remembered the multitude of swords hanging around the wall of the pit. Nemo looked up and reached for the closest sword to him, a sharp looking katana. He aggressively wrapped his hand around the hilt and took sword off the wall, only to have it immediately fall to ground, taking his arm with it. Nemo stood to his feet and tried to lift the sword with two hands this time, but despite using all his strength he could barely lift the blade off the ground.

"Why the hell is this sword so heavy, it must weigh fifty pounds! I can barely pick it up, never mind swing it."

Somehow Rufus overheard Nemo. "These are official Fratello della Spada training blades. They're made using a mixture of special alloys to maintain the balance and structural properties of the weapon but increase its weight tenfold!"

Still struggling to lift the katana, Nemo bumped into a sword still on the rack and caused it to fall next to him. He turned around and stared at the six inch deep impression the weapon made in the ground. The realization occurred to him that there was no way he could fight with these swords. He only hoped that meant they were too heavy for his opponent to use too. It was then that he noticed number eight was no longer standing in the same spot.

Nemo was so focused trying to lift the sword that he didn't see number eight approach him from behind. She calmly tapped him on the shoulder before grabbing the katana from the ground with one hand, and swinging it over her shoulder.

"Wow, are you really that weak? I thought you would at least put up a little fight. Well stop wasting my time and stay down already so I can move on to stage two."

After seeing her easily pick up the sword he struggled with, Nemo put all the energy he had into his legs and started running. He managed to dodge her first swing, and took off around the edge of the pit wall.

"What kind of monster am I in this pit with! I can't believe she can lift that heavy sword so easily? I have to stay away from her until I can think of a plan."

Number eight immediately started chasing Nemo. Although she was much faster than him, Nemo was able to outrun her while she was carrying the training blade. Unfortunately, he was still trapped in the pit. No matter how much he ran, he couldn't get away. It wasn't long before Nemo began to tire. Number eight's strikes were coming closer and closer as he dodged each one at the last second. He knew he wouldn't be able to dodge forever. Nemo couldn't come up with any kind of plan while he was running for his life. The differences in strength and ability were just too large for him to overcome. Suddenly, a sharp pain ripped down his back. His next few steps looked like an infant still learning to walk, but he managed to keep from falling as he recovered from the shocking pain.

Nemo could see light reflect off the edge the blade behind him. He didn't know how close that meant she was, but he knew it was too close. If he got hit again, he doubted that he would be able to stumble through it and keep running. Her last strike sapped what little energy he had left.

Not to mention the pain he felt from the top of his shoulder down through his back was steadily getting worse.

Nemo got one final boost of adrenaline from his fear of being cut again. He ran halfway around the pit before slowing down and dropping to his knees. Nemo could barely breathe. He hadn't run like that since he was a little kid. Number eight hadn't even broken a sweat chasing him. Her eyes were wide with the prospect of an easy target.

Nemo knew his time was up. He had no energy left to run, was too injured to quickly dodge, and nowhere near enough strength to stop her. Soon it would be over. He just wished he could see his parents one last time and let them know how much he was going to miss them. They probably would miss him even more, never knowing what happened to their son.

Number eight was nearly on him. A couple more steps and she would be there, and then it would be over for him. He prepared himself for the final strike. He wanted to close his eyes, but instead he stared her down. Somewhere along the way he had found the courage to want to see his final moments before death. Number eight was nearly one step away. The katana was high above her head, ready to deal the final blow. Right before she swung, her foot landed in the six inch deep hole made by the sword Nemo knocked over from the rack. Nemo saw her trip right before his eyes. The katana flew from her hands and hit the wall beside her, knocking down every weapon on the rack. Before number eight could get back up, three hundred pounds of weapons fell on top of her.

Nemo sat there, staring in disbelief. The crowd around him shouted with cheers, boos, and everything else in between while Rufus rushed over to Nemo to assess the situation.

"Doesn't look like she's dead, but she won't be fighting anymore. Ladies and gentlemen, that means we have a winner, applicant number twenty! What a surprising turn of events for the first fight. This is guaranteed to be a great year for the Trials. The final betting odds were an amazing 26:1! Congratulations to those of you that won. To those of you that lost, better luck next time. Give it up for applicant number twenty as he moves on to stage two!"

A mixture of cheers and boos resounded around the pit as Nemo walked out. His heart was still pounding at the thought of how close he had come to death just a few seconds ago. Several attendants came over to treat his wounds and guide him to the waiting area for stage two. He still had no idea what kind of test stage two would be. All he knew was that he was alive, and it was the happiest feeling in the world.

CHAPTER 6

Nemo wasn't really paying attention as while he walked, so he was surprised when they ended up outside. A crowd of people followed behind him and the other applicants. Rufus lead the way, walking them through the fields behind the Citadel until he came to an abrupt stop. Rufus motioned for all of them to line up side by side. In front of them was a large area of swamp land. Skinny trees poked out of large expanses of water, dotted by small islands of land in between the marsh. Water soaked logs bobbed up and down in the murky water. Nemo could see mosquitoes buzzing and frogs jumping across lily pads, but it was the sounds he heard that scared him the most. The sound of dead trees swaying in the wind, the hissing and croaking of creatures hidden in the water, and the eerie quiet moments in between it all were unfamiliar sounds to him. Part of him wondered if there were alligators in there. Another part of him wondered if alligators were the least of his problems. Nemo shook his head to banish the ideas from his mind. He had to focus on the next challenge.

"At least it's day time" said the applicant next to him. "I wouldn't want to be left in there when the sun goes down."

Ten applicants had made it to the second stage. Nemo didn't get to watch the other fights, so he still had no idea who he should try to avoid. By the looks everyone gave him, they all could tell that he was the weakest person there. Thinking back to what *A* had told him about the Trials, the first stage had to be the physical test. That just left mental and spiritual trials. A bit of relief came with the knowledge that he probably wouldn't have to fight anyone else, but the unknown challenges ahead still worried him.

Rufus stepped in front of the applicants and began to hand out long candles. He took his time lighting each of the applicant's candles, and one for himself. Then he began to explain the rules for the stage.

"Welcome remaining applicants, and congratulations again on passing the first stage. Your showing of superior fighting prowess over your opponent has gotten you this far, however time will be your opponent in this challenge. The candles you have in your hands will burn for approximately thirty minutes. You must make it through the swamp and to the other side before your candle goes out. The distance between here and the other edge of the swamp is about five miles. Take special care to keep your candle lit the entire time. If your candle goes out in the swamp you will have a tough time finding a way to relight it. Show up at the finish line with a lit candle and you pass this stage. In regards our betting members watching from the sidelines, you may place bets on whichever candidates you think will make it through the swamp with their candles still burning. The current odds were distributed to you beforehand. Best of luck to you all!"

Nemo saw his opportunity to escape. He completely forgot about the challenge and thought if he could sneak out the side of the swamp, he could run off and find his way home. It was a foolproof plan, until Rufus sat his candle on the ground and turned around to face them.

"Oh yes, one more thing. For any of you thinking about travelling along the side of the swamp in order to run on dry ground, this will not be allowed. If anyone is found outside of the swamp at a place that is not the beginning or end area…"

As Rufus finished his sentence the sound of a gunshot rang through the air. The candle that he placed on the ground was now several shards of wax melting against the ground. All the applicants looked around but no one could find where the shot came from.

"Well I think you get the picture. Cheating of any kind will not be tolerated. I hope to see you all at the finish line. Ready, Set, START!"

As soon as Rufus said start, three applicants rushed to edge of the swamp away from everyone. Two other applicants rushed to the center. Nemo was still feeling the disappointment of realizing his escape plan wouldn't work, he didn't even notice as one of the applicants who rushed to the center reached for his candle. At the same time, a bead of hot wax ran down the side of his candle. Right before his candle was taken from him, the bead of hot wax hit Nemo's hand and he dropped his candle on the ground. The sudden burning pain on his hand jolted him into noticing his surroundings. He looked around and finally realized what was happening.

"The three applicants that ran to the outside somehow knew that two of the applicants would try and steal candles. That way they would have plenty of time to make through the swamp."

Nemo knew that if he allowed his candle to be taken he would never be able to get it back. Luckily when he dropped his candle, the applicant trying to take it moved on. The wet grass threatened to extinguish his candle's flame, but he quickly picked it up while it was still lit and took off into the swamp.

Everything around him was wet and muddy. Odd vines and roots from trees stuck out from the water at every turn. At first Nemo tried to stick to the dry bits of land that dotted the landscape of the swamp, but soon he found himself with nowhere to go but in the water. It wasn't that deep initially, only coming up to his ankles. However, he quickly found out some parts were deeper than others when he slipped off a steep edge and felt the water rise to his waist. He knew that if he fell in the water, his candle would be impossible to relight. Still, he had to try and move faster. At his current pace, he wouldn't even get halfway before his candle burnt out.

Ten minutes had passed and Nemo's candle had burned a third of the way down. He had walked about half a mile, nowhere near the pace required to make it to the end of the swamp before the candle finished burning. So far, he'd been traveling in the shallow sections of the water, using a stick to check in front of him for unexpected drop offs. There was hardly any breeze so he didn't have to worry about his candle being blown out. The other applicants were probably way ahead of him. He hadn't come into contact with anyone else since they started. Other than mosquitoes, he hadn't run into any dangerous wildlife either. All things considered he was actually having a good time. The sounds that were frightening at first were now relaxing and quiet. Out here, it was just him and the sounds of nature. Nemo quickly reminded himself that he needed to pass this challenge or else he would be executed. He needed to find a way to travel faster.

Nemo stopped at the base of a nearby tree, and quietly listened to hear if anyone was nearby. When he was satisfied that no one was near his position, he sat his candle on the ground in a place where it wouldn't tip over and began to climb up the tree in order to get a better view of the swamp. From the top of the trees, he could see a bunch of roots that made a small path through the swamp. Nemo quickly climbed down, grabbed his candle, and took off towards the path. The tangled mesh of roots was solid enough to allow him to run. Throwing caution to wind, Nemo took off running. He needed to make up time.

Twenty-five minutes had passed since the start of stage two. Nemo guessed he had travelled about two miles, but he really had no clue how much farther the finish line was. His candle was starting to reach its end, and the pain from the injuries he received in stage one was returning. Without warning, the sound of an explosion brought Nemo to an abrupt stop. Whatever caused it was ahead of him. But before he could decide what to do, a loudspeaker broadcasting the Rufus' voice came on.

"Ladies and gentlemen we have our first explosion! Courtesy of applicant number ten. His candle must have burned a little faster than normal. Oh, did I forget to mention that the candles are packed with gunpowder and explode when the flame gets too close to bottom? Of course, you can always blow out your candle before it burns to the bottom, but if you don't show up with a lit candle at the finish area you will fail stage two. Let's see which of you applicants really has the guts to risk your life and finish this stage!"

Nemo looked at the candle he was holding with a new found fear. It slowly dripped wax, melting further with each passing second. He thought it ironic that even the simplest things in this place still conspired to kill him. He didn't know how much time his candle had left, but he knew he couldn't waste another second if he was going to finish in time. Nemo took off running again. He needed to move much faster if he was going to reach the end of the stage before his candle decided to make him a human firecracker.

He had been running on the tree roots for over a mile now, his candle's flame was looking weak, and didn't look like it would last much longer. Nemo knew he needed to do something, so he ran with all his strength while hoping his candle would hold on until he could make it to the end. Each minute that passed caused Nemo to look at his candle, wondering when exactly it might explode and if he should blow it out to keep himself from blowing up. Finally to ease his thoughts, he made a line with his fingernail at the bottom of the candle and told himself he would blow it out and throw the candle in the water if he hadn't reached the end by the time the candle burned down to that point. At least he could still try running away out the side of the swamp if he tossed his candle. Although the idea of being shot didn't seem much better than being blown up.

Running on the roots had increased his comfort level with the terrain. However, his confidence was short lived. With his next step, a section covered in dark moss caused him to slip and nearly fall in the water. Instinctively, Nemo held what was left of his candle high in the air, giving every bit of effort to keep the flame from being extinguished. Nemo expected to feel the splash of water around him. Instead, he felt the sharp impact of falling right on top of the tangle of roots. The force of the fall caused him to drop his candle right onto his chest. While everything from his waist down was wet from travelling through the swamp, his thin cotton shirt had remained relatively dry. As soon as the candle make contact with his shirt, he felt it.

Nemo immediately got up and started running, looking for any piece of solid ground. He had been taught in school many times what to do if your clothes were on fire. Stop, drop, and roll. He just needed to find somewhere to do that.

As he ran the flame on his shirt started to grow. The intensity of the heat was no longer concentrated on his shirt, but on his burning skin. Nemo contemplated just jumping in the water, but without a safe place to put down his candle he couldn't risk getting it wet. Finally, after running the quickest quarter mile of his life, Nemo found a patch of dirt and dove into it like a fish into water. He rolled around and covered himself in mud to put out the flames on his shirt. Once the fire was out, he just laid on ground trying to catch his breath and soothe his burned skin.

"I've been kicked, cut, and now burned. This is easily the worst day of my life, and to top it all off I still might die before it's over."

Nemo laid there in the dirt. His candle was nearly at the line he had carved in it. The way things looked now, it was hopeless. He would never make it to the end in time. Nemo prepared himself to follow through with his plan. He opened his mouth, took a deep breath, and brought the candle towards his lips. Just before he was about to blow, an idea came to him. He could burn his shirt instead of the candle. That would give him more time, maybe even enough to make it through the swamp. He quickly got up and grabbed the stick he had been using to guide him through the water, and wrapped his shirt around it. Using his candle, he lit his shirt on fire at the very edge, making sure to keep it away from the rest of the fabric so it would burn slowly. He then blew out his candle and started walking back on the roots towards the end of the swamp.

It had taken him over an hour, but he could finally see the end of the swamp. Many times he needed to stop and relight his candle just so he could sprinkle water on the shirt to keep it from burning too fast. Then he would blow out his candle and continue walking again. Mosquitoes had feasted on his skinny body as he walked through the swamp without a shirt. The bug bites barely bothered him though, the sight of the finish area took his mind off of everything that was irritating him at that moment. Nemo didn't know how many applicants had made it. He had heard at least two explosions but was so focused on his candle that he didn't know if those two were the only ones.

Nemo could see the other ten applicants waiting in the finish area, two were unconscious but alive. Their faces were covered in black soot from being too close to the explosion of gunpowder in their candles. He was the last one to emerge from the swamp and certainly looked like he had the hardest time making it there. There was hardly any time to spare. As soon as he handed his candle over, Rufus threw it high into the air right before it exploded. Nemo fell to the ground and nearly collapsed thinking about how close he was to being next to that candle when it detonated. Still, he was satisfied by the fact that he made it.

With all the applicants at the finishing area for stage two, Rufus stood to announce the completion of the stage.

"Congratulations to all six applicants who passed stage two! For our betting members, if you picked any of these six that makes you a winner! Congratulations and enjoy the spoils from your winnings. Now, I need the medical team to check on the unconscious applicants, and escort those who failed back to the manor. Better luck next year."

Nemo saw the two applicants who had their candles taken at the beginning of the stage get up, and the two that were unconscious being carried off. Somehow, he had managed to succeed where those four had failed. For once in his life, he was actually proud of himself.

Rufus resumed speaking once the medical team removed the four applicants that failed the stage. "Now that they're out of the way I'd like to highlight the fastest and slowest times of those that passed this stage. The fastest time of seventeen minutes and fifty seconds belongs to applicant number four! That is a new course record. The slowest time of one hour, twelve minutes and thirty-two seconds belongs to applicant number 20. Also, a new course record for the slowest time. Congratulations again to you all who are moving on to stage three. Let us hope your good fortune continues."

Nemo felt that Rufus' last comment was directed at him. Still, even with the slowest time, Nemo was proud of himself. Nothing could shake his confidence. Despite his injuries and his fatigue, he was ready for whatever challenges awaited him in stage three.

CHAPTER 7

Nemo was given a new shirt and led into a small room. His confidence was soaring from the last stage. But after sitting down and letting his body rest, he was really starting to feel his injuries. So far all he had been told to do was wait in this room. Typical, the majority of his time in this insane place was spent waiting. The room was dark. The only light came from several candles arranged around the perimeter of the room. After everything he went through in stage two, candles were the last thing he wanted to see right now. But these gave off a sweet aroma and for some reason put him in a good mood. However, there was something odd about this room. It had two doors. There was the one door he came through, and another one on the other side of the room facing him. Just as Nemo was pondering what could be behind that door, someone walked in.

"Hi, you must be Nemo right? My name is Janus."

Nemo stared at the person who walked in. He was a tall, well built man with short blonde hair. Muscles bulged from his neck, shoulders, and down through nearly every part of his body. A long broadsword hung from his hip, fitting him as naturally as his dark blue eyes. Nemo took his time standing up before walking over to introduce himself.

"Yes, I'm Nemo. Nice to meet you Janus. Are you here to take me to the next stage?"

"No, this is the final stage." Janus said in confident tone. Surprised by his words, Nemo looked around the room.

"But where is the Rufus and the other applicants?"

"Stage three is a bit different" replied Janus. "There's no moderator, no other applicants, no betting. Just you, me and this room."

Nemo could feel his anxiety starting to rise again. All the confidence he had built up slowly started to fade away just by being in the same room with this goliath of a man.

Janus could see the fear building on Nemo's face and tried to calm him down.

"Don't worry, I know I look pretty intimidating but I'm actually one of the nicest directors for stage three. I'll even let you pick."

Nemo's speeding heart started to slow down as he let out a long deep breathe. He was relieved to hear those words and looked to the sky to say a quick thank you to whatever god that finally gave him a break.

"So nice people do exist in this place, for a while I thought everyone was trying to kill me. What do I need to do to pass this stage, and what are you letting me pick?"

Janus walked closer to Nemo and spoke with a reassuring voice.

"It's really simple actually. All you have to do is defeat me. I'll let you pick what arm you want to lose first, you right or your left?"

Several seconds passed before what Janus said actually registered with Nemo. When he finally understood, his anxiety shot up so fast he thought his heart might explode. Immediately Nemo jumped back, trying to put as much distance between him and Janus as possible. When he was far enough to what he thought was safe distance, he noticed a trail of blood on the floor. A large pool of blood remained in the spot where he first stood, in the middle of that pool sat his right arm. Nemo slowly looked to his side, fearing what he already knew to be true. His right arm was gone.

Janus was still standing in the same spot, as if he hadn't moved at all.

"You took too long to decide, so I chose for you. Your next choice is your left arm or your left leg?"

Nemo wanted to run forward and grab his arm lying on the floor, but before he could move every nerve on his right side lit up in excruciating pain. The sensation immediately dropped him to his knees. Even in his wildest nightmares, he couldn't have imagined that pain this intense existed. All his other injuries were paper cuts compared to the feeling of losing his arm. The pain was so strong, he couldn't even scream. He opened his mouth but nothing came out.

Nemo tried to reach over and stop the bleeding with his left hand, but he suddenly couldn't feel his left arm anymore. Right next to him, in an even larger pool of blood, lay his left arm. If it weren't for the tremendous amount of pain keeping him awake, he would have fainted just at the sight of his arms on the ground. Janus still stood in the same spot, looking as if he had never moved.

"You took too long again. Honestly if you're going to just waste my time and generosity I'm going to stop giving you a choice."

Nemo could barely hear anything that Janus said. The pain was blurring his vision and blocking out everything but his own internal screams. It was all happening too fast.

Nemo couldn't even see him move, there was no way he had any chance of beating him.

"If you want my advice, just give up now. Plenty of people live full lives without arms. If you give up now you can still walk away with your life." said Janus.

"Give up" was all Nemo heard. It was an idea he had nearly forgotten about. Part of him welcomed giving up. He welcomed anything that promised to deliver him from this hell and make his pain stop. Nemo tried to form his mouth to say the words "I give up", but he could barely think straight. His thoughts transitioned to when he was back in stage one. He thought about how he was ready to die at that last moment, and how many times he had been close to death in the past two days. Somehow, even as Nemo was thinking of saying 'I give up', the word that came out his mouth was "No".

"No? Did I just hear you say no?" Janus asked laughing, as if he couldn't believe the kid's answer. "Alright, but you must be pretty stupid to want and continue this fight. Since you're no good at choosing, I'll let you know it will be you left leg this time."

Nearly as soon as the words left his mouth, Nemo felt the pressure on his left leg disappear. He immediately fell over on the ground, lying in a pool of his own blood mixed with the scattered remains of his limbs. Nemo was already in so much pain that he hardly felt it when his leg was cut off, but at that point it didn't matter. In that small space of time, Nemo had relived all the challenges he conquered earlier that day. In that small instance, he steeled his determination to know he wasn't going to give up, even if that meant dying. Nemo finally understood what Neith had told him that morning, "Every day is a day I might die, so why should I treat it any differently than the rest?"

"How about now, ready to give up? If you do it quickly we might be able to get you to a doctor in time to reattach some of your limbs." Janus said as he stared at Nemo, struggling to move in the growing puddle of his own blood.

Nemo lifted his head away from the mess on the floor. It was all he could manage to stay conscious.

"No, you'll have to kill me."

Janus looked at Nemo in complete surprise and burst out in laughter.

"I don't know want kind of honorable death you think you're giving yourself, but you should really rethink your decision. This is your last chance kid, give up now or you won't be able to go back and regret the decision you made."

The whole time Nemo had not seen Janus move from the spot he was standing in when the battle first started. His sword looked as if he hadn't touched it the entire fight, still sitting in its scabbard.

Janus slowly walked over to what was left of Nemo's body. It was the first move Nemo had seen him make. Nemo wanted to move away, but the ability to move his body was long gone. Only his right leg was still attached, and it had gone numb from the pain of losing his other limbs. Janus slowly pulled his sword from its resting place on his hip and pointed it at squarely at Nemo's heart.

"I came close so you can hear me clearly. This is your last chance boy, hurry and give up so we can get you to a doctor before you bleed out. If you insist on being stubborn this will be the last moment of your life. Is this how you really want to die, lying in pool of your own blood in some unknown room?"

Nemo wanted to make sure he got the words out before he passed out, if these were his last words he wanted to make sure they were heard.

"I'm not giving up!" he said with every last ounce of conviction he had left.

"So be it then." Janus said as he drew his sword back for the final strike. Nemo felt the blade touch his shoulder and then heard the words he least expected to hear.

"You pass".

CHAPTER 8

Nemo opened his eyes to find himself kneeling on the floor in the middle of the room. He didn't remember closing his eyes and he certainly didn't remember kneeling down. Sweat pooled below him as large drops ran off his face and down his arms. His shirt was thoroughly soaked. Beads of sweat dripped off the bottom of it. All the candles had been blown out except for one, giving off just enough light to barely see. In that light, Nemo saw that his arms and legs were still attached. In fact, none of the injuries he received in that room were there.

"Did I imagine the whole thing?" Nemo thought. "No the pain was all too real. I couldn't have imagined that."

He touched his face expecting to feel blood. Nothing was there. Even though he couldn't care less how he regained his limbs, part of him needed to know.

"What happened?" Nemo asked Janus.

"You passed, that's what happened. But I guess you're referring to why you're sitting here in one piece instead of bleeding out on the floor."

"Yea, what you said" was all Nemo could manage to respond with while the memory of everything that had just happened was still fresh in his mind.

"It was all so real. It felt so real that I'm wondering if I'm dreaming now, or maybe I'm dead."

"You're not dead." replied Janus "Like I already told you, you passed. You couldn't pass if you were dead."

Janus could see that Nemo still didn't really understand what he was telling him.

"Hmm, let me start from the beginning and explain. The fragrance from the candles in this room causes hallucinations. You were told to wait in here for a while before I came in, giving you plenty of time to be exposed to the effects of the candles. Also, this room has no windows and hardly any ventilation, ensuring you would be good and stoned by the time I came in. These hallucinations can be powerful and extremely vivid. All it takes is a little suggestive wording, like saying I'll cut off your arm, and your mind does the rest.

"What about the pain I felt, how could I hallucinate something I've never felt before?" Nemo asked.

"Oh the pain was real. You'd be surprised what the mind can be tricked into experiencing. Let your brain think your arm was cut off and it will send the appropriate response as if it was."

Nemo rubbed his elbow and felt down his arm. Not even a scratch from earlier remained. He still couldn't believe it all happened in his head.

"Well, how come you didn't start hallucinating? Shouldn't the candles have affected you in the same way?" Janus held up three fingers.

"Three reasons. One, you weren't talking to me to guide my mind into a hallucination. Two, I know that the candles are supposed to cause hallucinations, so I can focus my mind to counteract that. And three, I'm a goddamn member of Fratello della Spada. No simple trick like that should work on me. You'd do well to remember that too, now that you're one of us."

That last part caught Nemo's attention. "You mean, I'm a member now?"

"How many times do I have to tell you kid, you passed. Stage three is a test of your fighting spirit, and you have plenty of it. You refused give up no matter what I said. That means you pass. Keep that determination, you're going to need it in the future as a member of this organization."

Nemo's eyes went wide with understanding. "So this means I can go home!"

"Sure, if that's what you want. You can come and go as you please, but you'll probably want to stay for the ceremony first."

"Ceremony, what ceremony?"

Janus was quickly becoming tired of answering Nemo's everlasting questions. "Come on just follow me, unless you want to stay here and redo the stage all over again."

Hearing that, Nemo stopped talking and jumped up to follow Janus.

Nemo was led into a large banquet hall, the smell of good food roamed through air as people celebrated all around. He could see four other applicants standing at the front of the room. As usual he seemed to be the last one to finish. *A* was the first one to come up and greet him.

"Well done Nemo! Who knew you'd actually make it through the Trials. I hate to admit it, but I didn't have much faith in you making it here. But despite my reluctance, I bet on you each stage. I'm glad I did too. You've made me quite a bit of extra coin. Clearly no one thought you would survive because the odds on you were absolutely fantastic."

"Ugh, Thanks *A*... I guess." said Nemo, not knowing if he should be grateful or offended.

"Oh nonsense, call me by my real name. After all, you're one of us now. My name is Arthur, Arthur Cunningham. It's a pleasure to formally make your acquaintance Nathaniel."

Nemo felt weird anytime someone besides his parents used his real name. It was rare that anyone called him anything other than Nemo. As Arthur finished introducing himself, *B*, *C*, and *E* ran up to him as well.

"I always knew you could do it!" said *B* "The others had their doubts but I knew you would make it through. By the way, my name's Percival. Pleasure to meet you."

C and *E* introduced themselves, equally as excited that Nemo made it through the Trials.

"My name is Lancelot."

"And my name is Tristan. Boy, I'm glad we didn't have to kill you."

All the interrogators let out a hearty laugh at Tristan's statement. Nemo still didn't find it very funny. Just a few hours ago he hated all of them, but for some reason he couldn't find the motivation to hate them now. It seemed they were all genuinely happy for him.

"Now gentlemen, let's stop wasting Nemo's time. He has to get to front with the other four applicants. They've already been waiting for fifteen minutes. Go ahead Nemo, head to the front of the room so we can officially get this banquet started." said Arthur

Nemo walked to the front of the room and stood by the other applicants. Rufus was at the front patiently waiting.

"Good you're finally here, let's go ahead and get started. Ahem, ladies and gentlemen. After a long day filled with danger, excitement, and surprises, I present to you the newest members of Fratello della Spada! Let's go down the line and have our newest members introduce themselves by giving their name and the master they'll be training under. Let's start with you, applicant number four!"

Applicant number four stepped forward and spoke. "My name is CJ Bregdon, I'll be studying under master Saint Georges"

"Congratulations and welcome to Fratello della Spada. For anyone that wasn't watching stage two, applicant number four set a new record time for clearing that stage. I'm sure we can expect to see wonderful things from you in the future. Next, applicants number one and two. Go ahead and introduce yourselves."

Applicants one and two stepped forward together.

"Greetings I am Tai Liu, the oldest of the Liu twins."

"And I am Xiu Liu, the prettiest of the Liu twins."

"And we will be studying together under master Hao Jiang."

Nemo remembered the boy and girl from stage two. They were the ones who rushed in and tried to steal candles from the other applicants.

Rufus continued with his introductions, "Congratulations to you both, and welcome to Fratello della Spada. While it's rare for a master to take on more than one disciple at a time, I'm sure master Hao is up to the challenge. Next up, applicant number seventeen introduce yourself."

Applicant seventeen stepped forward. "……."

The room was silent. Rufus stared at applicant seventeen as he waved his hands around without saying anything.

"Go ahead don't be shy, now's the time to let everyone know your name."

"……."

Rufus continued to watch applicant seventeen sign in the air before realizing his mistake. "Oh my apologies, I forgot you are mute. Allow me to introduce applicant number seventeen, his name is Tommy Faulk. He will be studying under master Absolon Bissette. If you saw his astounding performance in the Trials, then you know that this applicant doesn't need to talk a big game. Congratulations and welcome to Fratello della Spada. Last but not least, applicant number twenty introduce yourself."

Nemo stepped forward and looked out at all the people in front of him.

"My name is Nathaniel Lake, but everyone calls me Nemo. Umm, I don't know who I'll be studying under because I was kind of forced into this…"

As Nemo was speaking Neith shouted from the back of the room.

"He'll be studying under me!"

Everyone turned around, surprised by the sudden outburst. Whispered voices broke out through the crowd and could be heard talking from where Nemo stood. He didn't know what they were saying, but none of it sounded positive. Rufus quickly started speaking again to maintain the composure of the room.

"Well as we all just heard, you will be studying under master Neith Mansour." Rufus said to Nemo before turning around to address the crowd.

"Everyone this boy had undoubtedly the worst performance I've ever seen in the Trials. Yet somehow he still stands before you now. I think we can all agree our doubts were no match for your determination. Congratulations and welcome to Fratello della Spada!"

The interrogators and Neith near the back of the room were the only ones to clap at the announcement. Everyone else looked either indifferent or confused. Nemo could see that even though he made it through the Trials, many people still didn't think he deserved to be there.

Rufus didn't bother to wait for the small group of applause to finish before moving to conclude the ceremony.

"Well let's go ahead and finish this up. By the rules and bylaws of Fratello della Spada I now confer upon you all the rank of *Ombra*. May you learn and grow from those that came before you, and teach those that come after you as you endeavor to advance the art of the sword and the goals of this organization."

The room erupted in applause with the induction of the new initiates. Nemo felt the applause were mostly for the other four, but he made himself believe that they were clapping for him as well.

The five new initiates walked from the front of the room to join the crowd. Nemo cautiously looked around at all the unfamiliar faces. He still barely understood everything that was happening. Neith walked up to him and slapped him on the back.

"Congratulations! I'm sure you've heard that enough today, but I thought I'd tell you anyway. Me and those dummies you call interrogators had a discussion and decided that since it's my fault you had to go through all of this, I'd become your master if you survived the Trials. If you want to become my disciple that is. You're an official Shadow now so you're free to leave and never come back if that's what you choose to do."

Nemo looked down and thought about everything that had happened that day. There wasn't one thing that he could honestly say he enjoyed. The whole time, throughout each of the stages, all he wanted to do was return to his normal life. But maybe this was just what he needed to break out of being normal. All his life he'd been average, never expecting much from himself. After everything he had been through, the only think Nemo was sure about is that he no longer wanted to be just normal. However, he wasn't ready to let Neith know that just yet.

"I don't know. It's a lot to think about. Right now I'm just happy to be alive. I can't think of anything else I would want more than that right now."

Nemo decided to change the subject so he didn't have to do anymore hard thinking. "What's an *Ombra*?"

Neith smiled at the question. She could look in his eyes and tell he had grown a lot in a very short period of time. His whole view of the world had been turned on its head, and somehow he still was able to maintain his boyish innocence. It was still too early to tell if she would actually like him as a disciple, or if he would just annoy her. At the very least, she could always use a new errand boy.

"*Ombra* means shadow, it's the first rank given to every new member of Fratello della Spada."

Neith paused to notice the look on Nemo's face. He was clearly hoping for give a more detailed explanation of what he was just risked his life to join. Knowing how little he knew of what was going on, she couldn't help but indulge him.

"You were kind of thrown into this, so I guess now is a good time to tell you some of the history of our organization. Fratello della Spada was founded as a club for sword masters to pass on their techniques. Over time the organization grew to have members around the world, all dedicated to preserving and advancing the arts of swordsmanship. With so many master swordsmen gathered together, eager to test their skills, duels were a common occurrence. Eventually a ranking system was developed.

"All new initiates are taken as a disciple under a master to be trained in a specific style of swordsmanship and given the rank of Shadow. To advance to the next rank requires a test similar to the Trials, except much shorter and without all this parading and pageantry. It's called a Master Trial, and you must pass it before you can be recognized as a true master of the sword. Once you pass the Master Trial you are promoted to *Cavaliere Ombra* or Knight Shadow. The Knight Shadow rank has four distinctions. The first is no star. This distinction is for newly minted masters and usually lasts less than a year. Enough time for you to get used to your new rank and responsibilities. Percival over there is a no star Knight Shadow. He just passed his Master Trial a couple of months ago. Next is one star, this is the rank both Arthur and I currently hold."

Neith gave a condescending look in Arthur's direction. "Although we are far from equal."

This wasn't the first time Nemo noticed that Neith always had a sense of superiority about herself. He didn't know if that was just her personality, or if it was well deserved. After firmly stressing her point, she continued.

"Above one star is of course the two star rank. I believe you met Janus, he's currently a two-star Knight Shadow. Finally, there's the three star rank. This class is reserved for those you hear about in legends. It's far from easy to attain. To become a three star your skills must truly be world renowned. A three star ranking puts you in league with some of the best swordsmen of all time!"

Neith paused to let the gravity of her explanation sink in.

"The last rank isn't really a rank at all, more of a title. That is the rank of *Grande Fantasma* or Grand Phantom. It's the title of those elected to the council, the governing body of Fratello della Spada. All major decisions that involve the organization as a whole go through the council."

Neith shook her head as if she had other thoughts about the council that she refrained from saying.

"You only become a Grand Phantom if you want to play politics. Anyway, all this is just for your information. All you need to worry about is doing what I say, when I say it. This will be my first time ever having a disciple, so concepts like leniency and mercy might take me some time to get used to. You are officially my new play thing."

Neith's eyes lit up as she referred to Nemo as a play thing. He already didn't really like the sound of that. One could only imagine what kind of sick and twisted things this woman had planned for him. Just the look in her eyes made him want to quit and never come back, but since he was already in he figured he might as well give it a try. Hopefully he didn't regret his decision.

"I guess I'm your disciple then, when do we start?"

"Well there's nothing I can do with you with the shape you're in now. Go home and let your injuries heal. We'll start your training next week. Besides, I'm sure your parents are worried sick by now."

Nemo had forgotten all about how worried his parents must be. It had been almost two days since he left home to get butter. His mom was probably throwing fits by now.

"Crap, I have to get home to let my folks know I'm ok!" Overhearing the conversation, Arthur walked up and interjected.

"Why don't you allow me to take your new disciple home. I'm sure his parents will be a little more relaxed if an officer shows up with their son, rather than some random stranger."

Nemo immediately turned around and asked Arthur, "You're a police officer?"

"Actually I'm a detective." Arthur responded

Nemo's eyes betrayed his skepticism. "Like a real detective?"

"Why yes, you didn't think we just sat around here and talked about swords all day did you? Some of us have real jobs. Besides, I wasn't lying before when I told you no one would look for your body." The look in Arthur's eyes said more than his words ever could. He slowly turned around and motioned for Nemo to follow him.

"Now let's get you home."

After Nemo and Arthur left, Neith stayed behind to enjoy what was left of the food from the ceremony. She could hardly believe she agreed to take on a disciple, and a really weak one at that. She must be getting old. Still, it might be fun having someone to boss around, even if he was a pathetic little thing. That just meant he had all the room in the world to improve, and it would be all due to her amazing teaching prowess. Neith's daydreams about her new disciple were abruptly interrupted by a sharp, high pitched scream. Everyone rushed down the hall to see what was going on. As Neith ran to look among the crowd she saw what had caused the scream.

Janus was dead.

CHAPTER 9

"The charge is treason" said Megas' aide to the three men in front of him. All at once they started to shout curses and explanations. The rattling of their chains only helped to drown out their already colliding voices. Even if they were to scream in unison, the winding passages of the caves they were in ensured that no one would ever hear them. A single torch hissed on the cave wall providing just enough light for the men to see each other.

"Where is Megas? Let me speak to him" One of them demanded. "If I could just speak to him I'm sure we can clear this entire misunderstanding—"

"Megas will not be coming here. He has instructed me to deal with your punishment in whichever way I see fit." said the aide. He made sure to look each of them in the eye, and speak slowly, so they could understand the finality of their situation. The one chained in middle was the first to understand the context between his words. Megas' aide could see it on his face when he realized that all three of them were about to die.

Immediately he started to rip at his chains, putting all of his muscle behind each attempt to break them from the stone walls behind him. Megas' aide was content to sit there and watch him try. He had more than a few minutes to spare to enjoy the grief of dying men.

"You can keep struggling all you want, those chains have been stuck deep in that stone for centuries. It's truly amazing what you can find in some of these ruins. Just think of the countless men that have died in this very room. You should be honored."

The man on the right was still seething with anger. Hopelessness had not reached him yet. In due time it would come to all of them, he would make sure of it.

"How dare you treat us like this!" shouted the man chained on the right. "We three have served under Megas' for years. You think just because you're related, you can show up in the last few months and take over what we've spent years building!"

"Now is no time to argue your position. Your replacements have already been chosen. Megas has no need for those that don't agree with his plans." said the aide

The gravity of everything finally reached the man on the left. He slumped to the ground as tears streamed from his eyes.

"We were mercenaries. We fought to make money, this new plan of his would get us all killed. And for what? Petty revenge…revenge for some woman. You put this idea in his head, and you've wanted us out of your way since you showed up by Megas' side. I bet you planned all of this. I should kill you with my bare hands."

Megas' aide simply watched the three struggle against their chains. He sat right in front of them, so close he could feel their fingernails scratch his skin. He watched them claw for him with everything they had, exerting every ounce of strength in their bodies trying to grab him. When they finally grew tired of reaching for him, all three quietly sat back against the stone wall that anchored their chains. The moment he was waiting for had arrived, the moment they realized pure hopelessness.

"Go ahead and kill us already" said the man in the middle "You've had that gun behind your back since you walked in. Go ahead and show us how much of a man you are and shoot us already."

Megas' aide couldn't help but laugh as he sat the gun down on the ground, just beyond their reach. "Why I never planned to shoot you, where's the fun in that? Besides this gun only has two bullets."

The three prisoners looked at each other in confusion, wondering if maybe one of them would survive after all. Megas' aide made sure to trample on those hopes almost immediately.

"While you can't reach it now, given a few days without food and water I'm sure one of you will find it in you to stretch for it. First one to reach to gun gets to die quickly, and take one person with him. Loser gets to starve."

Megas' aide turned to walk out of the small cave that held the prisoners. His appetite for grief had been fully satisfied. He might even crack a smile as he enjoyed his walk back to the main cavern. He took a few steps in to the darkness of the tunnels that connected the cave before stopping.

"You know it's a shame we never got around to putting in the wiring for lights this deep in the caves. I wouldn't want to get lost on my way back so I'll need this torch. Guess you men will have to enjoy your last living moments in the dark."

As he walked back through the tunnels, Megas' aide heard two gunshots followed by a scream. It was a sweet music to his ears.

CHAPTER 10

"Commander Megas, the three replacements for your captains have arrived."

"Who?" Megas replied without bothering to lift his head from his work.

Megas' aide didn't expect Megas to hear him the first time. When the commander was focused on a problem his concentration was nearly impossible to break. He walked closer until he was right in the commander's ear, making sure Megas wouldn't miss what he said this time.

"The ones you requested, the boy, the Irishman, and the warlord, are here!"

The sudden outburst disturbed Megas from his deep thoughts.

"What... Oh yes, I'll be there in a minute"

"Fine... I'll be waiting outside the conference room if you need me." replied the aide.

He wasn't going to argue with him. The man was just as stubborn as he was brilliant. Those qualities are probably what made him one of the best military strategists alive. Ever since they were kids, Megas was always one step ahead of him. Things he worked hard to learn seem to come naturally to his younger brother. But despite all of his strategical acumen, Megas lacked people skills. That's where his role came in. He helped Megas 'deal' with people.

"Just try not to keep them waiting long." said the aide as he paused in the doorway.

"The three you picked don't seem like the patient type, and we still have to convince them to go along with our plan. I suggested a number of well qualified people that would be undoubtedly loyal to us, but you went and picked the three people you wanted. Getting them here was no small endeavor. Sometimes I wonder if you purposely make things difficult."

"That's why I'm the leader and you're the second in command" said Megas. "Trust me brother, you'll see the rewards from all our efforts in due time."

He loved to see the look of frustration on his older brother's face. It was one of the few highlights in his day. Lately, all of his time was spent meticulously planning their next move. Different scenarios, different strategies based on different enemy attack patterns, the possibilities were near endless. He needed to account for them all if they were to succeed. Without the one, single goal that fueled him, he would have stopped this a long time ago. Now it was all he lived for.

Megas reached into his pocket and felt the folded up picture he always kept with him. He didn't need to look at it anymore. He had stared at that picture so often that feeling each crease, each individual bend, on the picture brought the image to the forefront of his mind. He slowly pulled his hand from inside his pocket and refocused his thoughts on the task at hand.

"Alright, let's go. I'm sure they're all anxious to meet the man who made them come all the way out here."

Megas walked into the conference room with his brother behind him. A long oak table with four chairs surrounding it sat in the middle. The three people he requested were already sitting on one side of the table. Megas walked up to the single chair on the other side of the table and sat down before mentally gauging the people he'd been waiting for.

The first person that caught his attention was a thin boy sitting directly across from him. Thin was an understatement. His body looked frail, possibly malnourished. His cheeks sunk into his face, giving him the ominous look of a skeleton with skin. But the strangest thing about him wasn't how he looked. Megas could feel a strong, dark energy radiating from him. Even as the boy just sat there quietly, this energy pulsed and vibrated the air around them. Just being in the same room with him felt like being pulled deeper into a bottomless pit with each passing second. Megas could only guess that meant he had the right person.

Next to the boy sat the Irishman. He was the exact opposite of the leprechaun stereotype, tall and well built. His lean frame emphasized his strong physique, undoubtedly developed from numerous battles. His short red beard and red hair were the only things that were noticeable Irish about him.

Closest to Megas sat a dark-skinned man with the look of royalty. He had spent the last few minutes scrutinizing the décor of the room as if he was used to a much finer setting. Still, there was something deadly about him beneath his royal, stuck up personality. It was the look in his eyes that said he held no value for anyone's life but his own. Probably not the best attribute for a ruler of a country, but just what Megas needed. He could always use someone with particular tastes and talents, especially when they were in a predicament that gave him leverage.

He would need all of their cooperation to achieve his goals. Each person had their own unique set of skills that would be vital for what he had planned.

"Gentlemen, thank you all for coming. I am Commander Megas Krav, and the reason we are here today is because we each have a certain goals we want to accomplish. Now while our goals may be different, the means to achieving them are the same, which is why it only makes sense for us to work together."

The Irishman was the first to break the silence from the other side of the table.

"Let me stop ya right there. Yous say our goals are the same, but why should I believe that. I'm sure me goals are a bit more vague than yours, so why the hell should I be following your advice?"

Megas smiled before taking out a folder from under the table.

"Fortune favors the prepared."

He slid the folder over in front of the Irishman and stood up from his chair. "Open it" he said as he began to walk around the room.

"Oh, I know what your goals are, Garland O'Shea aka Mad Cutter. You're wanted for seventy-nine murders in eighteen countries. Of those eighteen countries, nine of them have you on their most wanted lists. The bounty on your head is around $2 million, maybe more after that last incident of yours. You'll have to tell me later how you managed to hang a man with his own intestines without killing him."

"Sorry lad, trade secret. Besides, that was special for him. He had it coming." Mad Cutter interjected

"What's more impressive than your track record" Megas said talking over Mad Cutter, "is that you travel with complete disregard to these warrants for your arrest. You show your face in public and dare anyone to try and catch you. Yet no police agency of any country has even come close, despite the trail of bodies you leave in your wake."

Mad Cutter leaned back in the padded leather chair and thumbed through the papers in the folder as Megas spoke from across the table. Long strands of red hair fell over his forehead as he read everything that Megas said from the different papers in front of him. The file contained even more information about him than what Megas was saying. Date of birth, relatives, blood type, medical history, it was all there. Somehow this man had managed to collect all the information that he had spent a long time trying to erase. Even the hair in front of his face could not hide his surprised expression. How anyone could have gathered this amount of detailed intelligence on him, he didn't know. But now he was intrigued. He just didn't know yet whether he should join the man that stood in front of him, or kill him.

"I see you've done your homework laddie. Hardly anyone knows me real name is Garlan'. I never liked dat name, which is why all the people dat knew it are dead."

Megas wasn't paying attention to anything Mad Cutter said. He was more interested in watching his reactions. He tossed two more folders on the table, sliding one towards the boy and the other towards the warlord before he continued talking.

"Jean-Vis Mugabe, the self-proclaimed king of the very small but surprisingly violent country to the south, Maiteir. Your people see you as a savior, while the rest of the world sees you as a warlord desperate to conquer anything you can get your hands on."

Jean-Vis leaned back in his satin coated, gold and ivory embroidered chair that he specifically requested in exchange for his attendance to this meeting. His dark lips gave way to a wide bright smile as his eyes looked from behind gold rimmed, tortoise shell glasses. He didn't even bother to open the folder as he kicked his feet up on the table, revealing his custom crocodile loafers that he would bet cost more money than the oak table he was sitting them on.

"Flattery will get you nowhere mon'ami. However, I feel insulted that you seem to know so much about this nobody next to me, yet fail to tell me anything I couldn't look up about myself in the tabloids."

Jean-Vis turned towards Mad Cutter and started to slowly clap his hands with his trademark wide grin on his face.

"Garland was it, well good work on your seventy-nine murders. Mr. Megas must think you deserve a gold star and smiley face sticker to go with it." He stopped clapping as the grin dropped from his face, "I've killed hundreds. How dare you include me with this amateur."

Mad Cutter, still looking through the papers in his folder, responded in a deadly calm voice.

"Call me Garlan' again so me new count can be eighty, and I'll take me gold star from the frames of those cheap glassies."

Without warning, the table in the middle of the room flipped over. Papers from the folder on Jean-Vis flew through the air before gently floating to the ground. Mad Cutter and the quiet boy at the ends of the table both held their folders in their hands, keeping anyone from seeing the information inside. Both bickering men went quiet at Megas' sudden, unexpected display of brute strength.

"Don't interrupt me" said Megas

The three guests, still sitting in their seats, nodded in agreement. Megas' aide was standing in the back of the room, going mostly unnoticed while Megas talked. All he could do was hang his head in disappointment. The meeting was obviously not going as smoothly as they had hoped.

When Megas was positive that he had everyone's undivided attention again, he continued.

"Jena-Vis for the past ten years you have tried, and failed, to take over the country to your west, Tralone. Since a direct war with them would be suicide, you resorted to sending your own assassins for Tralone's prime minister. You needed his death to look like an accident. That plan failed three times, and resulted in all of your men being executed. Luckily for you they were killed without revealing who sent them.

"Next, you tried bribing ordinary citizens of Tralone, except each one you bribed was quickly found out. Again, none of the money could be traced back to your country. But your latest scheme was even more ambitious, perhaps too ambitious even for you. You provided chemical weapons to rebels in Tralone and encouraged them to start a revolution. That plan almost started a war, and lead to the slaughter of hundreds by the Tralonian government. However, this time you didn't cover your tracks completely. They'll be able to trace where the rebel's weapons came from, and then it's only a matter of time before Tralone's army comes marching to your front door. Of all the people here in this room, you need my help the most. Without it, that little town you call a country will be nothing more than a dust mound in six months' time. Luckily for you, I'm willing to offer a solution to your problems. Provided that you help me of course."

That brief speech seemed to convince Jean-Vis to joined Megas' side. His trademark grin was now a scowl on his face, and his crocodile loafers were planted firmly on the floor. Apparently, he didn't like having his dirty laundry aired for everyone in the room to hear. He mumbled to himself as he leaned on the armrest of the pompous chair he requested, "Dead. My security advisors are dead when I get back home."

Megas heard the man's whisper loud and clear.

"Don't bother executing anyone. You'll need all the men you have. You've made too many mistakes to think that you could keep this entire thing secret. Anyone could have found out the information I have, they just aren't looking for it yet."

Jean-Vis' scowl became even more pronounced. He mumbled to himself in an even quieter voice this time. This Megas person had given him no other choice. As much as he didn't like it, he would have to work with him if he enjoyed having a country to rule.

The boy, sitting at the other end of where the table once stood, had been quiet the entire time. He still held his unopened folder in his hands, completely uninterested in what was inside. He hardly even looked surprised by anything that had been said during the meeting. Even when the table was thrown across the room the unimpressed look remained on his sullen face. Megas walked back over in front of him.

"Leo, that's what I've resorted to calling you since no one I found could give me your real name. There are no records of your birth, so no one knows your exact age. Judging from your build and face, I'd guess you're about sixteen. On paper, it's as if you don't even exist. I'm sure more than a few people have found a use for someone like you, but I'm going to offer you something they never could."

The boy hardly acknowledged that Megas was speaking to him. He looked past Megas and stared across the room at nothing.

"Everything is black. All I see is ugly, black darkness around here. Whatever your plan, whatever job you want me to do, I'm not interested."

"I'm not offering you a job. I'm offering you a purpose." Megas replied.

The boy's eyes briefly looked in Megas' direction before returning back to staring at nothing. Megas wasn't bothered by his lack of attention. In fact, he expected it from someone like him. He turned to address the entire group. "The boy that sits beside you two has a very rare talent. Those eyes of his can peek directly into the future."

Both Mad Cutter and Jean-Vis looked at the boy in disbelief. Mad Cutter was eager to test his ability for himself, but he decided to let Megas finish speaking first. Besides, there would be plenty of time to play with him in the near future.

Megas leaned in towards the boy, looking directly in his eyes so they could no longer avoid him.

"I'm offering you a home by my side. No more peddling your services to those that use you and throw you away. No more running and living on the streets. I'm offering you a home. No longer will you be a person that doesn't exist. Come work with me and you'll no longer have to bear your burden alone. I see the darkness in you, the madness you're constantly running from. Let me carry the burden of your darkness for you. I will be your shield to protect you from all those that fear someone like you, someone they could never understand. In return, you will be my arrow, striking down our enemies before they know what's coming."

For the first time the boy's head looked up as if he finally found something that he had been looking for.

"I like the name Leo… I think I'll keep it."

Megas nodded at Leo, knowing his response meant yes. Now he just had one last person to convince, Mad Cutter. He expected Mad Cutter to be the hardest one to reason with. The man wasn't motivated by money, fame, or any other common thing that motivates most men. What interested a killer like him was a mystery. Despite that, Megas still needed him for his plan to succeed. He needed a logical argument to somehow convince a psychopath to join him.

"I'm in, but don't be trying to offer me that same load o' garbage you just told him." Mad Cutter said as he pointed to Leo.

Megas was so lost in his own thoughts that he barely heard Mad Cutter.

"Wait, what did you say?"

"I'm in" replied Mad Cutter as he leaned back in his chair, mimicking Jean-Vis' previous arrogant pose.

"You've assembled an intriguin' wee group here an' I'm interested to see what ya have planned for us. So, I'll play along with ye people for now, at least until I'm bored. I can't promise how long me cooperation will last."

Megas was surprised by this sudden change of heart. Controlling Mad Cutter would be even harder than he thought. He would need to watch him closely to make sure he didn't suddenly decide to change his mind again.

"Fair enough. Gentlemen, welcome to the group I call Guiding Light. For only light can cast out Shadows. Now that you've all agreed to work for me lets go over what I expect of you."

Megas' aide, who had been standing quietly in the back the whole time, stepped forward with three more folders.

"Enclosed in this folder is the plan to annihilate the organization known as Fratello della Spada"

Mad Cutter open the folder and smiled, "Very interestin', very interestin' indeed."

CHAPTER 11

"Faster, faster, no you need to be more explosive." Neith shouted.

Nemo looked to be on the verge of passing out "Neith we've been at this all day. This is as fast as I can go."

"We'll do it all night if we have too! If you can't master these simple movements how do expect to learn anything after this?"

It had been two weeks since Nemo passed the Trials. When Arthur brought him home his parents had been worried sick. His mom was sure that something terrible had happened and was frantically going door to door, asking everyone in the neighborhood to help look for him. Nemo felt a pit in his stomach at the thought of making his parents worry so much, but it's not like he chose to be kidnapped by this crazy woman. Arthur told his parents that he had been at the store getting butter when a group of people came in and robbed the place. They took Nemo hostage to make their escape, but the police managed to catch up with them and save Nemo. Sadly, the criminals escaped. Arthur made it a point to emphasize that the entire police department was tirelessly pursuing them. It all sounded pretty unbelievable. But after seeing Arthur flash his badge and bring their son home, his parents barely even questioned his story. It was like they had just seen it on the news themselves. Nemo doubted that they even listened to the whole explanation before rushing to hug him. He was ok, that was all that mattered to them. Arthur said Nemo bravely tried to fight the thugs off, and in the scuffle received all of his injuries. That should have been even more unbelievable, but again his parents bought the story hook, line, and sinker.

Right before leaving, Arthur gave him his official Fratello della Spada ring. He told Nemo,

"This ring bears the crest of Fratello della Spada and is given to all Shadows. It grants you access to all Fratello della Spada buildings, and certain special rooms. Use it to return to the Citadel in a week if you want to start your training."

That first week as his injuries healed was surreal. Normal life didn't seem the same anymore. Everything seemed to move slower than he remembered. The more he thought about it Nemo realized that his life was the same as it had always been. He was the one that changed. After what seemed like the most boring week ever, he told his parents he was offered free self-defense lessons by a gym that heard about his hostage situation. His parents were all for it. Using that as a cover, he couldn't wait to return to the Citadel and start training. If only he could have known what Neith was about to put him through.

"Annnnnnd Time! Two minutes and eleven seconds. That's still pretty slow, but at least you're improving." Neith said as she looked at Nemo laying on the ground gasping for air.

"C'mon it isn't that hard. I could do this obstacle course in under a minute. We're not going to move on to anything else until you can finish this course in less than one minute and thirty seconds."

Nemo could barely hear anything she said. His lungs were on fire and his muscles felt like they wanted to fall off his bones.

"Explain to me why I'm running around this obstacle course again?"

Neith was becoming annoyed by his constant need for explanations. When she was a disciple, she had enough respect not to ask her master why she was doing something and just do it. She would have to drill that quality into him later.

"I already told you, your fundamentals are pretty much nonexistent. Your strength, speed, and endurance need to be enhanced before you can even think about learning sword techniques. The other disciples that passed the Trials with you have already been training in the basics for years. If you want to catch up to them we'll need to build your muscles more efficiently. The quickest way to do that is using this obstacle course. Now get up, break time is over."

Nemo could barely move, he had been through the course at least ten times already. It was a grueling experience designed to strengthen all his fundamental skills by brute force and repetition. There were rope climb transitions, heavy walls he had to lift and roll under, treadmills that he had to run at top speed to get past, and a stationary bike connected a tower of light bulbs that he had to power by constantly peddling. All in all, it was a pretty high tech obstacle course that could be scaled to test the limits of anybody.

As he slowly stumbled to the starting line he heard a familiar sound. From a far off distance, it sounded like barking. Slowly it got closer and louder, until Nemo realized exactly who the sound was coming from. He immediately took off from the starting line as *D* from the interrogation team rounded the corner frantically chasing after him. Neith could hardly control her laughter at how quickly Nemo moved with *D* behind him.

"I figured you needed some extra motivation. Had I known it would be this effective, I would have brought *D* out when we first started."

As soon as Nemo crossed the finish line for the obstacle course, Neith grabbed *D*. The dog had been so close behind him the whole time that Nemo had scratches in places where *D*'s teeth almost caught him.

"One minute and fifty seconds!" shouted Neith. "Your fastest time yet. I guess a bit of motivation really did help."

Nemo didn't hear a word Neith said. He passed out on the ground as soon as he finished the course. *D* was still barking at the boy's unmoving body on the ground until he finally got tired and sat down. Neith bent down to check Nemo's pulse and make sure he was still breathing.

"Out cold. I guess he really did give it everything he had on that last run. Maybe I should ease up on how hard I push his training."

Neith tapped her cheek and looked up in the air for a moment. "On second thought, nope."

Several weeks passed with Nemo coming to the Citadel every day after school to train with Neith. The place had become near empty since Janus' death. Accusations ran rampant through the halls, and most weren't shy about publicly accusing whoever they thought was responsible. Most of the masters left the Citadel, fearing they might be the next one found dead in the halls. The ones that stayed behind were high on everyone's suspicion list. Champ would have been one of the people everyone suspected. He had a habit of causing trouble. Luckily for him, he left town after Bulo's funeral and hadn't returned since. Neith had her own reasons for staying behind, but she let Nemo believe it was because of his training. He was still oblivious to everything that was going on and she intended to keep it that way for as long as she could.

It had only been a few weeks, but Nemo was already starting to see the definition in his developing muscles and noticed his speed was increasing. Still, he had only been training his fundamentals. He wondered when he would actually start his sword training. As he prepared himself for another day of pure exercise, Neith surprised him when she said,

"Follow me".

They walked up a flight of stairs and back to the end of the hall until they approached a large wooden door with intricately carved designs. Sections of stained glass surrounded the door in a beautiful archway. Neith reached for a thin gold chain that hung around her neck and down between her breasts. On the end of the chain hung a ring bearing the Fratello della Spada crest. She grabbed the ring from inside her shirt and turned to Nemo.

"Here's something about your ring that you probably didn't know. Each of these rings is coded with the information of the member it belongs to. The rings can be updated to allow access to restricted areas in the building. The one you're wearing on your hand now won't allow you access to this room. Only those that have passed the Master Trial can be in this room unattended. Otherwise you must be escorted by someone. The area I'm about to take you in now is our weapon room. It's time for you to pick your first sword."

Nemo walked through the door to find a large dome capped room with swords of all shapes and sizes arranged along the walls. Rays of sunlight passed through the top windows of the dome ceiling, and reflected off the polished blades. Every weapon was arranged in an organized fashion, like a perfectly assembled puzzle. Some of the weapons he had only seen in pictures. Others he could have never even imagined.

Neith escorted him to a large open area within the room before she turned to face him.

"Here in this room is where you are going to pick your own weapon. When you pick a sword, it should feel like you're meeting an old friend for the first time. The sword should feel comfortable in your grip, and you should feel comfortable with it. Don't feel pressured to pick a weapon similar to mine just because I'm your master, in fact I'd prefer it if you didn't. You are your own person and you must pick what is right for you. You may use this open area to test whichever weapon you pick. Take your time, this is all we will be doing today."

Nemo looked around at all the blades in the room. To have to pick from such an arsenal was almost overwhelming. He didn't know where to start.

"Neith if I pick something drastically different from the type of sword you fight with, does that mean you won't be able to teach me how to use it and I'll be assigned to a different master?"

Neith rolled her eyes at the question, "If it were that simple, I would have passed you off to someone else a long time ago. No, any master here could train you in the fundamentals of almost any style. You may study under other masters to learn more advanced techniques, but that will be much further down the line. In your case much, much further."

"Ok, good to know" Nemo responded, ignoring another one of her constant insults about his lack of skills. Part of him was relieved to hear that Neith was stuck with him. He didn't really know what is was, but something about Neith kept him coming back. Somehow, he had become attached to this narcissistic woman and wanted to continue learning from her. Although everyday she worked to make him regret that decision.

"One more thing" Neith said just as Nemo was about to pick up his first sword. "These weapons aren't some old relics we had lying around. Each of these swords was forged here, in this very building, with the latest smithing techniques and highest quality metals available."

Nemo stood and listened as Neith informed him of all the technological advances that made the weapons forged by Fratello della Spada far superior to other weapons. He had always thought of sword making as an ancient art done the same way for thousands of years, but it was clear that modern technology had greatly improved the process.

His mind quickly focused back to the decision at hand. He needed to pick a sword. First he picked up a scimitar like Neith's. He immediately could tell that it was no good. It felt awkward and unwieldy in his hand. After a few minutes of trying it out, he put back and moved on. His next few picks weren't any better. The saber made him feel like a pirate, and any variation of a rapier he chose felt entirely too flimsy. After about thirty minutes of testing out swords, Neith became tired of watching Nemo struggle and stepped in to offer some more guidance.

"You know, you're pretty clumsy. Uncoordinated people like you sometimes need an extra hand to help them, so maybe you should stick to two-handed swords."

Nemo didn't know whether she just enjoyed making fun of him or if she actually was trying to help. But he decided to take her advice anyway and move to the section with two handed swords. The first weapon he picked up was an

English longsword. It felt better than the others. It was heavy, but for some reason he liked the weight. As he swung the blade all his movements with the sword were deliberate and natural, but something still wasn't right. He put the longsword down and continued to look around, until one sword in particular stuck out to him. His hands gripped the handle and immediately felt at home. The weight of it made him feel strong, the length of it made him feel protected. With each swing of the blade, each imaginary strike he made, he felt powerful. This felt like meeting an old friend for the first time.

Neith walked over to Nemo when she saw that he had decided on a sword.

"So you picked a claymore? Something slow, long, and heavy. Are you sure this is what you want?"

Nemo looked at his reflection as he held up the blade in front of him. "I'm sure."

"Well I guess we'll have to double up on your strength training so you can actually hold that thing. I hope you enjoyed the previous pace of your training because it's only getting harder from here."

Nemo almost fainted at the thought of training more brutal than what he had already done. It was either that, or the devilish smile that Neith had on her face when she talked about it. It was as if she enjoyed making him suffer. In fact, he was almost sure she did.

As they turned to leave the weapon room, Neith glanced over and saw a dark blue glow in Nemo's eyes. She turned directly towards him to take a closer look, but the bluish glow was gone.

"What, what is it? Do I have something on my face?" Nemo asked.

"It's nothing. Just the light in this room playing tricks on me." Neith said as she forced herself to believe her own words. She rationalized that it couldn't be what she thought she saw. It must have been a trick of the sunlight.

CHAPTER 12

Neith sat in a plush quilted chair watching Nemo as he meditated with his sword in his lap. She made him add thirty minutes of meditation to his regular training schedule for the past few weeks. While meditating, he was supposed to visualize the skills he had learned, visualize how he would execute them and correct any imperfections in his form. This continuous meditation would not only help to perfect his technique, but it would strengthen the bond between him and his sword so that it would start to feel like an extension of his own body. Of course, in typical Nemo fashion, he didn't understand the purpose of the meditation. Thinking it was just some boring exercise he was forced to do. What was really boring was having to sit there and watch him meditate. Although she did get to enjoy herself by finding amusing ways to wake Nemo every time she caught him falling asleep. He must have gotten tired of being slapped and kicked awake because he hardly ever fell asleep during meditation anymore.

She leaned back the chair and closed her eyes. Long forgotten memories of Bulo and the time they spent together filled her thoughts. Flashbacks of his funeral passed through her mind along with images of his casket being lowered into the ground. Before she knew it her hand was around the hilt of her sword, squeezing it with all her strength in an effort to surpass her rage. The scar above her eye throbbed as her anger threatened to spiral out of control. Before she could descend further into her madness the timer on her phone went off. Meditation time was over.

Nemo opened his eyes and stretched his long thin arms. The meditation was surprisingly relaxing and made him feel renewed with energy. Out of the corner of his eye he could see that Neith looked the opposite of relaxed. When she noticed him looking, she seemed to calm down. He wondered what it was that had her stressed so often. He had asked about it before, but could never get a straight answer from her. She was hardly ever in a sharing mood. The last time he asked her a personal question, she flipped out and promised to train him so hard that he wouldn't have time think about anyone other than himself. She kept her promise that day. He lost count of how many times he passed out from exhaustion. The next day she said that she might have overreacted, which as close as he would get to an apology. But the damage to his psyche was already done. He was too scared to ask her anything personal again. Still, whenever she would space out at random times he could tell that something was bothering her.

Neith started to look through her phone, checking messages and emails when something grabbed her attention. Immediately she jumped up in a surprisingly happy mood.

"Follow me." she said as she happily skipped down the hallway. Nemo had never seen Neith skip before. He knew this couldn't mean anything good for him. They stopped in front of a common looking wooden door near the middle of the hall. Neith grabbed the chain that held her ring and pulled it up from between her breasts. She merrily twisted it around her finger as she scanned the ring and opened the door.

"This room leads to the job board. People post requests for assistance with all types of matters. Although some people like Arthur have steady day jobs, others like myself make money from the odd jobs posted on this board. I just got an email about an interesting job."

It had never occurred to Nemo to ask what Neith did for work. He just assumed that she was at work during the time he was at school.

"What kind of job is it?"

Neith continued to play with the chain around her neck as they walked towards the job board. She went straight to the post she was interested in and began to look it over.

"It's a good one. I was starting to get bored around here because there hadn't been any interesting jobs in a while."

Nemo dreaded to ask what qualified as an interesting job to her, but before he could ask, she told him.

"We're going to stop a bank robbery, Friday at 5pm."

Nemo's mouth dropped open.

"A bank robbery! What do you mean we, why not just you? Why do we have to stop it, why don't we just call the police?"

Neith continued to look at the paper like a happy schoolgirl, enjoying the first piece of good news she had received in a while.

"First, I said we because I mean we. You're coming with me. It'll be good experience to witness some actual combat on your first mission. Second, usually the people who request these kinds of jobs aren't the type to go to the police. Maybe it's a rival gang member, or someone who has grudge against the crew robbing the bank. Either way, it doesn't matter who requested the job as long as we find the conditions acceptable. Third and most important, if we called the police we wouldn't get paid! Besides, any member of Fratello della Spada is better protection than a squad of police officers. Whoever requested the job is better off paying us, than tipping off the police."

Nemo was still in shock. He had done some crazy things up until now, but it still surprised him every time he was forced into a new, highly dangerous situation.

"Won't they have guns? How are we supposed to stop them when they'll be shooting at us?"

"Don't worry, I have a plan."

If Nemo was looking for comfort in her words he didn't find any. He knew anything he said wouldn't change her mind so he might as well mentally prepare himself, and hope he didn't get shot.

"Just another day where I try not to die" Nemo mumbled to himself.

Before he knew it, it was Friday and he was standing in the middle of a bank he knew was about to be robbed, with baggy clothes and a guitar case. It was 4:47pm. No matter how many times he went over the plan in his head, he couldn't stop himself from nervously shaking. Neith lifted her shades and shot him a glance from across the room. He knew what that look meant. If he didn't stop shaking and act natural, Neith would make his life hell when they got back. Nemo tried to calm down. All he had to do was wait in line for a bank teller and follow the plan. Neith was sitting on the other side of the bank pretending to be waiting for a bank manager. Her disguise made her look like somebody important, somebody rich and important. The gray pencil skirt she wore followed the curves of her hips and drew your eyes down her legs. Every man in the bank was distracted by her mere presence. Whatever business had brought them there was now an afterthought in their minds. The color of her heels matched her shirt, which showed just a glimpse of cleavage to catch the attention of anyone passing by. Nemo looked around again and noticed it wasn't just the men staring at her. Everyone in the bank was focused on Neith as if she was the center of the universe. Nemo wasn't sure if her outfit was part of the plan, or if she just liked the attention.

He checked his watch, 4:52pm. Just eight more minutes, he had to keep it together for at least eight more minutes. Luckily, he was wearing his custom bulletproof body armor Neith ordered for him under his clothes, or his shirt would have been dripping in sweat by now. Fratello della Spada seemed to have everything you could ever need at the Citadel. They had world class chefs that could make any meal you wanted, blacksmiths that could forge top quality blades, and even a tailor that sewed clothing from bulletproof material. Even without many of the masters around, the staff alone seemed to keep the place lively.

Neith had warned him that his bulletproof body armor would only stop small caliber rounds, and the thieves would probably be using high powered automatic rifles. Still, he thought it was better than nothing. Looking back at Neith, he couldn't figure out how she fit her bulletproof combat gear under the tight clothes she was wearing. He looked closer. The panty line on her skirt let him know she wasn't wearing any bullet proof gear. Nemo's pale face started to blush, he quickly turned his head towards the teller and recited the plan again in his mind.

4:54 pm, six minutes to go. The bank teller shouted, "Next" as the person in front of him finished their business at the counter. Nemo froze, he still couldn't believe what was about to happen. Everything thing seemed so peaceful, just another normal day with normal people at a normal bank. However, their mere presence broke any hope of that day in the bank continuing to be normal.

"Next", the teller shouted again, looking directly at Nemo to step forward. He took a deep breath, and told himself it was now or never.

He stepped forward. The teller greeted him and asked what she could do for him today. Nemo didn't say a word. He just slid a note through the slot under the glass and waited for the teller to read it. As soon as she read it, her eyes got big. She quickly looked around the bank and back down at the note. Faster than he expected, her face returned to a calm expression and she said,

"I'll have to check with my manager to see if we can process this request".

Nemo nodded his head, and the teller took off into the back. He was sure that she was going to scream when she read the note, but Neith had said that bank workers were trained on what to do in case of a robbery. However, what Neith had written on the note could shock anybody into making a scene. It said,

"This is a robbery. This boy has a bomb strapped to him that will detonate if you don't clear everyone out of the bank in the next five minutes. Use the back door and get as far away as you can, no alarms, no cops. If I get the slightest feeling that you touched an alarm or called the police, you and everyone in the bank die!"

Within the same minute the bank manger came out and announced that the bank had a gas leak and he would need everyone to evacuate the building through the back immediately. By 4:59pm, everyone but Neith and Nemo were out of the bank. Nemo popped open the guitar case he was carrying, passed Neith her scimitar, and slung his claymore over his shoulder letting the sheath rest on his back. Neith kicked off her heels and slid down her skirt, revealing the tight shorts she was wearing underneath.

"Good job clearing the bank. Now I can fight without having to worry about any hostages. Let's hope these thieves are punctual, I'm sure that note bought us ten minutes max before the police show up. You and I don't want to be the only ones here without the real criminals to pin that note on. Now stand back and pay attention, this shouldn't take long."

5:00 pm exactly. Six people rushed through the bank doors spraying bullets into the ceiling and screaming,

"This is a robbery! Everybody down on the ground!"

Nemo quickly looked over at Neith and saw the smile on her face. She looked back at him and said,

"Just another normal day".

CHAPTER 13

Before the first person through the door could notice that the bank was empty, Neith came running from the side. With two long strides, she jumped up and kicked him square in his jaw. Without any pause in her motions, she used her momentum to spin around and kick the next closest assailant directly in the neck. Both men went tumbling clear across the room. Barely five seconds had passed since they entered the bank and already two of them were down. Nemo looked in utter amazement. Even though he had seen Neith move like this in practice, looking at her in a real fight was completely different.

The other four assailants still didn't know what was going on, but it was clear to them that this wasn't going like they planned. All at once they started shooting at Neith, spraying bullets in every direction they saw her move. Bullet holes began to appear on the walls and every other surface in the bank. Nemo flipped a desk and ducked behind it for cover. He was so scared, he could swim in the pool of sweat dripping from his face. A line of bullets pierced the desk right next to where he was taking cover. He quickly rolled to the side and got up sprinting towards the nearest cubicle. During that brief moment, he could see Neith running between cover drawing their bullets away from him. The gunmen moved as a unit, hardly giving Neith an opening to attack. These weren't amateurs she was dealing with. If she hadn't caught two of them off guard first, dealing with the group would have been a problem.

Nemo peeked from behind his cover. He saw Neith finally draw her sword that had been resting on her hip as she ran around the room. The distinct sound of it being drawn reminded him of the first time they met, except this time it would be someone else on the receiving end of her fury.

Neith yelled, "Nemo stay down!"

She didn't have to tell him twice. Running directly into bullets was never one of his strong points.

Neith picked up and threw one of the small sturdy tables that dotted the bank floor. In the brief amount of time it took the thieves to move out of the way, she had the opening she needed. She quickly ran diagonally towards the wall as bullets followed her every step. Nemo thought she would have to turn around when she reached the wall, but to his surprise she kept running along it. In just four steps she was in the air, sword overhead, ready to cut down the next person in her way. At the same time, the gunman closest to her rushed to reload, but she was too close for him to make it in time. He quickly moved his gun above his head to try and stop the blade rushing towards him. Instead of coming straight down like he expected, Neith spun her sword around to cut under his guard. Neith traded places in the air with the gunman's newly severed hand. Fresh warm blood sprayed across her face following the arc of her blade as she landed on the ground, while the now one handed gunman fell down clutching his arm in pain. As the next assailant turned his gun on Neith, he caught a hard knee to the groin followed by an elbow to the back of the head. Now there were only two left.

Nemo ducked back down behind his cover. Everything was moving so fast. He crawled across to the other side of the cubicle before peeking his head up again to get a better look at the action. Just as his eyes focused on last place he saw Neith. He heard an unfamiliar voice yell,

"Move, ye in me way!"

Less than a second after he heard the yell, one of the gunmen came flailing through the air and crashed into the desk Nemo just left. Nemo looked over to see that it wasn't Neith that had thrown the guy. She was standing directly across from the last remaining gunman as he removed his mask. Strands of long red hair fell over his forehead matching the short beard stubble on his face.

"Hey there lass, 'ows about ye and me have a party."

Neith didn't bother to respond. Instead she ran directly towards him with her sword ready to eliminate the final threat. Her face was splattered with blood, yet she looked completely at ease. It was as if she was in her calmest state in the heat of battle.

Nemo stared intensely, expecting to soon hear the sound of metal severing flesh and bone, and the fight to be over. Right before Neith's blade struck, the red haired thief pulled a large, cleaver like knife from his back. He quickly brought it up to block Neith's attack, but it was the second blade in his other hand that caught Nemo's attention.

"Watch out!" he screamed

Neith hardly heard him. Her attention was already focused on the new threat. Neith jumped back with her sword merely inches away from striking its target. Had she taken one more step, the second blade would have impaled her thigh.

With some distance now in between them, Neith briefly stopped to survey the increasingly chaotic situation. Four of the thieves were unconscious. The one that lost his hand was quickly losing consciousness as blood gushed from his fresh wound. The creative combinations of curse words from his mouth managed to surprise her, although she was used to being called all kinds of names from men begging for their lives. Instead of waiting for him to quietly slip into silence, the man with the red hair stepped closer to take matters into his own hands.

"Shut up! 'ow am I supposed to enjoy me scrap with all that screaming?"

He said as he sliced a clean line across the man's throat. His last few moments were spent gurgling blood though the large opening in his neck. Nemo could barely watch the brutality unfold before his eyes. This was his first time seeing someone die right in front of him. It wasn't an experience he was mentally prepared for. Neith however looked unfazed. She was completely familiar with the empty gaze in the dead man's eyes.

"Twin butterfly swords, not exactly the normal tools of a bank robber." said Neith

The red haired man looked away from his most recent victim and focused his gaze on Neith, taking time to look her body up and down before responding.

"I guess me wouldn't be ye average bank robber then. Ye can call me Cutter, Mad Cutter. It's what all me friends call me."

Neith's face didn't show the slightest hint of emotion.

"I didn't ask for your name, nor do I care."

She immediately launched into a barrage of attacks. Each thrust, strike, and slash meant to end the fight with a decisive blow. Mad Cutter responded to each attack in kind, dodging and parrying while sneaking in his own attacks. In between the flashes of steel, Neith could see his eyes looking directly into hers. A twisted smile grew on his face with every exchange of blows. There was no doubt in her mind that he was enjoying this.

Neith feinted a straight thrust with her sword, but stopped right before she impacted his guard and punched him the face. Just as she was about to follow up her successful attack, Mad Cutter grabbed the hand she used to punch him. In one fluid movement, he swept her legs from under her and threw her hard against the wall. The sudden impact on her body knocked the air from her lungs. Her head bounced off the wall and everything in her vision started spinning. She could feel blood dripping down the back of her neck. It explained the wet thud sound she heard when she hit the wall. She could hardly believe his throw was that strong, but before she could finish her thought he was on her.

Mad Cutter grabbed Neith by her wrists and pinned her on the wall. He pushed his knee between her legs and raised it up to her groin. His twisted smile grew halfway across his face, which was so close to hers that she could count each stained tooth in his mouth as he licked his tongue across his lips.

"Now there's a good lass. Feisty too. Good, I like 'em when they struggle."

He leaned in and licked the side of her face from the bottom of her cheek to the top of her temple, then whispered in her ear.

"I like it even more when they scream as I cut 'em open."

That was the last straw. A red glow started to fill Neith's eyes. She broke her arms free from his grip, and forcefully slammed the palm of her hand against his chest.

Immediately, Mad Cutter was thrown to other side of the bank, knocking over tables, chairs, and everything in between him and the opposite wall.

Neith cracked her knuckles before grabbing her scimitar off the ground and sheathing it. The red glow in her eyes had grown to a blaze, making her eyes look like fiery red circles.

"I'm going to make you regret each letter of every word you just said to me"

Mad Cutter got up and steadied himself from the last blow.

"Bring it on them lass."

He rushed at her, attacking with both blades at once. It didn't matter. Each strike, each slash Neith saw, now looked like it was moving in slow motion. Mad Cutter's wide grin was gone. In place of the grin was a look of confusion as he struggled to figure out why he couldn't hit anything other than air. Neith hadn't planned on using this. It was hardly worth the effort for just one person. She preferred to save it for times when she was grossly outnumbered, but he had managed to really get under her skin. She would show him just how big of a mistake that was.

Instead of dodging the next strike that came her way, like she had done with the last dozen, she grabbed his wrist as the blade went past her face. She could hear each one of the bones in his wrist crack like a weathered twig as she squeezed it tighter. Without giving him a chance to react, she spun around so that she held his arm behind his back. The speed of her spin caused his shoulder to pop from its joint. In one smooth motion, she tilted his weight backwards and lifted him up in the air before violently slamming him back down into the ground.

The sound of the impact was deafening. Nemo didn't understand what could have caused the sudden change in Neith. Out of nowhere she had gotten insanely faster and stronger. But it was her eyes that held Nemo's attention. He had never seen anyone's eyes glow the way hers did at that moment. Neith's demeanor had also changed. Before she was calm and calculating, now it was if she was letting her emotions run wild. Nemo was sure Mad Cutter was nothing more than puddle of bone and blood on the floor at this point. He didn't see how anyone could have survived the force of that throw. Just as he finished that thought, Neith's head leaned back to dodge a slash at her neck. Mad Cutter emerged from the impression in the ground, his shirt soaked in blood as it streamed from his mouth and ran down his chin. His arm that Neith grabbed was barely hanging from his shoulder. Sharp points of bone jutted through his skin in several places. Yet there was no expression of pain on his face. His eyes just stared out into an endless void of nothing.

Even if he was still on his feet, Mad Cutter's movements had slowed considerably, and he could only use one arm. He was hardly a threat to Neith in her current state. This was no longer a fight. It was more like an execution. Mad Cutter ran his blade across his chest, covering the edge with his own blood. He brought the blade up to his mouth and licked it clean, before his face returned to its trademark grin. Then he started to giggle, until it turned into a full on laugh.

"Well I must say, it's been a long time since me been this banged up. What a rush!"

Neith looked at him in utter confusion, not knowing how or why he was still standing.

"I can see why they call you mad now, you definitely earned that title. Any other last words before you die?"

Out the corner of his eye, Nemo saw the gunman who was thrown into a desk, starting to wake up and reach for his gun beside him. Without thinking, Nemo rushed over and kicked the gun away. At the same time he drew his sword and held it at the gunman's neck.

"Don't make me kill you." Nemo said, doing his best impression of Neith's stern tone of voice. The gunman nodded his head and put his hands up showing he surrendered. One less problem to worry about Nemo thought. He turned around to see if Neith had finished what was left of Mad Cutter, only to see Mad Cutter standing directly in front of him. All the color drained from Nemo's face. Mad Cutter's imposing figure was even more terrifying up close. With blood dripping from his mouth, and an arm that looked like it was about to fall off, he was the last thing Nemo expected to see. Behind Mad Cutter, Nemo could see Neith running at full speed in his direction, wiping away blood from her eyes. He knew she wouldn't make it in time.

"Yous drawn your sword laddie, that makes you no longer a bystander and fair game. Now scream real pretty for me."

Nemo saw the blade in Mad Cutter's hand coming towards his chest, but he couldn't move. He saw Neith still running, using everything she had in her to try to get there in time. She would be one step too late. The last thing he saw was a white flash of light.

CHAPTER 14

When the white flash of light cleared from Nemo's eyes, he found himself in the arms of a familiar looking dark skinned man. The man's eyes had a glow in them similar to Neith's, except they glowed a luminous white color. The contrast between his eyes and his skin made them seem to shine even brighter. Long tightly wound dreads, thick with black hair, swung from his head down his back.
"Am I dead?" Nemo asked.
"Not even close." said the dark skinned man holding Nemo.
Mad Cutter stood in the same place, his blade thrust into the spot where Nemo's body once stood. Before he had time to figure out what happened, Neith's fist, with all of her strength and momentum behind it, connected with the back of his head. His body flopped around like a ragdoll as it went tumbling through the glass teller windows and into the back of the bank.

"That's what you get for spitting blood in my eyes!" Neith said as she wiped the crimson splatter from her hands.

The fight had clearly taken its toll on her. She was breathing heavy and the red glow in her eyes had faded to little more than a dim light. She looked over and saw that Nemo was unharmed and there was someone with him.

"Saint Georges, what are you doing here? Whatever the reason, thank you for saving my disciple. I should have never let him get in harm's way like that."

At the sound of his name, Nemo realized why he looked familiar. He remembered him from the celebration after the Trials. One of the other applicants that passed with Nemo was disciple under him.

Saint Georges put Nemo down and looked around the rubble of the bank.

"Quite the mess you've made here Neith, as usual. You might be fine with your reckless actions, but you should keep in mind how the consequences might affect those around you. Your disciple should have never been brought here. He's far from ready for this kind of work."

Neith looked Saint Georges straight in the eyes. "I'm grateful for your assistance, but you have no right to tell me how to train my disciple. I and I alone will determine—"

"If it weren't for me you might not have a disciple anymore." Saint Georges interrupted

Neith began to wipe the blood from her face as she caught her breath.

"I would have made it to him in time."

"If that is what you want to tell yourself go ahead. Just be more careful next time." replied Saint Georges

Nemo wanted to speak up for Neith, but he knew she wouldn't have made it to him before Mad Cutter's blade did. He was just ready for this whole ordeal to be over, but the sounds of movement he heard in the back of the bank told him it wasn't. Everyone turned to see Mad Cutter limping towards the back exit. Neith started to move in his direction, rekindling the rage still burning in her from their unfinished fight.

"Come back here and die like man!"

"Three's a crowd lass, I'll make sure to repay ye later for the beating ye gave this time. Ye can count on it."

Saint Georges grabbed Neith's arm before she could take off after him.

"You know how you get when you're in that state, calm down. Let him go, we have to leave now. The police will probably be here any second."

Neith started to object. She hated leaving unfinished business, but she knew Saint Georges was right and they needed to leave. She was far over the time limit her plan allotted. The smartest decision was to leave.

"Let's go Nemo."

The red glow completely faded from her eyes as they all turned toward the exit. CJ, Saint George's disciple was waiting outside with a car.

"It's about time you guys came out. I can hear the sirens. The cops are on their way. I don't think we want to stick around to explain what happened here."

Saint Georges nodded in agreement, "Step on it, we're headed back to the Citadel."

Once they were clear of the bank, and everyone seemed to calm down. Nemo decided it was a good time to ask about everything that just happened.

"How'd you do that thing in the bank?"

Neith didn't seem to be in the mood to talk. Her gaze stared straight ahead, never taking her eyes off the scenery in front of them.

"What thing?" she said quietly.

Nemo scratched his head trying to think of a way to explain it.

"You know, the thing where your eyes started glowing red and you suddenly became faster and stronger. Saint Georges did it too, well I think he did. I just remember his eyes glowing white after this bright flash of light."

CJ chimed in from the front of the car.

"You mean you don't know about fighting spirit?"

Nemo was getting tired of everyone except him always knowing what was going on.

"No, what's fighting spirit?"

Saint Georges answered this time, "Fighting spirit is the essence of a warrior's soul. It is that which turns willpower in actions. By strengthening your spirit you also strengthen your will, thereby strengthening your actions."

Everyone in the car silently looked around at each other until CJ chimed back in.

"Don't worry, I didn't understand it the first time he explained it either."

Neith tried to resist, but couldn't help but laugh.

"Great explanation o' wise one. You almost confused me with that complicated metaphorical definition."

A sigh of relief came from Nemo as he realized he wasn't the only one confused.

"So, does anyone want to tell me what fighting spirit is in simpler terms?"

Neith finally decided to address his question, and turned towards him to explain.

"Fighting spirit is exactly what it sounds like, the spirit of willpower inside of a fighter's body. Normally our spirit is released in short bursts, giving power to our everyday actions. But if your spirit and body are in sync you can draw out more than the normal amount of spirit that your body emits. Monks first discovered this long ago through meditation, but could only maintain this balanced state while meditating. Once they moved, their body and spirit would no longer be perfectly in sync. In order to maintain this state of harmony while fighting you must be able to perceive changes in your spirit and constantly correct for them, keeping your spirit in sync with your body. It's kind of like balancing a bucket of water on your head. Keeping both in sync while still being able to focus on your surroundings is far from trivial, but the result is it allows you to draw out the entire amount of your fighting spirit giving you extraordinary abilities."

Nemo was starting to understand what Saint Georges meant in his first explanation.

"So being able to use all of your fighting spirit, instead of the normal amount, gives you superhuman strength and speed?"

Neith put her hand to her chin as she searched for the best way to explain.

"Well not exactly. Just like everyone is different, everyone's spirit is different as well. The abilities that manifest themselves from being able to use all of your fighting spirit are different for each person. Since you've seen my and Saint Georges' abilities, I'll use those for example. When I'm using my fighting spirit, all of my senses increase. In addition to my strength, speed, and stamina I can hear, see, and smell better than any normal person. In Saint Georges' case, none of this happens. When he uses his fighting spirit, it is channeled into nothing but speed. Instead of increasing all of his abilities, it pours everything into one ability. Increasing it far past anything I could come close to. Because of this he is easily the fastest person in all of Fratello della Spada."

Saint Georges turned around to look at Nemo through a pair of dark sunglasses.

"The way I see it, in this world speed is king".

Neith quickly shot Saint Georges a glare from the sides of her eye.

"I gave you one compliment, don't let it go to your head. Like I was saying, these are just two examples of the differences in a person's fighting spirit. There are many more. Some are much harder to recognize than others."

Nemo wasn't sure what Neith meant by 'harder to recognize' but he decided to think about it later. He still had other more relevant questions to ask.

"So why do your eyes glow when you're using your fighting spirit?"

"Well they say the eyes are the window to the soul. Bringing out so much of your spirit at one time allows the true color of your soul to become visible, at least that's the theory behind it." replied Neith

Nemo scratched his head again. For every answer he got, ten more questions popped into his head.

"So was that last thief using his fighting spirit? His eyes didn't glow, but he certainly seemed to be able to survive things I'm sure would kill just about anyone else."

Neith started to recall moments from her fight with Mad Cutter. It all seemed like a blur at the time but now she could remember specific things that definitely weren't normal.

"No, that was something else. I'm not exactly sure what."

"We're here" Saint Georges interrupted. Neith looked pleased to have an excuse to end the conversation.

"Nemo it's been a long day already. How about you go home and get some rest."

Nemo was happy to hear any sentence with the word rest in it. He wasn't in the mood to do any training after everything that just happened. As he turned to leave, another question entered his mind.

"Is all this mediation I've been doing to help me recognize my fighting spirit?"

Neith rolled her eyes at the realization that he just now understood the reason behind the meditation they had been doing the past month.

"You're finally catching on. Maybe now you'll realize there's a purpose behind everything I make you do. Keep your sword with you when you meditate, it helps to have something to focus on and draw your spirit into. It also helps if you have some emotional connection to your weapon, but that doesn't really apply to your case. Go home, and get some rest. Continue with your meditations if you wish. I'll see you tomorrow."

As tired as Neith was, she wasn't nearly as tired as she led Nemo to believe. What she really wanted was to talk to Saint Georges, alone.

"Mind if talk to you for second?" she asked Saint Georges.

"Sure, CJ go start practicing your forms in the training area. I'll be there when I'm done talking to Neith."

Neith and Saint Georges went through several doorways. She wanted to make sure they were someplace where no one would be listening. As they walked through the halls, she could hear the staff whisper to each other.

"Is that him?"

"It is! It's him, the hero from the battle of Tralone, Saint Georges."

"Wow, I wonder what a big shot like him is doing back here?"

"I heard he took a new disciple."

"Wow, that kid must really be something for Saint Georges to accept him as a disciple."

Neith and Saint Georges both acted as if they couldn't hear them whispering. Neith had more important things on her mind, and for some reason Saint Georges didn't seem to enjoy the attention.

Finally, after walking halfway across the building, they arrived at a room where she knew they wouldn't be interrupted. Once the door closed behind them Neith couldn't contain herself any longer.

"Ok spill it Geo. Why were you at the bank and how come you brought your disciple back to train at the Citadel? You and the other masters with new disciples said it was too dangerous to stay here with a murderer on the loose. So what brings you back now?"

"How many times do I have to tell you don't call me Geo? I'm surprised you were able to wait this long to ask. My guess is you didn't want to explain to your disciple why you haven't told him about the murders that happened in this very building?"

"And have you told yours?" Neith replied, anxious to hear Saint Georges answer.

"CJ knows what he needs to know to keep him safe. He's no baby lamb like your disciple. He also knows why we're back here so he won't go wandering around blissful ignorant like you're letting your disciple Nemo do."

"For you to be judging me, what you're doing doesn't sound all that different." Neith responded. "Nemo also knows what he needs to know, and I never let him out of my sight. You let me worry about my disciple. Now stop avoiding my question. Why are you here and what were you doing at the bank?"

"The council has appointed a special investigation team in response to Bulo and Janus' murder. I'm here because I was selected to be on it, I'm sure you can guess why this is being kept quiet when the killer may be one of our own."

Neith took a step closer to Saint Georges. Even though she had to look up at him, she wanted to be in his face as much as she could.

"So how come I wasn't asked to be a part of this special investigation team? No one wants to find Bulo's killer more than I do, and I was one of the first people to discover Janus' body. I should be on this special team, unless you have a reason not to trust me."

Saint Georges didn't move. He stood his ground and stared directly back at her.

"Neith how long have we known each other? If I didn't trust you I wouldn't be telling you this now. Anyone with a personal relationship with the victims was banned from the team, this includes you. This is an investigation, not a witch hunt. The council doesn't want riled up members having an excuse to kill each other. Likewise, they also want this solved before any more murders can occur which is the reason I'm telling you this. I know you've probably been looking into Bulo's murder yourself, so if you find anything please come to me and I'll take care of it."

"Come to you so you can solve my problem. That's a good one." Neith shot back

"I'm serious Neith" replied Saint Georges. "Both the council and I want this handled as quickly as possible. Letting me help you is in everyone's best interest."

"Sure it is" Neith said. "Just like I'm sure the council took my interests into great consideration when deciding all of this. Just who else is on this special investigation team?"

Saint Georges patience with Neith was wearing thin. Whenever she was serious about something she wouldn't stop. He admired that about her, but wasn't in the mood to play twenty questions.

"I'm not going to tell you. It wouldn't do us much good to have everyone's cover blown before we solve this thing."

Neith raised a single eyebrow. "I thought you trusted me?"

"I do." said Saint Georges. "But I'd rather not burden you with that knowledge."

Neith took a couple of seconds to analyze his answer before stepping back.

"Fair enough, I'll be able to find that out on my own anyway. Now exactly what were you doing at the bank? Somehow, I feel like that weirdo I fought today has something to do with you showing up there. He never even made a move for the money, which either makes him the worst bank robber I've ever seen or he was there for a completely different reason."

"They call him Mad Cutter" said Saint Georges.

"Yea, I got that part" replied Neith

Saint Georges took off his shades so Neith could see he was not amused. He was quickly tiring of Neith's sarcastic commentary.

"They call him Mad Cutter. Some newspapers gave him that nickname after a string of gruesome murders that followed in each town he visited. We have been unable to find his real name or any other identifiable information so far, however we believe he's connected to the recent murders in the Citadel."

Neith drummed her fingers on the hilt of her sword as she thought.

"He doesn't seem like the kind of guy that works well with others. Hard to believe one of us would be partnered with him."

"I had similar thoughts." replied Saint Georges. "But with him being at the bank today proves he is connected with this somehow. As you said before, he clearly wasn't there for the money. There has to be some other motive we're missing. We also found several mentions of a demon while looking into his background. It seems some people believe he's either a demon himself or possessed by one."

Neith took another step back to lean against the wall.

"Probably some local superstition. He did seem to have a high tolerance for pain and survived some pretty heavy blows, but I've seen men survive worse. As far as motives, maybe he just wanted the chance to take out another Shadow. Someone put out that contract to stop the robbery at the last minute. It could have been a trap meant for anyone." Saint Georges turned towards the door. "Maybe that's the case, but we can't know for sure. Right now, we still have a lot more questions than answers."

CHAPTER 15

Mad Cutter stumbled into the underground hideout. Dim artificial light hit his eyes as he came to the end of the dark tunnels that converged into a large cave. Megas was using this place as his base of operations. The cavern split off into several rooms that had been outfitted with furniture, rugs, lamps and other small items to add touch of warmth to the dry rock walls of the cavern. Tables, chairs, and other utilitarian furniture covered the floor of the main opening in the cave. On top of each table were stacks of papers. Maps covered whatever space remaining that the papers left open.

Each step Mad Cutter took looked more painful than his last. His arm was hanging by the skin that bound it to his shoulder. His left leg looked deformed and trembled at any attempt to move it, and large splotches of dried blood covered the last pieces of tattered clothing left on his body. The cavern walls kept him upright as he slowly made his way towards everyone assembled inside.

Megas' aide let out a long whistle.

"Looks like someone got worked over real good".

Jean-Vis peeked over the edge of the newspaper he was reading and slowly removed the lit cigar from his mouth.

"Well look at this! All that talk and you come back here with your tail between your legs."

"Shaddup, the both of you" said Mad Cutter as he held onto the wall and gasped for air. When he reached a spot on the edge of the room, he slid his back down the wall until he was seated on the floor.

"The important thing is that I still accomplished me goal."

The aide's eyes opened wide at hearing the news.

"Quickly, let me see it then!"

Mad Cutter took two fingers from the hand on his only working arm, pulled a thin strip of plastic out of his mouth, and shook it to dry the spit before handing it to Megas' aide. He hesitantly grabbed it between his index finger and thumb, trying to touch it as little as possible.

"What is this? I told you that you only need to touch the person's skin with the plastic. What did you do, lick them?"

"I did. A pretty lass showed up to stop me, so I improvised a more exciting way for me to get your DNA sample."

Jean-Vis, still laughing at Mad Cutter's injured state, stood from his chair and walk over towards the center of the room.

"Maybe if you had kept your tongue in your mouth you wouldn't have gotten your ass handed to you by a woman."

"Eh, hindsight be 20/20." Mad Cutter quipped through a partial grin on his face before addressing the aide again.

"So 'ows about you tell us why I went through all this trouble to get a sample of some random person's DNA?"

Megas' aide took a long look at the sample before opening a clear case and laying the strip of plastic in it. He closed the case and buried deep in his pocket.

"You all have no need to know at this time. If in the future you develop a need to know, you will be informed about it then."

Jean-Vis' whole body tensed up in a look of frustration from the lack of answers.

"You will not talk down to me like I am some commoner. I'm fed up with your need to know nonsense. If I don't start getting some answers about what you and your boss are planning, you can count me out for the rest of this scheme. Where's Megas at? I'm certainly not going to listen to some glorified secretary who hasn't even told us his name."

The aide raised his voice in return, "My name is of no concern to you, and as the second in command here I am no mere—"

Out from the shadows of the cave, Megas walked in. His overbearing presence rendered everyone silent. Without even having to raise his voice, everyone stopped speaking and immediately focused on what Megas had to say.

"Gentlemen, gentlemen, there's no need to argue among ourselves. Ultimately, we're all on the same side here. Brother stand down, I expected that our associates here would want more details sooner or later. Go ahead and ask your questions, what would you like to know?"

Through his gasps for air and spattered coughs of blood Mad Cutter managed to get his words out.

"Did I 'ear that right? You two are kin?"

"Yes we are, I the younger and he the older." replied Megas

Jean-Vis interrupted before Mad Cutter could continue his line of questioning.

"I don't care if you're brothers, cousins, or long lost lovers. Someone tell me what we're doing here!"

Megas started to slowly pace around the cavern as he continued to speak.

"Jean-Vis have you ever wondered how I know so much about your country and the neighboring countries surrounding it?"

Jean-Vis was quickly growing tired on this game Megas was playing, asking questions he clearly knew the answer too. However, since it seemed to be leading somewhere he decided to indulge him a little while longer.

"Why that thought has been on my mind since I got here, would you care to explain?"

"Your country, Maiteir, borders Tralone on its east side. I was stationed on the eastern border of Tralone five years ago. I commanded a small special ops unit tracking black market weapons that were smuggled into third world countries. We had been there for three years, stopping the occasional black market merchant, but were unable to find the real source. It was there in eastern Tralone where I met Anya."

Megas' hand slid into his pocket to let his fingers rub against the picture he always kept with him. He found himself unconsciously touching the picture whenever he was in a stressful situation or just let his mind wander. Bringing up old painful memories put this moment in the former category.

"Never have I met a person who cared so much for her people. Anya was the elder leader of her tribe of Tralonians. She was designated as elder leader not because of her age, she was only in her mid-twenties, but because of her ability to lead and her deep love for protecting her people. I once saw her stand in front an attacking army, arms outstretched as people fled behind her. She told them that if one boot were to step on Tralonian soil it would be over her dead body. Somehow, she managed to talk down an entire army and prevent a war. Even the official Tralonian government respected her. They granted her a special position equivalent to governor over the land her tribe inhabited. Yet, the most dangerous and surprising thing she ever did was agreeing to marry me."

Megas took his picture of Anya from his pocket and unfolded it. He slowly rubbed one finger over her smiling face, imagining the warmth of her soft skin against his rough hands. Every time he looked at the picture he felt empty, knowing that this one and only possession of hers would be the closest he could ever come to seeing her again. After a long intense look at the picture of Anya, he set in down in front of Mad Cutter and Jean-Vis and continued his story.

"The last day in Tralone I remember, we had just discovered where each merchant we captured was coming from. Some small bordering nation called Maiteir."

Jean-Vis' face scrunched together as if someone had poured salt down his throat. He didn't like where this story was headed. He wondered how much Megas knew that he was leaving unsaid. Whatever he knew, it was already too much.

"Calm down Jean-Vis." said Megas "I didn't bring you all the way out here just to kill you. I could have done that a number of ways, at any time, while you were home in your mansion."

That statement helped Jean-Vis regain some of his composure, but he was clearly still on edge about what other secrets Megas might be keeping to himself.

"If you're done trembling I'll continue" said Megas.

"No one was trembling. I'm not sure I even believe this story of yours. Where's the proof?" replied Jean-Vis as he tried his best to appear calm and composed.

"My team and I weren't the only ones that found out about your illegal weapons. Tralone discovered the rebel group you were arming, and needed to deal with the problem immediately before they had a civil war on their hands. However, they couldn't send their army in to kill their own citizens. It would make the rebels martyrs for their cause. So, they outsourced the job to anyone that would take it. Mercenaries, security forces, and most importantly the Shadows of Fratello della Spada. What followed was a massacre."

Megas paused to look at everyone's reaction. All the attention was focused on what he would say next.

"Apparently the Tralonian government had no problem with hiring people to kill their own citizens. No due process, no attempts to find out who was innocent and who was actually guilty. Tralone wanted the rebels dead, that was all that mattered. They killed every man, woman, and child in the entire region!"

Megas slammed his fist on the table beside him. The unexpected release of anger caused everyone to step back, only Mad Cutter who was already on the floor and barely conscious remained in the same spot.

"Anya, my team, and her entire tribe were wiped out along with thousands of other innocents. Ten thousand people, that's a conservative estimate on the number of people they killed in the span of a few months. They granted no mercy. Men, women, and children were killed without regard to what side they were on. To Tralone's government, we were just nameless bodies not even worth warning before letting their fear of a potential threat run rampant. They covered it up as a horrific terrorist attack. They had parades and memorials for the victims and then pushed everyone to forget about it. I had to scrounge every hell hole around that god forsaken land before I found out the truth of what really happened. I questioned a lot of people. Most of them aren't alive to remember the experience. My brother found out through his own contacts how Fratello della Spada provided support to Tralone then turned their backs and washed their hands from the situation. So, you asked what this was about. What my grand plans were? Well, I plan on giving Tralone the war they so desperately tried to avoid. First, I'm going to take out every last member of Fratello della Spada, and then I'm going to let you wipe Tralone off the map."

By this time Jean-Vis was smiling from ear to ear.

"Well mon'ami you know what they say. The enemy of my enemy is my friend. I wish you had told me this earlier, I would have been more eager to assist in our little endeavor. I promise you will now have my full resources at your disposal. I just have one question, why take revenge on the whole organization, Fratello della Spada? Wouldn't it be much easier to find the one's that were in Tralone and kill them?"

Megas could barely hear Jean-Vis speak. Anger and sadness threatened to overwhelm him the longer he stared and her picture. Telling the story had ripped open old wounds and reminded him of everything that was taken from him. Before he completely lost himself in those emotions, he folded her picture and stuffed it back into his pocket. He forced himself to calm down, taking deep breaths and focusing on his one and only goal. Revenge for Anya and all those that died that day. He was an avenger whose only purpose was bring to light those who thought they could cast dark shadows upon the world and get away with it.

"No. All of the Shadows must die. Any organization that willingly allows its members to participate in the slaughter of innocent people doesn't deserve to exist. I plan on wiping them all out like they did Anya's people."

Mad Cutter lifted his head and started to slowly clap his hands together, "What a nice speech. If you two are done strolling down memory lane, would you mind getting me some medical attention? I've nodded off at least three times while you two flap your gums, and if ye want me to be here to see your grand plans fulfilled I suggest you find someone to stop me bleeding."

"I was actually hoping you'd die there on the floor, then I could use your body as a footstool." said Jean-Vis

Mad Cutter kept his head down and replied in a deep otherworldly voice.

"Why don't you come down here and say that to me face."

Before Mad Cutter and Jean-Vis decided to tear each other's heads off, Megas scooped up Mad Cutter's body and threw him over his shoulder.

"I'm going to take him to Leo. The kid is pretty good at stitching wounds. I'm glad we all had this chat because from now on I don't expect any more questions about my plans or my methods. Are we clear?"

Megas didn't bother to wait for an answer from Jean-Vis. He simply turned around and walked out of the room carrying Mad Cutter over his shoulder. Jean-Vis still stood in the cavern next to Megas' aide, not sure what he should do next. They both continued standing there halfway expecting Megas to return, but he did not. The aide finally broke the silence between them.

"Well there, you have your answers. Now can you get back to work, we're still waiting to see that equipment you promised us."

Jean-Vis waived his hand, brushing off the comment.

"Don't worry about that. It will be here. There was however one question I never did get the answer to. What's the DNA Mad Cutter stole for?"

Megas' aide rolled his eyes. "Hard to believe that question is what started this whole conversation. We're going to use it to break into Fratello della Spada's fortress. Each member has their own ring that gives them access. By using this sample we can recreate that ring and bypass their security system."

"And how do you know so much about their security?" Jean-Vis asked skeptically.

Without stopping what he was doing Megas' aide replied,

"Simple, I used to be one of the Shadows".

CHAPTER 16

Nemo ducked, then rolled across the ground. He quickly recovered back to his feet, just in time to parry the next attack. The next three strikes came quickly in succession. He skillfully dodged all three, waiting until the final possible moment to dodge the last strike in order to maximize his opening for a counterattack. As soon as the last attack missed him, he rushed in. The point of his sword was dead center in the opening he created. Nearly two inches before his sword tip reached its intended target, Nemo was halted by the touch of cold, sharp metal. Although he stopped immediately, Neith's sword was close enough to leave a thin red mark across his neck.

"You got too excited." Neith said with her sword still at his neck. "That last strike was a feint. Also, you're still too slow on your counter. I could have hit you three times before you reached me."

Nemo dropped his sword and fell to the ground in exhaustion. "Man, I really thought I had you this time".

This was the seventh round of sparring they'd done this week. Each time he thought he was doing better, but the gap between their skills was too great. It hardly looked like she was trying when they fought. Neith gently slid her sword home into its sheath and extended her hand towards Nemo.

"Don't be so hard on yourself. You are getting better. You just need to keep practicing. Take a break, then let's go again. Last time, you pushed me to half speed. That's pretty good considering you're using a twenty pound training blade. All your movements will be much faster with your real weapon."

Nemo forgot he was using a training blade. It was all he used in his regular practices now. He had become so used to it that he forgot what the weight of his real sword felt like. Neith had ordered a set of five training blades forged for him that looked just like his claymore. Each sword in the set was ten pounds heavier than the last. He was already strong enough to wield the twenty pound blade, and daily sparring with Neith was sharpening his reflexes. The only thing he still used his real sword for was meditation, which he did faithfully every day.

Neith stopped him just as he was moving into position.

"On second thought, that's enough for today. You look too tired to put up any real fight. Finish today's session with another twenty minutes of mediation and think about eliminating all the extra movements from your actions."

Nemo turned to leave, but heard Neith shout something else as she reached the door.

"And clean up all this sweat on the floor! I've seen fish drip less water than you do."

Neith left and waited in the meditation room for Nemo. Lately, she found herself diligently watching him meditate. He would manage to work himself into a trance and meditate the entire time with his eyes open. The first time it happened she thought he had found a way to sleep with his eyes open. But right when she was about to kick him square in his chest, she looked in his eyes. They had a faint blue glow to them, meaning his body and spirit were in harmony with one another. A disciple being able to sync their body and spirit after so little training was extremely rare. Those that could were either very gifted or had been trained to control their spirit since birth. Neith knew her bumbling disciple hadn't trained a day in his life before he started under her. That only left one option, however she had a hard time believing this boy was some kind of genius. Even that was an understatement. It was impossible for someone like him could learn to perfectly sync his body and spirit in such a short time. Still, the evidence was staring her in the face. Each time when he finished mediating, he had no knowledge of what he was doing. She didn't dare tell him either. She wanted to figure out exactly what this was before bringing it to his attention.

Nemo walked in and sat down. As he started to settle into his meditative trance, Neith put her face close to his. She looked deep into his eyes and tried to sense the fluctuations in his spirit. She could feel a steady flow of energy being emitted from his body. The glow in his eyes was stronger this time. It was still faint but clearly visible. Neith leaned back and whispered to herself,

"Maybe it wasn't just dumb luck that you were able to pass the Trials. Guess I'll have to push you even harder and find out."

The next day Nemo traveled to the Citadel right after school, showing up thirty minutes early before his practice with Neith was supposed to start. It was just beginning to dawn on him how large the Citadel really was. There were several floors, not including the underground levels. The main floor seemed to have the largest rooms. There were at least six of them almost the size of a basketball court. The weapons room took up most of the second floor. The rest of it consisted of meeting rooms and temporary living quarters. The few times he had been to the floors above that, were uneventful. Nothing distinct about them stuck out in his mind and without Neith with him, he didn't even have access to areas above the second floor. It all had an air of mystery about it, leaving him with thoughts of what secrets hid behind all those locked doors.

Down the hall on the main floor, he could hear the voices of CJ and Saint Georges. Since he was early, Nemo decided to peek in on their training session. He heard Saint Georges' voice call out, "Enguard".

Nemo could see two rapiers crossing blades in the distance, one held by Saint Georges and the other by CJ. What followed was a blur. The way CJ handled his weapon was like an extension of his arm. His motions were entirely fluid and very fast. His movements weren't as fast as Neith's, but it was clear CJ's abilities were far beyond his own. He could barely see their swords. Only flashes of light reflecting off their blades, and the sounds of collision as they parried each other's attacks allowed him to keep track of what was happening. Neither Saint Georges nor CJ moved one step. The subtle movements of their wrists guided the flurry of blade actions happening between them.

While he was concentrating on trying to follow CJ's movements, Neith silently walk up behind him and put her arm on his shoulder.

"Watching their close combat drill?"
Nemo simply nodded his head trying not to miss any of the action.

"It's an interesting thing to see. The first one that takes a step backward, or gets cut, loses. An ideal drill for two quick rapier specialists."

Neith could see the earnest look in Nemo's eyes as he watched how CJ was able to keep up with Saint Georges. He didn't know that Saint Georges could move much faster, but that didn't take away how impressive it was that a young disciple like CJ could still move as fast as he did. Whatever reasons that kept Nemo from quitting before were burned away by the sight of CJ and Saints Georges battle, and replaced with the motivation to surpass his own limitations.

"Seems like you've found yourself a rival."

Nemo sighed in disappointment. "I doubt I'd be much of a rival against him. Do you see how fast CJ is? I don't know how I'd be able to keep up."

Neith gently squeezed his shoulder. "Look at each one of his movements. There's hardly any more motion than necessary. No superfluous actions, no big flaring gestures that might give his opponent an opening. His only objective is to eliminate the enemy in the fastest and most efficient way possible. I wouldn't expect anything less from a disciple of Saint Georges. In the same regard, if we were to eliminate all the extra wasted movements you do while fighting, you would be twice as fast as you are now."

Nemo's face brightened at the sound of what Neith was telling him.

"So, you mean I could be just as fast as CJ is now?"

"Well yes, with hard work you can become even faster than he is now. But if I'm to be honest, it's likely that CJ will always be faster than you, and the gap in speed between you two will only widen as time goes on. The sword style that Saint Georges teaches is designed to be incredibly fast. Against your weapon and fighting style, it will always be the faster of the two."

Disappointment washed over Nemo's face. Before he settled on the wrong idea, Neith went on to explain.

"Contrary to what Saint Georges believes, it is not always the fastest one who wins the fight. Don't worry about how the other disciples are training. Put your faith in me as your master, and I promise you that I will make you just as strong as your resolve is."

That wasn't exactly the answer Nemo wanted to hear, but he trusted Neith at her word. He turned to look back at the bout between master and disciple.

It had been over a minute, and they were still going at full speed. Neither had moved a step from the position they started in. Doubt started to creep in Nemo's mind about how he would ever attain that kind of speed, or the strength and ability to fight against someone even faster. He quickly dismissed the thoughts from his head and pledged to himself that he would surpass CJ and the other disciples no matter what it took. Neith said she would make him as strong as his resolve, so his resolve needed to unbreakable.

Neith removed her hand from his shoulder and leaned over so that their eyes met, before giving him a piece of advice.

"Nemo no matter the gap between you two, if he pushes you to be better that makes him your rival. You know, I used to have a rival too. She was this girl from the far east branch that came here to train for a few years. I couldn't stand her. She thought I was lazy. I thought she was entirely too serious about everything. She was hands down the most uptight person I'd ever met. Always kept going on about her long noble bloodline, honoring her family, and blah blah blah. That attitude of hers annoyed me the most, which is why I refused to lose to her. I guessed I annoyed her too because she would go to almost any extreme necessary to keep from losing to me. Before we knew it, we both ended up pushing each other further than either of us would have gone by ourselves."

Nemo was about to ask the name of Neith's rival when CJ suddenly jumped backwards. His face was thick with sweat as he went down one knee and struggled to catch his breathe. Nemo noticed that CJ's shirt was split open right across his torso. He had narrowly dodged his stomach being split open just like his shirt.

Saint Georges deep voice echoed through the room as he spoke.

"Wonderful! You did well keeping up with me for that long. I'm sure our guests enjoyed the magnificent demonstration we put on for them."

He pointed one finger in the direction of Neith and Nemo, directing CJ's attention to his hidden spectators.

"Unfortunately, the exercise was over at least thirty seconds before we stopped. There should be another six holes in your shirt where I was able to penetrate your guard. As soon as you got tired, your actions got sloppy and lost that crisp edge to them. Your assignment for tonight is to go home and find those holes."

CJ's eyes started to scour his shirt, surprised to hear that he had been stabbed six times without knowing it. Nemo was also looking for the holes on CJ's shirt. He could see two in the area right above the cut in his shirt but couldn't find the other four. After a few seconds, he gave up looking for them. He was more concerned with figuring out at what point during the fight Saint Georges was able to hit CJ six distinct times.

When it was clear to CJ that he was not going to easily find all the holes in his shirt, he saluted and bowed to end his lesson.

"Thank you again master for allowing me to test and refine my skills against you. Goodnight."

Neith and Nemo stepped aside as CJ walked out the door. As he passed by them, Nemo heard him say, "Hoped you enjoyed the show, weakling."

Nemo was about to follow him, but Neith held her hand out gesturing for him to stop.

"Let him go. No need to chase after him, you'll see him around later. Now wait here while I go talk to Saint Georges for a second."

Neith walked over to the back of the room where Saint Georges stood.

"How's it going Geo? That was a nice little exercise you and your disciple went through. If I had to guess, I'd say you were using about sixty percent of your normal speed. That's pretty fast for a young disciple to keep up with."

Saint Georges sheathed his rapier and let it drop to his side. He removed the glove from his left hand, and grabbed a towel to wipe the beads of sweat from his forehead.

"He is pretty quick, isn't he? I knew he had potential when I saw that him surviving by himself on streets. He's even faster than I was at his age. Of course, I didn't have someone like me to train my younger self. But, he's never been that fast before. I think he wanted to show off once he found out you and your disciple were watching."

Neith brushed strands of hair from her face as she listened.

"Funny, and here I thought Nemo was the only one taking a bigger interest in your exhibition. Sounds like my disciple's little rivalry might go both ways."

"Not exactly" said Saint Georges. "More like CJ wanted to show his dominance over your disciple. He believes himself to be the strongest that came in with this last class. I can't say I disagree with him."

Neith folded her arms stared back at him with unwavering eyes.

"Guess my disciple will have to instill some humbleness in yours if they ever get a chance to spar against each other. Anyway, I didn't come over here to talk about our students. Have you discovered anything new about killer?"

Saint Georges face turned serious.

"I can't say. Information from the investigation is being held in secrecy by the special investigation team."

Neith released her mental hold on the anger that had been boiling under the surface since Bulo's funeral. She grabbed Saints Georges shirt and pulled him down so he met her eyes.

"Cut the crap Geo! If you know something, anything, you better tell me. Same goes for Arthur, Hao, Absolon, and whoever else I find out is a part of this secret investigation team."

With one swift motion, Saint Georges moved Neith's hand away from his shirt and held it above his head, letting her fingers dangle in front of his face. His eyes stared back at hers, taking in all of her features.

"I told you to stop calling me that."

He wanted to ask how she found out the names of the people assigned to the team, but seeing the scar on her face up close again reminded him of a different question.

"How long has it been since you called off the engagement?"

"Not long enough" said Neith

"Trust me, I understand. No one could have expected Bulo to change like he did. The time we spent in Tralone affected us all, but I didn't know how much that environment influenced him until it was too late. He was my friend too, but I couldn't excuse his actions after what he did to you. Then to have him die all of sudden—"

Neith slapped him across the face before he could finish speaking, tilting her head down so he could no longer see her eyes.

"I didn't come here for you to walk me down memory lane either. I came for information. Like I said, if you know something you better tell me."

Even with her head bowed, Saint Georges could see the tears starting to form in her eyes. He knew no matter what, she wouldn't let one tear would fall in front of him. Neith was too strong. No, too proud to cry in front anyone.

"Neith, what I told you before I told you as a friend. And as your friend I would appreciate if in the future you didn't ask questions you know I can't answer. Unfortunately, we haven't found any new information or any leads. I wish there was something to keep from you, but there isn't."

Neith leashed her emotions and stuffed them back down inside her. Calming down was never something she did well. Her feelings still lingered, waiting under just under her skin to be released in all their fury.

"Some investigation team you guys are, stuck at a dead end already." she said as she lifted her head to meet his eyes again.

"I didn't say we were at a dead end, just that we didn't have any new information." Saint Georges said as he began shuffling through his coat pocket. He smiled when until he found the scrap of paper he was looking for.

"Here look at this."

She quickly snatched the paper from his hand and unfolded it.

"What is this? The number for a job posting?"

Saint Georges grabbed a stool from the corner of the room, sat down, and folded his arms.

"Yeah, it's a job. It came through in some strange language, but we managed to translate it. We know it has some linkage to the killer's motives, we just can't figure out what. I was going to take it on, but since you seem so interested in this you can have it."

Neith took out her phone to look up the job referenced by the number on paper.

"This is a pretty low rank job. You sure it's connected to killer?"

"Do you want it or not?" Saint Georges asked. "I shouldn't even be letting you know this much."

"Ok I got it, I'll take the job. Thanks."

"Yeah yeah, if anyone asks you didn't get that from me." he shouted as Neith turned to walk away.

Neith hardly heard him as she hurried back towards where Nemo was standing.

"Oh Nemo, guess what I have for you..."

Nemo had been waiting by the entrance to the room the entire time. He couldn't hear what Saint Georges and Neith were talking about, but he could tell from their actions that it was more than a friendly chat. For Neith to come back happy all of a sudden probably meant trouble for him. Nemo didn't know what she had in her hand, but he already wanted to run for the door.

CHAPTER 17

Raindrops were just starting to fall from the cloudy sky above. Most of the light from the moon was obscured by the clouds, enhancing the darkness of the night. Nemo always liked the rain. It comforted him, helped him focus, and made the world seem quieter. Tonight the world was almost silent.

"*Nemo, do you copy... Nemo can you hear me?*"

Nemo adjusted the volume on his radio earpiece before responding.

"I can hear you loud and clear Neith"

"*Good, are you in position?*"

"Yes, I'm on the rooftop by the entrance. I'm ready to go whenever you give the signal."

"*Great. I've scoped out the building for you. There are twelve guards. Four on the first floor, and eight on the second. The second floor is where the package is being held. Remember, this is a quiet grab and go mission. Get in, get the package, and get out. I don't want you spending any more time in there than necessary. Stay in radio contact, I'll* be on the adjacent rooftop watching you if you need anything."

"Copy" Nemo responded

He looked up at Neith from his position and waited for her to give the signal. She stood on the roof of the next building over, looking back at him through a pair of binoculars. Her black outfit made her outline disappear in the background of the night sky. The hood of her cloak covered her long black hair, and most of her face, so that only her eyes could be seen in between the gaps of the raindrops. On her hip as always was her long handled scimitar resting in its sheath. Nemo hoped it stayed that way. If everything went according to plan he would be able to sneak in, reclaim the package, and sneak back out without anyone noticing. Neith was going to be his eyes, warning him of any unexpected dangers while he was in the building. However, if something went wrong it would be at least three minutes before she would be able to get to his position, probably more. It didn't matter, this time he was ready.

When Neith first showed him what was on the paper Saint Georges gave her, immediately he thought about the last job in the bank. Back then he was sure if the random gunfire didn't kill him, that crazy guy that fought Neith would. There was no way she was going to get him to go on another mission like that again. She must have seen the trepidation on his face because she didn't even bother to ask him. Instead, she said she would ask CJ to help her. Maybe it was jealousy, or maybe he just didn't want to prove CJ was right for calling him a weakling. Whatever that feeling was that boiled inside him, it made him snatch the paper out of her hand and say, "I'll do the job by myself!".

It was just now occurring to him how well Neith knew how to press his buttons. For the next three days, he trained with Neith to prepare for this job, learning to move quietly without being detected. Granted it didn't make him any less scared of going in the building now, but he was determined to do it anyway. None of the other disciples would run from a job, so he wouldn't either. No matter how scared he actually was.

Neith made a motion with her hands, giving Nemo the signal to get started. As soon as he saw it, Nemo opened the air vent below him and jumped in. Using his feet, he slid down the winding shaft as quietly as possible. Once he reached the bottom, he crawled through the duct until he found another air vent.

"I'm inside the building."

"*Good, the floor you're on is all clear.*" Neith responded

"Roger. Ok, here I go"

Nemo took a deep breath before exiting the air duct and dropping to the ground. The fear in his mind had him thinking as soon as he dropped out of the air duct, he would be surrounded by people aiming guns at him. But it was just as Neith described, the whole floor around him was empty.

"The first step is always the hardest" Nemo whispered to himself.

Now that he was actually inside, he regained some of his composure and started to look around. All the lights were off. Office doors lined the walls, and cubicles covered the rest of the open area on the floor. The place was probably full of people during the day, but at night it was empty and quiet. The only noises Nemo heard were the sound of rain crashing into the large windows, and wind roaring by outside. Light streaked though the windows, flashing over Nemo as he ran to the nearest corner. He made sure to stay low to the ground as he moved around in case someone was nearby. If someone were to spot him before he could get to the package, it would only make getting it out of the building that much harder. As he moved down the hallway, it dawned on him that he never was told what this 'package' actually was. The details probably weren't important. Neith would regularly keep him in the dark on things she thought he didn't need to know. This was probably one of those times. When he got to the package, he would be able to see what it was for himself. All he had to do was get there without anyone seeing him.

Once Nemo reached the first flight of stairs, he grabbed the handle of his sword and pulled it from the scabbard resting on his back. He made sure to do it as slowly and quietly as he could. Finally, when his blade free, Nemo positioned the sword in front of his face and used the reflection in the blade to see down the stairs and around the corner. He did the same thing at every other corner he encountered, checking to make sure the coast was clear before moving forward. Neith watched Nemo from the other rooftop as he snuck through the building. Her view from above helped her to direct Nemo through each turn, and around any potential obstacles until he made it down to second the floor where the package was being held.

When he reached the second floor, Nemo started to take cover behind the desks and chairs as he snuck around the building. Unlike the floors above it, all the lights were on. He could hear the rustle of footsteps against the ground and voices talking nearby. Those noises reminded him of the severe consequences of getting caught. After checking first to see if the coast was clear, Nemo rounded another corner just as three guards exited one of the offices and started walking in his direction. Nemo quickly ran back and hid in the shadow of a tall plant. Fear and anxiety rushed back to the front of thoughts.

"Neith, can you hear me?" Nemo whispered into his earpiece. "I'm on the second floor. There's three guards in front of me."

"*You'll have to find a way to sneak past them. There's no other route to the door you need.*" replied Neith.

Nemo tried to think of any possible way he could sneak past them. Between the three of them, there were no blind spots he could take advantage of. He thought about throwing something to distract them, but there was a good chance one of them would see where it came from. With each passing second, he could hear their steps coming closer. He was quickly running out of time. He needed an idea, but nothing came to him. The mission had barely started and he was already about to be caught.

"Neith I could use a little help here" Nemo whispered, hoping Neith could hear the urgency in his voice.

The radio was silent. Nemo crouched down as low as he could behind the plant in hopes that they wouldn't spot him hiding in the leaves. At the same time, he tightened his grip around the handle of his sword and prepared to fight. At the very least, he could catch the first one coming around the corner by surprise. Maybe even the second one if he was fast enough.

Time seemed to slow down as he saw a foot cross the threshold into his vision. Nemo readied himself to strike. His sword felt light in his grip, and he could visualize the path of his blade unfold in his mind. Nemo shifted his weight, ready to put all the momentum he could behind his sword. Just as the tip of his blade left the ground he heard something.

"Hey Mickey, you're going the wrong way. Look at this guy, two drinks in him and he can't find his way back to the loot."

"Up yours Roy, all these stupid hallways look alike. Just lead the way back."

The foot that had stepped beyond the corner retracted back into the hallway. The echo of their footsteps told Nemo that they were walking away. After nearly a minute, the sound of their footsteps faded. Nemo slumped down to the floor, releasing all the built up tension inside him. Neith's loud voice in his ear made him quickly jump back to his feet.

"That was close. Looks like you got pretty lucky just now."

"What happened to you? How come the radio went silent all of a sudden?" Nemo asked, slightly annoyed that Neith chose to ignore him when he needed her help.

"Calm down" Neith responded *"The sound of your radio could have given away your position. I wasn't going to take that chance. However, I was watching the whole time. I like the look you had on your face. It was the look of someone ready to put their life on the line."*

Nemo calmed himself and focused back on the objective.

"I was ready because I thought I had no other choice. What else could I do?"

"You remember that feeling. You'll need that same determination next time when you actually have to follow through with it." said Neith

"Got it" replied Nemo as he moved down the next hallway.

After a few more turns through the hallways of the second floor, he arrived in front of the door Neith had been directing him to. The tall oak frame was outlined with thick fogged glass panes that blocked the view inside. The door was the same dark oak color as the frame. By just looking at it Nemo knew it was too thick to break down without making an immense amount of noise.

"Neith I'm in front of the door, but it's locked. What do I do?"

Neith sighed in disbelief that her disciple could be this forgetful.

"Check the top pocket on your jacket."

Nemo fumbled through the pockets on his jacket until he found what Neith was referring to.

"Oh, the automatic lock pick tool. I guess I was so nervous sneaking around the building that I completely forgot you gave this to me."

"Everyone just calls it an A.L.P. tool for short. Just use it to open the door. Need I remind you the quicker you can get out of there the better." Neith said as she watched Nemo through her binoculars.

Nemo put the tool on top of the lock and listened to it make a quiet whirring sound before a series of clicks. A dim light on top turned bright green when it was done. Nemo twisted the handle on the large oak door and gently pushed it open.

"Oh I'm definitely holding on to this." he said looking down at the A.L.P. tool in his hands.

Nemo walked into the office and shut the door behind him.

"Ok I'm in, what next?"

"Great, listen carefully. Go into the closet. The office you're in is directly behind the office where the package is being held, the closets share a wall. All eight guards on this floor are standing in front of the office door where the package is. You'll need to quietly break through this office's closet wall and sneak back out the way you came. Let me know as soon as you have eyes on the package."

Nemo had been practicing slicing through wooden targets since he first picked his sword, so a few layers of drywall wouldn't be a problem. He found an empty space between the studs, and with two slashes and kick he was through the closet and into the connecting office. What he saw inside took him completely by surprise.

"Neith, now might be a good time to ask what the package I'm taking is supposed to contain?

"*The contract described the item as some kind of family heirloom, it didn't give much detail beyond that. Why? Do you not see it in there?*"

"Neith I think we have a problem."

"*What's wrong? Is the package missing?*"

"No, it's here. Except I think the package described in the contract, is actually a person."

CHAPTER 18

Neith muted the radio as she spit out a series of curse words. Most of them directed at the situation her and Nemo were now in.

"Of all the times something like this could happen, why now?" While she was busy cursing her luck, she could hear panic rising in Nemo's voice over the radio.

"Neith are you there? What should I do now? Neith...Neith!"

"*I'm here*" she responded. "*Just needed to vent for a bit. Describe what the person in the room looks like.*"

Nemo took a long look at the person passed out in front of him. For the first time, he noticed it was a girl sitting in the chair. Strands of long blonde hair fell down the sides of her face and onto the arms of the chair. She didn't look to be much older than he was, maybe fifteen or sixteen. Her skin was fair and smooth, looking like an unbroken spread of vanilla cream. Rosy spots dotted her skin with each breathe she took. The way her ears, eyes, and nose complimented the shape of her face only added to her angelic look. By all accounts, she was the most beautiful girl he had ever seen.

Nemo stuttered as he tried to relay what the girl looked like to Neith.

"Well umm... she's a young girl with blond hair, and she's really pretty. She's sitting in a chair with pajamas on passed out in front of me, as if someone kidnapped her right from bed. She has an oval shaped face with a cute, delicate looking nose. The way her hair frames her face is really pretty and—"

"*You mentioned how pretty she was already Nemo.*"

"Right, I guess I'm just surprised that's all" Nemo nervously replied. "So, what am I supposed to do with her. If she really is the package, it's going to be a lot harder to carry her out unnoticed."

Neith took a deep breath and wiped the water that dripped from the hood of her cloak away from her face. She could hardly believe the situations that seemed to happen exclusively to her.

"*Someone must have messed up the translation. Saint Georges mentioned that they had to translate it from another language, but I didn't expect them to get such a key detail wrong. We should have charged a lot more for this.*"

Neith thought about all the options before deciding on the next course of action. There was really only one choice.

"*Nemo, get out of there now. You aren't prepared for a hostage situation. There's no way you can make it out with the girl undetected.*"

Nemo listened to everything Neith said. There was nothing he wanted more than to get out of the building unseen and uninjured. He turned around to look directly at the girl in the chair. Somehow, she reminded him of how he first got into all of this.

"Neith, I heard everything you said and I know this isn't what we originally came here to do, but I'm still going to finish the job and save this girl."

"You can save the hero routine for someone else Nemo, this isn't a comic book." Neith shouted through the Nemo's earpiece. *"Do you really want to risk your life for some stranger?"*

Nemo turned away from the girl and faced the door. He knew on the other side of that door were eight people who wouldn't hesitate to kill him if he tried to leave with the girl in this room. Not to mention the other four on the floor below that he still had to worry about, if he made it past the first eight. Yet none of that changed his decision.

"Neith I know the risks, and I just couldn't live with myself if I turned around now and left this girl here. If I make it out of this building she's coming with me."

A smirk crossed Neith's lips. Sometimes he surprised her with how strong he really was. Guess that was one of the things she actually liked about her disciple.

"Ok then, I see you've made up your mind. Let me see what I can do to help get you out of there. We'll talk later about how much extra we're going charge whoever submitted this job."

Nemo breathe a sigh of relief that he had Neith's support in this. He knew he wouldn't be able to do it without her.

"Well first you can help me by—"

Nemo felt something smash into the back of his head that knocked him to the ground. It didn't keep him there for long. Nemo rolled over and saw a pair of green eyes staring back at him. The girl, who was just slumped over in the chair, was now staring down at him with a broken lamp in her hand ready to hit him again.

"Wait!" Nemo shouted.

The girl with the green eyes hesitated at his sudden outburst. For a brief second, they both looked into each other's eyes. That second could have been an eternity to Nemo. As soon as he saw them, he was lost in her green eyes. Nemo's face started to blush as he became lost in his thoughts. His mind quickly snapped back to the situation at hand when the girl drew her arm back to hit him again.

"I said wait! I'm here to rescue you so don't hit me." Nemo shouted.

She paused again, unsure of what to do.

"Who are you?" she asked.

"My name is Nemo, I found you unconscious in that chair over there. Someone hired me to get you out of here."

Nemo raised his hand to grab the broken lamp from her grip, but she jumped back and held it closer. She was ready to swing at the slightest sign of aggression.

"I wasn't unconscious, I was sleeping." She said as she looked Nemo up and down. "You don't look any older than me. Who would hire a kid to rescue me?"

"Well I was actually supposed to get something else and I ending up finding you...well it's a long story. I'll tell you all about it once we get out of here. Unless you want to stay here and see what plans those men outside have for you."

The girl's green eyes darted between Nemo and the door, unsure of what to do. Nemo prepared for another blow from the lamp. He didn't want to hurt her, but he didn't plan on being taken out by the hostage he was supposed to save and some fancy lamp that she picked up. He could see her deciding if she should trust him or not. The decision to trust him must have won that inner battle because she soon dropped the lamp on the floor and walked over to him.

"My name is Jennifer, but everyone just calls me Jen for short."

Nemo extended his hand towards hers.

"Nice to meet you Jen, everyone calls me Nemo".

Nemo had been so distracted after being hit by the lamp, he was just now hearing Neith shouting thru his radio earpiece.

"Nemo!...Nemo are you there!"

"I'm here Neith, everything's ok." Nemo responded.

Neith's voice relaxed after hearing he wasn't hurt. *"I heard a commotion, what happened?"*

"The girl, well her name is Jen, decided to attack me with a lamp. Knocked me on the head pretty good, but I'm ok."

Jen winced at hearing that she hurt Nemo. "Sorry about that, I thought you were one of the men that kidnapped me. Who is that you're speaking to?"

Nemo covered the microphone part of the radio. "I'm talking to my partner, she's my eyes on the outside."

Neith still heard him despite his attempts at muting the receiver.

"Partner! I am your master and you will address me as such. If I hear such disrespect from you again you're going to run the obstacle course until the blisters on your feet have blisters!"

Nemo hurried to remove the earpiece from his ear before his eardrum burst. Her shouting through the radio was so loud that even after he removed his earpiece he felt like he could still hear her voice from outside. Jen stood on her side of the room laughing as she overheard Nemo being screamed at through the radio.

"She sounds like she could be your mother." said Jen

"If she was, I don't think I would be alive right now." Nemo replied, making sure he fully covered the radio this time.

He put it back in his ear just as Neith was done ranting.

"Yes master... I understand master" Nemo said in a halfway sarcastic tone. If Neith heard the sarcasm in his voice she chose to ignore it.

"Good, seems like you are finally learning some manners. Now find out what that girl knows about the reason she was kidnapped, and you two get out of there."

"Roger that."

Nemo grabbed Jen's hand and led her towards the opening he made in the closet.

"Let's go. The quicker we get you out of here the better."

Nemo and Jen quietly exited through the back office. Nemo put his finger over his mouth, motioning for Jen to be quiet as they walked down the hallway. He was being extra cautious to avoid any guards in the building. Once they had made it a floor up Nemo felt safe enough to talk.

"So why were you being held hostage by those guys?"

Jen looked down at her bare feet, letting her blonde hair fall around her face.

"I don't know. I woke up to a bunch of men standing over my bed. They taped my mouth shut and put a bag over my head so I couldn't see where they took me. I was put in the trunk of a car, but on the ride over I kept hearing them say 'Her father will pay. Once he finds out he'll definitely pay.' I don't know why they would say that. My family doesn't have much money. Certainly not enough to warrant all of this."

"Who's your father? What does he do?" Nemo asked

"Both of my parents run a small restaurant. I doubt the men that kidnapped me would go through all trouble for the little bit of money my family has. But I've been thinking about it for the past few hours, and I think it might have something to do with my real parents. I was adopted from Tralone when I was a baby."

"Tralone? Never heard of the place." said Nemo.

"It's a small country west of here. I've never been there, but I was told it used to be a very dangerous place. My parents were killed shortly after I was born, but my current parents adopted me and took me away from all of that."

While Nemo was interested in her story, he was still waiting to hear how this related to her being kidnapped. She must have noticed the confusion on his face because she jumped to her point.

"I think these men have me confused with someone else. By the way they talk around me they think I'm someone important. I tried to explain, but they wouldn't listen. I'm scared to see what they'll do when they find out my family doesn't have any money to pay them."

Nemo shook his head. This job was becoming more confusing by the minute, but he didn't have to understand to know what they needed to do. He looked back at Jen and grabbed her hand.

"Regardless of what they believe, we need to keep moving. I don't want to be here when they discover you've escaped."

Nemo kept thinking about her situation as they walked together, but decided against asking anymore questions. He didn't want to upset her by making her worry about what might have happened to her family. It was best if they just remained quiet. However, walking in silence together didn't help make the situation any less awkward. The whole time they walked, he couldn't stop staring at her. Each time her piercing green eyes looked back at him, he would turn away in embarrassment.

"Your face is red" said Jen.

"Huh...What, no its not." Nemo said, fumbling over his words.

Jen stopped and took a closer look at his face. "You're blushing!"

"Sorry, I just think you...you're really...I mean you look nice."

Nemo wanted nothing more than to keep his mouth shut. He was never any good at talking to girls, and his current life threatening situation didn't make him any less nervous. He was so focused on what a fool he was making of himself that he didn't even notice when she leaned over, pressed her face against his, and kissed him on the cheek.

"Thanks, for saving me I mean. It's really sweet of you."

Nemo was speechless. For the next few moments, he felt like he was floating through the air.

They were less than fifty feet from where he first snuck in, and there hadn't been any signs of trouble. Nemo realized that they might just make it out without confronting anyone. Unfortunately, his feelings of euphoria were ruined by the sound of a toilet flush. The door in front of them swung open, as a man with his hands on the zipper of his pants and a gun hanging from his right shoulder exited the bathroom.

Before he noticed, Nemo had his sword out. His perception of time slowed. He had one chance to eliminate the threat in front of him before they were caught. Nemo knew exactly what he should do. The guard was distracted, still focusing on his zipper. All Nemo had to do was strike and they would be on their way without even breaking stride. Nearly everything in him was ready. Ready to protect Jen, and ready to protect himself. Yet he still paused. Something in him didn't want to kill another person. Nemo stood their frozen, with his sword in his grip as he looked at the guard slowly turn towards them and realize what was going on. Nemo expected him to go for the gun at his side. Had he gone for his gun, Nemo would have run him through before he had a chance to fire a single shot. Instead the guard went for the radio on his left side.

"Everybody up here now! Someone's trying to break out the girl!"

Before he could say another word, Nemo dropped down and swept his feet from under him. With the pommel of his sword, he smashed the guard's forehead into the ground. A hard, but less than fatal, blow. He wouldn't be waking up from for a while, but it didn't matter. Nemo knew that his moment of hesitation meant that every guard in the building was about to be on them. Neith confirmed it for him.

"You need to get out of there now. All the guards are approaching your position."

"Hurry, let's go!" Nemo shouted at Jen

They quickly ran to the air duct leading to the rooftop. Nemo gave Jen a boost and told her to climb until she saw light from the outside. Faster than he expected, six guards rushed around the corner to stop him. Five more followed after them. Each person carried at least one assault rifle, one or two pistols, and extra ammo on clips around their belts. Those were just the weapons Nemo could see, he didn't want to think about if they had anything else hidden on them. All he had was his sword.

As the first one reached him, Nemo ducked and stabbed his foot. His advantage was that they saw two children trying to escape. They didn't expect him to put up much of a fight. Unfortunately for them, they were wrong. Two more rushed in and tried to grab his arms. With his sword already low to the ground, he stuck the point in the floor and used it to vault him forward. Their momentum running towards him only added to the strength of his kick as he planted one foot in a guard's face and his other in the second guard's throat. He could feel a nose snap under his foot before both guards collapsed to the ground. Blood poured across the floor from the guard with the broken nose. The other clutched his throat while his eyes jutted wide open in shock and fear at his sudden inability to breathe. Nemo had either knocked the wind from him, or crushed his windpipe. He didn't stop to think about which. Taking out three of them caused the other guards to pause for a second. They had discovered he wasn't the easy target they expected him to be. The remaining guards drew guns from their holsters and pointed in his direction as he ran back to the air duct and climbed up as fast as he could.

"Neith I'm going to need a getaway plan once I get back to the roof." Nemo yelled

Neith was watching the situation spiral out of control as she looked for a way to get Nemo and Jen to safety.

"There's a fire escape directly to your left when you come out on the roof. I'll meet you at the bottom of it."

All Nemo could think of was how he would grab Jen's hand and take off as soon as he got to the roof. He could see light from outside shining through the opening where he first came in. Nemo grabbed the top of the vent and pulled himself up and outside. Raindrops splashed across his face as lightning and thunder roared through the sky. He saw Jen nearby waiting for him, her thin pajamas getting soaked by the downpour of rain. Her bare feet slid in the puddles of water as he grabbed her wrist and ran immediately to his left where Neith said the fire escape would be.

Right before they reached the edge of building, the sound of gunfire erupted behind them, drowning out the thunder from the storm.

"Stop right there or we kill you both!" a man shouted in Nemo's direction.

Nemo pulled Jen behind him as the other eight guards came from the stairwell that led to the roof, and stood in front of them. Every gun was pointed at Nemo. The barrels were so close to his face that he could see smoke drifting off them when raindrops hit. There was nowhere for him to run.

A bald man moved forward and held up his fist, a signal for the rest of them to hold their fire.

"I got to hand it to you kid. Mickey's nose is banged up pretty bad, and you kicked Roy so hard he almost choked to death on his own spit. You got spunk kid, but playtime's over. Her rich daddy is going to pay us well to get her back. So hand over the girl, and we'll let you go."

One of the men in the back started to protest. "Like hell we will! That little pisser broke my bloody nose!"

The bald man didn't bother to turn around. He simply pointed his gun behind him and fired.

"I told Mickey about talking back to me."

A splatter of blood was left where Mickey once stood. His body tumbled over the edge of the roof and fell down onto the street below. The bald man pointed his gun back at Nemo.

"Guess that one less share of the ransom we have to split off. Now boy, if you don't want to follow Mickey over that ledge, I suggest you hand over the girl right now. I won't ask again."

Nemo still had his sword out. Although he knew it wouldn't protect him from gunfire, it was the only thing he could depend on right now. Neith would be there to help him soon, but he had to somehow hold them off by himself until then.

He whispered behind him to Jen, "On the count of three I'm going to make an opening. You run for it and don't look back."

"I'm not going to run while they stand here and shoot you." Jen whispered back.

"Don't worry about me, just run. One...two..."

The last thing Nemo heard was a gunshot.

CHAPTER 19

Leo waited on the rooftop, looking through the scope on his sniper rifle. Megas gave it to him specifically for this job. With a high end scope, carbon fiber lightweight frame, and a special alloy heat dissipating barrel, this wasn't your run of the mill hunting rifle. Megas knew he was an admirer of beautiful things, which is why this master crafted rifle suited him perfectly. Not that the accuracy of the weapon he used had any bearing on the success of his task. Even if he was given an old musket, the result would be the same. Using his ability to peak into the future, he could see the bullet's path. All he had to do was aim until his vision of the bullet was where he wanted it to be. Unfortunately, his gift to see the future trailed off the further in time he looked. While he could see a few seconds into the future with complete certainty, he only had a fuzzy view of things occurring months in the future. Trying to see years into the future was like looking through a keyhole with the sun in your eyes. He hardly could see anything useful that far out. Still his ability came in handy for jobs like this one.

The rain was just starting to fall harder, and the sound of thunder filled the sky. It didn't bother him. He knew within the next few minutes he would be done with his work, then the real fun would begin. As he scanned the rooftops he saw his target appear.

"Right on time as usual." Leo casually whispered to himself.

The large box radio beside him came to life with the voice of Megas' aide as if it had heard Leo speak.

"*Has the target appeared yet?*"

"Yes, I have eyes on her now. She's surrounded by a large group of males. One with a sword is standing in front of her."

The voice from the radio paused before responding "*Are they a problem?*"

"No" said Leo as he put his rifle in position.

"*Very well then, describe the target.*" replied the voice from the radio.

"Pale face with Tralonian features. Long blonde hair, thin build, looks to be no older than sixteen. She has green eyes, although I can't see to confirm."

"*If you can't see to confirm then how do you know she has...never mind. I don't even know why I bother asking you to explain yourself.*" said the voice on the radio

"Ready to eliminate the target on your command." said Leo

There was another long pause from the radio until the voice finally came back. "*No, that's not her. Do not engage. Pack it up and come home.*"

"Copy that."

Leo took one last look at the girl through his scope. Even in the rain he could tell she was beautiful. Like a delicate flower sent to grace the world with her presence. Regrettably, he knew all too well that the world was not suited for beauty. No, the world that he knew was very ugly indeed, and anything beautiful in it was slowly crushed out of existence. The longer he looked, the more pain he felt for her. He didn't need to see her future to know that pain and suffering awaited to embrace her. He knew pain, and he knew suffering. They whispered to him how they couldn't wait to become acquainted with her. His finger slid closer to the trigger on the rifle. Somehow, he desperately wanted to save her from this world, from seeing her be slowly ripped apart by life's cruel humor. His finger gently tapped the trigger. It would be easy for him to spare her from all of this. But he had his orders, and he didn't want to upset Megas. Still he continued looking at her through the scope, watching her. His thoughts lingered on one thing. If she were to die right now, the memory of her beauty would stay with him forever. Forever pure, unable to be tarnished by the violence and cruelty of the world. If she truly knew how horrid this world was she would want that. He knew she would. In that moment, Leo made up his mind and decided to do her a favor. He pulled the trigger.

****

Neith heard shots as she ran towards Nemo's position. Her eyes were already glowing bright red. She anticipated a fight when she arrived. She just hoped she wasn't too late.

"I should have intervened earlier. As soon as he found the girl I should have come in to help him."

That thought kept looping through her head as she ran between rooftops. When she was halfway to Nemo's position, she heard another shot. It was a single shot that sounded completely different from the barrage of bullets she heard earlier. Judging from the sound, she could tell it came from farther away as well. Neith slid to a stop when she realized just how far away the shot had come from. Her senses were already heightened by letting her fighting spirit flow freely, so she could judge the distance and direction of the shot by its sound. She turned and stared intently into the rainy darkness, searching for any sign of movement. About half a mile away she saw a person with a rifle.

"Well isn't this great. On top of everything else, we've got a sniper."

As much as she wanted to rush and help Nemo, it would do him no good to save him from the guards on the building only to let him be taken out by some sniper from afar. She needed to get rid of the sniper first, then she could come back and help Nemo. She silently prayed that his first shot had missed.

"Hold on just a little bit longer Nemo."

Neith turned around and sprinted in the direction of the sniper, effortless jumping between rooftops. The dark silhouette of a person in her vision became clearer as she steadily moved closer to the sniper's position. It was odd that he was just standing there. She expected him to try and escape, or use his gun to get a second shot off before she reached him. He must have seen her running towards him by now. But instead of making a move to defend himself, he was just standing there. Almost as if he was waiting for her.

Neith didn't bother think too hard about what the sniper's reason for standing there could be. She was more concerned with eliminating him as a threat. As soon as she reached the sniper's building, she went for his rifle. Without that he would effectively be useless, and she could rush back to Nemo. She immediately grabbed the weapon, and using all her strength threw it far as she could. It soared past two adjacent buildings before slamming against the third and falling to the ground in pieces. Neith had paid no attention to the sniper this whole time, and prepared to turn around and rush back to Nemo. Out of the corner of her eye, she saw a sword rushing towards her neck. Whatever restraints were left on her fighting spirt were released as soon as she drew her own sword to block the attack against her. For the first time, she looked to see who the sniper and impromptu swordsman was. It was a kid.

"Fiiiiiiiiiiinally" He let out in a long deep exhale "I've been waiting for you. Shame what you did to my rifle, but such is life. Beautiful things are fleeting before they are crushed out of existence."

Neith looked into the eyes of the child that stood before her. They seemed to stare off into the distance, but somehow still focused directly on her. Dark circles rested under his eyes. From the looks of them he hadn't slept in days. He was just a few years older than Nemo, maybe sixteen or seventeen. But the wrinkles etched into his face, and the sullen look in his eyes, made him look years older than he was.

"Who are you?" she asked

Leo cocked his head all the way to the side touching his ear to the top of his shoulder. "I've gone by several names before. None of them I cared for, but I like my new name. They call me Leo."

From the weird way he spoke, Neith couldn't help but ask. "and who might 'they' be?"

"Ahh..." Leo said as he paused and tilted his head forward. As he looked down rain dripped off the ends of his hair. Once he seemed to be done thinking, his head slowly raised back up to look Neith in the eye.

"They wouldn't want me to tell you. They'll already be upset with me once they find out what I did."

Behind Neith, a large bolt of lightning streaked from the clouds down to the ground. She could hear it hit something nearby, but she didn't dare to turn around and look. Not when there was a clear and present threat in front of her. Whoever 'they' were probably had some answers about recent events. At the very least this kid knew more than he would say. She was interested in finding out exactly how much more. Now was no time to try and pull answers from this child's mind that was quickly spiraling into madness. She would have to take him back with her.

Neith rushed forward, feinting for his chest. She didn't plan on drawing this fight out. Her first strike would end it. She needed to get back to Nemo and make sure he was alive. Right before her blade reached his chest, she moved her aim to just above his kneecap. Once he was immobilized, she could easily capture him alive for questioning. She made sure to regulate her strength so that she wouldn't completely rip his leg off. Although in her current state of mind, regulating her strength was a tall order. The target area was open. She could visualize her sword piercing flesh and prepared for the impact of bone against her blade.

None of those things happened. Instead of flesh and bone, the longsword that was raised above Leo's head moments ago was all of a sudden in the way of her scimitar. Surprise quickly flashed across Neith's face. Almost instinctively she stepped back and redirected her attack to his shoulder. Just as before, the blade of his longsword seemed to appear at the last second between him and her sword. Neith was past the point of restraint and launched into a barrage of piercing strikes and slashes, each one more devastating than the last. Each one was blocked at the last second just like her first attack. What was even more remarkable than just blocking her attacks, he was repositioning his body so that the force of the blow was either transferred or absorbed. It was the only thing keeping his bones from shattering under the strength of her blows.

Neith broke her assault to figure out just what was going on. The movements of his body clearly reflected some type of training, but his swordsmanship was awkward at best. It was mostly him just waiving his sword around and somehow managing to be in her sword's path. He looked like he had never even held his weapon before today. Yet somehow he was able to place it in exactly the right spot at exactly the right time.

"They said you people were good with a sword, so I brought one with me to test if that was true. I figured you could provide me with at least a few moments of entertainment." Leo said, breaking Neith's concentration.

Until she could figure out what was happening, she thought it best to indulge him.

"Who do you mean 'You people'?"

Leo's emotionless face started to betray a smile across his lips,.

"You know, you Shadows, members of Fratello della Spada. There's no reason to play dumb, they already know everything about your organization. It almost laughable that we know so much about you and you know nothing about us. That's exactly why Guiding Light will be the ones to purge the Shadows from this world."

Neith looked at the boy's eyes again as they shifted. Looking off into the distance but focusing on her at the same time. As improbable as it seemed she could only come up with one answer as to why he was able to block all of her attacks.

"You can see what move I'm going to make next." she calmly stated as if she had already proven her theory. "You have some kind of ability for clairvoyance."

Now it was Leo who was surprised. He relished the emotion whenever he felt it, no matter how small. It was rare that he felt surprise, sometimes going years with nothing but a faint sense of it. But this was genuine surprise, and he was enjoying every ounce of it.

"Wow, never has anyone figured it out so quickly. Usually I tell people right before they're about to die as a last wish, but you seem to have ruined the surprise."

Even after he confirmed her suspicions, Neith still couldn't believe it. But she had eliminated every other likely possibility. Whether if she believed he could really see the future or not was hardly the problem. The real problem was if it was true, what was she going to do about it.

There was only one course of action. Even if he could foresee her next moves, that didn't mean he was quick enough to keep up with them.

Her next attack she made sure was twice as fast, and the one after that three times as fast. Leo managed to block each one, but that didn't stop her volley. Neith grabbed the sheath from her side and used it to add to her volley of attacks. Leo was starting to get sloppy trying to defend against them all. It was just the mistake she was looking for. In a split second Neith focused all of her attack power on one side. Leo's hasty movements, trying to keep up with her speed, put him in a bad position for what was coming. He was knocked off balance trying to control the swing of Neith's sword and sheath. Not by much, but enough to open the particular spot she was targeting. Neith knew there was one vital area he would have trouble guarding if he was off balance. In that narrow opening she created, Neith aimed for the fingers on his sword hand.

Leo's eyes suddenly shifted their focus to his hand. It was clear he knew what was about to happen, but he couldn't do anything to stop it. Neith saw his eyes widen in pain as his pinky, ring, and middle finger tumbled to the ground along with the weapon he was holding.

Leo stumbled backward, again he relished in the ocean of emotions currently flooding his senses. A mix of pain and pleasure threatened to overwhelm him. Leo squeezed his bleeding fingers as his face returned to a calm emotionless stare.

"Well well, it seems I've underestimated you people. You're just as good as he says."

Neith wasn't in the mood to talk, she focused purely on ending the fight. All she needed was one good strike to the head to knock him out, then she could bring him back and let Arthur and his investigation team go to work. In the midst of her thoughts she was distracted by the sounds of metal scraping against the ground.

"Megas sent me here with a few more toys than just that rifle." Leo said with a wide grin stretching across his face.

Neith immediately saw two grenades roll on each side of her. She didn't know how she could have missed them being thrown.

"Even though I couldn't stop your attack, I still knew it was coming." said Leo. "You didn't expect to me to not have some countermeasures prepared did you?"

There was no time to finish. Both of them would die on that rooftop if he wasn't bluffing. He was crazy enough not to be. Neith put her hands over her face and jumped off the side of the building. She didn't know how far she would make it before the blast caught her, hopefully it was far enough. Instead of the bang she expected to hear, smoke engulfed her as she went over the edge. Right before she succumbed to gravity pushing her onto the concrete below, she saw Leo mouth the words "Tricked You" with his head cocked to the side. Even with the smoke clouding her vision she saw Leo grab his fingers from the ground and take off in the other direction.

"This really isn't my day." Neith thought as she fell past the edge of the rooftop.

Neith hit everything from railings to the side of the wall on the way down. Her fall was the exact opposite of graceful, ending with a hard landing top of on a dumpster. Plastic pieces shattered from the dumpster lid. It was the only thing that saved her. Had she landed on the concrete, she would be dead. Pain radiated through her back as she arched it away from the sharp plastic piece stabbing through her side. Resisting the urge to blackout, she rolled off onto the wet concrete. Rain falling into her wound only added to the sting of pain in her side. She could feel blood welling up in the back of her throat as she tried to breathe. Fitting for the day she was having. Her best lead so far had escaped into the wind, and she didn't have much to show from the encounter besides a couple of names. Neith struggled to her feet and began to limp in the direction where she last heard from Nemo. She couldn't let the pain keep her down for long, she still had to get to him. She just hoped he was still alive.

CHAPTER 20

The last thing Nemo heard was a gunshot, until he opened his eyes again. He had lost count of how many times he expected to die, only to open his eyes and realize somehow he was still alive. The first thing he saw was blood. Blood covered the right side of his shoulder and ran all the way down his arm. It seeped between his fingers as he fought to keep a tight grip on his sword. Strangely he didn't feel any pain from his wound. Anatomy was one of his best subjects in school, so he knew exactly what arteries the bullet needed to pierce for him to be bleeding this severely.

"Adrenaline must be blocking out his pain" he thought. Whatever injury that caused him to lose that much blood had to be serious.

Nemo's eyes glanced up at the gun still pointed firmly in his face. Spots of crimson blood stood out on the man's bald head as he held the gun inches away from Nemo's forehead. As close as he was, Nemo couldn't believe he missed him the first time. He could only hope to be as lucky if a second shot came. Nemo thought about what Neith would do in this situation. There hadn't been any radio contact from her since he and Jen made it to the roof. No matter how long he waited to hear her voice in his ears, nothing but silence greeted him. He had no plan, no one telling him what moves to make. In this situation, he was all alone. Attempting to mimic her actions was the only hope he and Jen had of making it out alive.

He thought about everything he had learned and seen Neith do. He tried to focus his mind on what moves she would make in his position, but the expression on the bald man's face completely diverted his attention. The bald man's demeanor had changed from the confidence of being in control to the look of complete surprise. That didn't immediately register as awkward to Nemo. He was more concerned with escaping. The entire time Nemo was noticing subtle things in his surroundings, he was also raising his sword to knock the gun away from his face. He hadn't forgotten the fact that he was still in a battle. He had already learned that the slightest hesitation could get him or people he cared about killed.

"I can do this. I can hold on until Neith gets here. No matter what happens I'll protect Jen." Nemo resolved

He briefly looked to his right to check where Jen was. She should have been running for safety like he told her to do, but he couldn't see anyone moving in the darkness. He kept looking, searching around in all directions for where she could have gone. What he saw next shook him to his core. Right beside him lay Jen's body. Her head was split open in jagged pieces, like something had exploded near the back of her skull. Bits of hair and wet bone fragments were scattered in front of her body. Large pools of blood, diluted with rainwater, gathered around her top half and ran off into a drainage pipe on the side of the roof. She had only taken one step to move from behind Nemo, her last step. Both Nemo and the bald head man stared at the body without moving. He finally realized it was Jen's blood covering them, not his own.

Nemo could still picture her face through the carnage. Not a drop of blood had splashed on her clothes. Her body still look pristine, as if she had just fallen down and decided to rest. He silently whispered for her to get up, despite knowing the truth.

"Get up Jen... I said I would get you out of here so you have to get up." His soft whisper turned into a loud sob as he screamed, "Get up Jen! Get up. You have to get up, you have to."

Nemo didn't need the rain to hide his tears, none fell from his eyes. He wouldn't shed any tears while the ones responsible stood in front of him.

"Why...Why, Why, Why?"

Nemo turned back to face the bald man. A dark blue color started to fill his eyes, bubbling up from some unknown source. Sadness and anger battled to take hold of him as his eyes were coated in a blue color so rich that they looked as if you were staring into the depths of the ocean. Trails of dark blue energy sparked from his eyes as he continued muttering, "Why...Why...Why..." Finally, Nemo gave in and lost himself in his anger.

"Why did you kill her?" he whispered

The bald man stepped back, "You've got this all wrong kid, I didn't shoot her. That girl was my payday, why would I kill her?"

His reasoning fell on deaf ears as Nemo was already lost to his emotions. With one hand he thrust his sword toward the sky. Thunder roared as clouds started to circle overhead. The bald man took another step back, unsure of what was happening around him. His gun was shaking in his hand as he tried to hold it steady on Nemo.

"You've got to believe me! I didn't shoot the girl." Again, his pleading fell on deaf ears.

In one quick motion, Nemo brought the tip of his blade to the ground. Lighting crashed down on the bald man. His loud screams were drowned by the wave of thunder following the broad bolts of lightning that hit the rooftop. Everyone could see his body twitch in pain as electricity coursed through his limbs. Their imagination filled in the screams they couldn't hear. Once the lightning stopped, the smell of burnt flesh filled the air. A charred black corpse stood among a pile of ash and soot before collapsing to the ground.

Men dropped their weapons and ran for the door leading back inside. A few tried to climb down the side of the building, preferring to fall on the concrete below than end up a lighting charred corpse. None of them would make it to safety. Before any could reach the door, Nemo struck his sword to the ground again, sending electricity flowing through the water that covered the rooftop. Anyone standing on the rooftop was immediately paralyzed as current flowed through their bodies. It was spread over a large enough area that the electricity alone wouldn't kill them, but that didn't make it hurt any less. Burns started to appear through their skin as their bodies flailed around like ragdolls. Nemo stood there and watched.

When he picked his sword up from the ground again, it was to end it all. Nemo rushed in and skillfully cut down every man left on the rooftop while they were paralyzed and defenseless. Their blood finished covering every clean spot on Nemo that wasn't already soaked in Jen's blood. It dripped from every part of him and splashed across the roof like a fresh coat of paint. Once he was finished, he walked back over to Jen's body, knelt down, and began to cry.

****

Neith hobbled to Nemo as fast as she could. After her fall, she could tell she had a few broken bones, maybe a fractured rib or two. She didn't care about her injuries right now, they could be addressed after she saved Nemo. Unable to jump across the rooftops, she traveled along the ground and went through the front door. Just an hour earlier, the lobby of this building was heavily guarded. A man at each door watching for intruders. Now it was empty, Nemo had lured them all to the rooftop. Once inside the building she took the elevator to the top floor. When she reached the top floor, Neith ran for the rooftop. The lack of guards on the top floor hopefully meant that Nemo was still alive. She prayed again, something she was making a habit of today, that she wasn't too late. Through the windows, she could see that the rain had slowed to a light drizzle. Neith was already soaked so it hardly mattered. Her sword was in her hand ready to save her disciple as soon as she burst through the door. What she arrived to was a bloodbath.

"One, two, four…no seven bodies. Did he take out all seven by himself? And what happened to the body in the middle?" she asked herself.

The smell of burnt flesh was thick in the air. Neith could see Nemo kneeling over a body in the middle of the roof. It was the body of a young girl. She cursed under her breathe for her inability to capture Leo. But even if she did, it wouldn't have prevented the girl's death. That was the second person that got away from her in the past few weeks.

That was two, too many. The next person she found that was involved with whoever was doing all of this wouldn't leave her sight alive. She swore it.

After making sure the area was indeed safe, she walked over to Nemo and put her arm around his neck. Nemo turned towards her and buried his tears in her chest. Neith could do nothing but wrap her arms around him and hold him against her.

"C'mon Nemo, let's go home" was all she could say. They left in silence and headed back to the Citadel.

CHAPTER 21

Neith rested on the chesterfield in her room back at the Citadel. Her bare feet dangled over the edge in the air. Everything that had happened still weighed on her mind. She hadn't seen Nemo in three days. Things must have still been weighing on his mind too.

Just as the tranquility of her thoughts was about to lull her to sleep, Arthur burst through the door interrupting her peace and quiet. He was carrying his zweihänder with him, a giant two-handed sword with a cross in the middle of the blade. It was something he rarely did while inside the Citadel walls. The look on his face told her that he was not there for a friendly conversation.

"Mind telling me exactly what happened on that rooftop?"

Neith sighed as she sat up from the couch. "I had a feeling I'd be seeing you soon. Didn't take much to guess that the higher ups made you the head of the special investigation team."

"You've been collaborating with investigation team members after you received explicit instructions against it." Arthur yelled

Neith simply rolled her eyes, "If your team was doing their job I wouldn't need to interfere. It's been weeks, and you're no closer to solving this thing than when you started. At this point, you should be here thanking me for my interference. Seems like you need all the help you can get."

Arthur was visibly getting more irritated by the second. A deep breathe passed through his lips as he ran his fingers down his face. His other hand went for the hilt of his zweihänder, pulling it clear of the scabbard in one smooth motion. Neith leaned back from the sheer size of the weapon. It was nearly as tall as he was and stretched halfway across the room.

Arthur put his second hand on the hilt and held it high above his head.

"You're going to tell me what you were doing on the rooftop, or else we're going to have a vigorous conversation that will end with you telling me what I want to know while my blade is at your throat."

Dark circles surrounded Arthur's bloodshot red eyes. Neith could tell he hadn't been sleeping much lately. She didn't take being challenged lightly, but now wasn't the time to test him.

"It was messed up situation, and I take full responsi—"
Arthur rammed the blade of his sword into the floor. The sound of wood splintering rang throughout the small room as shards of hardwood floor flew through the air. Neith shielded her eyes, surprised by the sudden interruption.

"Actually never mind, you can start by telling me how a disciple of yours managed to massacre eight people, and how you both failed to complete a job that you two weren't even supposed to know about?"

"Arthur, I know how it looks but—"

Arthur slammed his fist against the wall before she could finish.

"No you don't. You didn't get a call at four in the morning to go clean up bits of brain and intestines sprawled across the top of a building. You didn't have to dispose of a body so charred that it was unrecognizable. You didn't have to cover your own ass in this mess that you and your disciple created. I did that! Now you better have a good reason for all of this, or else I'll arrest you myself."

Neith, tired of being interrupted, sat silently until she was sure Arthur was finished.

"Do you actually want to know what happened, or did you just come here to yell at me?"

Arthur relaxed his anger after finally seeing that Neith was taking him seriously.

"A bit of both I suppose."

"Whoever translated the request messed up a key detail. What was supposed to be a simple stolen item retrieval job turned into a hostage situation. The people on that roof kidnapped a young girl and Nemo tried to save her."

"And where were you during all of this?" Arthur asked

"I was watching Nemo from a few buildings over. When I saw he needed help I ran to him, but someone else got in my way."

"Yes, we were able to gather footage from security cameras in the surrounding area. Nothing close enough to make out faces, but enough to see two people dueling on a rooftop. Saint Georges filled me in on the rest of what happened after you came back and told him what you discovered that night. I don't know why I expect that man to keep secrets from you. I might as well have left a note on your door myself."

Arthur stepped towards Neith and sat down beside her. He left his sword jutting up from the floor.

"You were right about one thing. Until yesterday we hadn't come any closer to finding out the killer's identity. We've interrogated every member of Fratello della Spada we could find. As far as we can tell, every one of us is innocent. But the three names you discovered did turn up something interesting."

Neith jumped up from the couch in excitement. "Well what did you find?"

He gave her a stern look in return. "First tell me what happened to that charred body on the roof."

Neith could only look down as she thought about the events of that night.

"Nemo...he somehow called down lightning on him. Well, more like he directed the lightning in the sky towards a target and amplified its power using his own fighting spirit. I've never seen anything like it, especially from someone as inexperienced as him. I haven't spoken to him since that night so I'll need to ask him how he accomplished such a feat."

Arthur let out a long, high pitched whistle. "Well that is impressive, but troubling at the same time. I had a feeling there was more to that boy than we thought. You better keep an eye on him. Power like that can quickly spiral out of control. If it hasn't already that is."

Neith nodded that she understood. For once, she and Arthur agreed on something.

"So what did you find from the names I gave you?" Neith asked.

"Mostly a whole lot of nothing. The name Leo didn't turn up anything. At least nothing about a sword wielding teenage assassin that can see the future."

Arthur flashed Neith a look showing that he was still skeptical about that part of her story.

"Searching for references to Guiding Light didn't turn up much more, mostly just whisperings about some organization that's been buying up black market weapons en masse. Still, nothing I can concretely trace. But the proverbial needle in the haystack was Megas, that name did turn up something interesting."

Arthur pulled a small tablet computer from his coat pocket and used his fingers to scroll through digital pages until he found what he was looking for.

"Let's see here. Megas Krav, former military special operations captain turned mercenary. His file lists several deployments to warzones in Tralone during the time of their civil war. Then he disappeared and vanished from the face of the earth. No address, no bank accounts, the man is virtually a ghost. But its what's not here that's telling. No death certificate, no collections on life insurance, things like that are what lead me to believe he's been hiding and waiting."

"Waiting for what?" Neith asked almost instinctively

"I don't know, but it doesn't really matter. Now that we have a viable suspect for who's behind Janus and Bulo's murders, I'm calling everyone back to the Citadel. We'll find this guy and he's going to have a nice, long, and terribly painful time explaining himself."

Arthur stood up and headed towards the door. He effortlessly grabbed his sword that was still stuck in the floor and, with a flourish and a spin, returned it to the sheath resting at his side. Neith glanced over at the hole and noticed she had a clear view of the floor below her.

"This will be the only time I say this so listen closely" Arthur said as he walked toward the doorway. "Thank you."

Despite her best efforts to keep her emotionless stare, a slight smile came to her face. She hardly ever showed it, but she respected Arthur. One of these days she would find out just how good he was with that zweihänder of his.

Arthur stopped abruptly right before he exited the room. "Oh, one more thing. Nemo is downstairs, I think you should go see him."

Neith nodded, "Right, tell him to wait in the main hall. I'll be down there in a second."

****

Nemo leaned against one of the pillars in the main hall. He wasn't sure if he would ever come back to this place after that night. He still remembered everything that happened, in vivid detail, no matter how much he wanted to forget it all. The memory of Jen's body lying on the ground still brought tears to his eyes whenever he thought about it. That, and seeing all of the blood covering him every time he closed his eyes, kept him awake at night. There were only two reasons he came back to the Citadel. The first was to find out exactly how he was still alive. He didn't have the slightest idea how he was able to call down lightning and channel electricity through his sword. It was a question he couldn't leave unanswered, and the only place he could find answers was here. The other reason was because of Neith. Part of him he felt like he owed her at least this much after the way she treated him that night. He remembered crying the whole way back against her. Neith was silent the whole time, but there was kindness in her touch. Kindness was something he had never seen from her before.

It wasn't long before Neith came walking around the corner into the main hall. She walked up to him and put a hand on his shoulder.

"I'm glad to see you came back."

For a second Nemo wondered which Neith was greeting him. The normal Neith he was used to, or the kind Neith he saw a glimpse of three nights ago. It didn't take long for him to figure out.

"Now it's time to get back to work!" Neith said. "You've had three days off, so I don't want to see any slacking. I need five obstacle course runs as a warm up, and none of them better be longer than forty-five seconds. After that you're going straight into form drills, and if I see any weakness in your form I'll make you hold that position so long your body will sleep that way."

Just as Nemo was about to protest, Neith cut him off. "But before you start any of that, we need to talk. There are things I've been keeping from you, things that have put your life in danger this whole time. I should have told you from the beginning, but I didn't because of my own selfish reasons. There's no excuse for what I've done, but the only thing I can do is apologize and ask your forgiveness after I tell you everything."

Neith went on to explain the whole situation to him. Starting with Bulo's funeral, and how someone had been killing Shadows. She paused when told him about Janus' death. He could tell it was still hard for her to talk about it. Still she persevered through the details. Nemo could only nod his head as she talked, trying to take it all in. When she mentioned Jen, and that the men he killed on the rooftop didn't actually kill her, Nemo was the one that needed to pause and breathe. He killed all those men for something they didn't do. MURDERER, MURDERER, echoed through his head. The sound of Neith voice brought him back to reality, but it didn't quiet the thoughts in his mind. When she was finished, Nemo could barely put all the pieces together. However, he would rather walk away not knowing everything than hear her explain it all again. Nemo composed himself to speak when Neith asked him if he had any questions.

"So, you're telling me that all the new disciples and their masters left the Citadel because somebody has been targeting Shadows?"

"Yes" Neith responded, trying to look him in the eyes and not hide the shame she was feeling.

Nemo continued his question, "But we stayed here and went on those dangerous missions, just so you could try and catch that person?"

"Yes" Neith responded again.

Nemo stared directly into Neith's eyes, making sure she saw the frustration and anger in his. Neith stared right back at him refusing to look away.

"I can only ask for your forgiveness for what I've done." Neith said breaking the silence between them.

Nemo thought about all that had happened to him since that day he ran after Neith, thinking she was in danger. After a few moments, his face softened and he bowed his head.

"I can't forgive you. There's nothing for me to forgive you for. As my master and teacher, I trust you to know what is best for me. So, I cannot be mad at any decision you've made knowing that you had my best interests at heart."

It was the last thing Neith expected to hear. She waited until Nemo raised his head again in order to stare at the face of this person who was no longer the weak boy she thought he was. He had grown a lot over these past few months, more than she had bothered to notice. Before she knew it, Neith was blinking back tears from her eyes.

"You might just be the best disciple I've ever had."

Nemo raised an eyebrow, "I thought I was the only disciple you've ever had?"

"That still makes it true"

Neith bent down and wrapped her arms tightly around Nemo. He circled his arms around her and squeezed just as tightly. When she finally let him go, they both looked at each other confused about what to do next. Neith spoke first.

"Did you have any other questions before we get started with today's training? I know a dumped a lot on you just now so I'd rather clarify anything you want to know now, instead of waiting to address it later."

Nemo knew exactly what he wanted to ask. The question that was on his mind the past three days.

"How did I control lightning with my sword?"

Neith looked at him shocked at the question. "You mean you don't know? I don't know how you did it either."

That hadn't been the answer he was expecting. He thought for sure that Neith would be able to tell him how he was able to do the things he did on that rooftop.

"So you have no idea how I could control lightning?" Nemo asked again, hoping he would get a better answer.

"Well I didn't say that. I mean, obviously you were able to manifest your fighting spirit into a form of energy, the same way you've seen me or Saint Georges do. What I don't understand is how you did it without knowing yourself what you were doing. Keeping your body and spirit aligned in battle requires intense focus, it's not something that can be done unconsciously. Have you tried doing it again?"

Nemo put his hands in his pockets and leaned back against the wall.

"Yes. I tried a few times to channel electricity through my sword. I even tried meditating beforehand but I couldn't even produce a spark."

Neith tapped her finger against her cheek, trying to sort all the thoughts roaming through her mind at the moment. "Well I planned on teaching you this much later, but seems like it would be more helpful for you to learn about it now. Follow me."

Neith walked outside with Nemo to a large dirt area behind the Citadel.

"Hold out your arms." she said as she picked up a stick from the ground and began to drag it in the dirt around Nemo to make a circle.

Once she finished drawing the circle she took five large steps and began to drag the stick in the dirt to draw another circle encompassing the first circle Nemo was standing in. After finishing that circle, she took another ten large steps and began to draw an even larger circle. The whole time, Nemo stood holding his arms straight out. After about ten minutes, Neith finished drawing the third circle. She then drew three lines from the outside of the largest circle to the center, dividing each circle into three parts.

"Can I put my arms down now?" Nemo asked desperately, ready to relieve the fatigue in his arms.

"Sure, you could have put them down after I was done with the first circle." Neith said surprised he'd kept his arms up the entire time.

The stare on Nemo's face said what he was thinking before he could. "Then why didn't you say so?"

"Because a little extra training never hurts" she replied. Nemo could see Neith's sadistic streak starting to show again. After their emotional moment, he thought just maybe she would be a little easier on him. Clearly he was wrong.
Neith walked back towards Nemo, carefully stepping over the lines she had drawn forming circles in the dirt.

"What I've drawn is called the Three Tiers of the Soul."

CHAPTER 22

Nemo was clearly confused. Even though his head nodded that he understood, the expression on his face said he was completely lost. Neith simply looked at him and questioned how he could fail to understand such a simple diagram.

"I'll explain it once more for you so listen carefully. Each circle represents the amount of spiritual power needed to manifest certain abilities. The first circle is the Circle of Perception. Everyone has some experience with the amount of spiritual power inside this circle. Things like gut feelings, intuition, instincts, are all small forms of spiritual perception. The second circle is the Circle of Influence. Accessing it requires ten times the amount of spirit as the Circle of Perception, but at this point you can use you spirit to influence other people and their actions. Without training, very few people can achieve this level on their own. Even with training, influencing others is sort of a niche skill. I've heard of people that specialize in it can cause hallucinations and control minds. However, I've never seen anyone do it. The third circle is the Circle of Manifestation. This is the level of spirit needed affect things in the physical world. The threshold is about hundred times greater than the Circle of Perception. My enhanced abilities, Saint Georges speed, and your lightning control are all examples of getting your fighting spirit to spike past the Circle of Manifestation. It is impossible to achieve without having your body and spirit perfectly in sync, allowing you to surpass your body's natural limits."

Nemo listened as she explained the circles drawn in the dirt for the fourth time.

"Ok, I understood that the second time you explained it, but what about the three lines going through each circle?"

"Those are the three categories, natural, physical, and ethereal. Every person on this earth has spirit type that falls into one of these three categories. Your ability to manipulate lighting, if that actually is your ability, would fall into the natural category. The abilities of Saint Georges and myself would fall into the physical category. Ethereal abilities are harder to classify. I don't know many people that fall into that category, but they usually involve the manipulation of someone else's spirit against their will. It's kind of hard to explain if you haven't seen it, but once you see it you'll know what I'm talking about. Also it's important to realize, each of these categories overlap some. Natural and physical have the largest overlapping region showing how natural abilities can manifest themselves in physical ways and visa versa. Natural and ethereal have the second largest overlapping region. Nature inherently has some connection beyond this physical world. Therefore, ethereal abilities can also manifest themselves in natural ways. The smallest overlap is between the physical and ethereal categories. Nature serves as the bridge between the physical and the ethereal, but these categories are inherently separate from each other."

Nemo was finally starting to understand the diagram. He thought about what kind of abilities a person who fell in the ethereal category could have, but he had a hard time imagining anything. The one thing he did get from Neith's explanation was understanding how big of a jump in power was required to make to manifest his spirit to direct lightning. He needed to amplify his fighting spirit a hundred-fold to do what he did on that rooftop. Part of him still didn't believe it was possible, but the reoccurring visions of the men he killed were a steady reminder that this wasn't some fantasy he imagined.

"Neith how was I able to surpass the Circle of Manifestation before, and how come I can't do it now?"

"That's exactly what I've been wondering myself. I wanted to explain the Three Tiers of the Soul diagram to you so you would know just how big of an achievement it is to manifest your fighting spirit. I can only guess that the stress of the situation pushed you passed you limits before you were ready. Nemo, you have a natural talent. Otherwise your spirit wouldn't have responded the way it did when you were in danger. But your manifested spirit is still immature, which can be dangerous for you and anyone around you. Truth be told I've known about this for a while. I never told you, but your eyes glow blue when you meditate."

Nemo's mouth dropped open. "How come you never told me? How long has this been happening?"

"I never told you because you didn't need to know. What would you have done had I told you? Is there something you think you missed out on because you didn't know?"

"Well no, not exactly but—"

"I didn't think so. Your eyes glowing while you meditated meant you were somewhere between the upper levels of the Circle of Influence and the lower level of the Circle of Manifestation. I wanted to see if you would bring your fighting spirit out further without knowing. Looks like you did in a way neither of us could have predicted. So, the bad news is you seem to only know how to bring out you fighting spirit unconsciously. While impressive, it's also useless if you ever want to control your fighting spirit and be able to use it effectively. The good news is we know that you can manifest it, and we know exactly how you manifest it, through electricity. This should make it a lot easier to channel your spirit while meditating."

Nemo stared at Neith as she sat down in front of him and crossed her legs. "The even worse news for you, is that we're going to do nothing but meditate here until you're able to manifest your fighting spirit again."

"You mean I have to sit here until the end of practice meditating! And when I come back tomorrow I'll have to sit here and meditate again until I'm able to channel electricity?" Nemo whined

Neith simply smiled her sweet, yet sadistic way. It was a smile Nemo knew too well, and it always meant something bad for him.

"No, no, you misunderstand. You should call your parents before we begin. Tell them you won't be home tonight because you will sit here and meditate, without food or water, for as long as it takes for you to manifest your fighting spirit. Whether it takes three minutes or three days is up to you."

Nemo took a second to process what he heard. There was no way he could sit there for hours and still be expected to concentrate. He also knew any amount of protesting would do him no good. When Neith had that look on her face there was no changing her mind. There was only one option, sit down and get started.

The first uneventful minute passed by, then the first hour, followed by the next hour. Before he knew it, the moon was high and the sky was bright with stars. His claymore sat flat in his lap while his hands rested against the blade. He could hear crickets chirping around him, hidden by the darkness of the night and the long blades of grass that brushed against his legs. Neith's silhouette slowly appeared in his vision. The darkness of the night surrounded her like a thick fog. Even though he knew she was sitting right in front of him, her outline faded in and out of his sight.

"If you have time to worry about bugs, then you're not fully concentrating on synching your spirit and body." Neith said, sensing he was distracted. "Discard all of your senses and focus only on your spirit, you should be able to sense exactly where every cricket is once your body are spirit are truly in sync."

Another hour passed. Nemo could feel the air scrape against his tongue with every dry breathe. His stomach growled continuously to remind him that he hadn't eaten. The only thing keeping him going was the fact that Neith was sitting there with him. If she could sit there unbothered, then he could as well. Wisps of red energy strafed off of her body. Nemo could tell that she was channeling her fighting spirit, letting the energy of her spirit surround her body and engulf her. Then it occurred to him, how was he able to see it now? Before the color of her spirit never appeared anywhere outside of her eyes. Now it flowed around every part of her body.

Another hour passed by, or was it two? Nemo had completely lost track of time. It could have been mere minutes for all he knew. His legs ached from sitting in the same position for so long. Neith still seemed to be content sitting across from him. She hadn't moved or spoken for the past hour. He could clearly see her spiritual energy surrounding her, blazing bright like a hot flame. Her aura had been growing steadily around her since he first noticed it. Now, he could hardly see anything else with her energy radiating so strongly. That was until he noticed that there was nothing else around to see. No moon, no stars, no dirt, no grass, just an empty void of darkness around him. Before he started to panic, Nemo remembered that he closed his eyes after the first hour of sitting so he could concentrate. Whatever he was seeing was not by the sight of his eyes. Understanding dawned on him, he was using his own spirit to see hers.

"Finally!" Neith said. "I've been throwing off as much of my spirit energy as I could, trying to get you to sense me. Now stay focused and tell me what you see now."

Neith repressed all of her fighting spirit, extinguishing the blazing flame around her. Nemo's world went completely dark. Slowly, light started to appear around him. He could sense them all, everything from the crickets in the grass to the people in the Citadel. He could even discern the difference between those that were sleeping and those that were awake by the amount of energy they gave off. It was like all his senses had been combined into one total sense.

Neith wasted no time. "Now that you understand spiritual perception, sync your body and mind together to draw out as much of your spirit as you can and show me a spark form your sword."

Nemo focused his mind on creating a spark, one single spark was all he needed.

The sun was just beginning to rise. Nemo had been concentrating on drawing out his fighting spirit all night. Sweat soaked through his shirt from the effort. He had been sitting so long that his arms and legs were numb. His growling stomach was nothing more than a whimper, but that didn't mean he was any less hungry.

"Concentrate only on channeling your spirit through your sword" Neith said.

"What does she think I've been doing all this time" Nemo mumbled.

No matter how hard he concentrated, he wasn't any closer to producing static cling, let alone a spark. Nothing was working, and his patience for sitting in the same spot was long gone. Frustration quickly changed to anger. He was angry that he was hungry, angry that he had been sitting there so long, angry that he couldn't protect Jen. That last thought surprised him. Before he knew it, his mind had placed him back on that rooftop. He could see the bald man pressing a gun against his forehead. Jen pushed against his back as he stood in front of her. He could hear the words from his mouth telling her to run on the count of three. He tried to take his words back but couldn't. What happened next he had seen every time he closed his eyes the last three days. Jen's body lay on the ground. He could see the men surrounding him, pointing their guns in his direction. Emotion flooded his subconscious. He didn't want to kill, but he didn't want to die. But he didn't want to kill either. Finally, his urge to live won over and everything else fell away. He channeled all of his strength and rage into his sword, his one object of protection. He knew exactly what he was doing this time. He was defending his will to live.

Nemo's eyes popped open to see Neith standing directly above him. In his lap, his sword was cackling with electricity. Neith pulled her phone from her pocket and looked at the time.

"Fourteen hours. Not too bad, I thought we'd be out here for at least a whole day. I'll have to start expecting more from you Nemo."

Nemo exhaled to control his fluctuating spirit. After fourteen hours, he felt one step closer to the strength he needed. The kind of strength that would have saved Jen.

CHAPTER 23

Dig, dig, dig, that's all Megas' aide would let him do since he came back. It was his punishment for disobeying orders. Leo used his powers of clairvoyance to direct the crew where to dig next. The last thing they needed was the cave collapsing on top of them because someone decided to dig under the wrong rock. Each day, more of Jean-Vis' people showed up meaning they needed more room. They also brought equipment with them, some very large equipment. For the past few days they had been assembling it together in secret, as if he didn't already know what they were hiding. Leo watched as people walked in the tunnels behind him. More new faces he hadn't seen before. He couldn't imagine how Jean-Vis managed to sneak so many people down there without anyone noticing. He had never seen this many people at once before in his life. The space they were digging wouldn't be enough.

Three nights ago when he returned from his mission, Megas' aide was furious. He went on and on about defying orders and how insubordination wouldn't be tolerated. He nearly wanted to kill him for letting Megas' name slip out. If Megas hadn't made him do it, Leo was sure Megas' aide would have refused to reattach his fingers that were cut off that night, just to punish him. Mad Cutter was also furious, but not about Leo ignoring orders. Once he found out the woman from the bank was same woman Leo fought on the rooftop, he warned Leo to stay away from his prey. Calling it a warning was putting it nicely.

His exact words were, "If ye lay one grabby bloody finger on my girl before me get to her, I'll slit your eye balls and rub salt in them while your sleeping. I still be nursing me wounds after she nearly bet me to death. So if anyone is going to kill her, it's going to be yours truly."

The only person who wasn't angry with him surprisingly was Megas. In fact, Megas looked happy that Leo was able to enjoy himself. Megas was the only one that seemed to understand him. He didn't care what Megas' aide or Mad Cutter thought, everything he did that night had been worth it. The image of girl right before she died, was burned into his memory. Thanks to him, any memory of her would be while she still beautiful. Dying was easy, living was hard. Beautiful things need not suffer through living in this ugly world. As for his fight with the Shadow on the rooftop, that was just about having some fun. If there was anything he hated, it was being bored.

A smile briefly crossed Leo's face as he lingered in his thoughts. It disappeared just as quickly when his thoughts returned to all of the dirt that needed moving in front of him. He hated being bored, which is why his current punishment was absolute torture.

"Is the plan still on schedule?" Megas asked his aide as he walked through the new tunnels.

Leo could hear their conversation but, didn't bother to listen. He couldn't care less about their discussion. The only thing he wanted was to be relieved of dig duty.

"We've had to accelerate our efforts somewhat, but everything is still on schedule" replied the aide. "Everything should be ready to execute the plan soon."

"Good, I want to hit them before they see it coming." said Megas.

His aide pounded his fist against his heart and bowed his head, "Trust and believe it will be done".

Megas rounded the corner and walked into a large recently excavated room. Detailed carvings of animals and people in battle covered the stoned walls. Whatever civilization that originally built these tunnels was long dead. But instead of letting their legacy be reclaimed by the earth and forgotten, Megas was restoring it and giving it a new purpose. Jean-Vis stood off to the side with two women in thin lace garments fanning air around him as he shouted orders at workers in his native language. Megas could tell by the worker's reactions that he was shouting more threats than instructions. Once Jean-Vis saw Megas coming, he shooed his entourage of women away.

"You seem to be making yourself very comfortable down here." Megas said as he watched the women scurry away. "I hope that means you have what I requested?"

Jean-Vis pointed to collection of crates stacked behind him. "Take a look for yourself. It took me quite some time and maneuvering to get these supplies here. I needed to move a lot of things in very small quantities across the border to get it through undetected."

Megas scrutinized the cargo. It looked like it would suffice for what he had planned. Everything was falling into place. It was almost too easy, and that made him nervous.

Megas was inherently skeptical of things that looked good to be true.

"And you're sure this can do what you promised?" asked Megas

"Of course!" Jean-Vis said with a smile, "I wouldn't be a man of my word if it didn't."

"I'd worry less about your word, and more about your life if this doesn't work as promised." replied Megas

Jean-Vis' smile dropped from his face. He continued speaking, hoping Megas wouldn't notice.

"While we were working to get this in the country, I brought something else along. Think of it as a bonus, just for you."

Jean-Vis pulled a large sheet away to show what was hidden underneath. "Like I said, we had to move a lot of small pieces. If you break something down enough, no one knows what it is."

For the first time in ages, Megas smiled. "Yes, this will do nicely."

CHAPTER 24

Nemo waited patiently for Neith to exit from her meeting. Ever since all the masters returned, Neith and the others had been having daily meetings right before he showed up for practice. All the new disciples seemed to practice around the same time, starting just before the meeting ended every day. However, for some reason they never practiced together. Everyone else seemed to be stuck in their own little world, training by themselves until their master emerged from the meeting. Nemo thought about asking the other disciples to spar with him on several occasions, but everyone always looked so focused and busy. He was too shy to just walk up and interrupt them. But today was the day. Today he would ask for all of them to train together.

"It makes sense for all of us to train together." he thought. "Our masters work together, so we should work together too."

Nemo looked around at the other disciples, trying to gauge how he was going to go about asking the other disciples. He decided he would ask Tommy first, he seemed the most approachable.

Nemo calmly walked over to Tommy. He was stabbing the air and dodging imaginary strikes form his shadow as he trained in a corner by himself.

"Hey Tommy...hey, how about we spar together today?" Nemo asked.

Silence was the only response from Tommy. His back stayed facing Nemo as he continued stabbing and dodging at his shadow.

"Maybe he didn't hear me." Nemo said to himself. He shouted even louder this time to make sure Tommy could hear him.

"Hey Tommy! You want to spar together?"

Silence again. Tommy remained focused on what he was doing. Nemo knew Tommy was mute, but now he was wondering if he was deaf as well. He didn't bother to find out. Nemo slowly backed away and walked over towards Tai and Xui.

Tai and Xui were busy training together like they always did. Both of them moved in unison, as if they were performing a dance that only they knew. Nemo stood to the side, watching for a few minutes before speaking.

"Hey Xui, hey Tai, mind if I join in and spar with you two?"

Both of them looked at each other before muttering a few sentences to each other in Qxi-Chong, the language of their homeland. Each foreign statement ended with one of them turning to look at Nemo before continuing the conversation. Finally, Tai stepped towards Nemo.

"No thank you. My sister and I enjoy training by ourselves. Besides, we wouldn't want to you to slow us down."

"I think I'd be able to keep up just fine–" before he could finish Tai and Xui had already walked away and resumed their dance together.

Nemo didn't know what to say. His plan was quickly collapsing, but there was still hope. If could convince just one of the other disciples, he knew he could get the others to join him. There was only one problem, the only person left to ask was CJ.

Nemo walked down to the end of the hall where CJ was training by himself. In his right hand was the rapier he always carried with him. It's dull shine and worn, scratched up guard showed his dedication to constantly practicing. Behind his back, his left hand held a fistful of pennies. As Nemo approached him, CJ threw all the pennies from his left hand into the air and began stabbing each one. Only two hit the ground before his sword reached them.

"Looks like you missed two" said Nemo.

CJ slowly turned his head towards Nemo. "I don't remember asking you to count for me."

"Sorry, I didn't mean it to sound like an insult. I was just impressed that's all. You must have thrown like twenty pennies in the air at once. I didn't think you would get as many as you did." Nemo responded.

"Whatever" CJ said before turning back around.

Nemo stepped closer and grabbed CJ by the shoulder. "Hey, how about you and me train together today. I bet we can both learn something new from each other."

CJ brushed Nemo's hand off of his shoulder. With a flick of his wrist, CJ rested his sword across his back and flicked the tip of his blade with his left hand. He stepped closer until he was directly in Nemo's face.

"Nobody wants to train with you, weakling."

"Huh?" Nemo said instinctively, hoping he'd misheard what CJ said.

"You heard me. Nobody wants to train with you. It would be a waste of time." CJ reiterated.

Nemo wrapped his hand around the hilt of his sword, pulling it part way out of the scabbard on his back.

"Well why don't you try me and see. I think I might surprise you."

CJ took one step closer and whispered in Nemo's ear.

"I heard you tried to save some girl and ended up letting her die right in front of you. Is that the kind of strength you have? The kind that fails when people are counting on you?"

Emotion surged through Nemo. In an instance, his sword was free. "Take that back!"

A slick smirk appeared on the corner of CJ's mouth. "Looks like the rumors are true. Like I said, it would be a waste of time, weakling."

Nemo swung his claymore without thinking. He could visualize it travelling in smooth arc, making a smooth unbroken path across CJ's chest. CJ moved his rapier directly in the path of Nemo sword, stopping it right at the apex of his swing. It was so fast, Nemo barely saw him move.

"You should quit now. You can't keep up with me, so don't start something you can't finish."

Nemo could feel his fighting spirit deep inside him, waiting to be unleashed. The air around him became charged, and he could feel his hair standing on end.

"We'll see about that…"

Just before Nemo could release his fighting spirit, Neith came out of nowhere and grabbed his arm. Her other arm wrapped around his neck and pulled him back away from CJ. Saint Georges came from the opposite direction and held

CJ's wrist, stopping him before he could move his rapier any closer to Nemo.

"This isn't the way Shadows solve their problems. Unsanctioned fighting in the Citadel is strictly forbidden." Neith shouted at both of them.

She made sure her stares lingered longer on Nemo, so he knew how disappointed she was with his actions.

Saint Georges stared down at CJ. "I know you weren't planning on raising your sword at a comrade in anger. You know full well the punishment for violating the rules"

Nemo saw a glint a fear appear in CJ's eyes as he looked up at Saint Georges. It disappeared just as quickly.

"Calm down you two. Looks like they were just having a friendly squabble." Absolon said has he walked down the hall towards Neith and Saint Georges. "Boys will be boys you know."

Hao wasn't far behind him. "Actually, I think it would be a good for our disciples to test their skills against each other. There are things you can't teach in practice, but can only learn in real combat."

"We should set up tournament for our disciples then." said Absolon. "That way my Tommy could teach all of your disciples a thing or two."

Absolon looked around with a big grin on his face. The other masters were not amused.

"I'm not so sure that's a good idea" Neith said.

"Is that any way to show faith in your disciple?" replied Hao "Unless you think he's going lose, that is."

Neith rolled her eyes. She still held Nemo by his arm, but her grip around his neck had loosened. "Psst, he's my disciple. Of course, Nemo will win. I honestly wanted to save your disciples the embarrassment, but since you insist…"

"Wait…what, a tournament…umm…" Nemo interjected

"Great, then it's settled. I'll make the arrangements." Hao said before taking a few slow strides towards Absolon and Saint Georges.

The three of them whispered to each other before nodding in unison. Hao lifted his head with a smile stretching clear across his face.

"Since you're so confident in your disciple, you would wouldn't mind making a side bet on their tournament."

"What kind of side bet?" Neith asked

"Well I..." Hao looked around at all the disciples listening intently. "I prefer not to say in front of the young ones. You disciples run along now and get back to training. We'll come get you when we're done discussing the logistics of this tournament."

Nemo waited down the hall and around the corner for Neith. He waited for about ten minutes before he heard Neith storming down the hallway towards him. She was clearly not happy.

"I need you to win this tournament. Something very, very important depends on it." Neith said relaxing the scowl on her face.

"What happened?" Nemo asked

Neith put her finger to her lips, looking for the proper words to explain. "Well we placed a little wager on the outcome of the tournament. I said that if you win, I'd make them all my servants for a week. You can never have enough servants."

Nemo shook his head. That sounded just like the kind of bet Neith would make.

"So, what happens if I lose?"

That was the question Neith expected but didn't want to answer.

"Well those bumbling fools huddled together and asked what I was willing to do if you lost. I said 'Anything because it doesn't matter. My disciple is going to win.' I also added that I hoped they like their manservant outfits with tight spandex shorts. In hindsight, 'anything' might have been a poor choice of words and adding the spandex shorts part in didn't make it any better."

Nemo waited to hear what important thing the other masters wanted from Neith. "So…what did they ask for?"

Neith dropped her head and mumbled, "I have to… around…"

"What was that? You didn't say what I thought I heard, did you?" Nemo asked

Neith repeated herself louder this time, "I have to run laps around the Citadel naked, as many laps as they choose. Knowing those perverts, I'll be out there running all day. This is why it is of the upmost importance that you win this tournament! It is imperative, no paramount, that you…"

Neith looked at Nemo to see his face had turned completely red. She doubted that he heard anything she said after the word 'naked'.

Without warning, the hardest slap he ever felt landed across Nemo's face. The red in his face from blushing paled in comparison to the large red hand mark that now stretched from the side of his temple to the tip of his nose. He could still hear the sound of the slap echoing down the halls, or maybe that was just his ears ringing. Regardless, he was surprised that he was somehow still standing on his feet. Neith simply looked at him, as if nothing happened.

"Pay attention, you master's dignity and honor are on the line here! If that isn't reason enough to win then I'll also reward you with something when you win the disciple tournament. Don't bother asking what it is because I don't know yet, but I can promise you it will be something you want. Now meet me at the pit this time tomorrow. You know, the place where we held the first stage of the Trials. That's where we'll start the tournament."

Nemo didn't bother to mention that he couldn't hear anything because his ears were still ringing. Still, he was able to piece together the important parts of what Neith said. It felt like years since he'd been down to the pit, the place where his journey into Fratello della Spada started. So much had happened in the past couple months. He remembered how much more talented and prepared everyone seemed back then. Was it even possible for him to close that kind of gap between them in only a couple of months? He felt ready, but that didn't mean he was ready. But unlike the other disciples, he definitely had something to prove, especially to CJ. After what he just said, Nemo was itching to pick a fight with him. That alone was enough of a reason to win the tournament.

Nemo glanced up at Neith. She must have still thought he was listening because she was still talking. His face began to blush again as he thought to himself, "maybe losing wouldn't be so bad".

CHAPTER 25

The pit looked just like he remembered it, although it wasn't as scary without the threat of imminent death looming over his head. Word had spread through the Citadel about the disciple tournament and many of the other masters were gathering around the top of the pit to watch the action unfold. Nemo walked around the upper level with Neith as they headed to the bottom entrance of the pit. He recognized a few faces he'd seen before, roaming through the Citadel halls. Percival, Lancelot, and Tristan waved at him from the other side. He could faintly hear them wishing him good luck. The only person missing from their crew was Arthur. Nemo assumed he must have be off handling other, more important matters.

Food and drinks were being served all around, and distractions tempted him in every direction. The smells of freshly baked cakes and roasted meats teased his taste buds. This tournament was nothing more than a big party for the spectators.

"Focus" Nemo told himself.

He didn't have time to be concerned with people in the crowd and how much fun they were having. Every ounce of mental capacity he could use needed to be focused on his upcoming fight.

"So this is your disciple I've heard so much about." said a voice from the crowd in front of them.

Nemo looked up to see an unfamiliar face. Everyone around seem to be speaking in hushed tones in his direction, but no one else approached him. Neith pushed Nemo to the side before wrapping her arms around the stranger and embracing him.

"Champ! How have you been? I haven't seen you since the funeral."

Champ, surprised by the warm welcome, simply smiled as he wrapped his arms around her waist. "I've been good. I was taking care of some business in the northern region while everything was going on. Thought it best to not be around when there's trouble and I'm not the one causing it. I just got back yesterday, and everyone was talking about this disciple tournament. So, I figured I come see what all the buzz was about."

"Well it's good to see you!" Neith said, patting him on the back so he could let her go. "It was starting to get boring around here without you keeping everyone on their toes."

Champ leaned in to whisper to Neith, "I overheard Hao and Absolon talking about some bet you guys have. They seem to be pretty confident you're going to lose."

Neith cast a glance to the side, waving her hand as if she had forgotten about the wager. "We made a small bet about whose disciple would win. Of course, I picked my own disciple to win it all."

Champ looked over at Nemo and tried to gauge his strength. Nemo simply looked back with an empty stare.

"Well he doesn't look like much, but if he's survived this long under you I'm sure he's pretty strong. I look forward to seeing what he can do in tournament. Good luck, and I'll see you later."

"Bye Champ!" Neith said as they parted ways.

"Who was that?" Nemo asked.

He watched as people actively moved out Champ's way as he walked through the crowd. All eyes were glued on him until he finally disappeared in the larger crowd.

"Just an old acquaintance" Neith responded "C'mon we better get to the bottom level so we can get this show started."

When they arrived at the bottom of the pit, Nemo was surprised to see Rufus, the moderator from the Trials, arguing with master Hao. He hadn't expected to see Rufus here. A quick flashback of his time during the Trials ran through his mind.

"Focus" Nemo told himself again. "A lot has changed since then. This time things will be different." Rufus saw him and Neith come around the corner and broke his conversation with Hao to speak.

"Ah young disciple Nemo, how are you? I'm glad to see you still alive and in good health."

"Alive? Nemo felt all over his body as if Rufus words had a deeper meaning. "Why wouldn't I be alive? Is there something I should know about? There better not be any tricks like last time! I've had my fill of candles that explode and mess with your mind and…"

Neith grabbed the back of Nemo's shirt and pulled him behind her. It was her way of telling him to calm down. Hao grabbed Rufus' arm to direct his attention back to their conversation.

"I don't see why I have to choose, it's not fair to them."

"Master Hao, the numbers only allow for four participants. With you being the only master with two disciples I'm afraid we can only allow one to compete."

Neith stepped up to Hao to join the conversation. "I overheard what you two were talking about and I have to say, I think Rufus is right on this one. Even if they were to both compete it would only result in an earlier round in which both your disciples would fight each other. Whichever the case, the outcome remains the same. Only one of your disciples can fight in the tournament."

Hao's face dropped. His head hung down as he tried to think of another alternative. By the time he raised his head again, Neith could tell that he finally accepted the Rufus' point.

"They're going to be so disappointed when I tell them that they can't—"

"Let them both fight." Nemo shouted from behind Neith.

Both Neith and Rufus turned to address Nemo, but it was Neith who spoke first.

"We just explained why they both can't fight in the tournament. The numbers don't work to support a five person bracket."

"No, I mean let them both fight me. I'll take them both on at the same time."

Everyone's mouth dropped open. Even Nemo was unsure of what he heard himself say.

"I won't allow it." Hao responded. "Two verses one wouldn't be a fair fight, and I don't need Neith coming up with excuses to back out of our bet when her disciple loses."

"I don't plan on losing." Nemo said without an ounce of sarcasm in his voice. "Tai and Xiu both train together under the same master, let them fight together too. That way there won't be any excuses from master Hao when both of his disciples lose."

If Nemo's inner fire was lit before, it was blazing now. He was tired of being put down and underestimated. His words clearly struck a nerve. If Neith wasn't standing in his way, Hao might have struck him down right then and there for his arrogance. Meanwhile, Neith was stuck between being proud of her disciple, and being worried that he set himself up for much more than he could handle. She leaned over and whispered in Nemo's ear.

"Are sure this is what you want to do? You have a good chance of beating them one on one, but both of them... together? Are you sure, you're sure?"

Nemo simply nodded his head. His eyes had the look of complete confidence in them.

"Ok, then. Rufus set it up. Nemo will fight both of Hao's disciples at the same time." said Neith.

Hao looked around in disbelief before looking back at Nemo. "Well you got your wish. I'm sure you'll regret it later."

He walked off before Nemo could respond. Nemo didn't have anything left to say anyway. His mind was purely focused on the task in front of him. He was ready to take whatever was thrown at him and give it back tenfold.

"Let's do this." Nemo said as he took two steps towards the entrance of the pit, only to be stopped before he could enter. Rufus stretched his arm in front of Nemo to block his path.

"Wait just a second young disciple. I never said you were going first. Up first is CJ and Tommy. You should head back to the top level to watch their fight, then yours will be next."

Nemo struggled to maintain his composure as he and Neith ran back up the stairs to the top level. He had been ready to fight that very second. All the emotion and intensity he built up focusing on the upcoming fight was ready to burst out. But now, he needed to hold it all in until it was his turn to fight. It felt like trying to chain a wild animal. Every nerve and fiber in his body was ready to break loose and rampage through whoever was in his way. Neith put a hand on his shoulder to try and calm him, it helped a little. Nemo told himself to focus a third time. He wanted to pay close attention to this fight. He would need every advantage he could get to beat CJ. Seeing what Tommy was capable of would be helpful too if he ended up having to fight him instead.

They could hear Rufus announce the start of the tournament and the first fight just as they reached the top level. By the time they reached the edge of the railing where they could see, the match had already started. CJ immediately put Tommy on the defensive with a flurry of attacks. He clearly had an advantage in speed over Tommy, and Tommy wasn't moving slow by any means. Nemo figured it was safe to assume that CJ was the fastest of all the new disciples. Tommy's other disadvantage was his weapon. He was using a gladius, a type of roman short sword. That gave CJ a sizable advantage in striking distance. Strange symbols were carved down the center of Tommy's gladius. Nemo couldn't make out what they were, or figure out what purpose they served. However, by the looks of the fight, whatever they were for wasn't helping.

Tommy continued to be pushed back by CJ's unrelenting attacks. He was quickly approaching the wall behind him. If he ran out of room to retreat, the fight would be over. There was no way he'd be able to keep up with the speed of CJ's attacks to block them all. Tommy kept retreating until his back was about two feet away from the pit wall. Nemo could see it all unfold as if it were happening in slow motion. CJ unleashed a combination of thrusts and faints until he found an opening. The blade of CJ's rapier quickly advanced towards the center of Tommy's chest. Nemo hoped that CJ would stop short and let Rufus call the fight. It was clear he had won, he didn't need to follow through with his attack. Right before his sword connected with Tommy's chest, Tommy bent over backwards and pushed his head and sword arm though the middle of his legs. CJ's rapier was now aimed at nothing but air. He quickly shifted his momentum to move backwards right before Tommy's gladius could slash open his leg.

"So that was his game. He's a contortionist." Neith said as she cracked a slight grin.

"A contortion-what?" asked Nemo

"A contortionist. A person who is extremely flexible and able to bend their body into unnatural positions. He planned to get CJ close enough where he could surprise him with an unexpected attack to his legs, hindering his main advantage, his speed. Unfortunately, CJ was able to react in time. Now his element of surprise is gone. Although since he's a disciple of Absolon, he probably has a few more tricks up his sleeve."

Nemo just watched in awe, it was something he would have never expected if he was fighting against Tommy. It made him realize even more how much he didn't know about the other disciples.

After Tommy's surprise attack missed, he flipped the rest of his body over and kicked himself forward off the wall. He rushed toward CJ with a solid thrust, hoping to catch him before he had time to recover his composure. Despite Tommy's best efforts his attack simply couldn't keep up with the quick precision of CJ's movements. No matter how Tommy attacked or which direction he came from, CJ was able to dodge or parry while making it look effortless. Soon CJ stopped parrying all together and simply dodged each attack. Nemo could tell CJ had become confident in his ability over Tommy's and was just showing off now, typical of CJ. Tommy on the other hand didn't look amused. Even though he couldn't speak, his face showed everything he would have said. Nemo could see Tommy had something to prove as well.

With his next motion, Tommy's arm became like a whip. He started to strike from increasingly odd angles, dislocating his joints at will to attack unusual spots.

"That's the Serpents Fang technique" Neith said to Nemo. "Through joint dislocation and body manipulation, it allows the user to target areas that usually aren't guarded like the top of the head and the back of the shoulders."

Nemo nodded his head at Neith's explanation, keeping his eyes on the match in front of him. Tommy's wild attacks had forced CJ to start parrying again. A minor victory for Tommy, but it still didn't change the fact that CJ looked like he had everything completely under control. With each passing second Tommy looked increasingly frustrated by his inability to hit CJ. It started to hit home for Nemo that at any time CJ decided, the match would be over.

"Don't count him out yet." Neith said, as if she read Nemo's mind. "No matter how grim the outcome looks, it only takes once decisive blow to turn the tables. CJ may be a little too confident, he can still lose."

Tommy seemed to be trying everything he could. Kicks, throws, thrusts, and slashes. CJ effortlessly maneuvered through them all, letting Tommy waste his strength hitting nothing but air. Finally, Tommy backed away and stopped attacking. His expression said he was tired of playing CJ's game, and it was time to make CJ play his. Tommy retreated to the center of the pit and crouched into a weird position.

Nemo couldn't help but ask, "Neith what's that stance he's doing now? It doesn't resemble any fighting style I've seen before."

Neith leaned over the rail to get a better look. Her eyes got big when she recognized Tommy's pose.

"Oh! This is about to get interesting. Nemo pay attention, you may just get your first look at an ethereal ability."

The tip of Tommy's sword started to glow a greenish hue. The engravings down the center of the blade one by one started to glow with that same green color. If the building had been on fire, Nemo wouldn't have noticed. All his attention was on what Tommy was about to do next.

In an instance, it was over. If Nemo hadn't been so focused on the match he would have sworn he blinked. CJ seemed to disappear and reappear with his rapier at Tommy's neck. The greenish glow that formed around Tommy's sword slowly dissipated as Tommy dropped to his knees to surrender.

"Or not... I guess you won't be seeing whatever Tommy's ethereal fighting spirit ability is today." Neith said as she backed away from the top level railing. "Kind of an anticlimactic ending, CJ was holding back the whole time. As soon as Tommy was about to do something unpredictable, CJ moved as fast as he could to end the bout."

Nemo was trembling on the inside. "That's how fast he can really move? I couldn't...I couldn't even see it. How am I supposed to beat someone like that?" was all he could think about.

"Neith, are you sure CJ wasn't using a fighting spirit ability like Saint Georges?" Nemo asked

Neith barely even considered the idea before dismissing it. "No, Saint Georges is much faster. I could see CJ move the whole time, and I didn't feel any spike in his spirit. Not to mention the whole 'no glowing eyes' thing. Nope, I'm afraid that was just raw natural human ability."

The thought of what just happened continued to sink deeper in Nemo's mind.

"That was just his normal speed. What kind of frightening speed would he have if he used his fighting spirit?"

"I wouldn't worry about him being much faster than that though." Neith continued, interrupting Nemo's thoughts. "Most people don't learn to use their fighting spirit effectively until they're well above master level. You're what we call a 'special case' Nemo. By how long it was taking for Tommy to draw out his spiritual energy, I'd say he's just started learning to use it. Most likely whatever technique he was about to use only takes a fraction of the amount of energy it would normally take to pass the Circle of Manifestation. I doubt any of the other disciples can use any fighting spirit abilities at all."

Rufus ran out to the center of the pit to officially end the match. "And the winner of the first round is disciple CJ Bregdon! Why don't we cheer for him and his opponent, the silent warrior Tommy Faulk, for their fantastic display of ability."

Applause erupted from the crowd as every person watching clapped for the performance of the two disciples. Even Neith clapped a couple times to show her enthusiasm.

"Up next we have a special two on one match as the twin disciples of master Hao, Tai and Xui Liu, take on the disciple of master Neith, Nemo Lake! It's sure to be an interesting match and you don't want to miss it!"

Neith patted Nemo on the back signaling that it was time for them to head back down to the pit's lower level.

"You asked for this fight, so I expect nothing less than win. Don't let me down…or you'll regret it." Neith said to Nemo through gritted teeth.

If there was one thing Neith knew how to do it was strike fear into his heart. CJ's speed was nothing compared to his new thoughts of what Neith might do to him if he lost this next match.

CHAPTER 26

Nemo stepped out to the center of the pit. Tai and Xiu were already there waiting for him. The crowd was alive with excitement from the last fight. Now a two on one match captured their interest even further. Nemo lifted his sword slightly from the scabbard on his back. He wanted to be sure he could draw it as quickly as possible when the fight started. As he reached the center, Rufus started to announce the rules as he did before each match. As far as Nemo was concerned, the rules fell on deaf ears. No one appeared to be listening, they were all focused on the three disciples standing dead center in the pit preparing to face off.

Tai was the first to speak.

"I have to thank you for requesting to let me and my sister fight together. I promise we'll make your loss quick and try to spare you any embarrassment."

His twin sister Xiu nodded her head in agreement.

Nemo didn't hear a thing they said. The beast inside him, that he'd somehow managed to keep restrained until now, was finally free.

"I'm only going to warn you once. You better come at me with everything you've got, or else you're going to lose. I won't spare any embarrassment for either one of you." Nemo said as his gaze shifted between the two twins.

Xiu took a small step backward. Tai managed to stand his ground but was clearly shaken by what he heard. Nemo's powerful statement had made them unsure of themselves. They couldn't tell if he was bluffing, or if he was actually serious. They had expected an easy opponent, and an easy win. However, that is not what stood before them, staring them down with eyes filled with rage.

After a few seconds Tai said something to Xiu in Qxi-Chong. They looked Nemo up and down before regaining their composure. Nemo didn't know what they said but he could tell from their body language that they had settled on the fact that he was bluffing. That was fine by him, he tried to warn them.

"Nemo! Nemo!" Neith shouted from the entrance of the pit.

Nemo turned around to see Neith waving her hand for him to come to her. He quickly walked over to see what was wrong.

"I forgot to tell you one important thing. Don't use your fighting spirit at all in this match."

"WHAT!" Nemo shouted "But that's the main part of my strategy, how am I supposed to win without using my strongest ability?"

Neith, in her typical nonchalant manner, completely disregarded what Nemo had to say. "I'm sure you'll figure something out, but you don't want to show your trump card in your first match. If you want to have any chance at beating CJ you're going to need to save it for the finals."

"Might as well ask me to tie my arms behind my back while you're at it." Nemo mumbled

"I heard that." said Neith "Just remember you're the one that asked for this two on one fight. I still expect a win no matter the circumstances."

Nemo turned to walk back out into the pit, his mind still blown from Neith's instructions. Tai and Xiu must have sensed the change in his mood. Their exchanges in Qxi-Chong were mixed with snickering and sharp glances in his direction. Tai spoke in English when he returned to the center of the pit.

"We have decided to take back what we said earlier. It will not be quick. Your loss will be slow and painful, and everyone here will see you beg for mercy before it's over."

"Whatever you say, let's get started."

Nemo was still trying to figure what to do without being able to use his fighting spirit. It was just like Neith to somehow make things harder than they needed to be. However, she did have a point. He still had to win no matter what. His resolve to do just that still had not changed.

Rufus noticed the tense atmosphere between the three disciples as he stood in their midst.

"I think this might be a fine time to remind everyone these are exhibition fights and I reserve the right to step in at any moment I see fit. I'm sure both of your masters have taught you how to beat your opponent without killing them. I would like those teachings to be in the forefront of your mind. We're all alive now and I would like it to stay that way."

Rufus looked at Tai, Xui, and Nemo one by one to make sure they understood. Even though their heads nodded the expression on their faces still said they were out for blood.

He would need to have a talk with their masters about pushing their petty disputes onto their disciples when this was over.

"Now without further ado, let the fight begin!" Rufus shouted

Nemo immediately drew his sword and retreated to give himself some room. Tai and Xiu both spun dao swords to their hands out of nowhere. Nemo couldn't imagine where they had been hiding those swords this whole time. Immediately they split up and rushed toward him from opposite directions. They were slower than he expected. If he had faced either of them alone it would be pretty evenly matched. Against both of them however, the smallest mistake could be his downfall. He needed to be extremely cautious.

Xiu attacked high, aiming for his neck, while Tai went low aiming for his legs. Their timing was near perfect. Nemo knew he wouldn't have time to parry both attacks. Blocking one would just be giving an open target to the other. The only thing he could think of doing, was the exact opposite of cautious. In fact, if he missed it would probably mean the end of the fight for him. He was out of options, and out of time to think of anything else.

"Here goes everything" Nemo whispered to himself.

At just the right time, Nemo thrust his claymore towards the floor and pinned Tai's sword between the tip of his blade and the ground. The sudden force brought Tai to the ground still holding his sword. At the same time, Nemo jumped and kicked both of his legs into Xiu's stomach. His swords wide blade helped him keep his balance he laid out flat in the air. He could see Xiu's blade narrowly miss him, passing right above his face. Behind it he could see Xui's eyes bulge out in pain. In the next second Nemo fell to the ground, coming down elbow first on top of Tai as Xiu fell backward from his kick.

The crowd went wild! People on the top level jumped up shouting and clapping. Nemo was pretty surprised himself that it actually worked. Unfortunately, he didn't have time to pat himself on the back. He rolled off Tai and stood back up with his sword in a fighting stance. Tai and Xiu were still recovering on the ground, but aside from their pride, didn't look to be too injured.

Nemo didn't bother waiting for them to get back up before attacking again. He went directly at Tai, ready to deliver a decisive blow and turn this two on one match back into a one on one. Out of his peripheral he saw a several flashes of steel. Nemo dashed sideways, narrowly avoiding being cut. Xiu was on her feet and had come to her brother's aide. Had he been any slower, he might have lost an ear and maybe a few fingers too. What Xiu lacked physically, she more than made up for with her swordsmanship. It was like looking through a kaleidoscope. The reflections off her blade cast light in different directions, making it hard to judge exactly where it was at any instance. While he was distracted by Xiu, Nemo hadn't noticed Tai move. By the time he recognized that Tai wasn't on the ground anymore, it was too late.

Nemo turned around just in time to block Tai's sword coming towards him, but not enough to stop a punch from landing solid in his gut. Nemo was barely able to keep himself from heaving. He could taste vomit in his mouth as he bent over from the wind being knocked clean out of him.

"That was for that lucky kick you landed on my sister, this next one is for me." Tai said as his knee struck against the side of Nemo's face.

A collective gasp came from the crowd as Nemo rolled across the ground from the impact. Only Nemo knew that he purposefully rolled with the impact, so it didn't hurt as bad as it looked. If there was anything being constantly beat up by Neith had taught him, it was how to take a punch. In no time Nemo was back on his feet. Tai and Xiu were coming towards him together. Their blades seem to weave in and out of each other's space, leaving little room for anything else to pass between them. Nemo had no fancy plans for their attack this time.

Once they were on him he tried to block as many strikes as he could, but it was a losing battle. His claymore's wide blade made it easier to defend his skinny body, but against these two it was like sticking a knife in a blender. He could feel himself being cut little by little. While he was able to protect his vital organs, he just wasn't fast enough to keep up with both of them. Who was he kidding, he wasn't fast enough to keep up with the blade work of one of them. The thought of Tommy's fight flashed through his mind. If he knew he wasn't fast enough, then he shouldn't be trying to keep up with them. Why was he trying to beat them at their own game? He needed to make them fight his fight, not the other way around.

First, he needed to break them apart. They were trying to push him back towards the wall. If he ended up trapped between them and the wall there would be no escape. Nemo didn't know if his next action came out of desperation, or the simple pure madness of watching Neith for so long. All he knew was that losing wasn't an option. Nemo turned around and ran towards the wall. Tai and Xiu's swords were able to savor samples of his flesh from his wide open back. He didn't have to be facing them to imagine the look in their eyes. The look of bloodlust that said a taste wouldn't be enough, they lusted for more.

With his adrenaline going those shallow cuts in his back didn't slow Nemo down at all. In two steps he ran up the wall, and with his third kicked off the wall to launch himself over Tai and Xiu. It was anything but graceful. Nemo rolled across the ground, struggling to recover from his daring leap after making it over the duo. Even though he escaped having his back against the wall, it didn't buy him much time. In an instance Tai and Xiu were back on him.

The fight had only started a few minutes ago, but Nemo was tired already. Defending against both Xiu and Tai's attacks really took a lot out of him. He could feel the cuts on his back and arms sting as sweat dripped into the open wounds. There was no way he could keep up this pace. He needed to think of something to even the odds.

This time when they came at him, Nemo concentrated exclusively on Xiu. He brought his sword up to block her attack, but as soon as their blades met, he his let go and rushed in to grab both of her arms. Once he had them, Nemo squeezed her wrists with all his might until she was forced to drop her sword as well. Tai immediately came with a strike intended to free his sister, but he stopped midway when Nemo moved Xiu between them. That's what Nemo had been counting on. Now he had a human shield. She was light and thin and didn't take much muscle from Nemo to move around. However, that didn't make her any easier to keep a hold of. Everything in her fought against him to free herself from his grip. He couldn't hold her for long. Luckily, he didn't plan too.

Nemo turned her around so they were face to face, and started running towards Tai. Tai froze for a moment, unsure of how to attack without hurting his sister. Nemo ran at full speed holding Xiu in from of him. Her feet dragged through the dirt as she tried to stop herself from being carried by Nemo, but nothing she tried could stop their momentum. Tai moved out of the way right before the three of them collided. If he expected Nemo to stop, he was mistaken. Nemo kept running until he slammed Xiu's back against the curved brick wall of the pit, making sure to dip down and shove his shoulder into Xiu right at the point of impact. She screamed in pain as she crashed into the wall. Nemo didn't really know how hard he hit her until he realized the popping sounds he heard were Xui's ribs cracking as he pressed into her. Doubts about what he was doing, nor thoughts of mercy, registered in his consciousness. It's was either him or them, and he was going to do everything to make sure it wasn't them that lost today.

With everything he had left, Nemo brought the back of his head up directly under her chin. Xiu's teeth made a horrible clacking sound as they smashed together. The back of her head jerked back into the wall with enough force to knock her out.

Righteous rage consumed Tai at the sight of his sister slumped over against the pit wall. He ran towards Nemo with his sword aimed directly at the center of his back. Nemo saw him coming, but stayed where he was with his back turned. He needed to wait for him to get closer. Time seemed to slow down. Nemo could hear each step Tai took as he approached. Right before Tai reached him, Nemo turned around and threw Xiu's unconscious body at her brother. He was forcing Tai to choose. Either drop his guard and catch his sister, or let her flailing body fall to the ground. Tai wasted no time choosing the former. Before he could lay down her limp body, Nemo was on him. His sword still lay on the ground where he first grabbed Xiu, but at this point he didn't need it. Even without his sword, Tai wouldn't be able to fight on par with him while protecting his sister. Nemo knew exactly how hard it was to fight while protecting someone. It was an idea he had hoped he wouldn't have to use, but he had already made up his mind he would win this fight no matter what. Xiu swung wide hoping to hit Nemo, it was a desperate attempt. Nemo ducked, rolled, and came up directly behind him. One well-placed punch to the side of the head was all it took to drop him to the floor. Tai's body slumped to the ground with his sister still in his arms.

The sounds of shouting and cheering filled the pit again. Nemo walked over to grab his sword as Rufus ran out to call the fight. Out the corner of his eye, Nemo could see Neith smiling at him. He could see her mouth the words, "One fight down, one more to go."

CHAPTER 27

Everyone gathered in as close as they could to the upper railing. Any hint of open space was quickly snatched up by the first spectator that spotted it. Word had spread throughout the Citadel about Nemo's surprising win against Hao's disciples. That, combined with the tales of CJ's first fight, and everyone from visiting masters to Citadel staff all rushed to the pit to see the final fight. Nemo rested in one of the nearby rooms in the catacombs while Neith bandaged his wounds. Even down there he could hear the crowd chanting CJ's name. To his surprise, he could hear his name being chanted too. Although it was a much fainter sound. Still, people were chanting his name. That was something he never expected to hear in his life.

Neith finished wrapping the last bandage, checking to make sure they were good and tight. The last thing she wanted was for Nemo's wounds to open back up during the final fight. Unlike CJ, Nemo's win was hard fought. He had taken a minor beating and needed to recover as much strength as he could to try and close the already large gap in skill between them. CJ was the clear favorite to win this, but Nemo had his share of people cheering for him too. Regardless of what happened next, it was going to be one of best fights between disciples anyone had seen in a while.

"It's almost time Nemo, make sure you leave everything you got out there."

Nemo simply nodded his head in agreement. He didn't need to be told to leave everything out in that dirt pit, that was his plan from the beginning. Nemo stood up and started to walk back towards the pit. His legs felt heavy, and that short rest didn't revive him as much as he hoped. Still, Nemo walked on to face his greatest rival.

CJ stood out in the middle of the pit waiting for him. Most people would be basking in the limelight and enjoying the praises of the crowd, but not CJ. Nemo already knew that he wasn't one to lose focus of his goal, that's one of the things that made him so dangerous. CJ watched Nemo as he approached, taking note of the slow pace of his walk. When he reached the center of the pit, CJ extended his arm out for a handshake.

"I gotta say, I'm surprised you made it this far. After I heard you were fighting both of Hao's disciples at once I was sure I'd be facing them in the final match. It took some balls to challenge both of them, but you won…barely. I wonder if you even have anything left to fight me."

"How about when our fight starts I let you make the first move, then we'll see what I have left." said Nemo.

He would have added a sarcastic laugh for effect, but his ribs already hurt just trying to breathe. The truth was that he hoped CJ would make the first move. The less he needed to move the better.

To the crowd their handshake must have looked awkward. Neither would let the other's hand go, as if the fight would be decided by the first person to show any sign of weakness. Only the other masters watching knew the feeling of gauging your opponent's strength through the simplest of actions. Finally when Rufus started to speak, announcing the same rules they had heard many times before, they broke off their handshake and moved away to opposite sides.

Nemo pulled his sword from its scabbard and knelt down. The cheers and boos of crowd, the echo of Rufus' voice as he shouted out the rules, even the pain of his injuries, were all tuned out as Nemo focused on his sword. Just as he had done many times with Neith when they would practice meditating, he gathered his fighting spirit and held it behind the door in his mind so it could be released as soon as he needed it. He could see CJ take his 'en guard' stance, as he did before each fight. CJ's rapier settled in his hand like a tailored glove. The tip of his blade was locked in, pointing in Nemo's direction. As Nemo returned to his feet, he let all the noise of his surroundings back in just in time to hear Rufus start the match.

"Fighters ready! Begin!" announced Rufus

Fast was an understatement. It was one thing to see him from above at the top of the pit, but he didn't truly understand what Tommy felt until he was in the same position. It was as if CJ disappeared completely. Nemo's eyes darted left, right, up, down, and up again but he couldn't find him at all. Not until CJ was right in front of him. There was no way to dodge, and even less time to raise his sword to block it. CJ was preparing to end the fight immediately, leaving no opportunity for Nemo to devise a plan of attack. Even though he didn't see CJ's lips move, he could hear his voice as he saw the tip of his rapier approaching him.

"So much for giving me the first attack. I'm embarrassed that I thought you might actually be a threat. It seems you weren't even owed that much respect. I can't believe a weakling like you could even think to consider me your rival."

That was the mental trigger Nemo needed. He threw open door in his mind holding his fighting spirit at bay, letting it explode out like bursting dam. The concussive sound of thunder roared through the arena. Those watching from the top railing could feel the rumble in their stomachs from the release of Nemo's power. CJ was thrown back halfway across the pit from being so close to Nemo as he unleashed the depths of his fighting spirit. He was quickly back on his feet, but what he saw as he got back up froze him in place. Nemo's eyes glowed a deep blue color. Sparks of electricity cackled around him mirroring the storm CJ saw in his eyes. It looked as if Nemo was ready to bring destruction to anything in his path, and it was exactly what CJ had been waiting for.

CJ smiled as he took his en guard stance again. "Now this is more like it! Now I can show off a little."

Nemo watched CJ rush towards him, even faster than before. This time he was ready. Energy surged through every fiber of his body. The feeling of it was magnificent. Aside from the additional mental strain of keeping everything in sync while he moved, it was just like the feeling when he meditated only much stronger. He could even feel the reverb from sword, as he let his fighting spirit flow through it and surge back into his body. He could also follow CJ's movements now, even though he wasn't moving any slower. Something about being able to sense CJ's spirit made it easier for Nemo's eyes to follow him, and it also made it easier to see his attacks coming.

Nemo blocked CJ's straight thrust with ease. Anyone watching the fight would have a difficult time telling which disciple was more surprised that it happened. In that small pause, both boys looked in each other in the eyes while their swords were locked together in a stalemate. Quiet settled throughout the crowd as both combatants stood still, and then fury erupted. A wild exchange of blows followed from both CJ and Nemo, neither was able to land a solid hit on the other. Nemo was finding it easier to keep up with CJ as the fight went on. CJ was dodging less, and keeping his high speed movements to a minimum. For once Nemo saw a familiar look on the face that stared at him, CJ was becoming tired.

"What's the matter? Do a little too much running around?" Nemo quipped

Nemo had expected CJ to respond by viciously attacking him, instead CJ retreated backward. He dropped the point of his sword to the ground and leaned over, putting a hand on his knee. CJ let out small laugh through his heavy gasps for air.

"I think so. Never imagined I'd tire out before you would. Although I'm sure that glowing in your eyes has something to do with it. Guess you're full of surprises, but I still have some surprises of my own. If you don't mind, I think I'll try something different now."

That wasn't the reaction Nemo expected, but he didn't have to wait long to see what kind of surprise CJ was referring to.

"Shiva, shiva, shiva..." CJ chanted as he brought the blade of his rapier up to face. It almost looked like he was saluting Nemo for a good fight, except Nemo knew the fight was just getting started. As CJ brought his rapier back down from the salute, several after images of his arm holding his rapier started to appear as he moved. Foggy copies of CJ's weapon continued appear and disappear as waved his arms around, varying until Nemo could no longer tell which one was real.

"This can't be good" said Nemo.

He looked back at Neith standing at the entrance of the pit, hoping that she would shout something helpful. Her stone cold expression offered him no help. Either she didn't know what he should do, or she was going to make him figure it out on his own. Neither option made Nemo worry any less. Just like when he was fighting Xiu, Nemo found himself entranced by CJ's swordsmanship. Although this type of movement was completely different, unlike Xiu's kaleidoscope effect, he could clearly see each and every sword CJ seemed to be holding. He just couldn't tell which one was the real thing.

"Pretty cool right?" said CJ. "This is Saint Georges' technique that he personally developed, it's called Multipoint. It involves high speed movement to...well no point in telling you. I'll let experience it firsthand."

CJ took a slow step toward Nemo, at least it appeared slow. Somehow in that one step, he covered over half the distance between them. It was as if the ground had contracted under his feet. Nemo had no idea what was going on. He saw CJ take two more slow steps as he tried to back away, and suddenly CJ was right in front of him again. All the after-images coalesced into three distinct swords that came at him. Nemo didn't have time to think, he instinctively tried to block the one he thought was closest to him. Instead of feeling the solid connection of metal on metal, his claymore traveled through the sword like it was a puff of smoke.

A sharp pain on the side of his ribs arrested his attention from what he had just seen. Nemo looked down to see how bad it was. By the way it felt, he expected to see a clean hole straight through his body, but he was lucky. It was a shallow cut that felt a lot worse than it was. That was about the only bright side to the situation he was in.

"Looks like you guessed wrong. If I were you I'd be careful, all that hard swinging at the air can tire a person out." said CJ.

The irony of his humor was not lost on Nemo. Lines of blood ran across his bandages. All that moving around had reopened some of his wounds from the last fight. Adding fresh injuries to his body didn't help either.

While Nemo was distracted by his injuries, CJ set up for another attack. Again, Nemo found himself staring at three swords coming at him, and he still couldn't tell the real one. He swung for the one in the middle this time, hoping to connect against something. It was the same as last time. Nemo's sword simply passed through the image, leaving him with an empty feeling that was quickly replaced by the pain of being stabbed again. He could taste blood coming up into the back of his mouth. While his fighting spirit might have numbed his reaction to pain, it did nothing for the nausea he felt from tasting his own blood.

"Figured it out yet?" CJ asked while he looked at Nemo grab the top of his shoulder and fall to his knees in pain. "I'll give you a hint, they're all real."

Nemo looked up in surprise. "You can stop it with the mind games, that doesn't make any sense. If they were real then I would have been able to block at least one of them."

"Well it does if you think about it. Multipoint at its essence is just high speed coordinated movement, so at some point in time my sword is in all of those positions. As soon as I see you go for one, I can just move to another. This is the technique that made Saint Georges known as the Hero of Tralone. No one could stand against him while he was using this."

Nemo had seen and heard enough about Saint Georges' technique for one day. It was about time he used some tricks of his own. He remembered Neith describing how he called down lightning on the rooftop. Since he knew how to control his fighting spirit now, he should be able to do it again. Confidently, Nemo stood up and thrust his sword high into the air, channeling his fighting spirit through it.

"Time to end this." he shouted.

Any second now he expected a flash of lightning to illuminate the area followed by a deafening crack of thunder, but nothing came.

Before he had time to wonder where his lightning was, CJ smashed the bell guard of his sword into the side of Nemo's face. Nemo's legs buckled as he came crashing to the ground from the impact. His sword fell down in front of him as the blue storm in his eyes dissipated to their normal calm white color.

"C'mon, this can't be all you can do with your fighting spirit. You know I can see it glowing in your eyes. It's pretty hard for me to believe someone like you is able to use a skill it takes years to learn, and decades to master. That's if you actually can use it and this isn't just some trick. So far I haven't seen you do anything." said CJ

Nemo's head felt like it had been split open. He tried to fight through his blurred foggy vision and the pain throbbing in his head to regain the balance needed to draw out his fighting spirit again, but he couldn't maintain his focus. Not with his ears still ringing, and the struggle to keep from vomiting every time his tongue tasted the blood in his mouth. Everything had felt right. Granted he didn't know how he did it before, but he thought it felt right. Why lightning didn't come when he needed it was a mystery to him. While he lay there in the dirt, Nemo realized his only option was to return to the basics. Without his fighting spirit augmenting his abilities, he was no match for CJ. So he needed to draw it back out.

"The first step is Perception." Nemo told himself as he closed his eyes and focused his spirit. It came to him as naturally as breathing. Almost instantly he could tell where CJ was without having to look at him. Nemo skipped past Influence and jumped straight to Manifestation. He focused the majority of his spirit into the gap between his fingers until he could feel electricity arcing between them.

"Good, well at least that's still working." Nemo thought.

Now he needed to take same concept of making a spark and expand it down the length of his sword. Nemo reached his hand out to grab his claymore, taking great care to move as little as possible and concentrate only on refining the connection with his fighting spirit. Everything up to now he had practiced before, but this was uncharted territory. If he was going to beat CJ he needed to make this work.

He poured double the amount of spirit he used to make the spark between his fingers into his sword, nothing happened. Triple the amount, still no charge, no flow of electricity showed. Nemo took all his reserves of energy, everything that had kept him going through this fight and let it flow through his sword until finally he could feel a small current flowing through his blade. Even though he was still on the ground and could feel all of the fatigue from every single one of his injuries, he still couldn't help but smile at his success. After a few seconds he was able to build up a sizable charge in his sword, although it was much harder than he expected to keep the flow of electricity going through it. He wouldn't be able to keep his spirit manifested like this for long. It took every ounce of fighting spirit he could draw out just to keep it going. Any less wouldn't be enough. He had no idea how he was able to summon lightning previously on the rooftop if this was all he was able to achieve now.

Meanwhile CJ had been waiting for Nemo to get up. Saint Georges would have admonished him for not ending the fight immediately, but he seldom got to have this much fun testing his abilities. It would be a shame to end it so soon, but his patience was reaching its limits. It looked as if Nemo was barely conscious. Before he fell to the ground, his eyes had faded from their intense blue color to a dull white. Now they were closed. CJ couldn't tell if he was really unconscious or if he was up to something. Sections of the crowd yelled for CJ to end it already, and asking Rufus to call the match. Aside from a few twitches of his fingers, everything indicated that Nemo wouldn't be getting up anytime soon. CJ looked around at the crowd again before deciding to grant their wish.

"Well I guess in the end I expected too much. I thought you'd be able to hold on a few minutes longer, but I'm not one to pass up any opportunity to win." said CJ as he walked towards Nemo's body, still laying on the ground.

Rufus would probably call the match if Nemo didn't move before CJ made it over to him. He wouldn't let someone who couldn't defend themselves be attacked. Nemo had one shot to surprise CJ while he still thought Nemo was too injured to move, and he had to do it before CJ came too close.

As soon and CJ stepped in striking distance, Nemo hopped up and swung wildly. The arc made by the tip of his blade would have cut a man clean in half. It went from the bottom CJ's ankle to the top of his neck, and would have done some serious damage if CJ hadn't stepped back just in time to avoid it. CJ chuckled as he looked at Nemo blade swing past him.

"Did you think this blatantly telegraphed attack was going to hit—"

Before he could finish his statement, a white hot bolt of electricity discharged off Nemo's sword striking CJ directly in his chest and throwing him backwards.

Nemo dropped his sword in the dirt and fell to his knees. His body felt like it was going to completely shut down. He hadn't anticipated what it would feel like after using his fighting spirit to push his body past its normal limits. Everything hurt. Every single nerve in his body felt like it was being stabbed with needles. All his concentration immediately went to keeping himself conscious. Even if he was on his knees, as long as CJ didn't get up the match was his. That was all that mattered.

"Looks like I got you this time" Nemo said in CJ's direction, not expecting a reply.

"I guess you did. Got me pretty good too." CJ muttered in between fits of coughing, as he rolled over and pushed himself up onto his feet.

For the first time in the entire tournament, fear crept into Nemo's mind. He could hardly believe his eyes as CJ got up with a large burn mark streaking in multiple directions across his skin. Most of the material from his shirt was burned away, leaving only a few strands of fabric still connected and keeping it from falling off his back. In the center of where the bolt hit him, fresh blood oozed through the cracks in his burnt skin. It was a blow that would have kept most people of the ground for good. Nemo was starting to realize just how far CJ was from most people. While it was clear that he was seriously hurt, he could tell CJ had no intentions of giving up.

"I think I got enough in me for one more, which looks like one more than you have left in you." CJ said as he pointed his rapier in Nemo's direction.

"I'll let you make the first move, then you can come over here and see what I've got left" replied Nemo.

He didn't want CJ to know how right he was. Nemo had nothing left. He could barely move, let alone fight. Still, he didn't come this far to give up either. Nemo went to the depths of his soul and summoned whatever was left, scraping the bottom of his already depleted fighting spirit. His eyes threatened to close on him, sucking him into the void of unconscious. But he fought it to stay awake. Between each blink, he could see CJ approaching. The crowd was silent, every person waited in anticipation of their final encounter. There was one distinct voice shouting in the crowd that sounded familiar, but Nemo couldn't make out what it was saying. Suddenly all sound stopped, and Nemo was engulfed by darkness.

CHAPTER 28

Nemo opened his eyes to see bright stars surrounded by the darkness of the night sky.

"Strange" he thought.

He didn't remember being outside, but the brilliance of the stars distracted him from whatever questions rolled through his mind. Slowly, the voices behind the questions grew louder and louder, until it all came rushing back to him. Nemo lifted his head from the ground to look at his surroundings. He realized he wasn't outside, but still in the pit. A large hole was now present where the seamless stone dome, capping the top of the pit, once stood. It was then that Nemo noticed all the rubble scattered around him. A mixture of dust and smoke floated through the air obscuring his vision. The only person he could see was CJ, lying on the ground motionless. A group of large broken bricks from the ceiling covered his legs up to his waist. Each one was as big as his head. Nemo looked above CJ. More large bricks above him were starting to crumble away in pieces. It was only a matter of time before another one fell down on CJ. No sooner than that thought crossed his mind, one of the bricks from the ceiling gave way. Nemo could still barely move himself, there was no way he could move CJ out of the way in time. Another person was about to die right in front of him, and he was powerless to stop it.

Suddenly, Neith came running through the clouds of dust toward CJ. She slid through the dirt to make it to him in time, and with a strong kick straight up in the air, shattered the falling brick into harmless pieces. Nemo was ecstatic to see Neith, but his emotions were tempered by the alarm her face showed. She quickly scooped up CJ's limp body and ran over to Nemo.

"Nemo can you walk?"

"I think so, give me a second. Is CJ ok?"

Neith put two fingers against CJ's neck to check for a pulse.

"He's alive, but we need to get him some help. That burn you put on his chest needs to be treated and the rocks that fell on him look to have broken a few bones. He may be bleeding internally so we don't have much time."

Nemo tried to wrap his head around everything as he got up from the ground.

"Neith what happened? The last thing I remember is CJ getting up and coming at me."

"Right as you two were going in for your final attacks, Arthur came in screaming for everyone to get out as quick as they could."

A moment of clarity came to Nemo's mind. "Yes, I remember hearing a voice right before I blacked out. Why did he want everyone to evacuate?"

Neith looked around, hesitant to continue the conversation where they were. "I don't know. Before I could get over to him to find out why, this big explosion happened and collapsed part of the roof. I came rushing down here to you when I saw CJ lying under a pile of—"

Another deafening explosion ripped through the side of the wall, sending bits of stone hurling through the air like sharp bullets. This time when the dust cleared Nemo could see the arms and legs of people buried under the debris from the blast. He could only hope that most of them were able to escape in time. A deep mechanical rumble shook the ground. Nemo could feel the sound vibrating in his stomach. Through the hole in the wall, he caught glimpse of something outside. It looked like a large truck, but it was still too far away to tell. He had never heard that kind of sound come from a truck before. The longer he focused on it, the more he felt like he knew what it was. Realization washed over him like a cold shower. Nemo finally saw what was causing the explosions.

"Neith, there's a tank outside!" he shouted as loud as he could.

"Take CJ and run" she said to Nemo

"But what are you—"

"I said run! Get out of the building and as far away from here as you can!"

Nemo knew by her tone just how serious she was. There would be no arguing with her. He lifted CJ onto his back and took off.

Neith said a silent prayer for her disciple to make it out safely. Once he was out of her sight she rushed outside through the opening in the wall. She didn't know why this new threat was here, where it came from, or where the other masters were for that matter. Hopefully, there would be time for questions later, now was the time for action.

Outside soldiers in camouflage fatigues ran around the grounds shooting at anyone trying to escape. Neith drew her scimitar and began tearing through their ranks. There were hundreds of soldiers spread out across the area. It would take hours to try and stop them all. She could sense Saint Georges and Arthur nearby.

"Hopefully they'll know what's going on." she thought.

Neith fought her way across the front lawn of the Citadel to where she sensed Arthur. Each person that challenged her was cut down. She didn't bother to kill them, as long as they were no longer in her way so she could keep moving forward was all that mattered. Near the large double doors that served as the main entrance, she finally spotted Saint Georges and Arthur protecting people as they escaped. Just the two of them were carving a path through the enemy with their blades. Immediately she ran towards them to help.

"What the hell is going on?" she shouted as she approached Saint Georges

"Arthur discovered what Guiding Light's objective is, tell her Arthur." said Saint Georges

"They're building a bomb!" Arthur shouted towards Neith as he crushed a man's arm with the weight of his zweihänder. He swung it around in a large circle trying to clear a path. Neith moved over towards him and started cutting through the ones Arthur missed.

"How do you know?" Neith asked

"I noticed they were importing and lot of random items from a small country called Maiteir. They took special care to skirt main customs locations in favor of more remote ones with less scrutiny. Many of the goods listed aren't even exports that country produces, but the one thing that country does have a lot of is weapons. I was able to deduce that they've been smuggling in the materials to build it. Instead of taking us out one by one, they're going to try to kill us all at once."

Neith listened intently, waiting to hear the part of the plan where they stopped Guiding Light from detonating a bomb. Arthur remained quiet.

"And… so what are we going to do to stop it." Neith asked

"Nothing" replied Arthur as he looked down at the ground. "We have to get everyone to safety first. I won't take the chance of us trying to stop the bomb and allowing everyone to die if we fail."

"So were just going to let them destroy our home. No way, there has to be something we can do. "said Neith

"We won't have time. Look around you, there's hundreds of soldiers trying to get into the Citadel. How would we even find which one has the bomb? The safety of our people has to take priority." Arthur shouted back while kicking another man in front of him.

Neith looked around her. Soldiers were rushing into the Citadel through any opening they could find. The large hole made by the tank provided a convenient entrance for most of them. The others smashed through windows and broke down doors to get in. Watching them openly defile the place with such blatant disregard made her blood boil.

"No, there's no way I'm letting them get away with this. You and Saint Georges can handle getting people to safety, I'm going back in."

"Neith! No, you can't—" Arthur screamed. Just as Neith was turning away to run back into the Citadel, someone grabbed her shoulder stopping her. At the same time, she heard a voice behind her say,

"I like the sound of your plan, but there's one problem".

Neith turned around to see Champ staring her in the face. As usual she seemed to be the only one happy to see him.

"Champ…what are you doing here?" said Arthur.

"I'm here to help. I thought you'd be willing to put our petty differences aside given the situation." replied Champ.

Arthur's grip tightened around the hilt of his sword "Petty differences! Is that what you call—"

Champ didn't bother to let him finish.

"That tank is causing more havoc than all of these soldiers combined. If we can take that out we'll have an easier time holding them off, and I think I know just the woman for the job."

Champ made sure to take a long look at Neith so she knew he was talking about her.

"I'll go back inside and warn the other masters. We'll find the bomb and disarm it. You take out that tank so we don't have to worry about the whole building collapsing on our heads."

Saint Georges ran two soldiers through with his rapier as they charged towards the group. The dense forest surrounding the Citadel made it hard for anyone to get a clean shot from far away. If anyone wanted to kill them they would have to get up close. Most of them were finding out just how fatal of a mistake that was.

"How'd they get a tank up here without anyway noticing anyway?" Saint Georges asked the group.

"I don't know" Champ responded "but I'll make sure I leave a few of them alive so we can ask."

"Alive, ha. I didn't know you were capable of such restraint." said Arthur.

Neith jumped in before their war of words turned into something else. "Arthur, we could use the help."

Arthur exchanged a long look with Champ, searching for any other plan that didn't include him. Nothing came to mind.

"Very well then" said Arthur, turning the address everyone else. "Neith you take out that tank, Champ you find the other masters and have everyone start searching for the bomb. It will most likely be near some essential structural support in the building. Send all evacuees out of the west entrance so Saint Georges and I can guide them to safety."

Everyone nodded in agreement.

"Now let's show these bastards what it means to pick a fight with the Shadows."

Everyone broke off and headed towards their objective. Neith ran toward the tank. The darkness of the night shrouded her so well that many of the soldiers she cut down didn't even see her coming. She made sure to stay hidden in the trees until she was right next to the tank. There would be nothing she could do if it saw her out in the open field. At least she knew where the tank was headed. The Citadel was surrounded by trees on the front and sides. Towards the back was swampland. It would be difficult for the tank to travel through there without getting stuck in the water. That left one option. The tank would have to come in through the narrow clearing between the trees that served as their front entrance.

Neith made her way to the edge of the clearing. Once she heard the rumble of the tank coming closer she knew she was in the right spot. She patiently waited for the tank to drive by before hopping on the back. As soon as she jumped on, she climbed to the top of the turret and found the entrance hatch. Neith took a moment to focus her fighting spirit. The steel on the tank was thick. She would need to call forth more of her spirit than usual to break through. She would need to get through it quickly too, or else they might find a way to knock her off before she could get in and stop whoever was controlling this monstrous vehicle. Part of her wasn't sure she could do it, but all it took was one look at the smoke billowing from the Citadel to remind her of her rage.

Neith unleashed her fighting spirit, channeling all her emotion into her fists. She drew her arm back as far as it could reach and smashed her fist into the steel hatch with all her amplified strength. It barely made a dent. Neith tried again, reaching her arm back as far as it could go before hitting the same spot with even more force than before. This time the dent was more pronounced. It also had stains of blood from her knuckles. After two punches against the steel they were already rubbed raw and bloody. She knew this would a contest of endurance to see who would break first, her or the steel.

It didn't take long for whoever was inside to realize there was someone trying to get in. After her third punch, a sharp sensation of pain shot through her entire body, almost causing her to fall off. The outside of the tank was being electrified. Each part of body that touched the tank felt like it was being hit with a taser. Despite the pain, she still needed to maintain her focus to keep drawing out her fighting spirit. It was the only thing keeping her from feeling the full effect of the shocks. Every few seconds her muscles would tense up, followed by a few seconds where they would relax again. Neith realized that the electric shock must have to recharge every time it was used. That gave her window of a few seconds to punch at the steel hatch while her muscles weren't tense from the electricity flowing through them.

She kept punching at the hatch, enduring wave after wave of electric shocks. Surprisingly the shocks actually helped numb her hand against the steel. By the sixth wave of shocks, she couldn't even feel her arm anymore. With each strike she rammed her fist into the steel like a hammer, with no regard to how injured her arm might be. She was completely focused on breaking through the tank hatch. She could see the dent get larger and deeper with every punch. The small splashes of blood had started to coalesce into a pool that rested in the deepest parts of the dent she was making. Finally, just as she was beginning to think the steel would outlast her, she heard a loud pop and saw a crack in the steel. A crack was all she needed. Through the thin opening she could see her target beneath her. Neith drew her scimitar from its sheathe, letting the blood from her hand run down the side of her blade. She lifted it to the sky and thrust it down through the crack in the tanks armor, using the blood from her hand to grease its path. Her blade stuck solidly in the top of the tank driver's skull. Neith gave it a slight twist for good measure before pulling it back out and watching the tank roll to a stop.

Even with the driver out of the way, she still needed to get the person controlling the tank's gun. As long as the turret could still shoot, no one in the Citadel was safe. Neith waited atop the tank to see what her next move should be. Unexpectedly, the hatch that she put so much effort into trying to break through, opened. Bursts of machine gun fire rang out in every direction. Neith slid down from the top of the tank and rested behind it, using its own massive size for cover. By the way shots were being fired, everywhere instead of in one general direction, Neith could tell the gunner had no idea where she was. Only the barrel of his weapon peaked out of the top of the tank. He was smart enough not to stick his head out of the hatch and make himself an easy target. Neith crept around the opposite side and when there was a break in the gunfire, she jumped up the side and flipped into the open hatch.

The inside of the tank was barely big enough for her to turn around. Her arms could easily touch both sides of the wall if she stretched. Neith hated fighting in tight spaces. Mostly because she didn't have room to keep the blood of her opponents off her, and walking around covered in blood tended to make people ask questions. Whenever presented with the possibility of fighting in a confined area she would always find a way to lead her opponents to somewhere more open. This time she would have to make an exception. The soldier inside rushed to aim his weapon at Neith, but he was too slow. Before he knew it, Neith's sword had already pierced through his stomach. The confined space made it so her sword hardly had any distance to travel before reaching him. With his last few breaths, the gunner reached for something at his side. Neith only needed to hear the sounded of the pin being pulled to know it was a grenade.

"Shit" was the only word to pass her lips before looking back towards the exit.

A wicked smile of white teeth spread across the gunner's dark face. He clearly had no qualms about dying as long as he took her with him. Neith climbed from the inside of the tank as quickly as she could, and tried to shut the hatch behind her. Before it could close, the grenade went off. Neith felt the force of the explosion lift her into the air and slam her right into a nearby tree. Her entire body went numb on impact.

Neith fell to the ground, letting go of the last remnants of her fighting spirit that had kept her going. The fiery red color in her eyes faded to a pale white, and then to a dark blood red. Without her fighting spirit to block everything out, the stress and injuries she sustained almost overwhelmed her body. The bones in her hand were definitely broken. Her fingers still held a firm grip around the hilt of her sword, but no matter how many times she tried to move them they wouldn't let go.

"I just… I just need to rest… a little, then I'll go help the others." she spoke aloud in mumbled breaths. "Just a little rest…and… I'll… be…" before she could finish, Neith's head fell back against the trunk of the tree.

CHAPTER 29

Champ made his way through the hallways of the Citadel. So far, he hadn't found any of the other masters or their disciples. He could only hope they already escaped, although he wouldn't mind some help. No matter, he always worked better alone. Not everyone approved of his methods, but they were always effective. He needed to find this bomb soon before he became one of the casualties Arthur was worried about. Although he doubted that there would be many people shedding tears for him if he died. This whole situation had put a bad taste in his mouth. Something in him felt dirty, having to sneak around the very halls he normally walked freely in. Only one way to get rid of this feeling, he needed to break something. Someone would have to pay dearly for giving him this feeling of disgust.

Champ checked every large pillar he came across. He didn't see anything that looked like a bomb. Then again, he had no idea what the bomb would look like when he found it. As he rounded another corner he could hear footsteps coming towards him. Three, no four people, approached his position.

"Such a shame" he whispered to himself. "That's three more than I need."

Before the group of four reached the end of the hall, two of them were cut down. Champ's naginata severed through the necks of the first two men before retracting back into Champ's hand. With each kill, he paused to admire the efficiency of his weapon. It was one of the most complex in the Fratello della Spada arsenal. Using a high speed pneumatic actuator, the pole of his naginata was able to expand to its full length and retract back to its hand held size faster than the eye could see. Not only did that make it much easier to conceal, it also made it the perfect weapon for the kind of jobs that needed someone killed with discretion, assassination jobs.

The two men that he cut down had no chance to realize what happened. They were dead before their bodies hit the ground. The two he left alive turned to each other, both waiting for the other to make a move. Quickly, they each came to their own decisions. One dropped his gun and ran in the opposite direction. The other dropped down to a knee and looked through the sights of his rifle. Three shots were fired directly into Champ's chest as he charged towards them. It only slowed the inevitable. Champ made a habit of wearing some of the thickest body armor of all the Shadows. It always came in handy in his line of work. When the element of surprise didn't finish the job, things would quickly turn ugly. He'd been shot so many times that he didn't even bother to dodge anymore. It was that very quirk along with his immense size that earned him his nickname Mietitrice Leviatano, The Leviathan Reaper.

The soldier in front of him didn't even had time to rise to his feet before the pole of Champ's naginata smashed against the side of his head. An audible crack sound echoed throughout the hall as the soldier's body twitched and writhed in pain against the cold stone floors.

"Where's the bomb?" Champ asked in a deep threatening voice. The look on his face said he would only ask once.

"Ngeke ngiwaqambe yini…" were the sounds that came from the man's mouth as he choked on his own blood. A few seconds later he was dead.

"He bit his tongue off and choked on his own blood, what sad way to die." Champ said to himself.

He hadn't meant to kill him so fast. It seemed like his enemies were becoming more fragile lately. Still, the dead man told him more than he thought. He either didn't speak English, or chose not to. That meant they were foreign.

Champ took off down the hallway, chasing down the last man that ran away. The Citadel could be a maze of hallways if you didn't know where you were going. It could be hours before you found your way, especially if you didn't know any of the shortcuts. Champ saw the soldier run past as he came through one of the shortcut passages. It didn't take long to catch him. In two steps, he grabbed the back of the man's neck and threw him up against the wall.

"Where's the bomb?"

"I… I don't know what you're talking about" said the last surviving soldier, struggling to breathe with Champ's hand around his neck.

Champ tightened his grip. His large hand could almost close completely around the man's neck. "At least this one spoke English" he thought. Torture went much quicker when you could communicate properly. And as much as he would like too, he didn't have time to drag this out.

The man slowly gasped for air as Champ's hand constricted his throat. His legs and arms flailed against the rough brick behind him, but nothing would loosen the grip on his throat. Slowly his limbs became weak, then went limp. The world started to close in on him.

"Wait...Wait...I can tell you."

Champ let one finger off the top of his throat. Bruises around his neck had already started to form from the blood vessels ruptured by Champ's tight grip. The rush of air in the man's lungs must have felt like heaven.

"Talk, now!" shouted Champ

The soldier took in another luscious breathe of air before speaking. "They were headed down to the restricted areas, at the base of the building. That's where he instructed us to go."

Champ weighed the man's words carefully. He knew full well the lengths of lies that men would go to in order to save their own skin. The restrictive areas would be the best in the building place to detonate a bomb, but it was also one of the more secure areas. Not even all Fratello della Spada members had access to that area. Only the *Cavaliere Ombras* with at least one star were allowed down there. How these people even knew about it, not to mention planned to get in, was a mystery to him.

"Who instructed you to go there?" Champ asked, making sure to squeeze a little harder for emphasis. He could feel the trembling in the man's throat each time he prepared to speak.

"It was the aide, that what he called himself. Megas' aide. He told us what to do, and where to go. That all I know I swear!"

Champ didn't know who this aide was, but he seemed to be a little too familiar with the layout of the Citadel. He would have to worry about him later, right now he had a bomb to stop. Champ almost forgot about the person in front of him he still had pinned against the wall.

"I did say I would leave some of the enemy alive for Arthur to question." Champ thought as he lowered the man back down to the ground and loosened his grip around his man's neck.

He was ready to let him go, but then that familiar feeling came to him. Something he only felt when he held a man's life in his bare hands. It was exhilarating.

"There will be others I can leave alive to question." Champ said aloud

With one swift movement, he crushed the man's windpipe, watching him collapse to the floor to die a slow suffocating death.

"Assassins don't leave people alive." He whispered to himself, and ran off towards the restricted area.

The door looked like just another stretch of hallway. Unless you already knew it was there, you wouldn't notice it just walking by. Even if you did know it was there, it was still hard to find. Champ held up his ring to the scanner camouflaged as a normal brick. A section of the wall receded inward. Champ had to push it open the rest of the way. The door had a solid stone face, but was backed by an inch of steel. It took a substantial amount of strength to push it open. Another safe guard to keep someone from just stumbling in. Inside, a clean sheet of dust covered the ground directly behind the door. Steps leading into the restricted areas of the Citadel stretched down into darkness. Hardly anyone came down to this area, so the set of footprints Champ saw as entered stuck out like black ink on white paper. Someone had been through that door before him. Dust hadn't settled into the footprints yet, meaning they had been through there recently. There were no tracks leading out either. Whoever came in was still there.

Champ slowly walked down the steps. It didn't help that the looming threat of a bomb detonating before he could reach it was at the forefront of his mind, but he needed time to let his eyes adjust the darkness. Besides, he didn't want to give any hints that he was coming to whoever was down there. The bottom of the steps opened into a wide room, several pillars were spread evenly throughout the area. The pillars made up the foundation of the Citadel that was built directly on top of the catacombs. If someone wanted to destroy the Citadel from the inside, this would be the place to do it. Towards the back of the room, Champ could see someone's shadow stretched across the ground. He carefully moved into a position where he could take them out before they realized he was there.

"You might as well come out into the open. I heard you when you came in." said a voice from the shadows

Champ couldn't believe it. There was no way he could have been heard coming in. If there was one thing Champ was good at besides killing, it was being quiet. Champ stayed hidden, waiting to see what would happen next.

"I can already see you. You're behind the second pillar furthest from the steps." said the same voice from the shadows.

Champ rushed to change his position. The echo in the room made it hard to pin point which direction the voice was coming from. Still, he was able to make out the general area of origin. Whoever he was dealing with was either very skilled, or very lucky to be able to find him first. He would find out very soon which one it was.

"No point in hiding now" Champ said to himself before running out into the open.

What met him wasn't what he expected. In front of him stood a tall, thin framed, teenage boy with a longsword on his back. Behind him, Champ could see the assembled parts of the bomb he was searching for. A small box with a keypad sat in front of a larger box with wires connected at different points.

"I don't know how you were able to locate me kid, but you should have kept your mouth shut. Now that I've found you, whatever chance you had of leaving here alive is gone."

"Well that is a shame, and here I hoped we would have some fun first." said the boy "I didn't even get a chance to introduce myself, my name is Leo."

Champ wasn't the type of person to wait around for introductions. As soon as he saw an opening, he went for it. His fingers were already wrapped around the base of his naginata, all he had to do was extend it and cut down the boy in front of him. Then he could disarm the bomb.

"If I'm lucky, maybe the bomb won't even be armed yet" he thought. "This is turning out to be easier than I expected. Who are these people that thought they had even the smallest chance of destroying Fratello della Spada. Must be another overzealous group of weaklings. Arthur will have to find answers he wants on his own, this kid is going to be cut down right here."

The next thing Champ realized, he was on the ground struggling to breathe. He clutched his hand to his chest, only to pull it away and see it covered in blood.

"What could have possibly happened?" he thought.

Whatever his injury, he could tell it was bad. Each breathe felt like he was scrubbing his lungs against a cheese grater. Next to him, his naginata was on the ground barely a foot away. Still within his reach if he stretched for it. He still had a chance to eliminate this threat. At the very least he'd be taking one more person with him before he left this world. A boot stomped on his chest, causing Champ to violently cough up more blood.

"Ugly...I have no use for ugly things." Leo said as he kneeled down and put the full weight of his body on Champ's chest.

Two realizations came to Champ in that moment, both were equally frightening. The blood he coughed up wasn't coming from his mouth, it was coming from a large gash cut in his throat. He would most likely bleed out before he had a chance to suffocate. The second realization occurred to him as he stared at the boot planted on his chest. It was the wrong size. Whoever left the footprints near the entrance had much larger feet. That meant someone else was down there.

"Well well fella, guess it's true. Ye really are psychic." said Mad Cutter

"Fiiiiiiiiiinally he believes me." said Leo "You put up all that fuss about carrying me down the stairs on your back. I told you it would be worth it."

Mad Cutter looked down and Champ and spat on him. "Part o' me hoped yer were wrong. I was hoping that lass from the bank showed up. I still owe her a beating. This one here was too easy, relied on his size and his gammy instincts. Didn't even sense me strapped to the ceiling he didn't. I could 'av killed him wit me eyes closed."

Leo rolled his eyes. "Right... and I suppose me telling you to hide somewhere high up and drop down when he comes toward me had nothing to do with it. Look at him, the guy's a tank. The only part on him not protected are his neck and his wrists."

"Doesn't matter, I still would 'av taken him out just as fast." replied Mad Cutter

Leo restrained his tongue. He had to listen to Mad Cutter's ramblings all the way here and even now he still wouldn't shut up.

"Whatever, can we finish this job now?"

Champ was struggling to breathe. Even without the boy's boot on him, every breathe felt like it could be his last. His hand over his throat had slowed the bleeding, but it was only a matter of time. All those times he come close to death and this was how it ended. Ironic, he always thought he'd be hunted down by someone from an old job looking for revenge. Never did he think he meet his end in the place he called home. Champ rested his fingers around the base of his naginata. His weapon had never let him down, maybe even now it could still make a difference. While his two undertakers stood over him talking, Champ extended his naginata into the small box on the front of the bomb, destroying the keypad and whatever electronics were connected to it. With that last act, he dropped his naginata to the ground. He only hoped that was enough to stop them.

Leo delivered a swift kick into Champs side. "Look what you let him do Cutter, you distracted me with all your rambling and now he's gone and destroyed the keypad. How are we supposed to activate it now?"

Champ would have smiled if he had the strength. At least his final action was able to save the Citadel. Arthur and the others would bite their tongues knowing that someone like him, a killer for hire, was the one who saved them all.

"Guess we'll just have to set the other two and hope the third one blows up on its own." said Mad Cutter.

Two...there were two more bombs. Champ couldn't believe it. With his last breath, he prayed that everyone made it out safely.

****

Nemo laid CJ down in the grass. He'd been running for a couple miles with CJ on his back. Once he reached the top of a large hill where he could see the Citadel, he decided to stop and rest. Part of him wanted to go back and help Neith and the others, but he couldn't leave CJ alone. Especially with the severity of his wounds. Nemo started to treat them as best as he could. The only first aid training he knew was from school, and that dealt mostly with cuts and burns. At least CJ was still unconscious, that way he didn't have to worry about hurting him while he tried to clean his cuts and splint his broken bones. Nemo remembered what Neith said about CJ possibly having internal bleeding. He would need a doctor soon.

Nemo turned to look back at the Citadel. He could only hope someone would be coming after them sooner than later. Right before his eyes, a ball of light and fire shot up into the sky, followed by a deafening explosion. Nemo was temporarily blinded by the light that blanketed the night sky. When his sight returned, the Citadel was gone.

CHAPTER 30

The sun had just broken over the cusp of the horizon when Nemo stumbled into the temporary camp organized by Arthur and the other Shadows that escaped the Citadel. Hastily set up tents and flattened areas of dirt dotted areas between the trees. Mostly it was people just lying down in whatever spot they claimed. Nemo shouted for someone to come help CJ. He had drifted in and out of consciousness throughout the night. Even when he was conscious, he was barely functioning. Nemo tried not to think about what condition he was in, he just hoped someone was around to help him.

A few people rushed in and grabbed CJ from Nemo's back. Nemo recognized at least one face as a doctor from the Citadel. The others around him also looked like they knew what they were doing. They briefly looked CJ over before carrying him into one of the tents set up in the back. With CJ safely off his back, Nemo collapsed to his knees. It had taken him most of the night to find the camp. Sensing the fighting spirits of the others was becoming an invaluable skill, without it he'd still be wandering around in the dark woods.

Nemo hadn't eaten or slept since before the disciple tournament began. That was almost a full day ago. He was so tired, he barely responded when someone helped him up and told him to go get some sleep. The doctors would find him and let him know CJ's status when he awoke. Nemo shuffled his feet through the dirt, barely able to raise his head from exhaustion. His body wanted nothing more than to stop moving. While he was looking for a soft place to rest, Nemo gazed out at the smoking remains of the Citadel. With everything that had happened, sleep was the furthest thing from his mind. But as soon as he laid down, finally giving his body a chance to rest, he was out.

Four, maybe five hours had passed by the time he woke up. The sun was high in the sky indicating it was almost noon. His body felt like it needed a few more hours of sleep, but the sight of the Citadel in ruins reminded Nemo of all the questions he needed answered before he dared to sleep any longer. Immediately, he got up and started looking around for Neith. She would know everything that happened after he and CJ left the pit.

Nemo started to checked every tent he came across. All of them were being used to treat the injured. He managed to find the tent CJ was in. He was still asleep, but his steady even breathing gave Nemo a firm strand of hope to believe that he would be ok. Saint Georges was there, kneeling by his disciple's side. They had bandaged him up and properly splinted his broken bones. He would have to come back and talk to CJ when he was awake. Right now, he still needed to find out what happened last night.

Nemo continued frantically searching for Neith. Finally, he reached what he thought was the last tent. They weren't organized in any particular way, so he couldn't be sure he hadn't missed any. He would go back and check them all again if he needed to. As he opened the tent flap, it was Arthur's face he noticed first. A few others were around him. He recognized Percival and Tristan. The others he'd seen around the Citadel before but never actually spoken to any of them. Arthur motioned for him to come in the already cramped space as he continued talking.

"Did they find any survivors?" he asked the group of men facing him.

One of the men facing Arthur simply hung his head.

"No, but from our surveys of the area it seems that most people made it out before the explosion. We did find a number of bodies. Some belonged enemy, but most of them sadly were our people. Among them was Lancelot's…"

Nemo could see Percival and Tristan wince as the name of their friend was mentioned. They both looked up to Arthur who seemed to keep his composure while continuing to listen to the scout's report.

"So far we've counted twenty seven dead, all found in the surrounding area. We have no way of knowing if anyone is buried under the rubble, or if there would be anything left of them from the blast. We also gathered whatever supplies were still usable. Only the emergency responders on the list you gave me were allowed to stay. Any others that showed up were directed away as you requested."

"Very well" Arthur responded. "At least we can keep this internal for now. I need three men posted on the north, south and east corners guarding the Citadel grounds. We need to take several—"

"Arthur, where's Neith?" Nemo blurted out.

Normally he would have waited for him to finish, but after being unable to find her in the camp, he was running out of patience.

Instead of answering him, Arthur simply raised his finger, asking Nemo to hold on while he finished his conversation.

When they were done Arthur turned to address Nemo. Before, Nemo could get a word out Arthur rushed over and hugged him.

"I'm glad to see you made it through the night safely. I'd heard you and CJ wandered in here early this morning. How is he doing?'

"Better" Nemo responded. "He's had a rough night, but now he's bandaged up and sleeping about four tents over from here."

They both shared and momentary look of relief before Arthur spoke again.

"I don't know where Neith is. Last I saw her she was going to destroy the enemy's tank that was attacking us. I personally checked the area where she fought. The tank was dented and splattered with blood on the outside, the inside looked even worse. I even found body parts from the soldiers operating it, but there was no sign of Neith around. No one has found her body in the surrounding area. Either she had a good reason for leaving on her own, or most likely she was taken as a hostage. If it turns out to be the latter, we can only hope to find her quickly while she's still alive."

Without wasting a second Nemo turned to exit the tent, but Arthur stepped in front of him.

"Where are you going now?"

"Where do you think? To save Neith." replied Nemo

"Wait, just wait one second. You don't even know what happened, or who took her. You haven't eaten since yesterday. You look like you could barely walk a mile before you collapsed from exhaustion, and to top it all off you want to go after her by yourself. Since Neith isn't here to tell you herself, I'll tell you for her. That's a stupid plan you have."

Nemo just stood there and blinked. He expected Arthur to try and stop him, but he hadn't expected to hear that.

"I'll be fine, I'll rest along the way. We don't have time to wait around. You said it yourself, Neith could be still alive. We just don't know for how long."

Nemo could see Arthur getting ready to meticulously point out all the flaws in his 'plan', but at that exact moment Nemo smelled the most delicious smelling food he ever imagined. His stomach didn't help to hide his distraction when it growled as loud as it could.

Arthur seemed to forget what he was going to say and burst out in laughter.

"Why don't we sit down and have some lunch first. They'll be plenty of time for you to fall on your sword later. I'll explain everything that has happened up until now while we're eating, and then you can tell me what you plan to do about Neith after."

Nemo certainly didn't like the idea of waiting to go after Neith, especially if she was in danger. But his hunger got the best of him and he agreed to sit and have lunch first.

Before he knew it, Arthur had laid out a plate full of food in front of him.

"Where did all of this come from?" Nemo asked.

Arthur pointed to a broken crate in the corner of his tent.

"Our predecessors had the foresight to stash supplies in various areas around the Citadel in case of situations like the one we presently find ourselves in. Food, shelter, medicine, most of the main necessities needed in case of a disaster are readily available to us in limited supply."

Before Arthur had finished answering Nemo's question, he was already stuffing food in his mouth. Nemo hadn't realized just how hungry he was. He was sure the food was pretty ordinary, yet it felt like the best tasting meal he'd ever eaten. Arthur just sat across from him sipping a cup of tea.

Nemo briefly wondered how Arthur had time to grab tea while escaping the Citadel, but he didn't bother to ask. He was more concerned with filling what felt like and endless hole in his stomach. Arthur didn't bother to say a word until he was halfway done with his food. After Nemo slowed down eating, Arthur began.

"I'm sure you've heard some of this from Neith, but allow me to fill in the gaps. It all started with Bulo's death which happened a few days before you were brought in by Neith for questioning. Neith was on a war path, looking for anyone or anything to lead her to Bulo's killer. I don't know what she saw in you, but she was insistent that we question you and show no mercy to find out everything you knew."

Nemo swallowed hard on a bite of food he was chewing. The realization that Neith had nearly ordered him to be tortured at the mere suspicion that he might know something about Bulo's death surprised him. Although given the ways she managed to actually torture him during training, maybe it shouldn't.

"I was against it" Arthur continued. "Knowing the actions I would have to take after questioning you, even if you were found innocent. But she was insistent and agreed to be responsible for any repercussions that ensued. It was right then I decided that she couldn't be a part of the special investigation team. I had already been named to lead a team of my choosing to look into the questionable death of a Fratello della Spada member. I made the decision on my own to not include anyone who was too emotionally attached to the case. In hindsight, perhaps I should have made an exception for Neith."

Nemo could only nod his head and listen. He didn't know what stroke of bad luck put him in the middle of all of this, but it was nice to finally be able to put pieces of events together.

"After Janus was killed, most people fled the Citadel for their own safety. Only Neith and a few others stayed, she was the only master with a new disciple who stayed around. The investigation of the deaths that occurred in the Citadel became top priority. It was then that I started to find out about who was behind all of this, the group whose been calling themselves Guiding Light." Arthur paused to take a sip of his tea. Nemo barely blinked as he waiting to hear the next words out of Arthur's mouth.

"At first it was like smoke. You know how you can smell smoke and know there's a fire around without having to see it? Well I smelled the smoke that something was going on, but I couldn't find where the fire was to put it out before it was too late. They had been gathering intelligence on us for months by involving themselves in certain jobs we performed. I dare to say that they even put out some jobs themselves just to get a chance to observe how we work. One example you might be familiar with is the bank robbery gone awry. What you and Neith thought would be a simple bank robbery job, turned out to be something more complex because of one Guiding Light member being involved."

Nemo remembered the bank robbery all too well. As scared as he was, even then he realized something was weird about the way events unfolded. Another memory, one he would never forget, suddenly shot to the forefront of his mind.

"Do you know if Guiding Light had something to do with the mission Neith took involving a kidnapped girl?"

Arthur took another sip of his tea, "It was the information that Neith brought back from that mission that finally pointed me in the direction of the fire."

Nemo replayed what he remembered from the rooftop in his head. Even though Neith had told him what happened, he still couldn't help the feelings the boiled inside him upon finding out who was responsible for Jen's death. He could already feel his fighting spirit waiting to be unleashed again. It would have to wait for now.

Arthur continued, "From what she found out, I was finally able to put a name to this group and find out their objective. Unfortunately, my worst fears were confirmed, they weren't after any particular person. They wanted everyone and anyone who associated with Fratello della Spada destroyed. By linking together their strings of recent black market purchases with the materials they smuggled in from Matier, I was able to deduce that they planned on accomplishing this goal by detonating a bomb. By the time I figured this out however, their group had already started to attack."

They both sat in silence for the next few minutes. Arthur continued to drink his tea, giving Nemo time to process everything he'd said. Nemo looked to be deep in thought when he abruptly stood up from his chair.

"Thank you for telling me all of this, and for the meal, but it doesn't change my decision. I'm still going after Neith."

Arthur finished the last drops of tea form his cup. Nemo was expecting an argument from him about why he couldn't go after Neith, but what he said caught him off guard."

"Nemo, when was the last time you saw your mother?" With everything that happened, Nemo had completely lost track of time. He hadn't been home since yesterday morning. His parents were probably worried sick by now. Arthur clearly caught the worried expression on Nemo's face.

"Ah, that's what I thought. Why don't you go home and see your parents. This fight isn't a disciple's fight, and more importantly it isn't your fight. You need not worry about Neith. We will save her as soon as we can find her whereabouts."

"But how long will that—"

"Go home Nemo, go see your family. If you still want to save Neith come back later on tonight. But realize we don't need you, and this isn't your fight. Can you really look your family in the eyes and willingly put your life in jeopardy for no reason? Think about that while you contemplate coming back tonight."

Nemo weighed Arthur's words. How many times had he thrown his life needlessly in danger these past few months? If something happened to him, it would hurt his family the most. It felt like ages since he spent time at home. When he wasn't at school or sleeping, he was training with Neith. While Neith had become just like family to him, that didn't mean he had to abandon his real family that had always been there for him. As much as he wanted to immediately go after Neith, he knew he needed to go home first.

"Fine." was all Nemo said to Arthur before leaving the tent. He briefly stopped to see CJ, grabbed his stuff and headed home.

****

Nemo's mother hugged him so tightly, it felt like his spine might snap if she didn't let go soon. He barely made it into the driveway before she ran out to meet him, tears streaming down her face. His dad simply stood at the door watching the both of them. His face tried not to betray his emotions, but Nemo could tell he had been worried too. Knots of sadness filled Nemo's stomach. He hated the fact that he caused his parents to worry so much. He was their only child, of course they would notice if he disappeared for an entire day.

"Nemo, are you okay? I was so worried. No one could reach you and none of the neighbors knew where you were.

After everything that's happened lately, I started to assume the worst. I thought you might...I thought something might have..."

Nemo's mom could barely finish her sentence before bursting into tears again. He didn't know if they were tears of sadness from thoughts of what might have happened, or tears of joy form knowing her son was now safely home.

Nemo thought of everything that happened over the past few months. If his mom knew everything he'd been through, she would keep her arms wrapped around him and never let go again. Minutes passed with his mother still hugging him for dear life. His father, seeing that they were making a scene, calmly walked over to them and gently placed a hand on his wife's back.

"Honey, why don't we take this inside? I'm sure Nemo is exhausted from... well from wherever he's been."

He glanced over to Nemo with an expression that said he had some explaining to do.

"He also probably wants to take a bath." His next look let Nemo know it wasn't a suggestion.

After a long, warm bath and an hour of relaxing on the couch watching TV, Nemo sat at the kitchen table. His dad sat across from him as they waited for mom to finish cooking. Nemo had forgotten how it felt to just sit at home and be normal. But no amount of TV, warm baths, or home cooked food could make him forget about Neith, CJ, or anyone else from Fratello della Spada that might not see tomorrow. With each thing he enjoyed from home, he felt a little more guilt for even being there while the others we're still fighting for their lives. But when he looked at the excited smile on his mom's face just because he was home, he felt guilty for a completely different reason.

"What's wrong son?" Nemo's dad asked, noticing the addled look on his face. He leaned across the table to whisper, "I know what I said earlier about you have some explaining to do, but truthfully your mother and I are just happy you're home safe."

Nemo let his head drop down in his hands, trying to find the words to say.

"That's the thing Dad, as much as I want to be home here with you and Mom...I have to...well there's people that..."

Nemo had the full attention of his parents but couldn't bring himself to tell them he was leaving again, especially since he couldn't really tell them why.

"Dad, what would you do if you knew a really good friend of yours was in trouble and you could help them, but doing so might put you in a lot of trouble too?"

Nemo's dad looked him straight in the eyes, "What kind of trouble?"

Nemo kept his head down, letting it be known it was a question he didn't want to answer. After a few moments of silence his dad asked a different question.

"I really don't know son. Exactly how good of a friend are we talking here?"

"Definitely a once in a lifetime type friend Dad, of that much I'm sure." Nemo said looking his dad directly in his eyes.

He wanted him to know just how serious he was. Seconds passed as Nemo's dad looked back at him from across the table. Not as a father to son, but man to man. He wanted to gauge his resolve before coming to a decision. When he made up his mind, Nemo's dad slumped back in his chair and responded.

"Well in that case why are you still sitting here?"

Nemo cast a glance over to his mother in the kitchen.

"Ah I see" Nemo's dad responded. "Don't worry. I'll take care of your mother. I don't want you to go, but I can tell by the look in your eyes that I can't stop you. Just promise me one thing, that you'll come back to us safe."

Nemo hopped up from his chair so fast, it could have been on fire. He quickly ran upstairs and grabbed everything he thought he might need. He made sure to grab the bulletproof combat clothing from Neith, that he kept hidden under his mattress. Now was definitely a time he needed it. His sword was outside waiting for him under a large group of bushes two houses down. Walking in his parent's house with a giant sword on his back was not something he was prepared to explain today.

Nemo ran back down the stairs even faster than he did on his way up. Just as he touched the door to leave, his father called his name again.

"Nemo! Don't think I've forgotten about that talk we were supposed to have. You still have some explaining to do when you get back."

Nemo nodded his head that he understood. "I promise to tell you and Mom all about it when I get back. Thanks Dad."

Before his dad could say anything else, he was out the door. Overhead, he could see dark clouds rolling in fast. A storm was coming, and soon there would be rain.

CHAPTER 31

As she regained consciousness, Neith didn't open her eyes right away. As far as she could tell, there was only one person guarding her. She wanted to get a good sense of her surroundings before she gave him a reason to be more alert. Once they found out she was awake, there would be no more chances like this again.

She could feel the uncut rock floors digging into her back. Rusted iron shackles held her wrists above her head against a stone wall.

"At least my feet aren't shackled as well." she thought.

That allowed her to at least sit down while keeping her arms above her head. Had she been forced to stand, it would have quickly sapped any strength she hoped to recover while waiting for a chance to escape.

The rough, uneven walls gave her an idea of the type of makeshift dungeon that held her captive. Neith listened for any sound. Echoes from all around gave her a sense of the size of the room. They also gave her important clue to her location. The timing of the echoes and way they traveled before reaching her ears made her realize that she was being held underground. She would have to get to the surface somehow in order to find out exactly where she was. There were miles of disconnected old underground tunnels in the areas around the Citadel. Some of them had been excavated and used as wine cellars or storage. Others were turned into emergency escape routes. Even the Citadel itself was constructed on top of ancient catacombs built from a series of underground caves. But, for every known, well-used tunnel, there were at least another three that hadn't seen a human soul in centuries. A person could easily become lost in one of these uncharted underground tunnels and never find their way out. Neith gathered her thoughts. Someone brought her here, meaning they had been here before. If they knew the way in, then they knew the way out.

Neith slowly repositioned her wrist, trying to make as little sound as possible. As much as she wanted too, she hesitated to test their strength. The sound would probably alert her guard. Given enough time to recover, she could easily rip them from the walls. However, in her current state that wasn't going to happen. Strength wouldn't save her this time, she would need to use her wits and figure out another way to free herself.

When she was sure there was nothing else she could learn with her eyes still closed, Neith finally opened her eyes. The room was smaller than she thought. In fact, it was more like a cave than an actual room. Her feet, stretched out in front of her, reached halfway across the floor. There was no door, only a thinner hallway section that transitioned into a large opening connecting to the main caves. A single dim torch was her only source of light. Her eyes had been closed long enough so they didn't need much time to adjust, but for the first few seconds all she saw was darkness. As her vision became clearer, she could see the outline of something in front of her, something different from her surroundings. She could almost make out what it was, its outline was clearly the shape of a person, probably the person she sensed guarding her. But something about it was oddly familiar. Slowly the image of the person in front of her became clear. She immediately wanted to close her eyes again. For the first time in her life she thought she saw a ghost.

"Boo" said the person looking back at her, now merely inches away from her face.

Neith tried to ram her head forward into his. Ghost or not, she planned to go out fighting. But before she could move, a strong hand grabbed her by the chin. Warm lips pressed tightly against hers.

"Is this real?" she thought. "Can I believe what I'm seeing, what I'm feeling? Or are all of my senses working to trick me?"

Thoughts raced out of control through her mind. When his lips left hers, she could clearly see his face. It was no illusion. What she was seeing, everything she felt was real. Standing in front of her was none other than Bulo.

"If I didn't know any better I'd think you missed me." said Bulo.

By the look on his face, he took her surprise as a good thing. It was not.

"How are you alive? I was at your funeral. I saw your body." Neith said in disbelief.

Bulo didn't bother to acknowledge her question as he grabbed the ring finger from her left hand.

"I see you got rid of my ring. Tell me, what did you do with it?"

Neith paused. It was all happening too fast. The person whose killer she had nearly torn the world apart to find, was actually alive. Slowly her eyes stared back up to meet his.

"I put it in your casket at your funeral. Now tell me why you're not six feet under with it?"

Bulo dropped her hand, letting it fall against the hard iron of her shackle.

"Well, what a nice gesture that was, especially coming from you. Guess that means it's really over between us."

"It was over when you tried to kill me. This scar above my eye is a daily reminder of that."

Bulo took his time looking her up and down, taking in the sight of every one of her curves. Even bloody and bruised she was still a beauty to behold.

"I told you a long time ago that I'd never let you leave me, but you just had to test me. I loved you Neith, and what did I get in return? You and the others tried to expel me from Fratello della Spada."

Neith spit the blood dripping from her upper lip into the dirt. Half of her face was swollen, making it difficult to talk. But this was a conversation that was long overdue.

"Who do you think requested a full ritual for your funeral, even though you were about to be expelled? When I thought you died, I harassed everyone I could until they agreed to honor you as a full member in death. Even after everything you did to me, I still cared for you. After you tried to kill me, I still didn't vote for you to be expelled. But Saint Georges, Janus, Hao… all the other masters and everyone else voted against you. They couldn't forgive what you did."

Bulo looked at back her with piercing eyes. "Don't go painting yourself as the victim here. If I remember correctly, you put up one hell of a fight. I had a concussion, several broken ribs, and a pierced lung."

"And my head was nearly sliced open, so you'll have to excuse me for not feeling sorry for you." Neith interrupted.

Bulo slammed his hand on the wall next to her face. The sudden movement caused Neith to be quiet.

"Yet here you are back with me. Like I said, I'll never let you leave me."

Neith could feel a knot in her throat as she tried to speak.

"What happened to you? What happened to the man I fell in love with? I saw you changing right before my eyes, becoming more violent, isolating yourself all the time. But I chose to ignore it. That's my fault."

Her voice cracked as tears welled up in her eyes. "When I thought you were dead, that's exactly how I felt. I felt guilty that I watched you descend into madness and didn't do anything about it. Now that I see you here in front of me, I don't know what I feel."

The sudden reminder of the past almost made her forget her current situation, but the shackles pinning her arms to the wall when she reached for Bulo brought a vivid reminder of why she was there. Neith dried her eyes against her arm.

"Bulo tell me right now how you're alive. And if you still care for me like you say you do, release me from these chains this instant!"

Bulo bent back down to put his face close to hers and shook his head. "Tsk, tsk, tsk, same 'ol Neith. Now I don't think you're in any position to be giving orders. I'm afraid my brother and I have come too far to let you ruin our plans now. So, you'll have to bear with me and enjoy your accommodations here."

It was clear that he had no plans of letting her go. Neith changed the subject, hoping something he revealed might prove useful.

"So it was you following me after your funeral wasn't it?"

Bulo continued staring into her eyes as a smile grew across his face.

"Looks like you caught me. That day, I planned on finishing what I started when I gave you that scar, but I got a little too excited and you noticed me. But now, I'm glad I didn't kill you. Otherwise I would have missed out on all this fun we're having. Do you know how easy it is to manipulate the Fratello della Spada job postings? No one ever takes the time to verify where they came from before blindly putting it in the queue with the rest of the jobs. If they did, I might not have been able to set everything up so neatly."

"Is there a point you're trying to make, or are you just planning to talk my ears off while I'm chained here and forced to listen to you?" Neith shot back.

"Tell me, who do you think posted that bank job where you first met our associate, Mad Cutter?" Bulo responded. He watched Neith's eyes widen as she put the pieces together in her mind.

"I also sent over the kidnapping job that happened to be 'mistranslated'. There was a rumor going around about a girl being descendant of Tralonian royalty. The rumor was false, but my how the dominoes fell from that simple tale. When you really think about it, you'll realize my brother and I have been pulling your strings from the day you thought I died. You've been our personal puppet, happily dancing to our tune. Of course, I didn't know it would be you that took on those jobs I posted. I was just hoping to kill an extra Shadow or two before the big finale. But you made everything so much more interesting!"

"You sure talk a lot more than I remember." Neith said, refusing to give him the satisfaction of recognizing his grand plan. However, inside she wanted to scream. These past few months she had been chasing something that didn't even exist, and the person she wanted to avenge was actually the one manipulating her every action. Neith took a deep breathe.

"Now isn't the time to be angry at myself" she thought. She needed to keep Bulo talking to see what else he might reveal.

"And what's this nonsense about you having a brother? You never mentioned him before."

"Megas Krav, my brother and leader of our little group here know as Guiding Light. Perhaps you've heard of him? We reconnected some time ago in Tralone. Fate it seems has a sense of irony because we were on opposite sides during that decisive battle."

Bulo started to laugh as he reminisced about the past.

"I actually almost killed him before I recognized who he was, isn't that funny."

Neith stared back with a blank face as Bulo continued to laugh in her face. "Sorry, I'm not in a very humorous mood right now."

Bulo nonchalantly waved off her sarcasm, "Neith, I could hardly care what your mood is. Now you should listen closely because I'm just getting to the good part. My brother and I kept in touch and had a nice long chat after you all tried to expel me. Turns out we had a common enemy. We both agreed then and there that we would see Fratello della Spada burn to the ground, and from its ashes we could create something even better. Using our skills, and with the help of a few others, we've done just that. You'd be amazed at the things he's learned to do over the years. Things like forging death records, and mutilating a body so it can pass as your own corpse…"

"So then body we buried, was someone else?" Neith said aloud as she finally fit all the pieces of what was happening together.

"Bingo." replied Bulo. "Just some unlucky soldier donating his life for the greater good of our organization. He was more useful to us dead than he ever would have been alive."

Neith was quickly realizing that the Bulo she had known was no more. She briefly wondered if the person she'd grown close to even existed, or was this his true self finally surfacing. Instead of dwelling on the subject she asked about something more important to her.

"What about Janus? Is he alive too?" Neith asked, eager to find some silver lining in the clouds of despair that were now raining on her.

"No, he's definitely dead." Bulo said as he stood up from the ground. "I can say so with certainty because I killed him myself."

Whether it was confusion, or anger, she didn't know which she felt first. However, both were present in her.

"You killed Janus…Why?" Neith said through gritted teeth, her arms pulling against the chains that trapped her.

"Janus was one of the few people that had access to the restricted areas under the Citadel. Our plans required the ring of a high ranked individual. It just so happens that Janus was the target I stumbled upon first. He seemed surprised to see me, just like you were."

Bulo took two steps to turn his back towards Neith. "It was that moment of hesitation that got him killed."

"You're lying. Janus' body was found with his ring still on his hand." Neith said with confidence

Bulo turned his head just enough so Neith could see his wicked grin coming back to his face.

"Of course it was! Had I simply killed him and taken his ring, you all would have made sure to wipe anything he had access to out of the system. So instead, I took his DNA and created my own copy of his Fratello della Spada ring. I'm sure you know by now what we did with it."

An awkward silence fell between them before Bulo realized she actually didn't know what he was referring too. He almost shed a tear laughing at the irony.

"You really don't know do you? Well this has turned out to be a more joyous conversation than I thought. The home you knew as the Citadel is no more, we blew it up!"

Bulo made a small explosion gesture with his hands in Neith's face to further patronize her.

"Wouldn't have been possible without access to those restricted areas. No, to ensure the destruction of such a large building such as the Citadel you have to start at the foundation. I'm sure there a few stragglers running about. No matter, we will hunt them down too soon enough."

For the first few seconds, disbelief shielded her from truly understanding what Bulo was saying. As the realization slowly sunk in, Neith thought she was going to be sick. How many of her friends were dead already? She wanted it to be a joke, an idle bluff. But by the cavalier way Bulo talked to her about all of this, she knew deep down that it was true.

"Give yourself a pat on the back as well. Your DNA aided in our plan. While it couldn't get us into the restricted areas, it certainly helped my men move throughout the many corridors of the Citadel with ease. I'll have to thank Mad Cutter again for getting that for me. I'm sure he still has a lot to say to you after that beating you gave him back at the bank."

Neith could listen no longer. By this point she was pulling against her shackles as hard as she could. They didn't move. The chains connecting the shackles to the wall were buried deep in the stone. Rage welled up inside her and Neith summoned her fighting spirit. She was ready to kill Bulo herself. A red glow slowly covered her eyes, as if they were being submerged in a pool of blood and lit ablaze. Bulo never took his eyes off of her. In fact, he beckoned her to come towards him. He watched as her chains started to inch their way out of the stone. Cracks rippled across the wall. Dust that sat undisturbed for centuries, was sent flying by the sudden rush of air through the cracks. Neith planned to tear the entire wall to pieces if she needed too.

Without warning, pain shot through every nerve in her body. Her connection to her fighting spirit was instantly severed like cheap string, and the fire in her eyes was extinguished like a match dunked in water. Neith's body collapsed under its own weight. Blood and vomit seeped from her mouth. She felt like she might vomit up her organs if the pain didn't subside soon. Out of her peripheral, she could see Bulo approach her with his smug grin spread across his face ear to ear.

"You spent the better part of the day unconscious after an explosion slammed you into a tree so hard three of your ribs shattered, and you think your body can handle channeling your fighting spirit in that condition? Why don't you just save yourself the trouble and ask me to kill you now."

Neith took long, deep breaths to try and recover her senses. Slowly, the pain started to subside. She swallowed a gulp of blood and prayed that no more welled up in throat. As she leaned her head down in relief, Neith felt something sharp. Held directly underneath her chin was Bulo's sword. She hadn't seen him make any move to draw it, yet there it was right in front of her face.

"Did you forget that my shaska was one of the fastest drawn blades out of all of the Shadows? Judging by that hand of yours, you can barely even hold a sword now."

Neith looked up at her right hand. Several of her fingers were swollen and twisted in ways that told her they were broken. Dark purple bruises stretched down to the base of her hand and stopped right where the shackle held her wrist.

It was all coming back to her now, everything that had happened since the end of the disciple tournament. How long had it been? One, maybe two days since then? With no sun down there in the caves, it was impossible to tell. Her gut said it had only been a little over a day. Judging how she felt, it would take a couple weeks for her to be well enough to fight her way out of here, and that's if she was resting comfortably with proper food and medicine. If she was stuck in these shackles the whole time, it would take much longer. Longer than she knew she would last.

"If I were you I'd worry about saving my strength. A body doesn't last very long without food or water, especially one in your condition."

Bulo pointed his sword to the left of Neith. "I certainly hope you survive longer than the last people we had in here."

In the darkness, Neith hadn't even noticed the bodies besides her. They looked as if dried skin had been stretched on top of bone. What was left barely resembled a person. Shackles still bound the wrists of two corpses into the stone wall. If Neith didn't escape, this was the fate that awaited her, a slow death from starvation.

The sound of Bulo sheathing his sword grabbed her attention.

"Sleep tight. It will be dawn soon, although you won't know it. You may never see another sunrise again." said Bulo as he left the room taking the small torch, Neith's only source of light, with him.

Neith was left all alone in the dark.

****

Nemo made it back to the camp just as rain started to fall from the sky. He thought he might have trouble finding Arthur's tent again, but he was able to spot Arthur's tall frame standing outside. Nemo ran up directly to Arthur and dropped to a knee, too out of breath to speak. He hadn't stopped running since he left his parent's house. He was determined to let Arthur know what he decided, that goal had kept him going. He was going to go save Neith, tonight, from wherever she was. If Arthur and the others still wanted to wait that was there decision, but he was leaving out tonight. With or without them.

Once he finally caught his breathe, Nemo stood up. Arthur seemed to be waiting patiently for Nemo to gather his thoughts. Nemo had planned on saying everything he decided on to Arthur, but before he could speak Arthur beat him to it.

"So you came back, somehow I knew you would. How are your parents?"

Nemo looked up at Arthur with a serious expression. He wanted him to know exactly how set he was on his course of action.

"They are well. I've talked to them and they understand my decision."

"Really..." said Arthur, surprised to hear those words. "I wonder exactly what you told them. Do they know the entire gravity of the situation you are throwing yourself into?"

Nemo's resolve was unshaken by the question. He knew what had to do. "They know enough to understand the decision I've made."

"Well then, I guess I'll leave that discussion between you and your family."

Before he could change the topic, Nemo spoke up. "Arthur, I'm going to save Neith tonight. I don't know where she is, but the more time we waste the less time she has. I could use your help, but I'll still go without it. Will you come with me?"

Arthur looked down at Nemo, weighing the decision in his mind.

"No, I have things to do here."

"I see, well then I guess—"

"But that doesn't mean I'll let you leave without some help." Arthur said before putting his finger to his lips and letting out a high-pitched whistle.

Out of his tent walked a woman clad in full samurai armor. Next to her was a little girl who looked to be about eight years old, also clad in a smaller version of the same samurai armor.

Arthur looked back towards Nemo, trying to regain his attention as he focused on the woman and little girl walking towards them.

"When I found out about Guiding Light's plan I sent out a distress message asking Shadows from around the world to come back and help. Allow me to introduce one of the best ancient armor experts around, Atsuko Mizushima."

"Hello Nemo, nice to meet you." said Atsuko as she extended her hand out towards him.

Her foreign accent seemed to roll perfectly off her lips with every word. Long black hair cascaded from the top of her head down the back of her thick plated armor. The red and black wrapped handle of long katana rested at her side in a black sheath. Her helmet, resting under her right arm, was adorned with circular symbols that looked to connect with the symbols on the back and sides of her armor. Nemo hadn't thought anyone could look more intimidating than Neith did. Atsuko was making him reconsider that thought.

Arthur extended his hand and pointed, "And this little one here is her daughter Akiko. She's not an official disciple yet, still too young. But under her mother's tutelage I'm sure she can hold her own in any situation."

Akiko didn't say anything, but stayed by her mother's side. She looked like your typical shy little girl, aside from the armor covering her. She held her small helmet in both hands and her sword nearly dragged on the ground when she walked.

"Don't be shy Akiko, speak." Atsuko said to her daughter

"Nice to meet you" Akiko said as she finished a short bow in Nemo's direction. Her soft, high pitched voice matched her small thin frame nearly covered by long black hair just like her mother's.

Arthur leaned in closer to whisper to Nemo, "Don't be fooled by her shy appearance, the girl's a prodigy. She's probably stronger than you, so if you get scared I'd hide behind her."

Nemo could tell by Arthur's smile that he was only halfway joking. The little girl's armor had the same symbols as her mother's, although there were less of them.

"Since Neith isn't here to persuade her hard-headed disciple against going after her, I've asked Atsuko to look after you until you all can find and rescue Neith."

Atsuko took another step towards Nemo, "On my honor, I promise we'll save your master, Neith. Besides I can't wait to see the look on her face when her old rival shows up to rescue her. Knowing her, she might even refuse to leave. She'd rather remain a prisoner than give me the satisfaction of knowing she needed my help."

"You were Neith's rival?" Nemo asked, understanding why he felt intimidated by this woman just like he did around Neith. They were two sides of the same coin.

"Oh yes, back when we were both disciples. I'll tell you all about it on the way there." said Atsuko

Nemo looked back at Arthur, "On the way where? I have no idea where we're going yet."

Arthur, always one to keep information to himself, simply smiled. "As you said, time is of the essence. I managed to track down Guiding Light's base right before they attacked us. This whole time they've been plotting against us in our own backyard. They've been using sections of the underground caves as a base of operations. There's a good chance that's where Neith is being held. I managed to find the general area. You'll have to search through them to find exactly where Neith is. If you set out now, you all should make it there by dawn. I've already briefed Saint Georges on the details and directions."

Nemo turned around to find Saint Georges standing behind him along with master Hao, Tai, Xui, master Absolon, and Tommy.

"You didn't really think we'd let you go alone did you?" said Saint Georges.

Nemo dug the heel of his boot into the dirt while he hung his head, "Well I wasn't really sure…"

Tai chimed in, "If you think we're going to let you go off and outshine the rest of your disciple class, then you better think again. We're coming too."

Before Nemo could say another word, he felt a fist push against the back of his head. CJ was there behind him, his left foot and right arm in casts with one crutch holding him up under his left arm.

"I would go with you, but it would be unfair for me to still outrun you in these casts. So give 'em a good punch for me."

"I think everybody's here now" said Arthur. "Time for you all to head out and show these bastards why you don't mess with the Shadows of Fratello della Spada."

Nemo struck his fist against his chest, taking a line he liked from Atsuko. "On my honor."

Sunrise was still a few hours off. They would need to hurry if they were going to make it to Guiding Light's hideout by dawn. Then the real work would begin.

CHAPTER 32

Fog rolled over the wet grass as the sun broke the horizon. The group had been running all night and finally stopped at the ominous looking entrance to the system of caves. Atsuko checked on Nemo several times throughout the night. At first, he struggled to keep up with everyone. Having only a few hours of sleep in the past couple days was really starting to take its toll on him. But somehow Atsuko managed to distract him with stories of her and Neith when they were disciples. There was one in particular that almost had him falling on the ground laughing. Atsuko described how her and Neith jumped from the roof of the Citadel because neither one of them wanted to lose in a game of chicken. They both ended up jumping into a deep mud puddle and had to walk back past everyone in the Citadel completely covered in mud. Atsuko made sure to emphasize how long it took them to clean up all the mud they tracked through the building. After a while, Nemo forgot he was running. It felt like he was just moving while listening to her talk. By the time they arrived he felt relaxed, maybe even rested. That was until they stepped into the abyss of the cave.

Saint Georges walked in first, taking the lead. Everyone else followed close behind him, except for Absolon who stayed a few feet behind everyone to guard the rear. Water dripped down from the rock formations on the ceiling. The humid, damp darkness of cave made Nemo feel like he was entering the mouth of some viscous beast instead of cave. The fog covering the floor hardly put him at ease either. Soon, they were deep enough where there was no longer light from the surface to guide them. Nemo reached for the flashlight he carried in a pocket on his combat vest, but Atsuko grabbed his hand and shook her head.

"No lights. If someone is up ahead, we don't want to let them know we're coming."

As Nemo opened his mouth to ask how they were supposed to see where they were going, he noticed Atsuko's eyes glowing a sky blue color. He looked around and noticed all the masters and Tommy had activated their fighting spirit. Then it clicked. They were using their other senses in conjunction with their fighting spirit to guide them. It wasn't something Nemo would have thought to do on his own. Their fighting spirit allowed them to sense anyone nearby, while also increasing the sharpness of their other senses. Despite not being able to see, they would be able to keep the same pace moving through the cave.

Nemo quickly unleashed his fighting spirit as well. Letting the rush of energy flow through his body as his eyes changed from a dull gray to a glowing dark blue. It was an odd feeling. Like reading from a map inside his head instead of using his eyes. He could smell the granite as he approached closer to a wall. He could hear each individual water drop from the ceiling, and could pinpoint their locations. Every sense of his worked together to map his surroundings. Nemo turned back to where Atsuko had been standing.

"What about Akiko, Tai, and Xui? How are they supposed to see down here? They can't use their fighting spirit." He asked.

No later than he had finished his question, Tai and Xui came running by, holding on to the edges of Hao's robe. What they lacked in sight they compensated for in superior reflexes. With each turn their master made, they were able to feel the slightest change in his direction and follow it.

"I think they'll be just fine." said Atsuko

She looked down by her side and scoped up Akiko in her arms.

"Let go before we fall further behind."

Nemo nodded that he understood and took off running with her deeper into the darkness.

Almost an hour had passed since they entered the cave. Nemo was becoming comfortable running in the darkness, but maintaining his fighting spirit was sapping his strength faster than running. The other masters seemed to be able to draw out just enough power to amplify their senses, but all he had ever practiced was drawing out the maximum amount of fighting spirit he could. Trying to maintain just a slow trickle of spirit through his body had caused him to run into a wall more than a few times. The only way he could keep up with everyone was to just draw out a large amount of spirit and let most of his energy go to waste. Tommy also seemed to be dealing with this problem, although Tommy still looked to be in better shape than he was. Nemo could hear the heartbeats of everyone around him. His heart was beating the fastest by far. Nemo listened in to focus on Tommy's heartbeat. His was speeding up as he started to become tired as well. The strongest, most steady pattern however was coming from Atsuko right next to him. Even in full armor and carrying her daughter with her, her heartrate sounded slow and steady. Nemo couldn't imagine what kind of physical training this woman had been through to have such a high level of endurance. His thoughts faded into the time spent training with Neith and the things they had been through together. The more he thought about her, the more his fighting spirit poured out of him, responding to his need. He could hope only she was still ok, and that they wouldn't be too late.

Without warning, Nemo heard all of the master's heartrates shoot up. They all quickly came to dead stop from their sprinting pace. Atsuko and Absolon had to grab both Nemo and Tommy to stop them from running past everyone. Tai and Xui seemed to grasped the quick change in momentum from Hao's movements and stopped with everyone else. Nemo didn't know what just changed, but all the masters were on edge. He could barely see the outline of their bodies, but they all seemed to be focusing in a particular direction. Tai, Xui, and Tommy's body movements bore the same confusion as his own. They were probably trying to figure out what was going on too. Suddenly, the deep echo of Saint Georges voice cut through the silence that had persisted since they lost all light from the surface.

"They know we're here..."

Nemo quickly focused his fighting spirit to search for any other presence around. He didn't sense anyone nearby. Against his better judgement he decided to ask what was going on.

"Atsuko, I don't sense anyone. Why do all of the masters look as if trouble is around the next corner?"

Atsuko looked at Nemo, "You're fighting spirit is still immature. I imagine you can only detect people at a distance of two to three miles at most. All of the masters here can detect another's presence at a minimum of ten miles away."

Nemo never thought that the difference in their ability to sense others would be so vast. Even after all he had been through, he was still finding out the limits of what he thought was possible were much further than he imagined.

"So do you all sense someone coming?" asked Nemo.

Akiko jumped down from her mother's arms as Atsuko's hand gripped the hilt of her sword. She whispered to Nemo through gritted teeth.

"No, it's the opposite. Someone just let out a large amount of fighting spirit. It's like they're inviting us to come towards them, like moths to a flame."

Absolon chimed in from the back, "Well if someone's going to bother to invite us in, it would be rude of us to not come."

"You know it's probably a trap." said Hao

"Trap or not, it would still be rude. Besides I think we'll be ok. They don't call me 'The Prophet' for nothing." replied Absolon

"You only ever prophesy of one thing, so you can keep all your prophesies and predictions to yourself." shouted Saint Georges from the front of the group.

"It was a joke Georgy boy…wouldn't kill you to have a sense of humor." Absolon muttered just loud enough so Saint Georges could barely hear him.

Saint Georges shouted over Absolon's quiet voice, "But you're right. It would be rude not to go see whoever our host is that's invited us to come to him. I'd rather head that way instead of wandering around in the dark."

The group rushed towards the large presence they felt until they arrived in a large open area. The cave walls rose above them to form a dome at least twenty feet high. Nemo hadn't realized how far they had travelled underground.

"The presence came from this area, be on guard Nemo." said Atsuko

Light illuminated the cave and blinded everyone. The sudden transition from absolute darkness hurt Nemo's eyes, but after a few seconds they adjusted enough for him to be able to see his surroundings. Recessed pillars were carved into the stone at symmetric points around the room. It was clear the room wasn't a natural formation. People had been here before. Not only did they carve into the stone, but they installed lights too. Everyone looked around at the drastic difference between this room and the dark caverns they just emerged from. Everyone except Saint Georges, he looked forward with his mouth open. A paleness washed over his face that made his black skin appear ashen.

"Bulo is that you?" He screamed. "How are you alive!"

Bulo stood on a platform in front of them. His black gloves, black pants and boots offset his bright crimson shirt that struggled to stay buttoned across his broad chest. He crossed his arms and slowly stepped forward to look over them.

"Welcome to my humble abode." He said in a calm yet confident voice. "It's been so long since I've seen some of you."

Nemo immediately recognized the name. Neith and those around her had referenced him several times, but he was supposed to be dead. Nemo looked around at the other masters. Absolon and Hao stood still as stone, paralyzed by the sight in front of them. Their mouths moved to speak but no sound emerged, and their faces held the same confused expression as Saint Georges.

Seeing everyone else was paralyzed by confusion, Atsuko stepped forward to address the mysterious person standing in front of them.

"I don't know who you are, but we came here looking for a person. A woman with brown skin and dark hair. She also has a deep scar above her left eye. Have you seen anyone like that?"

"So this is the rescue party they sent after Neith. I honestly didn't think anyone would arrive for another day. Arthur must have had more information about us than I thought. A shame he didn't come himself. I would have relished the opportunity to kill him with my own hands."

At the mention on Neith's name Nemo drew his sword rushed forward. He could feel his fighting spirit surge to meet his need for power. Electricity sparked around him when he pointed his sword towards Bulo.

"Tell us where Neith is, now!"

"Boy be careful where you point that sword." Bulo said to Nemo looking directly into his eyes. "I hadn't noticed before, but you brought a few little ones with you. Saint Georges you should know better than this, to bring these children to their deaths. We must have killed more people than I thought when we blew up the Citadel if you let these disciples come with you."

In an instant, Saint Georges and Atsuko ascended the cliff and stood on opposite sides of Bulo. Saint Georges held his rapier mere inches from Bulo's left eye while Atsuko stood with her katana aimed to slice a clean line through his neck.

"You've made it clear that you are not on our side" said Saint Georges. "Even after our past history, I had hoped that seeing a friend I thought long dead again would be a more enjoyable experience. But make no mistake, I am here to accomplish a goal and you will tell us what you know. Willingly or unwillingly, the choice is yours."

"Let's start with Nemo's question. Where's Neith?" said Atsuko as she turned her blade to line up directly with Bulo's neck.

A sly smile spread across Bulo's lips. "Well this has been fun, but I see no reason to draw this out any further. It's a shame I have to say goodbye so soon, but you can take comfort in the fact that you all will die together."

A sudden hot flash of light blinded Nemo. He couldn't see anyone around him. He suddenly felt heavier, as if he was sinking into the ground beneath him. He could hear faint sounds in the background, but couldn't figure out where they were coming from.

Screams.

Nemo realized he could hear screams from someone around him. The sound of the stone pillars collapsing around them, and the ground exploding underneath him had masked it from his ears. There was nothing he could do as he fell into the depths below. Darkness encompassed him again in its cold embrace.

CHAPTER 33

The fall didn't last long. In mere seconds Nemo hit the ground, hard. Fortunately for him the ground was soft and muddy. Had it been stone like the walls around him and he would have broken his back. Nemo quickly released his fighting spirit to sense his surroundings in the darkness. Once he got up and looked around, he realized just how lucky he had been. Somehow, he managed to avoid falling on any of the large rocks created by the explosion. Sharp jagged edges of the large stones jutted from the ground where they landed.

Nemo could see light from the area above him where he fell. He wanted to make sure there were no surprises coming down after them.

"Doesn't look to be more than thirty feet." said Atsuko as she grabbed Nemo by the shoulder.

He almost jumped out of his shoes in surprise.

"Atsuko! Oh, it's just you. I'm still anxious after the explosion." Nemo said while he took deep breaths to calm himself.

He briefly wondered where Akiko had landed before he spotted her farther back behind Atsuko. The dim rays of light from above reflected off her clean armor as she walked up next to Atsuko.

Nemo looked down at his own clothes covered in mud.

"Hey, how come both of you aren't covered in mud like me?"

Akiko responded in a completely serious tone. "It's because we landed on our feet and not on our faces."

Nemo looked at Akiko, his eyes wide with surprise, before bursting out in laughter. Atsuko tried to hold it in, but couldn't help but laugh at her daughter's response as well.

"Thanks for the advice. I'll make sure to try that next time." said Nemo.

Saint Georges booming voice interrupted their brief moment of relief.

"Hey is everyone ok?"

Nemo looked around but didn't see him anywhere. He heard Saint Georges voice shout again.

"Hello, can anyone hear me?"

This time both Nemo and Atsuko could tell where it was coming from. It came from the other side of the wall closest to them.

"Yes, I have Akiko and Nemo with me. Is everyone else over there with you?" Atsuko responded

"No, I'm alone over here."

Before Atsuko could ask what happened to the others, Hao's voice came from behind the other wall furthest from them.

"We're ok over here. Tai and Xui are with me. Can anyone else but us can hear Absolon's voice? Its sounds further away, but I think he's saying him and Tommy are ok as well."

Nemo tried to focus his hearing on picking out Absolon's voice but couldn't hear any sign of it. He looked up to Atsuko who shook her head signifying that she couldn't hear it either.

"Apparently the collapsing stone separated us into different tunnels. Looks like Bulo's plan failed. He'll have to try harder if he wants to kill us off." Saint Georges said through the cavern walls. "Hao relay this message to Absolon if he can't hear me. We're all separated for now. It would be a waste of time to try and break through the walls that divide us. These paths probably intersect somewhere up ahead. Everyone switch priority to objective two, we'll cover more ground separately. If anyone finds Neith, find a way to alert to others and immediately head back to safety. The rest of us will finish the mission."

"Got it" Atsuko responded in the direction of Saint Georges voice before turning to Nemo. "Let's go, we've no time to waste. They'll soon figure out that we're not dead yet."

Nemo nodded, and they took off down the path in front of them.

Their path quickly transitioned from mud to dry rocky ground, and they soon went from travelling on a flat path to an uphill climb. Before long the slope of their path adjusted to where they had to climb on all fours to keep from falling backwards. The walls seem to close in tighter around them, leaving just enough space for Atsuko to fit through with her armor on. Rays of light peeked through the cracks in the wall, and provided enough light for them to see without them using their fighting spirit. Nemo could tell it wasn't sunlight coming through to walls. Wherever it was coming from, it was that same kind of light that was in the area where they saw Bulo. He hoped that meant they were getting closer to Neith, although part of him felt like they were approaching something else. He didn't know what it was, but his gut told him it wouldn't be anything good.

When the path became so steep that they were nearly climbing up the face of a cliff, Atsuko had Akiko lead and Nemo follow her. She took up the rear in case either of them fell. That same artificial light that was shining through the cracks of the wall started to become brighter as they ascended up the steep path in front of them. Nemo found that climbing was much easier now that he could actually see the ground. He could even see the end of the cliff ahead of them. Mere meters away, a flat plateau waited for them at the top of stone face they were climbing. A bright source of artificial light was coming from up there as well.

Akiko was the first to reach the top. As soon as her hand touched the edge of the plateau, she screamed. At the same time, something grabbed her arm and pulled her over the top. Before Nemo could rush to the top, Atsuko had nearly jumped all the way up there. Nemo quickly reached the plateau and rolled over the top, drawing his sword at the same time. Atsuko already had her sword drawn.

"Mommy help!" Akiko yelled as a man's arm grabbed her around her middle, keeping her from moving.

Nemo's heart dropped into his stomach. His eyes nearly popped out of his head with how wide he opened them. In front of them stood hundreds of people. Each armed with everything from machetes and pistols, to guns as long as his arm. The man holding Akiko had a long belt of bullets draped over his shoulder. His face had a wild expression on it towards Nemo and Atsuko, as if it wanted them to try something so he could have an excuse to kill Akiko.

Atsuko took a step towards him, but she stopped when he picked Akiko up and wagged his finger. He slowly drew the machete resting at his side and held it in front of her throat. All at once, the men and women behind him started chanting, "Damu! Damu! Damu! Damu!"

"What are they saying?" Nemo whispered to Atsuko hoping she could hear him.

If she did hear him she didn't respond. However, Nemo didn't have to wait long for and answer to his question.

"It means blood. It is the war cry of my people before battle." A loud voice said from the back of the crowd.

Nemo's attention focused on the man that stepped through the middle of the crowd. Everyone parted around him as he walked through. He took a handful of Akiko's long black hair and let it run through his fingers while he looked Atsuko straight in her eyes.

"A woman and two children. I had hoped to have more worthy opponents for my army. As much as I dislike it, I have killed women and children before, and I doubt you all will be my last."

Nemo stood there confused about who this person was in front of them. Atsuko however, remained focused on the man holding her daughter. Her gaze never left him. This man clearly didn't know what trouble he had set in motion for himself.

"Where are my manners" the man in front said attempting to get Atsuko's attention. "Allow me to introduce myself, I am King Jean-Vis Mugabe, and that is the last name you will ever hear."

Atsuko quickly looked at Nemo, "I going to make a path. When I do run past them and keep going. Don't worry about me or Akiko, just run."

Nemo couldn't believe what he was hearing.

"There's no way I'm leaving—"

Before he even realized what happened Atsuko's hand had already finished slapping him across his face.

"I wasn't asking your permission. I am your temporary master while Neith isn't here and you will follow my orders. You never asked me on the way here, and I doubt Arthur told you, so you must have figured out what objective two is already."

Nemo rubbed his cheek to soothe the stinging.

"I figured it out while we were running through the night. It's the only reason that made sense for Arthur to send you along with the other masters that were a part of the special investigation team with me."

"Good" Atsuko said while she looked directly at the enemy. "You just remember to stick to objective one. That is what you came for right?"

Nemo didn't have to respond. He had made his answer clear since the beginning. Nemo could feel Atsuko's fighting spirit surging. Whatever she planned on doing, she wasn't going to hold anything back. Jean Vis grabbed another fistful of Akiko's hair and pulled it hard to get Atsuko and Nemo's attention.

"Now you have me interested. What exactly are these objectives you're referring to? Think of this as your chance to speak any last words you might have. If it truly is something interesting, I may have them carved into your tombstones."

"Objective One…" Nemo said in a firm voice as he sheathed his sword, "is to save one star Shadow Neith Mansour."

The air around Nemo cackled as his eyes changed to a solid dark blue color. He dropped to a knee and assumed a sprinting stance. The surprise on Jean-Vis' face gave away that he had never seen anyone use their fighting spirit before.

"Boy, tell me how did your eyes change color like—"

"Objective Two" Atsuko shouted interrupting Jean-Vis, "is the completely destruction of the organization known as Guiding Light."

Had Nemo not been shrouded in his own fighting spirit, he wouldn't have been able to stand as close as he was to Atsuko. She hadn't released her fighting spirit yet, but just the potential of all that energy waiting to be unleashed had his hairs standing on end.

"How dare you interrupt a king!" Jean-Vis shouted in a brief outburst of anger. His mood quickly changed to indifference. "Enough of this, kill them both. We'll take our time with the little girl."

In a voice barely louder than a whisper, Atsuko ushered a command to her daughter. "Akiko, slay."

Several flashes of steel happened in an instant, followed by streams of blood pouring onto the spot where Akiko had been standing. The man holding her fell to ground while he watched his severed arms roll away from him. Blood spurted from a single cut across his throat as he attempted to scream. He didn't have to wallow in pain for long. Seconds later his eyes and mouth stopped moving. It had taken him just as much time to bleed out as it took Akiko walk back to her mother's side. Every other soldier paused at the sight of one of their own brutally killed by a small eight-year-old child.

Jean-Vis wiped the streaks of blood from his face.

"I've changed my mind. Make sure they all die slowly."

On his word, hundreds of soldiers ran at them all at once.

"Remember what I said." Atsuko mentioned to Nemo as the first soldier ran towards her with a machete held high above his head.

Nemo felt a rush of air move by him. At that moment, he knew Atsuko had released her fighting spirit. By the way they kept moving forward no one else had noticed. That would be a fatal mistake for them.

Atsuko brought down her sword in a straight arc directly in front of her. The closest soldier ducked to the side, barely letting the blade scratch him. His wide smile betrayed his confidence. He knew there was no way she could swing again before he would reach her. Nemo doubted the man even realized what was happening to him as his body exploded milliseconds before reaching Atsuko. Only a pile of wet tissue and bone fragments were left where he once stood. That and fine red mist hovering in the air.

Atsuko looked at all of those in front of her, "Single Point Focus. No matter how small the contact with my sword is, the person touching the blade will receive the blunt force of all my strength. That is my fighting spirit ability. Anyone attacking me better be prepared to suffer the same fate as this man."

All those running towards her had now stopped short. Each one of them looked around, seeing who would make the first move. But while their eyes were on Atsuko, they had forgotten about Akiko. From the left side of the crowd, spurts of blood shot in air as Akiko carved her own path through the mass of people. Anyone that approached her quickly lost a foot or an ankle. None of them were prepared to fight against someone that low to ground moving with such high speed. Any attacks that did manage to find her simply glanced off her armor. Nemo could see what Arthur meant. She really was a prodigy for her age.

Without warning Atsuko rushed forward, immediately heading for Jean-Vis. His followers quickly moved in front to protect him. The look in Atsuko's eyes however said she would cut them down to the last man if that's what it took. Gunfire sounded off in Atsuko's direction, but it was too late. She had already cut a path into middle of them.

Automatic gunfire followed a step behind her as she tried to cut her way towards Jean-Vis. Bullets began taking down those around her. The random sprays of gunfire in her direction were doing nothing but thinning their own forces. She had turned their biggest advantage of numbers against them by surrounding herself with human shields.

"Stop shooting you idiots!" Jean- Vis shouted "At this rate you'll shoot your own eyes out before you hit her. I swear the incompetence I have to deal with never ceases to amaze—"

Jean-Vis screamed in pain as a knife blade slammed into his shoulder. Through the chaos of the crowd he caught a glimpse of Atsuko's hand as she finished the motion of her throw. With her other arm she held the snapped neck of the soldier she had taken the knife from. She dropped his lifeless body to the ground before moving on to her next victim, all without ever releasing the grip on her sword.

Jean-Vis cautiously backed up through his horde of soldiers while holding his bleeding shoulder. His fingers held a tight grip on his wound around the knife still jutting out from his flesh. Only the handle and a couple inches of the blade could be seen, the rest of the blade was implanted deep into his shoulder bone.

"That was a good shot, but let's see how long you last mon'amie. I'm going to enjoy standing here and personally watching you die."

He winked at Atsuko as he took a confident stance behind all of his warriors. Nemo couldn't tell if Atsuko had even heard him. She was already consumed in the heat of the battle. Bodies exploded around her. The smell of blood filled the air. Nemo could taste it in his mouth as he waited for the opening Atsuko promised would appear. Even though she appeared to be holding her own, the numbers surrounding her were overwhelming.

A high pitched scream ripped throughout the room. Nemo turned to see that someone had finally managed to stab Akiko between the plates of her armor. The soldier's small victory was short lived. Even though she shouted in pain, Akiko still moved as if she were unfazed by the blow. With a quick spin, Akiko cut the soldier that struck her from his thigh up to his stomach. The man collapsed to the ground desperately trying to keep his intestines from spilling on the floor. Nemo knew it was a futile effort. Wherever Akiko cut, she aimed for a major artery. In less than a minute he would be dead from blood loss. Still the soldier's brief moment of success had emboldened the others. All at once they jumped on Akiko. Flashes of steel cascaded around her, but she couldn't handle them all. Nemo could hear her muffle cries through the crowd as small attacks started to reach her. He had to do something. Atsuko was still engulfed by the large crowd surrounding her. There was no way she would make it to Akiko in time. She was doing all she could just to hold to the bit of ground she had.

Without thinking, Nemo ran towards Akiko. The first person he encountered noticed him too late to do anything before his sword was already sticking through their gut. Everyone was still focused on Akiko, trying to rip her sword away from her grip any way they could. They didn't even notice Nemo as he slipped between them. The next person in his way didn't notice at all until their head was no longer attached to the top of their neck. This time everyone shifted their focus from Akiko to him. This was the part he had no plan for.

"Akiko run!" Nemo shouted

There was no way he could take on this many opponents at once. Even with the aid of his fighting spirit, there were just too many. Nemo struck two more people before he felt a boot in the middle of his back knock him to the ground.

Enemies circled around him, each one ready to deal the fatal blow. He could see the shadows of several machetes raised above him. Of all the times he had thought he was going to die, he never expected it to end like this.

Just before they all came down to pierce him like a pincushion. Akiko slid between the legs of one of the soldiers, took one step off of Nemo's back and jump high into the air. In one smooth motion, she spun and sliced open each of their necks. A hand pulled him to his feet before he had time to get up. Atsuko stood above him, her armor covered in blood.

"I told you to wait for an opening" she said.

"I thought you both could use some help" Nemo replied jokingly.

"Well this is as good of an opening as you're going to get." Atsuko said, directing his gaze to follow her outstretched arm.

Nemo looked around at the piles of bodies that littered the ground. Over half of Jean-Vis' soldiers had been annihilated. The other half stood about fifteen feet away unsure of what to do next. Most of them were probably questioning if this fight was worth their lives. Nemo had no idea how Atsuko could have taken out so many of them so quickly. Right before he went to save Akiko, she was still surrounded.

Jean-Vis looked just as frightened as his men. His mouth had dropped wide open in shock.

"What... what... just what the hell are you?"

Atsuko turned back towards Jean-Vis, "I'm the thing that haunts you in your nightmares. Hunting you no matter where you go, no matter where you hide. I'm a Shadow of Fratello della Spada."

One soldier must have come to his own decision. He dropped his weapon and ran in the opposite direction.

"Hey, where are you going? Come back here!" Jean-Vis yelled at the fleeing soldier.

He didn't get far before Jean-Vis pulled out a pistol and shot him in the back.

"Nobody is allowed to run! You hear me! Nobody is allowed to run! Your lives all belong to me, that means you fight until you or your opponent is dead. Now get over there and kill her!!!"

Atsuko turned to Nemo, "Go now! We'll handle the rest of them. Go find Neith."

Nemo nodded his head and took off into the dimly lit tunnel Jean-Vis and his army had been blocking. He didn't bother to look back. Somehow he knew Atsuko and Akiko would be ok.

Atsuko watched Nemo run into the tunnel until she couldn't see him anymore.

"Whew, I thought he would never leave." She turned to address Jean-Vis and his men directly. You know no one has ever seen that move and lived. I only used part of it when the boy was on the ground. I couldn't risk him seeing it too. The only ones who know of its existence are myself, my daughter Akiko, and now you. So I'm glad to hear that no one is running. It'll save me the trouble of hunting you down one by one.

Nemo thought he heard screams as he ran down through the tunnel. He stopped to listen to where they were coming from, but they stopped just as quickly as they had started.

"Must have been my imagination." He whispered to himself before taking back off running down the tunnel to find Neith.

CHAPTER 34

"Just where the hell are we going?" yelled Absolon.

Tommy made signs with his hands, but in the darkness of the tunnels Absolon could barely see them.

"I can't see a thing down here! I know you don't know where we're going either. That was a rhetorical question."

Tommy signed something else in dark, this time his signs were more frantic.

"I already told you I can't see your signs in this darkness so you can save your energy. Besides I sense it too." said Absolon. "Seems like we won't be meeting up with our friends before trouble finds us."

Light from up ahead began to infiltrate the darkness of the tunnel. Suddenly the walls around them ended, leaving only the path they were running on. Lanterns hung from the sides of the path lighting their way and revealing the abyss below. Absolon looked on both sides of them and let out a slow whistle.

"Looks like a long drop. Be careful not to lose your footing Tommy."

Up ahead they could see the path leading to a large area in the center of the chasm. A single path on the other side of the open area led into another tunnel. Climbing down or around it was impossible. The stone walls holding up the paths and the region in the middle dropped straight down. There was hardly a place for a foothold to make the climb. This place was not a natural formation. The sheer drop from the sides was evidence that someone had spent time making it this way.

A low dirt hill sat directly in the middle of the open area. On top of the hill sat a single person.

"Fiiiiiiiiiiinally, I've been waiting here for hours for someone to show up." said the person on top of the hill. He stood up and turned towards Absolon and Tommy.

"Welcome to my own little slice of heaven, but it will be hell for you two."

Absolon stared in the direction he heard the voice come from. The person on top of the hill barely looked older than Tommy.

"What in the world is he talking about Tommy? Is that some kind of new slang you kids talk in these days?"

Tommy quickly moved his hands and fingers in Absolon's direction.

"What do you mean stop asking you dumb questions? Is that any way to talk to your master? Kids today…No respect I tell you."

Absolon turned back towards the person standing on the hill. "In any case this is the one we were looking for, no doubt about it."

Absolon started to walk toward the hill. Tommy kept pace just a step behind him.

"Hey kid, you mind moving out of the way? We're kind of in rush and don't have time for any distractions." Absolon shouted from the base of the hill.

"Who are you calling kid, old man? My name is Leo and you won't be going anywhere." Leo said confidently.

His gaze turned to Tommy standing right behind Absolon. "And who is this defective being you have with you. You both stink of ugliness. You deserve to crawl through the dirt of this world until you die of old age. Fortunately, I have orders from Megas to eliminate anyone who crosses my path. Be not afraid, for I will give you an undeserved beautiful death with my own hands."

Absolon looked down and shook his head. "Why do I always get the weird ones" he whispered to himself.

Tommy punched him hard on his shoulder.

"Ouch! Hey I wasn't talking about you…this time."

Absolon looked back at Leo, still standing on top of the hill.

"Well, I thought you'd say something like that. Tommy I'll let you get first crack at him. I hate fighting kids."

Leo unsheathed the longsword from his back and pointed it at Absolon.

"I told you not to call me kid!"

"You should be worried about what's behind you instead of what's in front of you." replied Absolon

Just then Tommy wrapped his arm around Leo's neck and bound his legs using both of his own. Leo immediately felt his throat being clamped down. The feeling of being unable to breathe excited him. The grip around his neck was unyielding. Blood rushed to his head. Just a few more seconds and he would pass out. Another time and he would have welcomed the feeling, but not today.

Leo grabbed Tommy's arm with his right hand and gave him a shocking surprise. Tommy jumped away from him and rolled midway down the hill. His movements were stunned and sluggish getting up.

Leo waved his hand around in the air, letting the electricity jump across the tips of his fingers.

"How'd you like a taste of my stun glove? It's another present I got from Megas himself. One touch and your body gets a taste of 10,000 volts per second. I brought it just for you, so you can't use your little contortionist tricks on me."

Tommy immediately drew his gladius and attacked Leo with his Serpents' Fang technique. Leo stood in his spot on the top of the hill and blocked every attack Tommy launched at him, all without moving a single step.

"Well this is interesting. The way your arm whips around with that short sword is unnatural. I bet anyone would find it hard to predict and block every one of your strikes." said Leo

Tommy paid him no attention. He kept attacking, searching for an opening anywhere around Leo.

"I bet you're wondering how I knew you were a contortionist." Leo said as locked eyes with Tommy. "The same way I know exactly where your sword will be to block it. I can see the future."

Tommy's expression barely changed. He was relentless in his goal of attacking his target. Leo kept his eyes on Tommy's, waiting for some expression of emotion on his face. However there nothing but a cold uncaring stare, reeking of diligence and determination, in Leo's direction. He would have to work harder to draw out that pure expression of fear he loved to see on his victims faces.

"Looks like you don't believe me. Here, why don't I show you just how powerless you really are." Leo said as he closed he eyes.

Tommy dropped to the ground to sweep Leo's legs from under him. Leo responded by jumping over his leg with ease.

Tommy, now facing the opposite direction, quickly sprang back to his feet and threw the arm holding his sword over his shoulder. Leo, still in the air, parried the surprise attack and landed with his right hand on Tommy's shoulder, his eyes still closed.

"Believe me now?" said Leo before unleashing another 10,000 volts into Tommy's body.

Tommy collapsed and rolled back down the hill towards Absolon. His muscles were briefly paralyzed from the current flowing through them. With one hand Absolon picked Tommy up and held him upright until he recovered enough to stand on his own.

"Looks like the reports are true. This one can tell the future right before it happens. Sorry I had to make you the guinea pig Tommy, but I needed to see it for myself."

Tommy signed with one hand at Absolon.

"Yea, I know you volunteered to do it, but that doesn't make me feel any better about it. Still, it's good we found him first before anyone else."

Absolon drew his kopis, a short curved sword that rested at his side. A series of archaic symbols were engraved down the length of the steel blade. A dark green glow enveloped Absolon's eyes. At the same time, each symbol on his kopis started to glow the same color.

"You said your name was Leo." Absolon shouted towards the hill as he took a bow. "This is my disciple Tommy, and I am Absolon the Prophet. I must say I am impressed by your abilities, they are far beyond mine. In fact, compared to you I am quite untalented. I can only give prophecy on one subject, death. Would you like to know about yours?"

Leo almost laughed at the flamboyant introduction he had just witnessed. He didn't appreciate being mocked by some old charlatan.

"Will I have to give you a quarter first before you pull out your crystal ball?"

"I assure you young man the information won't cost you a penny, but it is far from free." replied Absolon

Leo was already tired of this game. "As much as I actually would like to know how I die, I don't believe lies from false prophets."

A sly smile formed in corner of Absolon's face. "Looks like I'll just have to show you then."

Both Tommy and Absolon ran up the hill at Leo. When they were right in front of him, they split up to attack from opposite sides.

"Futile" said Leo as he blocked both of their attacks with his longsword. He reached his right hand out to grab Tommy, but had to pull it back just before Absolon's blade came down on it. Just as quickly, Tommy thrust his sword forward. Leo jumped back to keep from being skewered. It was the first time he needed to move from his spot on the hilltop.

Absolon stepped up to the top of hill and looked down at Leo.

"Looks like you lost your spot. Even if you can see our moves before we make them, it'll be pretty hard to keep up with the both of us."

Leo charged back up the hill, his sword held straight in front of him. To Absolon, he might as well have been crawling. Leo's attack was so slow and so deliberate that it would have been harder to try not to block it. However, just when Absolon expected to feel the contact of Leo's longsword, he hit nothing but air. Tommy rushed in and blocked the tip of Leo's sword with the flat side of his blade. Had he arrived even a half second later, and Leo's sword would have pierced through Absolon's stomach.

"Well that was a close one" said Absolon facing Leo. "I see your powers of premonition are not the only skills you possess. To know exactly how I would parry, then deliberately slow your speed to throw me off your tempo, takes a fair amount of skill. Too bad it didn't work. Now that I've seen it, I won't fall for that trick again."

Leo grinned before pulling two pellets from his pocket and smashing them on the ground. Clouds of black smoke filled the air around them making it impossible to see. Leo's voice came from somewhere in the smoke.

"I think I still have a few tricks up my sleeve".

Absolon and Tommy pressed their backs together. They both struggled to keep from inhaling the smoke as they waited to defend against any incoming attack.

Leo's voice echoed through the chamber, taunting them.

"I can see youuuuu!" he shouted

Absolon felt the slightest touch on the top of his head. Desperately he pushed Tommy away and rolled down on the ground just in time to avoid Leo's sword coming down on top of him. Chaos ensued. Both Absolon and Tommy swung wildly at every touch they felt in the thick smoke. The smoke settled in their lungs, making them struggle for each breathe. Tears streamed from their eyes as they both tried to see through the black clouds. With no breeze underground, it was hard to see even the shape of a person moving through the smoke. It all twisted and rolled in random directions, making it hard to discern what was real and what was just the smoke playing tricks on your eyes.

Leo flicked two rocks simultaneously at the backs of Absolon and Tommy. Both turned around swinging their blades at the perceived threats behind them. They both stopped just as the smoked cleared, revealing their blades at each other's necks.

Leo burst out in laughter. "Man, you all were this close to killing each other. That would have really made my day."

Absolon gently dropped his sword from Tommy's neck. Tommy followed his lead and dropped his sword too.

"He's toying with us" Absolon said to Tommy. "I think it's about time we got serious."

Absolon ran and attacked Leo with lethal intentions. Each slash of his kopis was a killing blow if it landed, targeting vital arteries in the body. Behind him, Tommy followed each of Absolon's attacks with a flurry of his own. Leo blocked and dodged around each one. Absolon refused to let up. The gaps between his attacks became smaller. Tommy's attacks became quicker. They could tell it was becoming more difficult for Leo to block everything. He had started dodging more, and that was starting to tire him.

Absolon locked blades with Leo, looking him dead in his eyes.

"Even though you can see our next moves, you only have one sword. At this rate, unless you take one of us out, we're going to close in and get you eventually."

Leo reached out his right hand, barely letting Absolon's blade scratch his skin in order to get his hand around Absolon's neck in time.

"You talk too much." he said before letting 10,000 volts flow into Absolon's body.

Absolon let out a blood curdling scream. Tommy rushed in swinging his gladius, forcing Leo to either let him go or lose his arm. He chose the former. Absolon slid backwards down the hill until Tommy caught up to him, keeping him from tumbling any further. The electricity in direct contact with Absolon's skin left a large burn mark across his neck. He wheezed as he struggled to catch his breathe. Cold sweat poured across his skin. The dark green color that had swallowed the whites of his eyes began to recede, and the symbols engraved into his sword ceased glowing.

After a few seconds, Absolon gathered himself and stood to his feet.

"I must be getting old, that really hurt." He said before returning his sword to his sheathe. Tommy breathed a sigh of relief before sheathing his sword as well.

"Giving up and finally accepting your fate?" Leo asked. "I expected more from you Shadows, how boring. That girl Shadow I fought last time was a lot tougher than you two."

"Oh, we're not giving up. The fight is over, you've lost." replied Absolon

Leo screamed back in a fit of anger, "Just what the hell do you mean I've lost already. I've been running circles around you the whole—" Leo pressed his hands to head and dropped to his knees in pain. "What's going on?"

"Looks like the visions are starting to take hold." said Absolon to Tommy. Tommy nodded in agreement.

"I've poisoned your mind. Actually, I've poisoned both your mind and your body, but it's your mind that will kill you first."

Leo began to scream in pain. His hands clawed at his face as if he desperately wanted to climb out of his own skin. Absolon calmly walk towards Leo. He no longer posed a threat to anyone but himself.

"I should explain this while your mind is still able to comprehend it. I assume you've never seen an ethereal ability before. Tsk tsk, that's a shame. Otherwise you might have known that you can never be too careful when dealing with someone whose fighting spirit falls in the ethereal category. You never know what effects it might have on you."

Absolon took his time to walk around Leo's body that was now huddled on the ground in the fetal position, babbling incoherently.

"For example, my ability is called 'Unlucky Voodoo'. All it takes is one strike when using my fighting spirit. One cut to let my sword taste your blood and you are then branded forever as unlucky. Normally, it takes someone a couple days to even to notice something's wrong. But usually by the second day it becomes clear. You see my ability scales with time. So the longer you're alive, the worse off your luck is. Now I'm not talking about you losing your wallet or your keys no, no, no, my curse is much stronger than that. The first day you might break your toe or a finger. The second, you might lose your sight or hearing in some unfortunate accident. By the third day even the simplest and safest of things you do have a good chance of killing you. In fact, I've never known anyone to survive more than a week after being cursed by my ability."

Absolon put his fingers to his lips as a thought occurred to him.

"Well no one that I didn't perform the purification ritual for to cancel the curse, but I wouldn't get your hopes up for that if I were you. This is how I came by my nickname, Absolon the Prophet."

Absolon continued to circle Leo's body, watching him descend further into madness. "So now that I've shown you your death like I promised, what do you think?"

Absolon squatted down and grabbed Leo under his chin, he wanted to make sure he was conscious enough to hear him. There no point in explaining to a dead man. Leo's eyes darted around wildly. He was having visions, many at once. Absolon didn't know if he could still hear him, but at the very least he was conscious. So, he decided to continue.

"Like I said, normally the curse takes a couple days before it becomes deadly. You however are a special case. It's because of your gift of premonition that my curse affects you immediately. Right now, I bet you're seeing the infinite possibilities of time stretched out in front of you. Tell me, in how many of those scenarios do you die in the first three days? How about the first two? You may even die today in some of them. I would imagine those are particularly painful."

Leo's body starting to shake in convulsions. Tears streamed from his eyes and vomit started to drip from the side of his mouth. Absolon dropped his chin back to the ground, and shook off the vomit that had dripped on his hand.

"To view your death over and over and over again in an inescapable, eternal loop. I'm sure it takes a toll on the mind. I have to admit, I had no idea if this would even work. But if it did, that made me the worst opponent for you."

"I won't, I won't die like this." Leo struggled to whisper

"It's too late kid. Go in peace." replied Absolon as he turned towards the path on the other side of the hill that Leo had been blocking.

"No…No…No!!! I won't die like this!" Leo screamed as he jumped up and ran at Absolon. Tommy ran to stop him, but Absolon held out his hand for Tommy to stop where he was. Absolon slowly stepped to side and watched Leo dive off the edge of the platform and fall into the depths below. It was too dark to see the bottom, but he doubted there was any way Leo would survive the fall.

"Let's go Tommy, we still have work to do." said Absolon.

Tommy made several motions with his hands before take a deep breath and sighing.

"No, I don't think the rest of them will be this tough. But killing anyone never really gets any easier, especially a misguided youth like Leo. Had the circumstances been different, I think I would have liked to train him." replied Absolon

Tommy made a single motion with his fingers. Absolon simply hung his head as he started walking.

"Yea you're right, I knew that when accepted this mission. Objective Two, complete and utter destruction. Let's keep moving and maybe we can catch up with everyone else. I hope they're having an easier time than we are."

CHAPTER 35

"Be careful you two, the rocks look loose around here. Move the wrong one and we could find ourselves trapped beneath a mountain of rubble." Hao said as he slowly moved another large rock. Tai and Xui stood beside him moving the smaller rocks they could lift out of the way. What they thought to be a dead end quickly turned into a much needed shortcut.

It was Tai who first noticed the faint breeze coming through the gaps in the rocks. Until then it had been slow going for them through the tunnels, and they hadn't seen the slightest glimpse of light since being separated from everyone. Their predicament only got worse when they found themselves at a dead end. Their path was blocked by a large pile of rocks, most likely from a recent cave in. Hao thought that the path beyond had collapsed in on itself, so they had no choice but to turn back and find another way around. They had already been walking for an hour. Turning back now would ensure they were stuck in these tunnels for several more hours, or worse days. That's when Tai said he heard sounds from the other side and put his ear closer to the pile. In no time at all, he was able to find several spots where air was passing through small gaps between the rocks. This meant that the path beyond the hadn't collapsed, and they could still move forward if they could just get through the obstacle in their way. So they started moving the rocks one by one.

"Had I known we'd be doing grunt work, I would have brought a shovel instead of my sword." joked Tai while he passed a sizable stone back to Xiu.

"If you did less talking and more work we'd be through already." replied Xui. "Besides, as the only girl here I'm the only one who gets to complain about moving these heavy boulders."

"Diamonds are rarely found on the surface. Likewise, a man that avoids work also avoids his own reward." Hao calmly said to his disciples.

Tai and Xui both rolled their eyes. "There he goes again with another one of his proverbs." Tai whispered to Xui.

"I know. It seems like for every situation he always has some ancient proverb that we never understand." she replied.

"I still don't get the one he told us about the birds and the bees."

Tai felt around for more rocks nearby. "I didn't understand that one either, but he did say that maybe we weren't old enough to hear about that yet."

"That's enough chit chat you two. Any energy spent talking is energy you're not using to move rocks with. I shouldn't have to remind you that we're not here for a vacation." Hao said with a voice of authority.

"Yes master." They both replied.

He looked at them silently rush back to work moving rocks out of the way.

"Good, now when we get past this obstacle I want you both to—"

Just as Hao was removing the next large stone, the leftover pile of rocks tumbled backwards. A large gust of air blew in their faces as the passage opened back up, connecting with the rest of the tunnels.

"All right we're through!" yelled Tai as grabbed his sisters hand and ran ahead.

"That didn't take as long as I thought it would." said Hao. As happy as he was to finally have a path forward, something didn't seem right. When the rush of air came through he faintly smelled something. He couldn't remember what that smell reminded him of, but it immediately made his body tense up.

"Just wait a second you two. It's pitch black dark in these tunnels so be careful." He couldn't tell if they heard him at all the way the both kept running.

Hao's mind was still going through options of what that smell could be, and why he had such a strong reaction to it. He walked ahead past the collapsed pile, still thinking, allowing his hands to brush against the sides of the tunnel walls. A loose, thin wire passed under his fingers. The kind used to set tripwire traps. Hao quickly remembered what it was that gave off that particular smell, gunpowder.

"Stop!" Hao yelled at his disciples, but it was too late. In the distance, he could see a spark ignite a thick trail of gunpowder headed in their direction. Hao used all the power in his legs to run in front of his disciples.

"Please let me make it in time." He prayed

At the last second, Hao flung his body in front of Tai and Xui. Just in time to shield them from a violent explosion.

The entire tunnel shook from the blast. Cracks ran across the smooth unbroken walls sending sharp stone shards flying through the air. Hao took the brunt of the damage, using his own body to protect Tai and Xiu. When it was all over, and the dust had settled, Tai and Xiu lay on the ground under Hao's unconscious body.

"Well, well, what do we 'ave here?" said a voice that echoed from further back in the darkness.

Xui looked at Tai with big eyes and asked, "Who was that?"

"I don't know" said Tai. "But we need to get Master Hao out of here. I can feel his pulse, its barely there. I don't think he's breathing either."

Tai and Xui immediately rolled from under Hao, and spun their dao swords into their hands.

"Who's there...show yourself!" shouted Tai. Xui stood beside him searching for the source of the threat.

"I'm right in front of yer and yer can't even see me, must be the darkness. Tis a shame, I can see ye just fine."

Tai and Xui turned around in circles searching. Something was wrong, it wasn't just the echoes form the caves that were confusing them. Likewise, it wasn't the lack of light that hid whatever was speaking to them from their eyes.

"Last chance, show yourself or else" shouted Tai trying his best to sound more confident than scared.

Suddenly, a pair of black eyes opened right in front of Tai's face. He froze in place as the eyes in front of him seem to absorb the darkness around them, becoming something darker than black. It was like they cast a shadow on darkness itself. Everything else around him looked a muted grey color in comparison. The eyes transfixed him in their gaze, slowly ripping away his will to fight.

"Or else what?" whispered the voice from the darkness in Tai's ear

The sound of steel against steel awoke Tai from his hypnotized state. He looked beside him to see Xui blocking the large blade of a butterfly sword from piercing the side of his neck.

"What are you doing? Move!" Xui said as she pushed Tai out of the way and rolled backwards, letting the blade pass right over her head. She immediately got up and went on the offensive, swinging wildly in the darkness and looking for any sign of whoever had attacked Tai. Her technique was flawless. Her sword moved through the air as naturally as a fish in water, but in that darkness she might as well have been a child swinging a stick.

"Tai what are you doing?" Xui shouted when she noticed Tai still on the ground where she had pushed him.

"I... I can't... I can't move" replied Tai

Xui ran towards her brother. As soon as she reached her hand out to grab his, she jumped backwards. The butterfly's edge stopped just inches away from her chest. This time it came was close enough for her to see the hand that wielded it, but it quickly retreated back into the darkness. Another slash came from a different direction. Xui back flipped to dodge it again, noticing the subtle difference between this sword and the last one that attacked her.

"Twins" she thought "Someone's fighting us with twin blades. They must think themselves clever."

"I'm still waiting...or else what? What are you going to do wee fella?" said a voice coming from behind Tai. Its form started to take shape. In the darkness, Xui could see the outline of a person, a tall thin person.

Even though she could barely see his outline, there were two things she could see clearly. The all-encompassing darkness of his eyes, and the butterfly sword pressed firmly against her brother's neck.

"If I we're you I'd stop all that jumping around. Might be bad for your brother's health." He twisted the knife slightly against Tai's neck so that it was clear what he meant.

Xui simply nodded her head and lowered her sword to the ground.

"What do you want?" she asked

"First off the name's Cutter, Mad Cutter, they call me. Second, I'd like to say how ironic it is that you two kits think yourselves Shadows, but are as helpless as newborn babes in the dark. I come down here to set a few traps with a large amount o' gunpowder, just hoping someone would be stupid enough to set one off and let me 'ave some fun. And wouldn't you know it, someone did. Looks like your chaperon over there knocked himself out protecting you two. He might 'ave put up a better fight. Anyhow, that's the predicament we find ourselves in. So since I can't get a decent fight from you kits, you're going to answer a few questions for me."

"I'll answer whatever you want, just let my brother go." Xui pleaded.

Mad Cutter pushed Tai to his knees and pulled his head back as far as it could go. He gently stroked Tai's sun kissed neck with the flat of his blade.

"I'll let him go depending on how you answer me questions. Number one, do you know a dark skinned lass with long black hair, scar on her face, and eyes that turn red as the blood moon?"

Xui looked in her brother's eyes and thought carefully about her answer. "You must be talking about master Neith. She sounds like the person you're describing."

"Where is she?" asked Mad Cutter

"She's here..." Xui answered, confused by the question.

"I know she's here." said Mad Cutter. "I expected her to tag along with your little band. Where is she exactly? I owe her something."

"Why are you asking me?" Xui responded. "You should know where she is. She was captured by someone from Guiding Light and we came here to rescue her."

The blackness of Mad Cutter's eye stared back at Xui, deciding if he actually believed her. Her face said she was telling the truth.

"Curse that conniving Megas and his aide." Mad Cutter shouted. "They've had me prey here the whole time and kept her hidden from me."

Xui could tell by the change in his voice that he was upset. With his attention no longer solely focused on her, it might give her an opening. She readied her sword to charge in the second she felt he might cut Tai's throat.

Tai also recognized his chance to get away while Mad Cutter was distracted by his anger. With all his might, he forced both of his elbows into Mad Cutter's stomach. Spit shot out of Mad Cutters' mouth. His eyes bulged form their sockets like two odd shaped balloons. That blow created just enough space for Tai to drop down behind Mad Cutters' blade without slicing his neck open. Once he was free, Tai jumped up and ran to his sister's side. He didn't have to run far. As soon as he was on his feet, she was already halfway towards him. Her intent was clear. Tai immediately turned around with his sword raised, and joined his sister charging towards Mad Cutter. This was there chance. Mad Cutter was still bent over from the blow Tai gave him. His arms cupped his stomach and his head leaned over in pain. Now was the best time to attack him.

Tai match up with Xui's movements. Their coordination was perfect as always. Xui would go high, going for the back of Mad Cutter's exposed neck. Tai would go low, going for his ankles to limit his mobility. Just as Xui jumped in the air and Tai lowered his body, Mad Cutter lifted his head.

"Gotcha" he said as he brought both of his butterfly swords around directly at them.

Tai managed to dodge the blade headed towards him, but was caught by the back of Mad Cutters arm. His head made an ugly sound as it bounced off the ground like flat ball. Xui brought her sword up to block the one headed towards her, but the strength behind Mad Cutter's strike was something like she had never experienced before. Mad Cutter's blade plowed through her guard like it was wet paper. Her sword snapped in half right before her eyes. Xui felt a piercing sting as the tip of the butterfly sword pierced her chest and hit directly against her breastbone. It didn't pierce deeply, but the impact against her chest threw her backwards and made all the bones in her body throb with pain.

Mad Cutter wiped one of his blades against the side of his face as he laughed. "You kits really thought you had me didn't ya."

Tai lifted his head, to find his sister. Everything around him was still spinning.

"Xui, he's using his fighting spirit. Its unlike anything I've felt before. Something about it is dark...demonic. Something in him isn't human. I don't know how I know, but I can feel it. I can feel the hate and menace from his soul. That's the darkness that shows up in his eyes."

"Is that what this is called? Well next time I see this Neith lass, I'll give her a proper beating as thanks for unlocking me hidden potential. After that whooping I got last time by her hands, something changed in me. I never had me arse handed to me like that in me entire life, and I plan to return the favor."

Mad Cutter looked down toward Tai. "Quite a shame you'll never get the chance to see that day."

Xui screamed as she watched Mad Cutter thrust his blade through Tai's neck. He savored each and every labored breath that Tai tried to inhale with a sword piercing his throat, before savagely pulling his blade back out and watching the blood spill against the ground. Xui looked in her twin brother's eyes the whole time and watched the spark of life slowly fade from them.

Tai felt his lungs burning, desperate for air. No matter how hard he tried, he couldn't get a breath in. He stared back at Xui. For as long as he could remember, they were always together. All he ever wanted to do was protect her, but now she would be on her own. Tai gathered all of his remaining strength to lift his arm and toss his sword over to Xui. His lips struggled to mouth the word 'sister' as he pointed to his sword before his head dropped back into the dirt. By the time his head hit the ground, he was dead.

Xui screamed again as tears poured from her eyes. She looked at her brother's body, praying that this was all a dream, praying that she would wake up. But she knew it was not a dream, and she would never wake up from this grief that had gripped her soul.

Something in Xui snapped. Sadness, anger, fear, all of it blended together in one unnamable emotion. Her eyes turned a bright golden color. Everything in her vision was illuminated, as if sunlight shone directly from her eyes. She could see every detail of Mad Cutter, down to each greasy strand of red hair on his head and each fuzz of stubble on his face. Slowly, she pulled herself off the ground and got back on her feet. Stepping forward, she grabbed her brother's dao sword that he'd tossed in her direction right before he died. As soon as her hand touched the hilt, her spirit resonated with it. Somewhere in there she could still feel a part of Tai. Part of his spirit was still with her, and would help her survive.

Xui's fighting spirit suddenly exploded with power. The walls around them vibrated from her energy. Mad Cutter couldn't help but notice the change in her demeanor, as well as the sudden spike of aura around her.

"Well, well, looks like you got some more fight in you little lass. How about we test that out."

No sooner than the words had left his mouth, Xui was already running towards him. In an instant she was in front of Mad Cutter. All her movements up until that point had been like a calm stream, but now they were like a waterfall. Powerful, fast strikes rained down on Mad Cutter. A grin spread further across his face with each attack. His twin butterfly swords responded in kind to each and every attack that challenged him. Xui gave no ground, and responded to his counter attacks with her own. Her sudden increase in strength and speed made her a near even match for Mad Cutter. Both of their raw unfocused fighting spirits amplified their bodies as they battled one another for supremacy. However, one thing still in separated them and gave Mad Cutter a distinct advantage, experience.

Mad Cutter stepped in close to Xui. His tall thin frame towered over her as he threw bone crushing strikes, giving her as little room as possible to dodge. Cuts from Xui's sword started to cover Mad Cutter's body as she snuck in attacks between defensive dodges and blocks, but they didn't seem to slow him down. Mad Cutter had given up any attempts at defending himself. The darkness in him yearned for blood and didn't care how much damage his body took to quench its thirst. His tolerance for pain and punishment would prevail. He grabbed Xui by the hair while Xui's sword cut him deep cut across his forearm. With his other hand, he grabbed her sword arm and slammed it against the rocks surrounding them until she dropped her weapon.

Mad Cutter licked his lips as he held Xui by her hair. Xui tried punching and kicking with all the strength she had left, but one solid punch to her side knocked the wind from her lungs and rendered her helpless. Darkness started to return to her eyes as she struggled to keep up her fighting spirit.

Mad Cutter held her up, looking at her with bloodlust in eyes.

"Had I known this was in you, I would have killed your brother when we first started." he said

Xui showed no reaction to his words. She stared past Mad Cutter at her brother's body still lying on the ground. The thought of rejoining her brother in death crossed her mind. The more she thought about it the better it sounded. Xui looked into the black abyss of Mad Cutter's eyes. A quiet voice in her head whispered that she needed only to lie back and let it happen. "Why bother dodging, let him kill you. One quick moment of pain, then she would be reunited with Tai." the voices promised. They grew louder with their promises, beckoning her to give up.

Clear as day, Tai's voice resounded through her head like a ringing bell, clearing the fog in her mind. "Not yet" he said. "We will be together again, but not yet."

Illuminated vision returned to Xui's eyes as her fighting spirit came back like second wind. She could see every single bump and ridge on Mad Cutter's face staring back at her.

"Still got some more fight in yer? Just how much power does that wee body of yers have in it? In five or ten years, ye would have really been something. As ye are now though, ye still got no chance of killing me. Even with all yer resolve and strength, just what are yer going to do while I've got you by the—"

Xui saw everything happen in slow motion. Hao's boot came out of nowhere and smashed into the side of Mad Cutter's face with such force that she could hear bones snapping. She watched his face deform like putty. Her vision sped back up to real time as Mad Cutter's body went flying through the air and skidded across the ground before slamming to a stop against one of the tunnel walls.

Hao put his arm around Xui and made sure she was able to stand on her own before letting her go. Once he was sure she was ok, he turned around and stared at Tai's body. Xui could see tears drip down his face to the ground.

"How dare you lay a hand on my disciples." Hao said in a voice barely above a whisper.

In one smooth motion, quicker than Xui's eyes could follow, Hao unsheathed his sword and let his fighting spirit erupt from within. A wave of heat filled the tunnel. Small puddles of water quickly turned to steam. Rocks near Hao started to glow in shades of bright red and orange. Xui saw Hao's eyes glowing an even brighter golden color than her own. It brought back the memory of the time her and Tai we're following Hao through the village where he was born. There everyone referred to him as the Golden Phoenix. Hao said it was just some nickname they made up for him, but now she could see exactly where it came from. Even more surprising was that she didn't feel any hotter than she would on a nice summer day. Xui nearly burned herself trying to touch one of the glowing red rocks to make sure what she was seeing wasn't an illusion. Had she taken one look at Mad Cutter first, she would have known the heat radiating from Hao was no mere illusion. Patches of red boils began to cover Mad Cutter's skin. Drops of blood that dripped from his cuts began to boil as soon as they hit the ground.

Hao looked unwilling to grant even an ounce of mercy to Mad Cutter. His spirit raged as the heat only intensified. Xui could hear Mad Cutter's skin sizzle as he put his hand on the ground to get back up. The hot air must have burned his lungs as he coughed and struggled to speak.

"You got the drop on me, that you did. A shame I can't stay and finish this one out, but I think it's time I take me leave. I don't very much like my odds against you two right now."

"You're not going anywhere" Hao responded.

"I beg to differ" said Mad Cutter as he pulled a flare from his back pocket. It lit up with barely any effort in the already scorching heat. Mad Cutter dropped the flare beside him, igniting a small trail of gunpowder that seem to go no further than the wall beside him.

Another deafening explosion ripped through the tunnel, sending a rush of cool wet air with it. Shards of rocks skipped across the ground as the entire tunnel started to shake. Hao immediately knew what was happening. He rushed towards Mad Cutter, intending to finish him off quickly, but large slabs of stone started to fall from the ceiling directly in between them.

"Glad I kept some barrels 'o powder stored in reserve. I'll be going this way now." said Mad Cutter as he made his way towards the new opening made by the explosion. "You can either try and come after me, and risked getting you and the one disciple you have left crushed by the very stones above yer heads. Or you make it out of here alive the way you came. Choice is yours laddie."

Hao looked at Mad Cutter with rage still in his eyes.

"Don't think you've escaped, you've just made it to the top of a short list of people who'll die on the spot when I catch them."

"Come and get me laddie. I'll be waiting." shouted Mad Cutter as he took off through the opening.

Hao wasted no time scooping up Xui over his shoulder and running towards the part of the tunnel they entered from.

"Tai! We must get Tai!" Xui shouted.

"There's no time!" Hao shouted back.

Hao dove through the threshold leading back to the smaller tunnel just as the ceiling fully caved in. Xui silently said farewell to her brother as the rocks and dirt falling from the ceiling buried his body forever.

CHAPTER 36

Saint Georges could tell he'd made it into the heart of Guiding Light's base. The floors were no longer roughly cut stone and dirt, but smooth tile. Intricate symbols were carved along large stretches of the walls. By the look of them, the carvings were centuries old. Most likely from whatever ancient civilization originally constructed these tunnels. There were simple looking tables and chairs sprawled around and doors that separated the space into different rooms. As he expected, he was the first from the assault team to make this deep into the base. Although, what did surprise him was lack of resistance he encountered on his way here. After the shock of seeing Bulo alive, and splitting up from the others, he hadn't seen another person. That just meant he had been lucky so far.

He could sense the fighting spirits of his comrades fluctuating. That could only mean they we're fighting against Guiding Light's forces. Normally he would want to rush back and assist whoever was fighting, but the network of tunnels was like a maze. The battle would long be finished by the time he could get there. However, even if he could get to the others he still wouldn't have gone. The masters on the assault team we're some of the most capable people in Fratello della Spada. He had no doubts that they would be able to handle whatever came their way.

Saint Georges rounded another corner into a short hallway that looked to be a dead end. Thick electrical lines secured by simple metal clasps ran along the walls and broke off into different rooms. Holes in the walls and space in between the doors gave a glimpse into the rooms along the hall. Several computers, printers, and other electronic equipment were hooked up to the electrical lines through series of smaller wires. It was clear that someone went through a lot of trouble to set up a power system for all of the devices down there. One room in particular caught his attention. It was decorated with lavish furniture. A plush chair, gilded with gold and decorated with ivory and satin, sat in the center of the room facing the door. Exotic furs covered the floor, surrounding a small pit in the ground that contained remnants of firewood and burned paper. Saint Georges took his time going over each detail of the room, looking for any clue that might give him guidance on where to go next.

"Found what you're looking for in there, or just enjoying the view?" said a voice behind Saint Georges

Without the slightest hesitation, Saint Gorges drew his rapier and turned around before the last letter of the last word left the lips of the man behind him. The air whistled from the speed of his draw. He wasn't sure who was behind him, but whoever it was wasn't a friend. That automatically made them his enemy. The orders of his mission quickly flashed through his mind. He would execute Objective Two without prejudice. With one powerful thrust he planned to run through whoever was behind him.

A sharp ringing sound brought the two men face to face. The entire body of the man that stood in front of him was covered in a mixture of military style body armor and metal plates made of an odd looking black fabric. Even thicker plates covered the joints around his knees in elbows serving as both a weapon for attacking and a solid defense of the body's weak points. Saint Georges looked down to see a hand wrapped up to the wrist in the same strange black fabric, gripping his rapier by the blade without the slightest fear of being cut. His gaze slowly came back up to meet the eyes of the man standing in front of him.

"Megas" he said with a scowl on his face that could crack stone.

"So you recognize me. I expected as much" said Megas as he stared back at Saint Georges. He could feel Saint Georges trying to pull his sword away from his grasp, but the fabric on his hands made his grip like a fish hook. The more he tried to pull away the better hold Megas had on it. He would let of his sword when he was good and ready, but first he needed to let him know just how excited he was to see him.

"However, I recognize you too. You're one of the faces I can never forget."

That statement caused Saint Georges to raise an eyebrow.

"You were there that day." Megas continued. "That day in Tralone. Even through all the dust and sand blowing around in the desert I could see your face. You were a part of the legion that slaughtered my Anya and her people."

Saint Georges looked even more confused now. He wondered how anyone could have this much strength to hold on to his rapier by the blade. It had to be something with the black fabric that wrapped around his arm. The ringing sound his sword made on contact with it made it sound like a dense metal, but the way it moved and conformed to his hand was like fabric.

"I never thought this day would come. Up until now, I hoped that you all died in the blast back at the Citadel. But now that I see you in front of me… Nothing compares to the feeling of being able to kill you myself!"

Megas let out a deep throaty roar as he threw a punch with his other hand covered in the same metallic fabric. Saint Georges took the punch directly to his jaw, sending him flying. He managed to hold on to his sword until Megas finally let it go. Saint Georges crashed into the gold and ivory chair in the middle of the room, smashing it to pieces.

The force of the blow got his blood running. Saint Georges got back up and rolled his head around to stretch his neck. He casually threw one arm above his head, followed by the other.

"Been a while since I felt a punch like that." He said while working his jaw to make sure it was still attached. "At first I was going to ask you where Bulo is hiding. I still have much to say to him. But it seems you have your own vendetta with me. Rose colored glasses of nostalgia must be clouding your memory because you have your facts wrong. Nobody on the battle field that day was innocent."

"Oh, I'm quite clear on my facts." Megas said. "I saw it firsthand with my own eyes. I saw you slaughter innocent person after person. Men came that you in waves all fell by your sword. I will avenge them here today!"

Megas moved in close to Saint Georges and took a boxer's stance. He threw lightning quick jab after jab, mixing in devastating hooks that could kill anyone unlucky enough to be on the receiving end of them. However, despite all his fighting prowess and his destructive strength, each of his punches connected with nothing but air. Saint Georges effortlessly weaved between each blow, expertly judging his distance and timing so that every strike against him was just a fraction too late or a millimeter too far.

"You might have been able to hit me while you held my sword, but that won't happen again while I'm free to move. The gap in our speed is overwhelmingly in my favor." said Saint Georges.

His arm became a blur as Saint Georges made an 's' shaped slash across Megas' chest before he could even realize what happened. But instead of falling to the ground, Megas continued charging at him. Not even a scratch was left on him. His armor had completely withstood being cut by Saint Georges blade.

"You must be admiring my body armor." Megas said sarcastically. "It was a special order, just for you Shadows. This black lightweight material was originally intended to be used on vehicles. Enabling lightweight jeeps to withstand heavy artillery and mines like tanks. But I found another purpose for it more suited to my needs. Try as much as you want! No matter how hard you strike me, you'll never get through this."

Saint Georges visually inspected his sword to check for damage before turning back towards Megas.

"First you hide down here in these tunnels, and now you hide behind some kind of special armor. What's the matter, afraid to fight me like a man?"

"You can't blame an old soldier for finding a few advantages where he can. Besides, I'll use every method and resource at my disposal to make sure you don't leave here alive. I owe Anya that much." Megas shouted

Saint Georges barely entertained Megas' response.

"All that armor still won't protect you." he said

Megas motioned his hands, beckoning Saint Georges to come at him. In a flash Saint Georges was behind him. His arm in a twisted position that resulted in the tip of his blade angled down at Megas' neck. Megas barely had time to react. He grabbed for Saint Georges' rapier and missed, but managed to shift his shoulder so that he wasn't stabbed through the small gap in his armor by his neck. Before he had any time to compose himself, another attack from Saint Georges targeted the top of his left knee. Megas jumped back narrowly avoiding it, only for him to feel a sharp stabbing pain in his right knee. He ignored the pain, using all his concertation to focus on Saint Georges' next attack.

"Going for the gaps in my armor, typical. You used the same kind of tricks back then too. I can already see through your plan." Megas said while he rapidly took several steps backwards to set up a defensive stance.

"Shoulder again" he thought "That's where he'll attack next"

He could see Saint Georges coming towards him. All he had to do was time his dodge right and counter immediately after. With the precision of a surgeon, Megas timed his dodge perfectly. He instantly went on the offensive, putting all his force behind a punch into Saint Georges stomach. He could feel the fabric of Saint Georges' clothes graze his gloves before his opposite shoulder burst with stabbing pain stealing the strength behind his punch before it reached its intended target. Trickles of blood ran down his right leg and arm under his armor. Something was wrong. It was as if Saint Georges' blade would disappear and reappear in a different location. But that was impossible, he had to understand exactly what was going on. Recollection slammed into his mind of what he was seeing.

"So this is the famous Multipoint style of Saint Georges. I should have guessed from the beginning." Megas said through a grin while he held his shoulder waiting for the pain to subside.

"Multipoint? There you go getting your facts wrong again." Saint Georges replied "All I've been using are simple disengages. Had I used multipoint you'd be dead already. As it stands now I just want to immobilize you so you can listen to me. I feel that you should know the truth about Tralone before you die."

Megas clenched his fists together. His face turned crimson as his eyes bulged from his head.

"I know the truth!" he screamed "I will not let you spout lies about Anya and her legacy in front of me. I'll kill you where you stand right now even if it costs me my life!"

Saint Georges whipped his dreads from in front of his eyes.

"Suit yourself."

Megas charged at Saint Georges. He could see the clean unbroken white glow in Saint Georges' eyes as his dreads swung past them. Using the weight of his entire body, Megas tackled Saint Georges through the frail wooden door into the hallway. The door splintered into wooden scraps from the intensity. Pieces slid in every direction across the concrete floor. Megas could feel Saint Georges body under him. The power of his legs propelled both of them to the ground. He raised his arms above his head, preparing to bash Saint Georges' head in against the smooth gray concrete. But there was no soft feeling of flesh as his fists made contact. No crack of bone against his knuckles, no fresh wet blood staining fingers. His fist landed flat against the floor.

Saint Georges stood behind him, looking down at him pounding against the ground.

"Are you done?" he asked

Megas jumped up and lunged at him, swinging wildly.

"I'll kill you!"

Saint Georges took his time leading Megas towards him as he easily moved between his punches. Letting him get close, before quickly moved out of reach again. The hallway was narrow. There was barely any room to maneuver, especially with Megas' imposing body blocking off most of it. Yet Saint Georges had no trouble effortlessly dodging. It was as he said earlier, the gap in their speed was overwhelming. It had been several minutes and Megas' raged still burned, but his strength was waning. Each strike was slower than the last as he struggled to moves his arms. Large splotches of blood covered the areas by his shoulder and knee where he'd been stabbed.

Megas could tell Saint Georges wasn't even trying. He was toying with him as if he were a child trying to fight against the wind. From the beginning, he knew this was a fight he couldn't win directly. The only thing in his favor was his opponent's confidence. Saint Georges was taking his time, proving his superiority over him. That would prove to be a grave mistake. As angry as Megas actually was, his true plan was always at the forefront of his mind.

"Just a little bit further" he thought. "Continue leading me exactly to where I want you to go."

When Saint Georges reached the midpoint of the hallway, Megas pulled out a small remote that he had tucked in his belt. He calmly looked Saint Georges in his eyes.

"This is for Anya."

A shockwave of air rushed through the hall from the explosion. Hundreds of pieces of shrapnel tore through both sides of the walls in a two-foot section of the hallway. Megas had hidden dozens of claymore mines behind the walls. Whatever was between them would be annihilated. As fast as Saint Georges was, even he couldn't escape from the explosion of shrapnel surrounding him.

"You know there's a limit to how fast a person can be" said Saint Georges. "No matter how strong your muscles are or how light your body is, there's a limit to how fast the human body can move."

Megas could barely hear him. His words sounded like a garbled mash of blended sounds. It was a wonder that he could even speak. Any second he expected him to collapse into bright red puddle of his own blood.

"However, true speed is not only determined by how fast something is moving, but how fast you perceive it to be moving."

Megas labored for each breathe wondering when Saint Georges would fall. He could barely hear anything he said and his vision was starting to blur.

"The secret to a speed that surpasses human limitations is to change your opponent's perception. My fighting spirit not only augments the muscles in my body to make me faster, but changes the perception of those around me. You could think of it as a simple version of mind control, a very simple version since I can only influence your perception of two things, time and distance."

Megas dropped to his knees. He could barely breathe. It felt like he was drowning with each passing second. His vision started to turn red as his eyes filled with blood. It was all starting to come together now. He turned his head to see the holes in the walls from the shrapnel before falling forward on his face. Blood gurgled from his mouth as it filled his lungs. Despite all the chunks of metal logged in his body, he barely felt any pain. For all his planning, all his strategizing, never did he think he'd be done in by his own trap.

"I will be with you soon Anya" whispered Megas

Saint Georges squatted down next to Megas.

"You're Anya was no saint. None of us on that battlefield were. I'm certainly no hero. We each fought for our own ideals. They were being supplied weapons from a neighboring country, and were planning a coup. This girl Anya and her clan wanted to overthrow the government of Tralone. When the government found out about this they knew that using their own army to stamp out a group of rebels would only embolden others to take up their cause. So instead, they hired people to take care of it for them. It was a war, plain and simple. Neither side would back down. I killed many people during that time, and they all would have killed me had they gotten the chance. I'm not proud of what I did, but I'm not ashamed either. Despite whatever you think of me, I figured you should know the truth before you died."

By the time Saint Georges had finished speaking Megas was dead. A large pool of blood was growing beneath him. Saint Georges hoped he was alive long enough to hear what he had to say. He thought it important for a man to know truth before he died.

Saint Georges stood up and with one swift motion shook the blood from his blade. He slid his rapier back into its scabbard until the hilt rested firmly at his side.

"Guess I should move on and see what else I can find. With the others already engaging the enemy, it shouldn't be long now. Objective Two is nearly complete."

CHAPTER 37

Nemo snuck around another corner using the dim light from his torch, only to find another dark hallway. He had been following a path of unlit torches, and lighting them as he passed by to mark which way he came. Ever since he found the first torch hanging against a wall, he also had been seeing strange carvings and writings along the paths he wandered through. The carvings in the wall probably gave directions, but he had no way of deciphering what they meant. However, if someone bothered to hang torches this deep into the tunnels they must lead to something important. So, he continued to follow them.

He could barely feel the fighting spirit of the others anymore. Either he was too far away, or the battles had concluded already. Nemo wondered if everyone was ok. As much as he hoped everyone was alive and well, he couldn't help but have fearful thoughts jumping to the forefront of his mind. Thoughts of who might dying right this moment, or who might be dead already. He quickly focused his mind, now wasn't the time to let his fear influence his actions. He had to believe in the masters of Fratello della Spada. Absolon, Hao, Atsuko, and Saint Georges, there was no way they would lose after all that had happened. This wasn't a mere job, this was personal.

Barely audible sounds arrested Nemo's attention. He couldn't immediately tell what they were, but something about them was familiar to him. His gut told him to go the opposite way, but a thought occurred to him. What if the sound was some kind of signal from Neith? He couldn't take the chance of missing any signal from her, no matter how small, so he had to follow it. At first, the tunnels made tracking the sound nearly impossible. The echoes lead him down the direction of dead ends and around in circles before he could isolate the small differences between the source and its echoes. It gradually became louder and easier to follow as Nemo got closer. Surprisingly, following the sound was leading him down the same paths where the torches were hung. Once Nemo realized this he picked up the pace, barely stopping to light torches anymore except at key turns.

When he reached the dark opening of a small cave, he knew he was in the right place. The sound seemed to bellow from the opening. Nemo peeked his head in, using the light from the torch to see, but it was too dim to see all the way to the back of the room. He took a few more steps in, cautiously looking around for any sign of Neith. When he saw the bare foot of a dried corpse his mind immediately thought the worst. His heart skipped a beat as his eyes followed the foot up to see the rest of the body still chained against the stone behind it. Relief washed over him once he realized that it wasn't Neith's body. He felt silly for even thinking it could be her. It was too old. For a body to be this decomposed it would have been there for months. The scraps of military uniform left on the body were unlike anything he'd ever seen Neith wear, and the few features he could still make out looked distinctly male. Nemo said a quick prayer as he stood over the body, when another thought about the corpse in front of him came crashing through his mind. What killed him?

A sudden deep growl sent Nemo running back out the room. He ran back to where the tunnel curved around and hid behind a stretch of wall, confident that something vicious would be chasing after him. Nemo continued to wait in his hiding spot, peeking around the corner every few seconds, but nothing was there. No ghosts or vicious beasts were coming after him. The only sounds he heard were the quiet flicker of the flames from his torch and his own loud breathing.

Nemo tried to calm down. When he finally convinced himself that it must have been his imagination, he walked back into the cave. As soon as he was a couple steps in, Nemo heard the same growling sound right beside him. This time instead of running, his body froze. He immediately turned to his right, his hand gripped the hilt of his sword ready to fight for his life. In the farthest corner of the cave his eyes focused in the dim light to see Neith lying against the wall with her arms above her head, her knees curled up to her chest, and her mouth wide open bellowing the loudest snoring he'd ever heard.

Words couldn't express the joy Nemo felt seeing Neith again. It was as if all the pain and heartache of the past couple days melted away by just knowing she was alive. That joy was swiftly tempered when he moved close enough to look at her injuries. The skin around her wrists was gone from constantly rubbing against the iron shackles. Open sores trickled blood down her arms as they hung down from the chains like lifeless extensions of her body. Dark bruises and jagged lines of dried blood covered the rest of her skin, but none of that compared the horrid shape of her right hand. Her fingertips were black and swollen. Each finger was contorted into a position that assured him they were all broken. It must have been torture for her to even sleep in her condition.

"Wake up, Neith. I'm getting you out of here." Nemo said while he gently shook her.

Neith barely moved from the gentle rocking. He shook her again, this time forcefully.

"Neith wake up!"

"What…what's going on? Nemo, how did you get here?" Neith whispered in a dry, raspy voice.

"I'll explain later, right now we have to get you out of here." Replied Nemo

Neith moved her arms until the chains on her shackles were tight.

"You think I've just been sitting here because I enjoy the scenery?" she joked.

Nemo point to the corpse behind him. "Well I thought you might be enjoying the company of your new friend over there."

Neith didn't have to look to know what Nemo was pointing at. "I'm afraid he's not much of a talker. Now if you'd be so kind, can you tell me what you plan on doing to get me out of here? I know you couldn't have come all this way without a plan. Who let you come here by yourself anyway? Where are the others. Nemo don't tell me you came to a place this dangerous by your…"

Nemo reached into the front pocket on his jacket. "Be quiet. You'll have plenty of time to scold me when we get out of here. Besides I didn't come by myself. Arthur sent Saint Georges, Hao, Absolon, and Atsuko with me. Tommy, Xai, and Tai also came to help."

Nemo could see the irritation on Neith's face when he mentioned Atsuko, but he cut her off before she had a chance say anything else.

"I think I have a way to get you out. I just hope this works because I didn't come with a backup plan."

Nemo pulled out the A.L.P. tool Neith had given him on their second job. He had no idea if it would work on a lock as old as the ones the held Neith, but it was the only plan he could come up with.

"Hold still" he said as he held the A.L.P against the iron collar of her shackles. The gears inside the tool whirred back and forth, minute after minute, without any sign of progress on opening the lock. Fifteen minutes had passed when Nemo was starting to doubt his plan. He had managed to find Neith with hardly anything to go on. He'd made it all this way through Guiding Light's base, and now after all his effort he was being thwarted by an old iron lock.

"Just open already you stupid lock!" Nemo screamed

The A.L.P. tool went quiet and popped the first shackle open freeing Neith's arm. Her arm immediately fell to the floor, landing hard against the stone. She could barely feel her arms after having them trapped above her head for so long. It would feel good to finally be able to put them down, once she regained feeling in them.

Nemo quickly worked on the other lock with the A.L.P. tool and had it open in half the time it took for the first one. He grabbed Neith's other arm and gently lowered to the ground this time. When both of her arms were finally free, Nemo crouched under her armpit and wrapped his arms around her waist to help her up.

"How are you feeling? Can you stand?" Nemo asked

"I'll manage" replied Neith.

Nemo wasn't buying her typical answer. He kept his arms around her until he was sure the strength in her legs had returned. All of her injuries looked manageable, except for the fingers on her right hand, they needed a doctor right away. Nemo looked back up at Neith's face when he realized she had caught him staring at her hand.

"Alright let's get out of here. The others will meet us outside on the way back. I doubt they'll have any trouble catching up at the pace we're moving."

"Not without my sword." Neith responded. "I bet that bastard Bulo hid it somewhere in here. I'll have to find him and apply some 'aggressive' persuasion techniques until he tells me where it is."

"You've got to be kidding me! You can barely stand and you still want to try and fight. No way, we're getting out of here now." said Nemo

Neith stopped walking and looked him dead in his eyes. "That sword has been in my family for generations. I'd sooner lose an arm than leave it behind."

Nemo saw the determination in her eyes and knew there was no changing her mind.

"Fine. We'll find your sword, but we'll do it without confronting anyone. As soon as we get it, we leave. Deal?"

"Deal" replied Neith.

Nemo let Neith lead the way as they walked. He didn't know if it was some kind of sixth sense, but she seemed to be completely sure of the direction she was going. Each time he started down a different path she would correct him saying,

"I feel like it's this way."

Nemo simply nodded and followed her lead. Eventually the paths started to look familiar to him. He could see the glow from the torches he lit pointing out the way he came.

"Neith, are you sure you don't remember being brought down here." Nemo asked

"No, I'm seeing all of this from the first time" said Neith. "I can't explain how I know where to go, but it's like a kind of intuition. I always know where my weapon is."

It wasn't long before they reached a large door that looked out of place.

"This is the place. My sword is in here." said Neith. Nemo slowly opened it to peek inside, trying not to make any sound. The room was dark but he could see lights hanging from the ceiling. Electrical lines ran along the ceiling and around the walls before running through the floor to another room. Unlike the other areas they had walked through, the floor was paved with smooth tile. Ornate pillars, covered in the same strange symbol Nemo had seem in the tunnels, were carved into the stone walls. In the middle of the room sat a long, master crafted oak table, taking up the majority of the space inside. Someone had clearly put a lot of work into decorating this room. On top of the table Nemo spotted Neith's sword. There was no mistaking that curved blade that he had seem nearly every day for the past few months. All he needed to do was walk in and grab it.

Nemo motioned to Neith to stay where she was while he went inside. He slowly stepped towards the table, taking his time to be as quiet as possible. When he reached the table, he slid his hand along its edge, admiring its smooth glossy finish. There was hardly a scratch on it. He couldn't imagine how someone was able to move it down there while keeping it in such pristine condition.

He was mere inches away from grabbing Neith's scimitar and running out the room when Neith burst through the door behind him. He quickly turned to see her screaming something in his direction, but he couldn't hear her. Her mouth was clearly moving, but all Nemo could hear was loud buzzing sound growing louder in his ears. Before he knew what happened, he was on the ground. His face flat against the floor. Nemo looked up from the floor to see clouds of dust floating in the air. The table he had just been admiring was cut clean in two right in front of him. Another step and his head would have been able to see his legs from a completely new angle on the floor.

Light from the ceiling flooded the room showing the true extent of the damage. A deep crevice followed across the floor, through where the table had been cut, and continued a good distance up the opposite wall.

"Now how'd you manage to dodge that? Men that have been fighting longer than you've been alive have died by my draw. Yet somehow you still live." Bulo said as he walked through a cloud of dust concealing the new entrance into the room.

Nemo looked back by his foot and saw it was caught on the edge of the table leg. He had tripped right as he was reaching for Neith's sword. For once, his clumsiness had saved his life.

Bulo slid his short blade back into its sheathe. "No matter, you'll die soon enough."

Bulo saw Neith leaning against the wall near the door. A wide smile crossed his face. "Now I know that isn't my Neith roaming around untethered. After all of my gracious hospitality. I could have killed you, or given you to that psychopath Mad Cutter. You know he has some kind of creepy obsession with you after you almost beat him to death. But I didn't do any of that, and this is how my kindness is repaid. Well, maybe this time I'll chain you back up in that cave and invite some of the guys down there to see you. I'm sure after some time with them you'll come to appreciate how kind I am. Then when you're begging for it to all end I'll finish what we started when I was expelled from the Shadows."

Bulo paused to savor the emotion of Neith's face.

"Of course, I'll have to kill all of your comrades and your little disciple first. The fighters my brother recruited are probably finishing them off as we speak."

As if it were a natural instinct, Nemo rolled over, drew his sword and used it to push himself forward. He slid for Neith's sword that had fallen to the floor. With a swift kick backwards, he kicked it over to her before standing to his feet.

"Shut up" Nemo said through gritted teeth.

Bulo's fingers drummed the hilt of his sword. His hand came up to his chest in surprise.

"Boy, were you addressing me with that tone?"

"You're the one responsible for all of this" said Nemo.

Bulo chuckled at the threatening tone coming from Nemo.

"I know, are you not impressed?"

Nemo gripped the hilt of his sword so hard his hands were starting to blister. His jaw pressed together so hard he had to try and keep his teeth from grinding together.

"All this time Neith was looking to avenge you. She cried for you. She put her life in danger to find out who killed you, even after you tried to kill her."

Neith's mouth dropped open. She had never told Nemo about her and Bulo's fight.

"I'm going to kill you so you can never hurt her, or anyone else again." Nemo screamed

Bulo almost laughed. It would have been funny had he not seen just how serious Nemo was.

"Don't speak about things you have no power to accomplish."

Nemo shrouded himself with his fighting spirit and ran towards Bulo. He ran faster than he'd ever run before, jumped into the air, and put all of his power into swinging his sword down on top of Bulo's head.

"Pitiful" Bulo whispered under his breathe.

Before Nemo's strike could connect, Bulo punched him directly in the chest sending him flying back into what was left of the table behind him. It was so quick Nemo could barely see it.

"You were so open I couldn't help myself. All that talk about killing me, and this is what you come at me with. You'd have trouble killing a blind man with your basic attacks and rudimentary fighting style."

"Why don't you try telling me that." Neith whispered behind Bulo.

Her left hand was functional enough to hold her sword, and her right hand dragged her sheathe along the ground behind her. In one fast movement, she slashed Bulo clear across his torso. All her energy had gone to attacking him in order to make the most of the opening Nemo provided. She didn't even try to guard herself when a strong punch hit her in the side of the head. Neith dropped to the ground, hard.

"Almost darling"

Bulo said as he ripped the cut fabric of his shirt off. A thin scratch across his stomach was the only sign that Neith's attack had actually hit him.

"You know you always were a little more predictable when attacking with your off hand. Had you been at full strength, you probably would have got me. However, in the state you're in now you're just a little too slow."

"I told you to leave Neith alone!" Nemo screamed directly in front of Bulo.

His blade crackled with electricity as it whistled through the air towards Bulo. All he needed to do was make contact and Bulo would be paralyzed for at least the next few minutes giving them time to escape. Faster than he could see, Bulo drew his shaska sending a powerful wave of air to block Nemo's blade. Nemo pushed with all his strength to break through the thick wall of air blocking him, but the wind seemed to get stronger the more he pushed against it. Soon he was struggling just to hold on to his sword as the air rushed around it. Directly beside him the ground began to crack open from the force of the air rushing by. Finally, after a few seconds it subsided. Nemo regained control of his sword just in time to save himself form a flurry of kicks and punches from Bulo. The final blow knocked the wind from him and sent rolling him back across the room again.

Bulo held his arm out relishing the impact from the last blow against Nemo's chest. He quickly looked out the corner of his eye to see if Neith was still on the ground. As he expected, she was gone. Probably hiding somewhere waiting for another opening.

"Who would have thought I'd be having even the slightest bit of trouble with child and an injured woman. Dealing with both of you at the same time is actually going to take some work. Neith have you filled the boy in on my abilities or did you just leave it to him to find out? Clearly you told him about our history. I wonder what other personal secrets about me you've divulged?"

No one responded to Bulo's comments. The room was nearly silent as Nemo struggled to catch his breath and Neith hid in the shadows.

"Not going to tell me?" Bulo asked again, hoping Neith would make a move. "Guess I'll have to ask the boy myself. So much for granting him a quick death."

Nemo pushed himself across the ground on his back with his feet. He had managed to protect his vital organs but took the brunt of the hits in his face. He could feel his left eye forcing itself closed as it swelled up diminishing his vision. He could see flashes of Neith as she moved around the room, using the random debris for cover. Even he could tell she was moving slower than normal. Based on the way she was when he found her, he was surprised she was moving at all.

Nemo struggled back to his feet, using his sword to balance himself. He hadn't been able to put one scratch on Bulo, even though he was doing most of his fighting bared handed. He seemed to only draw his shaska to unleash a sharp wind to attack or defend himself, and immediately after that he'd re-sheathe it. That had to be something specific to his fighting style. His eyes would briefly glow silver every time he drew his sword, before quickly returning to normal. He clearly had a specialized style of using his fighting spirit exclusively to amplify his draw.

Nemo thought about his next move. If he couldn't damage Bulo himself, he would have to settle for making another opening for Neith. Nemo wiped the blood dripping from the side of his mouth.

"No matter how many times you hit me, a coward like you could never beat me. There's no way I'd ever lose to a coward that turned his back on Fratello della Spada."

For the first time Bulo looked Nemo directly in the eye.

"That's where you're wrong boy. I didn't turn my back on the Shadows, they turned their back on me. Allow me to impart this piece of wisdom to you. Fratello della Spada is only loyal to those who blindly follow their ideology. Start asking questions and you'll start to find out how fast your so called friends can turn to enemies."

Nemo stared at Bulo, not really understanding what he was talking about.

"Don't bother thinking too hard about it. It's not like you'll live to understand the meaning behind my words. Goodbye boy."

Bulo grabbed the hilt of his sword and prepared to draw it. Nemo knew another one of those strong winds would be coming his way. He also knew he wouldn't be able to dodge this one.

"You talk too much." Neith said as she dropped down from the ceiling sword first. Even Nemo hadn't seen how she made it up there. Blood splashed across the walls of the room. With one cut, it was over.

CHAPTER 38

He couldn't hear her. All he could hear was a steady buzzing sound. But he could see her face. He could see her look directly at him with a faced filled with worry and fear. He could see dust and rocks blown away as the wind cleared a path towards him. What was barely a second felt agonizingly long as he watched it creeping closer to him. Then he felt it hit him.

"Nemooooo!!!!!" Neith shouted

"I told you that you we're too slow." Bulo said as he grabbed her leg and threw her to the ground. Her blade left a deep gash down is chest. His blood barely stained his crimson shirt that was now cut wide open. But that wasn't enough stop him from drawing his sword and sending an attack towards Nemo.

Bulo grabbed Neith by the back of the neck and forced her head against the floor. With the full weight of his large body, he crushed her wrist under his boot until she let go of her sword. Neith slapped the ground with her broken right hand as she screamed. Those screams soon turned into muffled sobs against the ground. Bulo pulled her head up from the dirt just enough so she could see. Tears streamed down her face.

"Look at him" he commanded. "Look at what you caused. Had you told that boy to run away from here and leave you to me he'd still be alive right now. What a foolish thing. Knowing how weak he was and still coming here to try and save you. Brave, but very foolish."

"I'll kill you, I swear I will." Neith whispered through her sobs loud enough so Bulo could here.

"Maybe, but not in the state you're in now. Once I have you chained back up, Megas and I will have ample time to hunt down the rest of the Shadows. Whoever survived the blast from the Citadel won't consider themselves lucky for long. Fratello della Spada will fall by our hands.

Nemo could barely stay conscious. His vision was fuzzy, but somehow his eyes managed to stay open. He saw Neith being held by her neck and her face pressed against the ground. Then he saw her staring at him. There was sadness in those eyes, but he quickly lost sight of them as darkness swallowed him. He was cold. It started in his fingers, but soon his whole body was cold. His face felt a warm liquid flowing against it. It was the only comfort he had now. Everything in him said to relax and let go. As soon as he let go it would be over, no more cold, no more pain. Events from his life rolled through his mind like a highlight reel. The first time he met Neith in that alley, being questioned by Arthur and his team, the first time he stepped foot in the pit for the Trials. Janus, Neith, CJ, Tai, Xui, Jen, all the people he'd met since joining Fratello della Spada. All the people that made an impact on his life. He was letting them all down, by letting go. Yet, it still called out to him. The quiet voice inside his head begged him to let it all go, leave it all behind and rest. He had to make a choice.

Blue light engulfed his eyes. Nemo made his choice. He reached deep inside himself and chose to use whatever strength he had left to fight for those the people he cared about. Everything that didn't help him accomplish that goal he let go, just like the time on the rooftop. With one hand, he touched his chest and let electricity flow from his hands through his body. The surface of his skin burned and blistered, but he didn't stop until his hand made it all the way across his torso to stop the bleeding. It would hold for as long as he needed it too. Any notion of survival was thrown away with the rest of himself. His only purpose was to eliminate the threat to those he cared about. With a speed that rivaled Saint Georges, Nemo moved his body from the ground, took one step to adjust his momentum, and swung his sword in a smooth arc straight at Bulo's neck.

Bulo's eyes went wide in shock. Just a second ago the boy was on the ground, seconds away from death. Yet in mere milliseconds he was already up and in his face. Bulo dropped Neith's neck from his hands and instinctively drew his sword to slow Nemo's attack. A vicious, wild wind erupted from his blade, slowing Nemo's sword just enough for Bulo to dodge it. He immediately moved away from Nemo, putting some space between them. Sweat dripped down his face. It was too close of a call, even for him. Bulo return his sword to his sheathe as he composed himself.

"I don't know what happened to you boy, but you should know I had the fastest draw of all the Shadows. That was a good try, really good, but as long as I'm able to draw my sword from its sheathe you can't touch me. Now I advise you to take whatever energy you've mustered up and run while you still can."

Nemo had no more words for Bulo. It no longer mattered what he said, he was a threat to those Nemo cared about. That was all that mattered. Nemo raised his sword in the air, pointing it up towards the ceiling. The air in the room suddenly felt stiff as it became charged with energy. An odd quiet settled over Neith and Bulo. Neither knew what to expect next. Without warning lightning streaked down and connected to Bulo's shoulder running down his body. The edges of his torn shirt burst into flames. His fingers twitched wildly from the current overwhelming his body. Neith could see his eyes starting to roll back into his head.

Nemo dropped the point of his sword to the floor, cutting off the lighting as abruptly as it started. As soon as the lightning ceased, Bulo's body collapsed to the ground. Smoke rose from his charred extremities and still burning clothes.

"Is he dead?" Neith shouted across to Nemo, not entirely sure he could still hear her.

Nemo stood there staring at Bulo's body. Vivid blue light still coursed through his eyes. Blood dripped down his arm. The wound across his chest that he'd burned closed was starting to reopen. Nemo relaxed his grip on his sword.

Slowly, he tried to bring himself back from the edge of madness. The next thing he knew he was on the floor. His legs could no longer keep him standing. Every muscle in his body throbbed in pain. He had pushed himself far beyond his physical limits. Now it was time to pay the price.

"Is he dead?" Neith asked again. This time Nemo was conscious enough to hear her.

"I think so." said Nemo

"Neith look back the thin trails of smoke still rising from Bulo's body.

"Good, he got what he deserved."

They both shared a moment of relief that the fighting was finished. Nemo looked at Neith standing to her feet.

"Neith, I don't think I can move."

"Well I guess I'll just have to leave you here then." She said before smiling. "Don't worry we'll make it out of here even if I have to drag you behind me."

As uncomfortable as that sounded, Nemo smiled anyway.

"I'm sure someone will find us. I doubt the others would just leave without me."

"No one is going to find you." Bulo said through muttered coughs. "There will nothing left for them to find. I'm going to grind your bones to dust and grind your dust into a powder so fine that people will question if you ever existed."

Bulo struggled to regain control of his body, moving only his fingers at first. Slowly his motor skills came back to him, and within minutes he was back on his feet. His vision was blurry and a red tint of blood clouded his left eye, but none of that would stop him. Before he hardly cared if the boy lived or died. But now, after such insolence and humiliation, he would make sure he died in the most painful way possible.

"I'm going to take you apart piece by piece while Neith watches. I'll start with your hands, then your feet, and slowly work my way across your body until you're nothing but a barely breathing torso."

Neith didn't wait for him to start on Nemo. She was already up, sword in hand, moving towards Bulo. She aimed for his sword hand, but merely distracting him from Nemo was all she needed to accomplish.

Bulo saw her coming.

"You still try and attack me! You both are like roaches. No matter how many times I squash you, you keep getting back up."

He dodged her first attack and countered with a punch to her ribs. It only caused her a moment of hesitation before she spun into another attack. Bulo leaned back to dodge that one as well. It barely grazed him, leaving a small cut on his face. It didn't matter, he saw the opening he was waiting for approaching. When Neith planted her foot to set up for her next attack, Bulo kicked the inside of her leg. While she was off balance, Bulo threw a series of punches to her chest. Each one hit harder than the last. The final one left Neith hanging in the air for a moment. Just enough time for Bulo to draw his sword and unleash his wind upon her.

Neith flew backwards. She heard a loud crack when her body hit the wall. Immediately she thought her ribs had been shattered, but it was actually the stone behind her. The force of the blow combined with the previous damage to the room broke off large jagged pieces from the stone walls. Power lines, hung high on the walls, were torn apart by the breaking stone. One nearly fell on Nemo, just missing his elbow. Had it reached him, he would have received a quick death by electrocution. Ironically the same way he tried to kill Bulo.

Neith was done. There was no more fighting she could do. She looked over at Nemo who could barely move. They we're both in rough shape. There was nothing they could do, and no one to call to for help. As hard as she tried, Neith couldn't think of anything either of them could do to save their lives.

Bulo walked over and stood above Nemo.

"You should have run boy, but you wanted to fight. Even after choosing to fight, you should have just died quickly. But no, you had to struggle. Now you're going to regret it."

Bulo grabbed the hilt of his sword and in a very slow and deliberate manner, pulled it from its scabbard. It was the first time Nemo got a good look at his blade. Bulo placed it directly on top of Nemo's wrist, making his intent clear.

"Now make sure you scream real loud so Neith can hear. I want her to remember this long after you're dead."

Nemo stared directly up at Bulo. There was no more fear in his heart, he had let go of his ability to fear. Only thing he had left was his resolve.

"I was already dead when I got back up, I just wanted to take you with me."

Nemo grabbed the live power wire next to him and put his hand on Bulo's chest. Digging his fingernails as deep in his skin as he could. He felt the electricity flow through him and into Bulo. He didn't know whose heart would stop first, his or Bulo's. He wanted to see Bulo die first, but if he was able to take him out it hardly mattered what order they went in. Nemo looked over and smiled at Neith. It was that last thing he saw before darkness swallowed him for the final time.

CHAPTER 39

As they walked solemnly two by two, the iron black caskets drifted behind them. All of them carried by strangers. Neith watched as the bodies of friends and others were brought to their final resting place. They were all honored with the grand display reserved for members of Fratello della Spada that died in battle. All of them deserved it.

Arthur stood beside her as they watched the caskets pass by.

"Do you know which one belongs to Champ?"

Neith didn't bother to rise her head when she answered, "No I didn't take the time to ask."

"Ah, I see." Arthur responded before turning back to face the procession.

"That one there is Lancelot's." He pointed out as it slowly passed by them. "I can tell by the flowers we put on it."

"That was a nice touch. I'm sure he would have appreciated it." Neith said without looking up.

"I certainly hope so." Arthur responded. "We all lost someone close to us in this mess. Even with all our security, checks, and precautions, no one could have predicted all of this. Right now, the council is going through plans to make sure nothing like this happens again. If you ask me, it does no good to prepare for the last war after you've fought it."

"Well those sound like decisions I'd leave to those up high." Neith said.

Arthur folded his arms together and continued looking at the procession.

"You know the council wanted to meet with us and the other masters today to discuss everything that happened."

"And I told them, if they couldn't wait until after the funerals then there would be no meeting at all."

Neith took a moment to keep her anger from boiling over. She didn't want to waste one second not reflecting on those they lost at their funeral.

"Even now their insensitivity disguised as loyalty to the organization bothers me to no end. What are we to them? Just the expendable pawns for them to move around a board?"

Arthur frowned at Neith. "Don't talk like that, you'll set a bad example."

"Oh, don't mind me Arthur. I was looking for Tai's casket. I remember the flowers we put on top so I would recognize it when it passes." said Nemo.

"I think that might be it over there." Arthur pointed. "We still have some time before it reaches us. By the way, how are you feeling? Have you started to remember anything from that day?"

"Not really. Most of it is still a blur." Nemo said. In truth, his memories had started to come back. He remembered waking up with Neith crying over him, pumping his chest with all her strength. Tears rolled down her face as he faintly heard her shouting,

"Don't die! Disciples are not supposed to die before their masters, so you can't die yet!"

Saint Georges and the other masters stood around in disbelief when he woke up. Their only guess at how he survived was that his fighting spirit's natural element shielded him from most of the damage and allowed him to transfer it all to Bulo. Had anybody else tried the same thing, they would be dead ten times over. From there the next thing he remembered was being carried outside by Atsuko. Saint Georges carried Neith out on his back. That was when he also realized Tai wasn't with them. Fire engulfed the entrance of the tunnels behind them as they left. Saint Georges found anything that was flammable and lit it up on the way out. Making sure no one would use those tunnels ever again.

Everything after they got back was lost in a haze of medication and painkillers for his injuries. Neith advised him that if anyone asked, he should tell them he still didn't remember anything. Otherwise the questions about how he killed Bulo and survived would never stop.

"Well that's probably for the best then. Not all memories are good ones." said Arthur

They spent the rest of the afternoon saying goodbye to those they lost one final time before seeing them laid to rest. While Neith and the other masters went to a meeting with the council. Nemo went home. He had been in hospital four days since he almost died. Arthur made up something about an accident to cover him being in the hospital. Nemo's parents believed him without even questioning what he said. They were still as gullible as ever. During that time, he knew his parents visited him, but because of the painkillers and medication he didn't remember seeing them at all.

He was greeted by the smell of home cooked pot roast and mashed potatoes when he walked in. His dad sat in the kitchen while his mom cooked. Both of their eyes looked towards the door when he walked in. As happy as he was to see them, Nemo walked straight to the kitchen table next to his father. When his mother came over next to them, Nemo took the claymore off his back and dropped it on the table. Both his parents jumped at the sudden thud it made. His mom was the first to ask.

"Nemo what is that? Where did you get it from?"

His father wasted no time chiming in, "Is that a prop? Are you in some kind of play?"

"No, it's a real sword." Nemo said, staring at it on the table.

"Well why is it here?" His mom asked.

"You all better sit down. I have a lot to tell you."

Made in the USA
Lexington, KY
15 January 2019